Victoria Purman began her career as a cadet journalist at the ABC and since then has worked in varied jobs in the media, including as a media manager in the public sector, a publicist, a freelance journalist, a political adviser, a speechwriter and a consultant editor. In 2013, she was selected as a Writer in Residence at the SA Writers Centre and currently serves as the deputy chair of its board. She is also a long-standing member of the board of Carclew, South Australia's youth arts funding body. In 2014, Victoria was named a finalist in the category Favourite New Author 2013 by the Australian Romance Readers Association, and made the long list for Booktopia's poll Favourite Australian Novelist 2014. In 2015 and 2016, Victoria made the final 75 in that list. In 2014, Victoria was a finalist in the RuBY Awards – the Romance Writers of Australia's Romantic Book of the Year Awards – for her first book, *Nobody But Him*. In 2016, she was nominated for Favourite Contemporary Romance by members of the Australian Romance Readers Association for *Only We Know*. Victoria has been a featured author at the 2014 Adelaide Writers' Week and at the 2015 Sydney Writers' Festival. She has also appeared as a panel chair at the 2015 and 2016 Adelaide Writers' Weeks.

The Three
Miss Allens

VICTORIA PURMAN

First Published 2016
Second Australian Paperback Edition 2019
ISBN 978 1 4892 4846 6

THE THREE MISS ALLENS
© 2016 by Victoria Purman
Australian Copyright 2016
New Zealand Copyright 2016

Published by
HQ Fiction
An imprint of Harlequin Enterprises (Australia) Pty Limited
(ABN 47 001 180 918), a subsidiary of HarperCollins
Publishers Australia Pty Limited (ABN 36 009 913 517)
Level 13, 201 Elizabeth Street
SYDNEY NSW 2000
AUSTRALIA

Printed and bound by CPI Group (UK) Ltd, Croydon, CR0 4YY

To my mother-in-law, Vilma Halliday, with much love

CHAPTER
1

2016

Roma Harris clutched a cold collection of keys in her right hand, the sharp and unfamiliar edges digging into her palm. Her fingers were August cold, stiff and reluctant to unfurl, and the ocean winds were sweeping up off Remarkable Bay and blowing around her ears. The sleeves of her heavy woollen coat grazed her knuckles and she shivered inside it. It was winter in southern Australia, and it had been a bitter and long one; the kind of weather that sends you inside to hibernate until the first buds of spring appear on the almond trees and the winds finally swing around and come from the north and bring everyone and everything slowly back to life.

She didn't yet know the feel of these new keys in her hands. They were a way in to a new life in a new house. Well, an old house to be precise. An old, windswept and forlorn house in which there was more than enough work for its new owner. Roma wasn't scared of it and had laughed when the agent ('Remarkable Sales in Remarkable Bay') had looked sideways at her as if she'd taken leave of her senses when she'd made an offer on the place. She knew the house, had walked past it almost every summer of her childhood, but had never been inside.

'It should be knocked down, in all honesty,' he'd told her with a wrinkle of disdain on his ruddy face as he'd shown her through the property the first time. 'If things ever take off in Remarkable Bay again—and I'm predicting they will because I keep a very close eye on the market—it'll be the perfect place to build a couple, maybe three, modern beach houses. You know, with all the mod cons that people want these days. European kitchens, six bedrooms, three bathrooms. That's what this town needs. More places like that. Less places like this. They'd go for two million each, I reckon. You just can't get a view like this down here any more. Rare as hen's teeth. God knows what happened in here when it was a boarding house and just between you and me I tried to convince the owners they should do something about the ... smell. But the owner died and left it to a distant niece or some such person and she doesn't want it, lives in Brisbane now where the winters are a whole lot kinder, so that's why it's on the market.'

Roma had wondered how the agent made a living with a sales pitch so convincing and had tried not to smirk. The old guest-house had been on the market for two years with no takers, so she'd offered low, and it was accepted overnight. She'd suspected it then but she knew it for certain now, standing in front of the place, taking in the peeling paint, the weeds like bushes in the front garden and the sad disrepair of the place: it desperately needed rescuing.

The house was hers now and she was ready to be its saviour.

There was simply something about Bayview that Roma hadn't been able to walk away from. It sat facing the water in the best position on Remarkable Bay's only main strip, Ocean Street, the old, unguttered bitumen road which met the main highway to Adelaide at one end, and the cliff tops adjacent to the bay at the other. The views from every window and door at the front of the house were spectacular. Before she could bring herself to turn the key in the lock Roma turned to the outlook and took in a lungful of air, salty and cool, chilling her as she swallowed it. Across the road there were no houses but a lawned reserve with a shining and abundant low hedge bordering it, and then in the near distance the coastline down below curved like it had been cut by a scythe; with cliffs on either end of the bay and towering Norfolk Island pines reaching into the sky.

Why did this small seaside town still have a hold on her? As a child on holidays it was sun and the beach and family holidays and melting ice-cream. But now? It was so firmly stuck back in time that it still had a well-patronised video shop. A gust of wind chilled her more deeply through her coat and Roma examined her keys again. They represented some kind of new beginning. Not better necessarily, not shinier.

But new.

That's what she needed Remarkable Bay to be.

There were more keys on this key ring than she'd ever had in her life: front screen, front door, back door, various window locks and a storage cupboard which, the agent had assured her, she would need to keep locked if she was going to have strangers in her home.

It was a completely reasonable idea to put to someone who'd just bought a rundown old guesthouse at the beach. The agent had probably assumed that she might be after a sea change or a renovation challenge and would restore the old guesthouse to some kind of new life as a boutique hotel. He'd hinted at it but Roma had smiled politely and never answered him. The last thing she wanted was strangers in her home and, if she was honest, she didn't want old friends or new friends or family there, either.

You couldn't hide if people came to stay, could you?

Roma took a quick guess about which of her mysterious keys would open the front door and on the second attempt she heard the snick of the lock. The door opened reluctantly, catching against the tattered and worn floral hallway carpet runner. With a shove of her shoulder, she managed to open the door all the way. Light streamed into the hallway in front of her. There was a room to the immediate right, with an open double doorway, and she went in and dropped her heavy shoulder bag and her bunch of keys on the floor. The jangling noise echoed throughout the empty house. This might have been a living room once. Roma screwed up her nose. It was dim in the early afternoon light and motes of dust floated in the space, like tiny confetti from a ghostly welcoming parade.

She checked her watch. She'd made good time ahead of the removalists' truck and it should be arriving any minute. In a more perfect world, one in which she didn't have to finish up at work and settle on the house on the same day, she might have had time to get there in advance, to clean and paint and rip up carpets. But her life hadn't been perfect for a while.

'This is it,' she whispered to the dust and the air and the quiet. 'Welcome home.'

She went out the front door and walked the short cement footpath to the gate. Her car was parked on the street, packed with bulging suitcases, her computer safely boxed, and precious keepsakes she couldn't bring herself to entrust to the journey to the beach in the moving van.

She went to flip open the boot of her car but stopped, taking a moment to look back at her new home. The guesthouse would have been quite grand in the bloom of its youth. It sat on the most prominent point on Ocean Street, its two stories high and important, and its stonework once a symbol of expense and prestige. The wooden fretwork adorning the balcony above and the ground floor veranda was as decorative as lace on a collar, but its white paint was peeling and loose, revealing layers of ruby red and pale cream underneath. Once, the well-to-do families of South Australia had spent summers in it, but the house was no adolescent now; no classic in middle-age, or a grand dame. Like the town, it had slowly died as other towns in the region had thrived. Remarkable Bay had become the runt of the south coast. The town, and her house, seriously needed love, some fool to come along and spend money to bring them back to life. And for the life of her, Roma still hadn't quite understood why the fool had to be her. She was clear about why she'd left the city: there was no gotcha moment there. But why this place? Here in Remarkable Bay?

Cautious and sensible Roma Harris had never run from anything in her entire life. Until now.

Roma hauled her suitcases on to the footpath and placed them in a neat row. She lugged the first case to the front door, past the black wrought-iron gate and over the cracked footpath. The front door, designed to be a grand entrance, was surrounded by stained glass panels at the top and sides, thankfully still intact and made up of intricate floral designs in pale pink and forest green. Set into the plasterwork above the doorframe was a word which looked half worn away by years of salt spray and biting winds.

Bayview. And then underneath it the date, 1916.

The words and numbers were faded like a mirage or a memory; as if they'd been waiting for a hundred years for someone to come along and read them. A century, Roma realised with a little smile to herself.

Bayview. 1916.

All those fancy visitors from days gone by probably wouldn't recognise it now. Above her, the wooden frame supporting the upstairs balcony was strung with silvery spider webs, dust and age. Below her feet, the concrete of the front veranda was cracked like shattered glass and had sunk into potholes in other places. The fly wire in each of the double-sash windows at the front of the house, one on either side of the front door, was flapping loose in the breeze.

Roma sighed and let herself smile just a little. She would have to make a thousand decisions about the house in the next few months. New or old. Replace or repair.

Live or exist.

For now, for today, for this week, this month, she'd chosen to live.

Roma discovered, to her surprise, that all the downstairs windows opened easily and, before too long, she could smell the sea and feel its crisp chill inside the house. She'd unpacked her belongings from her car and they were crowded together in a pile down the hallway and at the bottom of the staircase. She looked up. Light streamed down on to the steps and illuminated the landing where the stairs turned. Each tread was worn into a slight curve. The honeyed hand-rail was warm to her touch, smooth and safe, and she slowly took the steps, looking around her at the doorways leading into the five rooms upstairs and the small, functional bathroom.

It was slightly warmer up there but she could already feel the breeze from the open downstairs windows swirling up the staircase and spreading its reach into every corner of the second floor. The room which would be her bedroom was at the front of the house, and as she made her way there with slow and hesitant steps, she felt a shuddering in her chest as she reached the doorway.

There was nothing more symbolic of her new life than this room. A room she'd never shared with anyone. She crossed the large, empty space, double the size of the one she'd left behind in the city. The ceilings were like every other in the house: pressed tin painted over with white. The walls were a mint green, scuffed and gouged in places where it seemed furniture had been ground against the plasterwork. As she unlatched and swung open the French doors that opened onto the front balcony, Roma held her breath. Even though she had paid for a detailed building inspection before agree-ing to the purchase and it had revealed the balcony was sound, she was nervous going out there. The area ran almost the length of the front of the house: about six metres long and two metres from door to railing. It had the best views of Remarkable Bay. Roma pictured herself sitting in a cane chair with a book and a glass of wine in the summer months, getting lost in the distant waves and the sleepy small town feeling of the place. When the weather warmed and the sun shone, this would be the perfect place to sit and think. Or maybe to simply sit.

The rumbling of a truck echoed in the quiet and peaceful street. It came to a slow halt behind her car and when the driver cut the engine and hopped out, she waved down at him.

'G'day, love.' The removalist tugged at his football beanie, pull-ing it close over his ears against the wind. 'I guess this is the place?'

'Yes, it is.'

'We'll start unloading. You know where you want everything?'

Roma nodded and felt scared and excited in equal measure. She was ready for her new life to begin right here in the musty rooms and empty spaces of Bayview.

'I'll put the kettle on,' she called back.

After a late dinner—takeaway hot chips from the pub—Roma had dragged a chair out to her balcony from her bedroom and slumped into it. She was exhausted. It had taken the removalists three hours to unload her furniture and all her boxes, the stairs having made things slightly more complex. Everything was now in the right rooms, if not the right positions. That would all come later. For now, for tonight, she had a mattress and a sleeping bag. And she had a red wine in her hand. In a proper wine glass. Priorities.

She had a blanket around her shoulders and she tugged it tighter as she took another sip of her glass of Barossa shiraz. Across the road, the reserve was dark now, sucked up into the blackness of the night. The night was so much thicker here without streetlights, something that had scared her on holidays in Remarkable Bay as a child unless she had her older brother Leo by her side. And then she had a flash of memory. Roaming children. Bright pinpoints of torch light in the scrubby coastal bushes. The scratch of branches on her arm. Mosquito bites and midges. Someone being kissed. She remembered there was a path across the reserve that guided walkers along the narrow steps down the cliff to the water's edge but she couldn't make it out now in the dark. All she could hear was the roaring white noise of the ocean.

This was the peace she craved; the peace she hoped would calm her thinking and every trembling, anxious thought that had filled her head for three years. For the nights when she couldn't sleep, when her memories became her nightmares and her jaw ached from the violent, crushing grinding of her teeth.

She willed those thoughts away with another sip of wine. There was so much here to distract her from those memories. She knew that in winter, the southern right whales arrived in the bay to give birth, to seek solace from the raging far Southern Ocean. Would she be able to see them from her balcony?

She held her glass high, made a toast to no one.

'Happy first day,' she called and her voice echoed in the street below.

And it was then the sadness hit her like a firestorm. Uncontrollable, it swamped her, rose up and stuck in her throat and then exploded out of her mouth in raging sobs and shudders. She gripped the cane chair while her body shook and her throat scratched hoarse with her sobs. There had been no way to prepare for what had happened; there wasn't the chance for the long, drawn-out, slow goodbye of an illness. There had only been the short, sharp shock of instant death.

She'd held it in for so long and now it came out of her in a tumult.

She had alienated all her friends with the depths of her grief. And now she'd left everything. She'd quit her job for a life as a widow at thirty-five, alone in a town where she knew no one. Roma let the tears fall, waited until the racking sobs receded and tried to feel every inch of this grief so she might grow to know it, get over it, move on from it.

She needed more good days, she knew that. She needed more happy days. That's what Remarkable Bay was for. Because if there weren't, Roma feared she would go under, silently and easily, like the southern right whales gliding and disappearing into the depths of the winter ocean.

CHAPTER 2

'Hey, Leo.'

Roma was still in bed when she answered the call from her big brother, her body complaining from the shifting and hauling and unpacking she'd done the day before. It had been a physically exhausting day but an emotional one too. This wrenching oneself from one life and dropping into another took a toll. A few times during the afternoon's unpacking, during which she'd directed the movers to put the sofa over there and the kitchen table here, the chest of drawers upstairs and the red velvet winged chair in what was going to be her bedroom (up the stairs, turn left and the one with the French doors), she found herself on the verge of more tears. She didn't sob—she was too controlled for that—but little thin tears had leaked from her eyes and drizzled down her cheeks. As she'd wiped them away with the dusty sleeve of her long-sleeved T-shirt, she'd fought the shudders which rattled her chest, and the fear that snaked up her spine and goose bumped her skin.

There was no going back. That's what she'd have to tell Leo.

'Good morning,' he said, his familiar voice clear and full of energy despite the early hour.

'Good morning to you, too.' The early morning light had Roma blinking her eyes. She pushed aside her sleep-mussed hair, pressed the phone into her ear and waited for the lecture. She was used to it from Leo, especially since their parents had died, and especially in the past three years.

'You still in bed?' he asked incredulously.

'Yes. I am.'

She imagined the judgement in his silence. You've let yourself go, Roma. You've got to move on. It's time.

'I suppose it is Sunday,' he finally conceded.

She stretched an arm out above her, yawned on purpose. 'And don't tell me. It's still almost the crack of dawn, despite the half hour time difference between you and me, and you've already been to the gym, run ten ks and had something biodynamic for breakfast, right?'

'Two out of three ain't bad. How's everything with you? It's hard to keep track of what you're up to since you never post on your Facebook page.'

She hadn't seen Leo in six months, since her birthday back in February, when he'd surprised her with a flying visit to Adelaide and then convinced her to put on a cocktail dress that was too tight and high heels that pinched and dragged her to drinks at a new bar in the city filled with men sporting hipster beards and women who looked like pin-up girls from the forties. She'd had fun that night. It had been such a long time since she'd been out on the town, since she'd let herself laugh without feeling guilty. She'd enjoyed it despite the fact that Leo had invited Addy McNamara. She wasn't sure why Leo had asked her to come along. They were related to Addy, distant cousins in fact, and Addy and Roma had been close as children and teenagers, but they'd drifted apart and hadn't shared a meaningful conversation in years. Apparently Leo had reconnected with Addy when she'd worked on a film in Sydney a couple of years ago and had needed somewhere to stay for a couple of months.

'I've sworn off Facebook,' Roma replied. The truth was, she didn't want to see how happy everyone else was, to be confronted with their good times and meals and holidays and humorous anecdotes because she had absolutely nothing to give in return. 'I'm good. Tired but good.' Roma stretched and yawned.

'So you've moved in?'

Despite the physical distance between the siblings, Leo still called every week. For much of the past three years, his calls were place markers for Roma. A call from Leo meant it must be Sunday night and that meant the weekend was over and she would have to go to work the next day which meant she had to put a load of washing on, make her lunch, iron a shirt. They helped her get through the worst of it.

And now, this morning especially, tucked up on her mattress on the floor, with the warmth of a sleeping bag her only comfort, alone in her new house, at the very beginning of her new beginning? It was so good to hear his voice that tears welled. She let them fall.

'Have I moved in? Well, my stuff's here. I'm surrounded by boxes and the place smells weirdly like possum urine, but it's all going great.'

Leo's deep laugh down the line lured her into a broad smile. 'Possum piss? How does that differ from regular piss?'

'It's more possumy.'

'Damn, you make it sound so attractive. I can't wait to come and stay. Hold on. On second thoughts, maybe I'll head to Noumea instead of Remarkable Bay for my summer holidays.'

She gasped. 'Too late. You promised. I believe we even did a pinkie swear over expensive champagne so you can't back out now.'

'Yes, well, I was drunk and I made that promise to you to come home for Christmas *long* before you came up with this harebrained scheme to run away to the beach. Remind me again why you did it?'

Leo was right. Six months before, on her thirty-fifth birthday, the night they'd had drinks in that hipster bar, she'd had a life somewhere else. In reality, it had become half a life, maybe even less. She was still getting up every day and going to work, doing all the boring administrivia that went along with being gainfully employed and having a house of one's own, and making it through each day. The idea of throwing that all in and moving to Remarkable Bay hadn't even been a glimmer of a notion inside an idea back then.

'I follow one of those real estate websites on Facebook and this house popped up in my newsfeed.' While that was true, she hadn't simply opened an atlas—or Google maps—and randomly selected Remarkable Bay as the place for her exile from her life. She'd been searching the web for houses to rent there, thinking that maybe one day soon in the future, possibly next year, she might go back there for a holiday.

And then one day, Bayview was on her screen, somehow calling to her.

'It just popped up in your newsfeed, like magic? And that was a sign or something that you should buy that old wreck?' Leo scoffed from fifteen hundred kilometres away. 'C'mon, Romes. We used to cross the street to avoid that place. You're not going to tell me you believe in fate and all that bullshit, are you? Especially after what happened to Tom.'

Three years and she still flinched at the mention of his name. And there it was, the grief, multiplying like some disease in a Petri dish. Roma's grief had grown big in her empty house in the city; in inverse proportion to the shrinking of her heart. It had taken time, months, years of sadness so overwhelming it was like trudging through quicksand, before she'd finally realised that quietness and a fresh start was what she needed; that a new life—or at least a new chapter—was within her reach. She needed to wipe the slate clean; to wake up in a room that wasn't one she'd shared with Tom; to cook in a kitchen where she didn't see him complaining about having to wipe the saucepans.

Leo understood the silence. She braced for the inevitable lecture. 'Listen, Roma. You shouldn't have spent all your money on that place.'

She hadn't, but she also hadn't told him that. She was far more savvy with her money than he would allow. She swallowed and said, quietly, firmly, 'I'll be fine.'

'You've still got your share from the sale of Mum and Dad's house although it's tied up in a term deposit for another year. Do you need any of it?'

Roma gripped the edge of her sleeping bag with her free hand. 'No, I don't. With the money from the sale of our house, and Tom's superannuation and the ... his life insurance ... I'm okay for a year, at least. You do know that I used to manage budgets at work, don't you?'

'Yeah, of course.' Leo paused. 'So I guess there's no need for me to start sending food parcels then?'

He always knew how to make her laugh. 'Hang on, let me double check. I seem to be out of chocolate and wine.'

'You'll have to wait for Christmas.'

'But that's four months away.'

'Toughen up, princess.'

'Well, in that case, it's socks and jocks for you then. White ones. Big old grandpa ones.'

They were silent for a moment, remembering one of their father's jokes. He'd been a happy father, a generous one. He'd had a good heart and a booming laugh. He'd always said he wanted for nothing: he'd won the heart of a woman he adored, fathered two children who were the light of his life, and worked in a job he could tolerate. 'All a man ever needs is new socks and jocks,' he'd announced every Christmas morning when they'd gathered under the tree to open their presents. He was never disappointed and laughed along when the socks became more cartoonish as the years went on. Dancing Santas. Surfing cats. Giant tomatoes.

'I still miss them, Leo,' Roma said softly.

'Me too, Romes, but ... you can't bring them back by buying a house in the place we used to spend summer holidays.'

'Of course I know that,' she huffed. But did she really? Was that the draw for Roma? Was that why she'd bought Bayview?

There were so many memories tied up in these streets, in the whispering fronds of the Norfolk Island pines in the distance, in the grains of sand on the beach and in the waters of the bay. The town had been sunshine and summer holidays during every summer of her childhood, and for her mother and her mother's family for generations before that. Her parents had rented a house right on the beach for two weeks from New Year's Eve until mid-January, and there had been years of holidays in which the winds blew in cool from the beach to calm tensions, and dripping ice-creams marked each afternoon. Roma and Leo enjoyed sun-kissed days and evenings filled with laughter and music and board games and holiday-home records on scratchy record players. Roma had loved it, the freedom and looseness of those two weeks every year. Leo's commanding personality was evident even then; within days he'd corralled together a troupe of holidaying kids and they'd roamed the beach and the cliffs all summer, following him. Those same kids returned every year: city kids, country kids, some from the State's southeast. Lawyers' kids and doctors' kids and farmers' kids. Boys and girls. For two weeks every summer, Roma had been part of Leo's tribe and she'd been in heaven. It was fun until it wasn't and then, once Leo had gone to university, and when the attractions of a city summer were so much more entertaining than the beach, those summers faded. Eventually, Roma stayed up in Adelaide when her parents holidayed down at the Bay, and finally their parents moved to Victor Harbor, the biggest town nearby, to retire. Remarkable Bay had already been too small for them by then: it was without a doctor and too far from the hospital for their liking. They'd ended up needing both: they'd died within a year of each other, of cancer, lung and breast.

'Hey,' she said. 'Remember that ice-cream shop on the corner of Ocean Street? The one by the church?'

'The one that had the waffle cones and the Golden North honey ice-cream?' Leo's voice sounded boyish, and Roma suddenly saw him as fifteen again, tanned and slender, his colourful boardshorts slung low for effect, his dripping cone between his fingers and the melting ice-cream dripping on to the black of the bitumen road like globs of tears.

'Yeah. That one.'

'Man, that was the best ice-cream ...'

'Don't get too sentimental. It's gone. And the church is a craft shop now.'

'What the fuck? That's it. I'm definitely going to Noumea. Listen, Romes, I've got to go. I'll call you next weekend and I'll see you at Christmas. Call me if you need anything, all right?'

'I will,' Roma promised and she half meant it.

But Leo didn't hang up. She heard a deep sigh. 'Damn it, it's probably a good thing about the ice-cream place. My personal trainer would kill me if he found out I was eating ice-cream.'

'You have a personal trainer now? How Sydney.'

'I know. I'm such a cliché but I look hot.' He still didn't hang up.

Roma knew what was coming. She unzipped her sleeping bag and tiptoed over the icy wooden floorboards to the French doors. The windows were fogged from condensation and she wiped a circle with her palm. It didn't do much for the view. The outside was filmy with sea spray.

'Listen. You really okay?' he asked quietly.

She tensed. There was no simple answer to his question. Some days, she was okay. Yesterday, moving into her new house in Remarkable Bay, she'd been ... okay. For a while. Other days she started out okay and then a smell, a taste or hint of memory would suck her back down into the void of grief. Her psychologist had told to expect this waxing and waning, this pull and push of happiness and despair. She'd hung on to that advice on the days when she felt there would be no heaven to her hell.

'Oh, you know. Each day is better than the day before until I have a bad day and then my life feels like it's snakes and ladders.'

'Shit, Roma ...'

She wouldn't say any more. She'd been too honest. It scared people, she knew that, and Roma chided herself for the slip. She knew first hand that people accepted that there would be grief at a funeral and then for perhaps a month or two after a terrible loss. But then you were expected to get over things, to move on. To find what people liked to refer to as 'closure'. Closure. How she hated that damn word. Getting over grief—if you ever could—wasn't like closing the last page on a book and putting it on a high shelf so you didn't have to look at it every day. Grief was like driving a car and the road ahead of you was endless and long and dark and there was nowhere to pull over and eventually, maybe one day, you might find that you weren't driving so fast anymore, your fingers weren't gripping the steering wheel until you were white-knuckled. One day, you might let go of that wheel for just a moment so you could reach for the gear stick to change gears. Fourth to third. Third to second. But you were always on that road. Every day.

And Leo's question was the subtext of every conversation she'd had with him for the past two and a half years. Are you really okay? he'd asked her over and over.

'Every day is better, Leo, I promise.' She knew Leo needed to hear the words. Roma was so used to saying them, so practised in automatically reassuring people who were worried about her, so used to pleasing everyone, that they came out as naturally as blinking. 'So, I'll see you at Christmas?'

'You just want a present,' Leo said, relief in his big-brother voice. Relief that he thought she was moving on, relief that she'd changed the subject.

'Damn right I do. You'd better bring me something good.'

'Don't I always, Romes?'

CHAPTER
3

Addy McNamara repositioned herself in an old grey office chair she was sure was two parts broken and stared at the chaos of her desk in the middle of the film production office. The film's producer and the accountant had offices but as production manager, she sat in the open plan office with her team. She liked it that way. It put her in the perfect position to see everything and hear everything. To others, it may have looked like mayhem but to Addy, it all made perfect sense. Everything on the desk was important and required her attention. Her shining silver laptop was at the centre and on the left, two black toaster racks full of different coloured manila folders looked like a rainbow. On the right, draft daily call sheets, printed on yellow paper, mapped out what would happen on set once they started filming. The film's script was in a folder under the call sheet, and the printed schedule from the first assistant director, which mapped out the whole production timeline, sat to her left. There were cost reports, hard copies of the crews' timesheets which she had to approve, and an old-school phone that sat at the back of the desk, dusty and lonely. She never used it: every call came in on one of her two mobile phones, at all hours of the day and night. When one of them rang, her personal one, she took a deep breath before checking the display. It was safe. It was Leo.

'Way too busy and important to be talking to you, Leo.'

'Aren't you always?'

'Yes, as a matter of fact I am.'

'I need to talk to you. Can you give me just a minute?'

Addy waved to a runner with a clipboard on her arm and a question on her lips. 'Sure. Anything for my favourite cousin. Hey, lighting department needs some more gaffer tape.'

'What?'

'Nothing,' Addy said as she watched the young woman nod and take notes. 'What's up?'

Leo hesitated. 'It's Roma.'

Addy stilled. The voices and activity all around her became white noise. 'Is she okay?'

'She says she is but I don't think so. I don't know what the hell she was thinking when she bought that ridiculous old pile down in Remarkable Bay. She moved in yesterday.'

In the craziness of her work, Addy had forgotten what Leo had told her about Roma's move. Her sensible cousin Roma. Boring Roma, if Addy was honest. Roma had gone to university, married her first boyfriend, found a job pushing paper in the government and seemed to get middle-aged at twenty-five. That was not Addy's life.

That's when Addy realised what Leo had said. 'Did you say Remarkable Bay?'

'Yeah. She bought that big old place at the top of Ocean Street. Do you remember it? I think it was a squat when we were there on holidays as kids.'

'That place? You're kidding me.' She was dumbfounded. Roma had pulled up stumps and moved to Remarkable Bay? It sounded like the least boring thing Roma had ever done.

'Not kidding. I was as shocked as you are. I mean, have you seen the Bay lately? It looks like a shithole.'

Addy leaned forward, hit Google and a few clicks later an image of the property filled the screen of her iPad. The previous owners had clearly not even bothered to tidy the place up a bit for the real-estate photos. The two-storey hulk of a building was peeling paint and had tall weeds in the small front garden and a wobbly looking wrought-iron fence. It looked abandoned and spooky.

'Damn, Leo. If we were scouting locations for *Murder in the Outback Part 23*, I'm sure we could use this as a set. You know, teens find an abandoned house only to be met by a deranged serial killer.'

Leo scoffed. 'I can't believe people make crappy movies like that.'

'I can't believe people *pay* to see crappy movies like that. But if they didn't, I wouldn't have a job.'

Leo paused and Addy could hear his concern in the silence. 'You know what she's been through, Addy, but this …'

Addy clicked out of the site and checked her Facebook page as she continued her conversation with Leo. It wasn't that she didn't care but he talked about Roma's state of mind a lot. He hadn't seemed to have listened the last ten times Addy had told him to butt out of her business and leave her alone, that she was a grown woman and she could do whatever the hell she liked, no matter if he agreed or not. 'But what …?'

'But quitting her job, selling her house, chucking it all in to move down to Remarkable Bay? I think she may have tipped over the edge.'

The production assistant walked by Addy's crowded desk and lobbed two thick yellow envelopes on her desk. Addy nodded her thanks.

'Look Leo. After what she's been through … I think she can be excused for going a little mad. Hang on, no, not that hotel, he hates it. Book that serviced apartment in the city. Sorry, Leo. I'm kinda snowed right here.'

'Are you at *work*?'

She sighed. 'Yep.'

'On a *Sunday*?'

Addy looked around her, taking in the organised chaos of the film's production office. 'What's a Sunday?'

'I forgot. You work in the creative industries. All love, no money, right?'

Addy leaned back in her ancient office chair to stare at the ceiling. It ratcheted back unexpectedly and sent all her limbs flailing and adrenaline pumping. When she straightened herself, she replied, 'I do it for the love, Leo.'

There was a long pause. 'Listen. Addy. I need you to do me a favour. You need to go see her.'

'Me? Why me?' This was a bolt out of the blue. She'd patiently listened to Leo's concerns about his sister over the past couple of years but never once had he suggested Addy get involved. There was no way Roma would take advice from her. If she'd known this was where all those conversations with him were leading she might not have been so faux sympathetic.

'Because I've been away too long and I don't know any of her friends well enough to talk to them about this. And, frankly, you're the nearest thing to a living relative she's got. I can't leave Sydney until Christmas. We've got a big merger going on and if I told you any more about that I'd have to kill you. You've got to do this for me.'

Addy bit her lip and slumped back in her chair. Leo had a way of just telling you to do things without asking you if you wanted to do them, and it grated. But he was half right: Roma was the nearest thing to a cousin she had. They were, in fact, third-cousins, once removed. Or was that fourth-cousins twice removed? They'd tried to work it out once when they were teenagers but Addy had never had any patience for facts and Roma had always insisted on being right so they'd let the topic drift away and they'd decided to call each other, simply, cousins.

Their great-grandmothers had been sisters: the two Miss Allens, the upright and well-bred children of Charles and Henrietta Allen. Addy had been the only one to inherit the red hair of her great-grandmother, Adeline. She'd not only inherited her hair colour, but something of a tribute in her name, Adelaide, as well. Leo and Roma's great-grandmother—Ruby—had been Adeline's sister, and the two branches of the family tree had spread far from them ever since. Generation after generation, the children and the children's children of Ruby and Adeline had grown up in Adelaide with fewer connections as the years went on. Their great-granddaughters— Roma and Addy—were only a month apart in age and had gone to the same school by sheer coincidence.

'C'mon, Addy,' Leo implored. 'I'm worried about her.'

Addy was about to answer that no, she couldn't possibly go to see Roma because she was a working woman with a responsible job, when a quiet descended on the office like the hush of a cool change in midsummer. People had stopped bustling. The TV monitors had been muted. She looked over her shoulder. A sense of resignation swept over her when she saw the blank expressions on the young faces of her team.

'Leo, I'm sorry. I've going to have to call you back.' She jabbed the screen on her phone and tossed it on to the desk. 'What's going on?'

The fifty-something producer, Sally James, stomped over to Addy's desk, her designer suit looking rumpled for the first time ever. She breathed a heavy sigh and tugged on one of her earrings. 'We're delayed, Addy. The money fell through.'

'Fuck.' Addy knew she had to remain composed. She was the calm eye in the storm, wasn't she? But damn it to hell. Things had been slow in the industry for a few years, and the odd short film and television commercial had got her through, just, but this was the first film she'd managed to pick up in a hell of a long time. An I-don't-know-how-I'm-going-to-pay-my-rent long time. 'For how long?'

'It could be months. The delay means we've lost Josh Kruger. He's off to do a TV pilot in LA. So now we have to factor in his availability and the money and, you know, it's a clusterfuck. As these things always are. I know this sucks, Addy. You'll score some other work until we can pick up, right?'

Addy bit the inside of her lip so hard she could taste the blood in her mouth. Her alternative option had recently dried up, for reasons that made her fists tighten and her gut churn. 'I'll be fine, Sally. Don't worry. And you know where to find me when you get the word, right?'

Sally looped an arm around Addy's shoulders. 'We're getting too old for this shit, aren't we?' They looked over at the production team, mostly young kids with stars in their eyes who were consoling each other with dramatic sighs and even more dramatic hugs. Like they were never going to see each other again. Addy knew she should go over to them and cluck sympathetically, 'We'll be back before you know it. This is the industry. It'll be okay and this film is going to win Oscars!' That was bullshit, of course. The film was a bad road movie featuring men in leather and women in not much at all. But it was a job. Addy corrected herself: it had been a job.

Addy suddenly didn't have the energy to try to make other people feel better. Sally was right: she was too old for this shit. She flopped down in her chair and this time it gave way, sending her sprawling backwards on to the floor. She saw arms flailing, her black Converse sneakers in the air as if she was tumble-turning and *bang*. The backrest hit the floor and so did she.

Within a moment, there was a crowd of people all around her.

'You okay, Addy?' Sally was kneeling at her side, her face white and concern crinkling her eyes.

Addy reached an arm out. 'I'm okay. Stupid fucking chair. Help me up, will you?'

When she was on her feet, patting the dust off her arse, she rolled her eyes. 'Perfect end to a perfect day, huh?'

Sally chuckled. 'Pack up your stuff. Go home. Unless you want to join us all at the pub for a drink?'

She would never usually say no to a drink, but Addy could feel the beginnings of a headache gnawing at her skull. Maybe she'd knocked her head when she toppled backwards. Maybe she was just tired. Maybe Leo's phone call had her thinking too much about things she couldn't change, about Roma.

'Thanks, but … no. I'll head home.'

The two women hugged. They'd worked together for years, off and on, and Addy knew Sally's word was good. She'd be back when the money was back. Which she also knew might be never.

'We're heading to the pub, kids. Drinks are on me!' Sally announced. The production crew suddenly rallied and followed the woman with the credit card out the door as if she were the Pied Piper and they were the children of Hamelin.

An hour later, when Addy had loaded boxes into the boot of her car, turned off the lights in the production office and locked the door behind her, she hesitated at turning the key to start the engine. Instead, she dug out her phone from her bag. Dialled Leo back.

'Hey Leo. My diary has suddenly opened up. I'll go to Remarkable Bay. I'll check up on Roma. What's the address?'

CHAPTER

4

Roma pulled on a thick jumper, a pair of comfortable jeans and her oldest sneakers and got to work in her kitchen. It seemed like the obvious place to start, the quickest way to make her new house feel like home and, while it would have been more sensible to wait until she'd painted, she needed to get started. She could live with boxes of her possessions stacked in one of the many spare rooms, rugs rolled into tubes and half her clothes in suitcases, but she needed somewhere to plug in her coffee machine. She needed to settle on a place for the toaster so she could make breakfast. The fridge had been rolled into place by the removalists and was chock-a-block with precisely one litre of milk, some butter, half a dozen eggs and ice cubes. That was a start.

Once she'd found her iPod and her sound dock, buried in a box with her laptop, Roma cranked up the sound on her favourite play-list and got to work. With a bucket of hot water and a bottle of sugar soap at her side, she scrubbed every surface, every shelf, every counter top, the tiles and even the walls. And once that was done and the walls were drying, she tackled the boxes. She pulled the first box into the centre of the room and popped open the taped up flaps. Platters and fine china tea cups. Not exactly essentials, but it was a start. She continued for hours, unpacking boxes and filling freshly cleaned cupboards; stacking plates, setting vases and colourful bowls on shelves. It was methodical work, but it required the kind of mechanical thinking that pushed every other thought out of her mind. Busy-work. That's what she needed, and Roma had a whole house full of busy-work to do.

As things started to settle into place, as the room started to look like her, Roma was pleased she'd begun there. She'd never exactly been a foodie but she'd liked eating well. She'd liked trying different foods and experimenting with some of the dishes she'd seen on cooking shows. At least that's what she used to do. She hadn't spent much time cooking—really cooking—during the past three years. Looking back, she guessed she'd eaten more packets of chocolate biscuits for dinner than real meals. It had been so much easier when she was cooking meals for two, when the quiet routine of preparing dinner was a ritual for her, a way to unwind after work, a way to fill in the evenings. Tom would pour some wine and sit on the other side of the kitchen bench, and they'd find things to say while she worked. She'd grown to love her city kitchen. At first, it had seemed too ostentatious, too unnecessary, with its stainless steel appliances and stone bench tops, the decorative overhead lighting and its huge work space. Tom had convinced her those features would add resale value to the house and he'd been right.

By contrast, Bayview's kitchen appeared to have been the height of sophistication sometime around 1976. Unfortunately now its lime-green bench tops and veneer cupboards were so old and chipped they wouldn't even qualify as retro chic. If only she had a mission brown slow cooker and some stone dinnerware. But it had a redeeming feature: it was big. Beyond the U-shaped kitchen workspace, there was enough room in the kitchen to fit a big table and perhaps eight chairs, which would be useful if she ever had seven people over for dinner. She wasn't sure if she had seven friends left.

By two o'clock, Roma was ravenous and the contents of her fridge were clearly not going to assuage her hunger, so she grabbed her purse, threw on her coat, locked the front door behind her and walked down Ocean Street to the bakery. It was a pleasant late winter's day. The light grey clouds hung in the sky and the overnight winds had settled. As she walked, she glanced down to the white sands of Remarkable Bay and saw little activity there. It would have been the perfect place to walk Charlie, she realised with an ache in her chest. Her beloved dog had died a year ago but she'd still inadvertantly looked for him every day since when she'd gotten home from work.

This really was a sleepy seaside town in the middle of winter. Ocean Street wasn't much of a main street. More shops in it were vacant than occupied, but a pharmacy, a pub, a bakery, a newsagent, a surf shop and small general store clung to life. Other buildings sat lonely and empty, sandstone and tin sentinels with fading advertising slogans on their windows and side walls. Some bore the scars of ambitious newcomers who'd taken chances on businesses over the years and failed: a bookshop, a sewing nook, a sushi bar.

Roma could smell the bakery before she entered it, the scent of sweet pastry and bread filling her nostrils as she approached. It was definitely a shock to the senses after a head full of sugar soap and antiseptic spray. Those thoughts were swept out of her head by the delicious displays of buns and pastries and crispy sausage rolls. She took a good deep breath, savouring everything about them. Above the counters, there were sign boards filled with products and prices, and behind her there were packaged biscuits and wrapped loaves of bread. So much about Remarkable Bay had changed in the past twenty years; Roma was so glad this business had survived the vagaries of small town economic rises and falls.

'G'day. What can I help you with today?' A young woman appeared on the other side of the counter, her purple hair and a nose ring slamming Roma's expectations of exactly who lived in Remarkable Bay in the off-season.

'I'll have a sausage roll with sauce. Thanks.' Roma hoped she was putting on a smile to show her appreciation. It felt unnatural sometimes to smile, but she tried. She wanted to make a good impression on these people. She hoped to be considered as one of them, one day. The last thing she needed was for word to get around that the woman who'd bought the decrepit house on Ocean Street was a snob or unfriendly. She had an inkling about how hard it would be to settle in a small town and didn't want to fall into anyone's stereotype of who a newcomer might be and how they would act.

The assistant slid the crisp pastry into a brown paper bag and popped it on the counter.

'Is there anything else I can get for you today?'

The staff here were well trained. There was always something else in a country bakery like this.

Roma let herself go, just a little. 'And a cream bun, thanks.'

Once Roma had paid, she took her purchases outside and found a spot at one of the wooden tables under the wide bakery veranda and ate her sausage roll hungrily. Crisp pastry, spicy meat; it was as delicious as it looked. Around her, the street was quiet, winter coastal town sleepy. The only traffic seemed to be people coming and going from the bakery. Passing tradies in their high-vis vests munched on steaming hot pies; locals with still-warm loaves of freshly baked bread; grey-haired couples clutching perfectly baked scones and heading hurriedly home to eat them with jam and cream. Roma watched all the comings and goings for a while and let her mind wander. She thought about how nice it must be to work in a bakery. Setting aside the obvious hard work of being on your feet all day, and no doubt some customers would be difficult, there would be a joy in providing people with comfort food all day, every day. Her job had involved working with files, not people. She'd sat behind a desk from nine till five, five days a week, and processed documents. They were very important documents, and she had to be responsible and meticulous, but it wasn't like working with living, breathing customers. It had got her through what had happened: knowing she could go to work and get lost in paper. Dealing with people had been too hard, was perhaps still too hard for her.

Roma took another bite, copped a hit of tangy tomato sauce, and sucked in a sudden breath to cool down the chunk of sausage roll burning her tongue. She had to think a moment about what day it actually was. Ah, it was Monday. These days, she suddenly realised, she didn't really need to know if it was a normal working day or not because she didn't have normal working days anymore. She had no Monday to Friday, nine to five routine; no timesheet to fill in and, as a consequence, her days had become a bit of a blur in just a couple of weeks.

She took this to be a good sign. She was filling her days with things now instead of thoughts. To others, Leo especially, her life might appear aimless. She knew people were worried about her, not just Leo but her former colleagues at work, and her oldest friends. She knew what they'd been saying, that she'd withdrawn from her life, that she'd shut herself up in grief and was wallowing in it. Some of what they said was cruel; some was true. It was easier to say no to friends than to go out and pretend. She simply couldn't act happy when she wasn't and attempting it was exhausting. So she'd burrowed away in her house, in herself, always asking herself the same questions, with no satisfactory answers.

How do I stop?

When does it stop?

When will it get better?

A car sped past, way too fast, and Roma startled, an icy shiver cracking her spine. A woman on her way into the bakery clucked her tongue and shook her head. Roma waited for her pounding head and her thumping heart to settle. When she felt calm enough to finish her lunch, when she thought she might not choke on the sausage roll if she took another bite, she realised she wasn't alone. Someone was standing in front of her. She looked up. It was a man. His eyes were hidden behind sunglasses and he was wearing a navy suit and a spotted burgundy tie. For a minute, she thought it was her real estate agent. Who else would wear a suit down here?

'Hello,' the man said with a broad smile.

Roma glanced from side to side, wondering if this stranger had mistaken her for someone else. She lifted a hand to her forehead to block out the sun so she could focus on his face. She didn't know him, she was sure of it.

'Hello,' she answered finally, hesitantly.

'I'm sorry to interrupt your lunch but you've just bought the old place up the top of Ocean Street.'

Remarkable Bay may be a little dot on the map and long past its glory days, but it seemed it wasn't so far from civilisation that mansplaining hadn't yet arrived.

'Yes.'

The man lifted his sunglasses and propped them on his long-ish, blondish-brown hair. He was still smiling. His teeth were very white. His eyes were a strangely mesmerising aqua blue. 'I saw you moving in yesterday.'

'Oh, right.'

'Hell, sorry. I should introduce myself.' He leaned down, reached a hand towards her. 'Not a stalker, I promise.' He chuckled. 'I'm Connor Stapleton. I live next door. That's how I knew you'd moved in. I saw the truck. "Smiths Removalists" on the side was a dead giveaway.'

Roma scrutinised this stranger. He was late thirties, maybe forty, judging by the flecks of grey at his temples, and she couldn't tell without a much closer inspection if the lines around his eyes were caused by too much laughing or age.

'Roma Harris.' She held out her hand and shook his politely.

'Welcome to Remarkable Bay,' Connor said cheerily. 'It's small but we like it. It's quiet too, but if that starts to drive you crazy, Victor Harbor's only twenty minutes away. And Adelaide's only an hour up the freeway.'

She knew the nearby town well from when her parents had lived there. It was a bustling retirement and holiday town further along the coast, with a hospital, a high school, banks, government services and shops. Roma had a loose plan in the back of her mind that when she wanted to go back to work, she might pick up a job in one of the government offices there.

'I know,' she said. 'I'm from Adelaide originally.'

'You are? Right. Well, let me fill you in on what our tiny town has to offer. You've obviously sampled the delights of the bakery. We have some quality offerings in the video shop.' Connor glanced across the road to the window filled with posters of the latest Hollywood action blockbuster. 'And what else do we have? The pharmacy. The general store. The surf shop, an oldie but a goodie. Then there's the pub and ... yep, that's about it.'

Connor Stapleton seemed to be Remarkable Bay's one-man welcoming committee.

'Thanks,' she said, deciding not to tell him that she knew Remarkable Bay. She'd quickly judged that if she mentioned that, it would lead to a longer conversation, and she didn't want a longer conversation. She hadn't been all that good at keeping the friends she'd had. This wasn't the right time to be making new ones. She reached for her purse and the brown paper bag holding her cream bun, stood and brushed the sausage roll crumbs off her coat.

'Well, it was nice to meet you, Connor,' Roma said, hoping it sounded polite. 'I've got to get back.' She slipped her purse into the front pocket of her jeans and pulled her coat closer around her.

'Sure. Me too.'

Connor was carrying a plastic bag from the bakery, which looked to be loaded with items. He hung back politely and then matched Roma's steps as they walked. She could hardly ask him not to as they were heading in the same direction.

It was a moment before Connor spoke. 'That's a great old place you've got. You doing a reno to sell it?'

'I'm not sure,' Roma said. And it was the truth. 'I'm living here for the moment. I'll see how it goes.'

'It had some pretty dodgy tenants for a while and no one was more thrilled than me to see them kicked out last year. All-night parties and lots of strangers coming and going and I'm pretty sure it wasn't tomatoes they were growing in the back yard behind the old chook shed. The whole town's been worried some investor would land in the Bay with a big cheque book, knock it down and build

luxury apartments in the vain hope that things pick up in the town.'
Connor stopped, held up a hand. 'Wait a minute.' He turned to her
and looked her up and down, clearly taking in her dirty jeans, her
old sneakers and her vintage coat.

'You're not some investor with a big cheque book who's going to
knock it down and build luxury apartments on it, are you?'

She looked down at her dirty sneakers. 'Do I look like an
investor?'

'No, you don't.'

'I'm not.'

Connor smiled. 'Now that is good news.'

They continued walking up Ocean Street.

Roma felt awkward with the silence and filled it. 'How long have
you lived in Remarkable Bay?'

Connor's bag from the bakery was swinging back and forth by
his leg, slowly, happily, like a child on a swing. 'That's a simple
question with a complicated answer. I'm from this part of the world
originally but I lived in Adelaide for a long time. I'm back now and
my son goes to my old school in Victor Harbor.'

'How old is your son?'

Connor chuckled. 'Angas is fifteen and he has the appetite of a
pack of marauding dogs. That's what this is for.' He lifted the bag.
'All for him to snort when he gets off the school bus. A salad roll, a
pastie and a finger bun. And that's just afternoon tea.'

'Boys, right?' and Roma smiled because that's the kind of thing
you should say when someone makes a crack about teenage boys
and their appetites. Not that she would know anything about that.
And then, she waited for the question from Connor about whether
she had any children, or a family, but it didn't come.

They continued up Ocean Street, past the shops and up the slow
incline towards Bayview and Connor's house. Connor pointed at
one of the old vacant stone buildings to their left. 'We hear this
one's about to become a Pilates studio.'

'Really? Here in Remarkable Bay?'

'I know. What next? A raw food cafe for our bustling metropolis?'

Roma let the laughter bubble up inside her. The unfamiliar sound of it surprised her.

Connor laughed along with her. 'I prefer surfing myself but, you know, whatever floats your boat. You into Pilates, Roma?'

'No,' she shook her head and grinned. 'Not in the slightest.' They stopped at her front gate. 'Well, here I am.' Roma held out a hand, wishing Connor to be gone as fast as possible so she could devour her cream bun and be alone again. 'It was nice to meet you, Connor Stapleton.'

'Likewise, Roma Harris. Welcome to Remarkable Bay. I'm sure we'll be bumping into each other from time to time.'

Roma smiled politely, turned and walked up her front path, the laugh they'd shared still ringing in her ears.

For the next couple of days, Roma worked solidly on the house. With the kitchen cleaned and unpacked, it was time to paint it. She'd chosen a warm white, knowing that no other colour on earth would go with the lime green of the cupboards. She set to work with her music blaring and sang softly to herself as she painted the ceiling—the first of two coats—the walls, the doorframes and the windows. There was a smallish window by the sink and then a double window next to the back door, which overlooked the back yard. It was slow work but she had time, and she approached her task like a project she had to manage at work. Every stage had to be planned, noted and ticked off. She liked the process of it, the way she could write a list of things to do and then complete them. After she'd finished the kitchen, she had a methodical plan to tackle the rest of the house. Downstairs, the hallway was next, then the living room, and the two spare rooms which would have been guestrooms a long time ago. The laundry could wait. Once they were done, she would head upstairs to paint her bedroom, the hallway and then, one by one, the other rooms. Five upstairs, in all, and five downstairs.

It was good to have a plan. To stick to it. With a plan, you knew what was coming next. There were no surprises. Sticking to a plan meant there was no time for thinking about the alternatives. Or, and this was really the object of it, no time for thinking at all.

Over two days, she made headway, slow but steady. Each night she went to bed with paint-splattered arms, the white splotches on them like freckles, her body tired and exhilarated from the progress she was making. Once she'd painted a second coat in the kitchen, she'd returned everything on to the benches. Her toaster. Her knife block. Her coffee machine. A row of colourful bowls on the open shelving on the wall near the fridge. She set a vanilla candle dead centre in the middle of her table and stood back, admiring what she'd done.

Next, Roma turned her attention to the hallway, which led from the front door, past rooms on either side, to the kitchen and laundry at the rear. Like everywhere in the house, the carpeting needed to be pulled up and decades of dust had to be swept away from underneath it. Nails from ancient underfelt would have to be pulled up with pliers and walls needed to be sugar-soaped. The worn carpet runner up the middle of the hallway was a floral Axminster in swirls of pale pink and mint green. It would have been luxurious in its day, she knew, but was now threadbare in places and torn in others, and she didn't even want to guess what had soaked through its fibres and down underneath it.

She wiped her hands down the front of her jeans and positioned herself at the kitchen end. She crouched down, pried her fingers under the end edge and tugged. The small piece she was holding pulled clean off in her hands, leaving her holding a knot of dusty threads that felt like hessian, and a waft of dust rose up and hit her throat.

'You're a genius, Roma,' she coughed. The carpet was nailed to the floor, and the small tacks were holding firm despite the rust which had sent them coppery. Roma kicked at the edge with her runners, and a little more of it gave way. She found her claw hammer in her red toolbox in the laundry and then got to work pulling up the nails. An hour later, she kicked the carpet into a roll like a magic carpet and dragged it out the back door. It was dumped on to the pile of refuse from all her work so far: empty paint tins, card-board boxes ready to be recycled and an assortment of other detri-tus that reminded her how much work she'd actually done. Roma allowed herself to feel a sense of achievement, a sense that she was moving forward; taking steps to reclaim a life for herself.

She fetched a broom, swept the hallway thoroughly and then considered it. The carpet runner had protected the floorboards underneath it and the space looked like someone had carved a pale landing strip into the wood.

Roma's days became a routine of breakfast, cleaning and paint-ing. She'd struck up a friendship with the staff in the big hardware store in Victor Harbor as she drove back and forth for supplies and advice. The pile of empty paint tins in the backyard began to grow higher. And each time she tossed one on to the pile, the clang attracted the attention of the dog next door. Its timorous cries—barking was hardly the word to describe how yappy and demure they sounded—led her to begin to reassure the mutt every time she walked outside. It had been hard, but she'd resisted looking over the low fence to see what kind of dog it was. The last thing she needed was another reminder about losing Charlie.

Each lunchtime she walked down to the bakery, telling her-self the exercise was all about the fresh air, and bought lunch. She varied the sausage roll every other day with a salad sandwich and rationed the cream buns. She didn't run into Connor Stapleton again, but the woman in the bakery with the nose ring, who Roma found out was called Lauren, had begun to make friendly jokes about whether or not it was a sausage roll day or a salad sandwich day and Roma let herself open up to this little piece of settling in to Remarkable Bay.

She'd finished the downstairs living room, cleaned and painted it, and moved her sofas into place. She'd even unpacked her precious books from their boxes and they filled the shelves of two book-cases which had come down in the removalists' van. She'd hung a mirror above the mantel of the brick fireplace and it bounced light around the rather dark room. On the shelf she placed silver trinkets and a photo of her parents in a silver frame, taken in their retirement home before they'd died. She hung a couple of pieces of original artwork on the walls and scattered some cushions on the sofas, before rolling out one of her old rugs and setting the low coffee table on it, and positioned the television on a small table in one corner. She flopped back on the nearest of the twin sofas and laid her head back, glancing around at all her familiar things. The room looked transformed. It had life in it now, and comfort. Roma hugged one of her throw cushions to her chest and sighed, bone weary, and allowed herself a minute to take it all in. This was a good room. The views from the window took in the grassed reserve across the road and Roma guessed that when the summer hit, this south facing room would remain cool.

She had a lot to learn about Bayview, she realised. Where the sun streamed in. How hot it would be upstairs in summer. The way the sea breeze flowed through it. She had time to learn its creaks and its foibles, its cracks and its secrets.

Her work continued. Roma cleaned and scraped and painted, transforming the hallway's faded custard-yellow stained walls into the palest blue with white trims. Wall by wall, she was making Bayview hers. She worked until sunset each night, threw together a quick meal and then went to bed with a book, where she barely made it through a couple of chapters before drowsing off, bone tired and feeling just a little bit satisfied with herself.

Two weeks after moving in, on a rainy Friday in late August, Addy arrived.

CHAPTER
5

Roma was upstairs in the room she'd set aside as her bedroom. She loved the space and couldn't wait until it was cleaned and painted and all hers. Big and light and airy, there would be room for her queen size bed, a couple of wardrobes and a sofa if she was inclined to set it up that way. Although they were faded yellow, the ceilings were perfect, patterns of pressed metal in elaborate forms and squares, and the French doors provided easy access to the balcony and the spectacular view across Remarkable Bay. She'd stood out there every day of the past two weeks, taking it all in in a sweep from ocean to sand to quiet street, and felt somehow, mysteriously, that this was where she was going to start her new life.

She was still sleeping on her mattress on the floor in her sleeping bag. She hadn't wanted to rush her bedroom but now she was eager to get it done, to set it up and luxuriate in the comfort of her own bed and this view.

She was inspecting the chips in the wall and wondering if she had the skills to plaster them over smooth, when she heard the knocking at the front door. She paused, then waited a moment longer for it to stop.

'Please go away,' she whispered. She didn't feel up to having to make conversation, to putting on a smile, to finding things to chat about with strangers.

There was another adamant knock.

Roma hoped it wasn't Connor Stapleton, stopping by to be neighbourly, then pushed the thought aside. It seemed like the kind of thing he might do. But she hadn't seen him since their encounter at the bakery the day after she'd moved in. He was obviously a busy man, what with his job that required the wearing of a suit and his teenage son who, by the sounds of it, needed constant feeding. And she'd been head down tail up in her own work.

The knocking continued. Roma really hoped it wasn't someone selling religion or a new electricity plan. She had no use for either.

Then a woman's voice drifted up to her. 'Are you there, Romes?'

Her memory fired up. Only two people called her that and one of them was Leo. It couldn't be.

Roma felt herself stiffen and tense. She opened the doors to the balcony and went outside. She peered over the railing into the front garden below.

'Addy?'

'Where the hell are you, Roma?'

'I'm up here,' Roma called.

Addy stepped backwards onto the path and into view, and peered upwards. 'Well, look at you. "It is the east and Juliet is the sun."' Addy dropped her voice an octave and lifted an arm skywards. Her red hair caught the sun and glimmered as it bounced on her shoulders. Her face was half covered by huge black sunglasses and her lips were movie-star red. A black woollen coat swamped her thin frame and the boots on her feet were polished to within an inch of their life. She looked like she'd just stepped off a movie set. She always did.

'What … what's going on?' Roma was still trying to process her shock. Should she have felt pleased to see her cousin, eight times

removed, here in Remarkable Bay? She couldn't find that emotion.
She felt her back go up and a suspicion set in, trepidation heavy in her
throat. Bayview was supposed to be her place to hide, not to entertain,
to perform, to step up, to compete. Especially with Addy. Because
experience had taught Roma that there could only ever be one winner
when it came to competing with Addy. And that was Addy.

"'She speaks.'" Addy replied dramatically, extending her arms
out to her sides, her flowing black coat and her wild curls blowing
about her as if she was caught in a tempest, not a stiff south coast
breeze.

Roma tried to smile so her questions would sound inquisitive
rather than accusatory. She wasn't happy to see Addy but was still
too polite to let it show. 'What are you doing here? Down there? In
Remarkable Bay, I mean?'

Addy swept aside the panels of her coat and propped her hands
on her slim hips. She took an exaggerated look over each shoulder,
perusing the quiet emptiness of Ocean Street. There wasn't much
to see, Roma knew. A lonely seagull hovered overhead and the
only two cars in the street were Roma's and now Addy's. There was
nothing else to interrupt the peaceful quiet.

Addy sighed audibly and avoided Roma's question. 'God. This
town hasn't changed a bit, has it? It's still a pimple on the backside of a coast in the middle of nowhere.' Her harsh critique was
undercut by the laugh in her voice.

Addy's words stirred something ancient in Roma and she gripped
the balcony railing. 'You can always get back in your car and drive
back to Adelaide, you know.' When she realised how the words
sounded out loud, she made herself laugh to lighten the mood,
trying not to let on that that's exactly what she needed Addy to do.

'Me? Go home? Not fucking likely now I'm here.' Addy pushed
her sunglasses back on to her head and looked back up to Roma.
'So, are you going to let me in, Juliet, or do I have to shimmy up a
drainpipe?'

It looked like Roma was going to have to invite her in. 'I'll be
down in a minute.' Roma took the stairs slowly, and stopped on

the landing, trying to give herself more time to collect herself, a moment more to breathe and figure out how she felt about Addy's arrival.

Younger than Roma by a month, Addy McNamara had been born with a flamboyant and dramatic streak. At school, Addy had excelled in everything but the curriculum. She was quietly removed with one year to complete and finished her high school education at an alternative school in the Adelaide Hills. In stark contrast, Roma had been a studious virgin well into university. There had always been a wildness to Addy, a barely restrained energy that people who should have known better had blamed on her fiery red hair. Roma had always known it had more to do with her parents than her genes. They had separated when Addy was in primary school, and continued to be at bitter odds for years over property and settlement of their considerable assets. But Roma's parents had opened their arms to Addy when she needed it most, and she'd been a regular guest of theirs during their summer holidays at Remarkable Bay. Addy and Roma had become best friends back then, or at least it had seemed that way to Roma.

When she opened the front door, Addy gasped her welcome. 'Well. Look at you.'

Addy's eyes slipped down to Roma's runners, stopping just a little too long on her thighs and the curve of her hips, before finally reaching her face. Addy had always been one of those people who seemed to say hello to your stomach before your eyes. This time, she knew exactly what Addy was thinking: that she'd got fat. It wasn't *fat* fat—she'd put on about eight kilos and had gone up a size or two depending on the brand of clothing but she was hardly *The Biggest Loser* material. And that one glance from Addy reminded Roma of how Addy had always made her feel. She gritted her teeth at the memories that came flooding back from those long ago summers ...

'No ice-cream for me. It's *so* fattening,' Addy had announced to Leo one year. The three of them had been walking down Ocean Street to the shops.

'What do *you* have to worry about?' Leo had said. 'You're skinny.' Leo hadn't been making a value judgement. He was a guy and he'd just been stating a guy fact in the no-nonsense way he'd always done. And he was right. Addy *was* skinny. Too skinny. So skinny she had hipbones that jutted out and created angles on her flat stomach. She had thighs that didn't meet in the middle. Addy had positively glowed at his words, and had flipped her long hair over her shoulder and skipped ahead of Roma to bask in the glow of Leo's attention. Roma decided then and there to buy two scoops of choc-on-choc just to show Addy she thought her obsession with the thinness of her thighs was ridiculous and anti-feminist. How could Addy not know she was skinny? How on earth could she still believe she was enormous? She'd always been slightly fixated on how she looked, but the summer they were fifteen she was out of control. She wouldn't even go for a swim anymore, much less go bodyboarding, because it smudged her mascara.

'Well, buy waterproof mascara next time,' Roma had argued, frustrated.

'This is waterproof,' Addy had explained, pointing to her eyes, 'But it still smudges and it's really hard to get off.'

'For god's sake,' Roma had huffed, and she'd grabbed her board and headed down into the water by herself.

Addy had been obsessed with finding the smallest bikini in just the right shade of blue and had dragged Roma to the Remarkable Bay surf shop, where she commandeered the single change room and paraded around the shop staring at herself in all the mirrors.

'What do you think?' she'd asked Roma, but it was a rhetorical question because she really didn't care for any answer that wasn't complimentary. And anyway, Addy wasn't even looking at Roma to wait for her opinion: she was too preoccupied looking over her shoulder checking out her own arse in the tall mirror fixed to the wall. She turned, ran her hands down the backs of her legs checking every centimetre for non-existent cellulite. Then she'd turned, sucked in her stomach, reached for the halter straps and tugged them upwards to lift her small but perky breasts.

Roma had turned away, pretending she was actually interested in the bikinis hanging tauntingly on the racks, slivers of strings and triangles she knew she would never dare wear. The idea of standing alongside Addy on the beach in one was mortifying. Roma had always preferred black racing bathers and a towel wrapped around her middle as soon as she'd come out of the water.

'Romes!' Addy had demanded.

She'd turned back, rolled her eyes teenage style and said, 'What?'

'Well? What do you think?'

That's when Roma had begun to fume. How dare Addy fish for compliments when she, well, when she looked like Addy? Didn't she see that all this posing, this preening, this showing off, was insulting and hurtful to the pear-shaped person with small breasts and thighs and a wobbly tummy? Did she even care? Roma held in the words Addy wanted to hear: of course you look good and you know it. She wanted to tell her to stop showing off and why don't you try saving the world for a change instead of being so obsessed with your body? But she didn't. Because she knew that Addy would assess her retort with pinpoint accuracy, that she would know how small and fat and envious Roma was. And Roma was desperate not to let Addy know that because that would have fuelled Addy's ego even more.

She's jealous of me because I'm so thin and beautiful. Of course she is. Poor Roma.

Instead, Roma found a smile. 'That colour looks great on you.' Addy had won. The attention was squarely back exactly where Addy liked it the most: herself and her non-existent thighs.

That summer was the beginning of the end. Addy didn't want to go bodyboarding anymore: she wanted to walk up and down the beach in her bikini. Roma didn't want to be the fat friend tagging along so she developed a sudden passion for surfing. She took lessons and fell off a hundred times before finally managing to get up on her board.

And that summer of the perfect bikini had been the second-last summer they'd spent together down at Remarkable Bay.

The second-last summer they'd spent as friends, before Addy had cut her off.

Which is why Roma was confused about why Addy was on her front doorstep now.

'I can't believe you're here,' she said with a pretend smile as she ushered Addy inside.

Addy glanced around at the hallway. 'Neither can I, but Leo told me all about this place and I had to come see for myself. For old time's sake.' She brushed past Roma and stepped into the hallway, taking in the space. She glanced up at the pressed metal ceilings, now crisp and white thanks to Roma's hard work, the pale blue walls, and as she walked up the hallway her boot steps echoed on the Baltic floorboards. Then she turned, looked again at Roma's paint-splattered jeans and her once black T-shirt which now looked like a Dalmatian's coat.

'I've been painting,' Roma said, somewhat unnecessarily.

Addy laughed. 'Of course you've been painting. You always were Little Miss Practical.'

Roma's hands became tight fists. She fought to make her voice light. 'And you've interrupted me. If I don't get back to it the brush'll dry and I'll have to go buy a new one.'

'Surely we have time for a coffee and a catch up?'

'Sure. Just let me deal with the paint.'

Before she could turn, Addy slipped an arm around Roma's shoulder and pulled her close. Addy's gaze was warm and direct and she paused, as if she was trying to read Roma, and she realised it was the first human touch she'd had in two months. 'It's so good to see you.'

The move startled Roma and she stiffened. 'It's good to see you, too,' she blurted, but she was only able to meet Addy's gaze for a moment. She shrugged out of her cousin's embrace.

'I'll be back in a minute.'

CHAPTER 6

Once Roma had put the lid back on the paint tin in one of the downstairs spare rooms and then wasted a couple more minutes unnecessarily fussing with the drop sheets, she began to feel increasingly more anxious about her interloper. She knew she had to face her, to chat, if she was to send her on her way back to Adelaide and out of her life once more. She found Addy in the kitchen, sitting at the table, one long leg languidly rested on the other, casually flicking through a magazine, way too fast to be doing anything other than looking at the photos.

Roma took a deep breath. It wasn't enough. She definitely needed a coffee. Maybe two. 'How are things in the film business?'

Addy waved a frustrated hand and returned the magazine to its pile. 'God, it's a nightmare. I've been knee-deep in pre-production on a film but some of the funding disappeared and we're in limbo now. The production office has been shut down and our leading man has flown off to Hollywood.'

Roma crossed the kitchen to the coffee machine and looked back over her shoulder. 'Who's that?'

'Josh Kruger.' Addy threw the name into the air and then raised her eyebrows, waiting for Roma to be impressed.

'Sorry,' Roma shrugged. 'I don't know who that is.'

'Really?' Addy splayed a hand to her chest. 'You haven't heard of Josh? He's extraordinarily talented. We were so lucky to get him, although,' Addy dropped her voice, 'between you and me he's a bit of a handful.'

She slipped a capsule into the top of the coffee machine and flicked it on. 'Would you like coffee or tea?'

Addy thought on the question. 'I don't suppose you have almond milk? Or green tea?'

What next? Goji berries? 'Sorry, no. Plain old supermarket tea bags, I'm afraid. And I only have the kind of milk that comes from a cow. Are you lactose intolerant or something?'

Addy lifted her chin and looked haughty. 'No. Not lactose intolerant. I'm just trying to eat clean, that's all. It's not paleo exactly but it's halfway there.' She paused. 'Wait. Okay, I'll have coffee. Black. No sugar, of course.'

Roma took two mugs from the cupboard and wished she had a biscuit barrel so she could plonk it on the table and stuff her face in front of Addy.

'So you bought this place, huh?'

'Yes. How did you know?'

'Leo told me but he didn't let on how rustic it is.'

'Rustic,' Roma repeated, suddenly cross at Leo. It felt like a betrayal, describing Bayview that way to Addy. It sounded like slick Sydney Leo and glamazon Addy had been laughing about her behind her back.

'It looks like it needs a whole lot of work.'

'I'm not afraid of hard work,' Roma said.

'I know,' Addy answered with a half-smile.

Roma made the coffees and warmed and frothed enough milk for hers, sliding a small silver jug around the silver tube from the coffee machine. She tried desperately to think of something to say. It had been so many years since they'd actually had a conversation that she was nervous.

'It's been a while,' Addy said matter-of-factly.

'Yes. Ages.'

'Hey, Romes?'

'Yeah?' Roma brought the coffees to the table and sat down opposite Addy, putting a distance between them.

Addy took in a deep breath. Her smile disappeared. 'I'm really sorry I wasn't at Tom's funeral.'

Leo had mentioned it, afterwards, that Addy wasn't there. Roma wouldn't have known and had hardly cared who was there and who wasn't. She had been too busy trying not to fall apart. That whole day was still a blur.

'It's all right.' She placed a reassuring hand on Addy's arm, although exactly why she should be reassuring Addy she wasn't sure. It was easier than talking about it, going back over that day, raking over those old coals. She didn't want to. She'd moved to Remarkable Bay to forget, not to have it all thrown back in her face so Addy could feel good and be redeemed for her behaviour.

Addy sniffed and her eyes welled. 'I'm so sorry. I was up in Broken Hill on a film and things weren't going well and …' She wiped her tears away with her delicate fingers.

'I understand,' Roma said. Even if Addy had been there, would Roma have wanted her to be? Lots of people didn't know how to handle grief, she knew that. People she'd thought of as friends had drifted away, especially those who'd been Tom's friends first.

'I knew you would understand,' Addy sniffed.

'So, this film you're working on has been delayed, huh?'

Addy nodded, wiped her eyes, found a smile that looked as false as a movie star's teeth. 'Yes. I'm now officially unemployed again.'

'I've never known how you do that,' Roma said.

'Do what?'

'How you cope with that uncertainly. Going from job to job like that. Never knowing what's next and how long it will last. All that insecurity. I couldn't live like that.'

Addy raised her eyebrows. 'Says the woman who's left her job and everything she knows to move into this place in the middle of nowhere. I mean, you're going to have to go back to work eventually, right?'

'Not until next year, I think.'

Addy glanced around the kitchen, at the lime-green bench tops and the ancient cabinetry. 'Was there nowhere more modern? With some amenities like, I don't know, a dishwasher?'

'I did look around at a couple of other places. Remember the one my parents used to rent, around the corner from here?'

Addy's face lit up and, for a moment, Roma saw through the glamour and the showbiz and the drama Addy had cloaked herself in for twenty years. She saw a glimmer of the young girl she had been, heartbroken about her parents, scared and alone. 'That little beach shack? The one with all the ants making that trail up the wall in our bedroom and those enormous moths?'

They both shivered at the memory and laughed. The house the Harrises leased every summer was a 1960s fibro shack. It had three small bedrooms, a living area and dine-in kitchen and a large front lawn on which the two girls and Leo used to play cricket with teams of kids Leo had dragged up from the beach. Roma and Addy had shared a bedroom and talked late into the night, still covered in sand and sunscreen, about what was happening on *Home and Away* and all the new music they'd heard on *rage*.

'I tried to find that shack, to see if it might be for sale. I was way too late. Like, a decade too late. There are two new places on that block now.'

Addy propped her chin in her hand. 'They were fun summers, weren't they?'

'Yes. Except you used to snore.'

'I did not!'

'Yes you did,' Roma said with certainty. Tom used to snore, softy and slightly annoyingly, if he'd had too much red wine. She'd poke him in the ribs and he would automatically turn on his side, away from her. She shut the memory away.

'I swear that was you, Roma. Not me.'

Roma finished her coffee. 'So why the visit to Remarkable Bay?'

Addy's eyes dropped to the table. 'I was hoping I could crash here for a few days. Is that all right?'

No, it wasn't all right. Roma didn't want Addy here. She didn't want anyone here yet. She'd been looking forward to welcoming Leo at Christmas, when the house was finished, when the front yard was tidied and she'd managed to paint the front veranda and clean all the windows. She didn't want people here when the house was a work in progress—when she was still a work in progress. This was supposed to be a place of solace, not Grand Central station.

Addy filled the heavy silence. 'That's okay. I understand. I've brought some things. I'll check in to the pub, or maybe drive to Victor and find a bed and breakfast or something.'

Her voice was brittle and proud and Roma winced inside. No matter what had happened between them, it felt wrong to be sending Addy away. Roma didn't want to do to Addy what her own parents had done for so many summers.

'Would you like to stay here?'

Addy's reaction was swift and unchecked. 'Really?'

Roma couldn't believe she was saying it. 'Yes. But although I have lots of rooms, I don't have any spare beds. You'll have to sleep on the sofa in the living room. It's not glamorous.'

'That sounds uncomfortable, but I'll take it.' Addy's smile was fragile. Roma suddenly realised that Addy must have been nervous about seeing her again after so much water under the bridge. She gave her some credit for her apology for missing Tom's funeral. There were other things to apologise for as well, but Roma filed her resentment away for the moment. Roma knew what a lost soul looked like: she was faced with one every morning in the mirror when she brushed her teeth. It was the least she could do.

'Can you give me the tour?'

'Shall we get your things from your car first?'

'Yes, which reminds me: I actually brought you a present. It's the most fabulous bottle of Kangaroo Island gin. Do you have any limes?'

'No limes,' Roma said with a shrug. 'Not even a lemon.'

'Talk about the boondocks,' Addy winked.

They brought inside Addy's leopard-print suitcase, a matching smaller carry-on bag and a laptop case and put them in the living room in a neat row before Roma led Addy upstairs for the start of the tour.

'Bathroom's at the end of the hall. There's a toilet downstairs off the laundry. There are spare rooms along here, which still smell kind of musty. And this room right here is going to be my bedroom.'

Addy slowly walked into the room, hesitating, taking in every detail: the space, the ceiling, the doors, the cracks. She turned to Roma with a beaming smile, her arms crossed, as if she was hugging herself tight.

'This is so beautiful. And the balcony!' Addy crossed the room and peered through the glass of the French doors. 'Look at that view. I can see right across to the other end of Remarkable Bay and all the way out to the ocean.'

'It's why I bought the place.'

'I can understand why,' Addy murmured. 'You know,' she turned back to Roma, 'I can help you.'

'Help me? With what?'

'This.' Addy waved a hand around. 'I can help you paint. I can also help you decorate this whole place. You don't spend fifteen years on movie and TV sets without picking up a few design tips. Especially cheap ones. And this house is huge.'

Roma tried not to say no immediately. She knew there were strings attached if she accepted Addy's help. She would want to choose the colours and furniture and placement of everything down to the last coat hook.

'I don't know quite why you wanted a place with so many rooms,' Addy pondered.

Roma shrugged. That was still a mystery, even to her. 'I like the space and the history of it. And the quiet. And I'm looking forward to the work, to transforming this house at my own pace. With my own ideas,' she added pointedly.

Addy raised her hands in defeat. 'I hear you and I promise not to be bossy. Please let me help. Think of it as me paying you back for letting me stay. Who knows, it could be months before I go back to work on the film. I'll have plenty of time.'

'Months?' Roma asked a little too quickly.

'Maybe.'

Roma's chest began to tighten, forcing her breaths into quick little pants. 'Oh.'

Addy laughed and her smile could still light up a room. 'I'm joking, Roma. But I do have some time. Why don't we have some fun? Just like we used to.'

Fun? That wasn't Roma's memory of her time with Addy.

Addy reached an arm around her and pulled her in close. Roma could feel Addy's thin fingers gripping her shoulder and she realised how comforting the touch was. The quiet solitude she'd created for herself was the only comfort she'd thought she needed. But her life and her emotions were still fragile. Once crack and she didn't know what might happen.

'Oh, Roma.'

'I'm okay. I'm fine.'

'That's not what your brother thinks.'

Roma swore under her breath. 'Is that the reason you're here? Did Leo tell you to come?'

Addy spun Roma around and gently pushed her out the bedroom door towards the stairs. 'You go paint. I'll unpack and try not to let this weird smell get into my clothes. Then I'm going to get supplies. Search for some limes. Then, we'll talk.'

Roma spent the rest of the day climbing up and down the ladder, rolling a fresh coat of paint over the faded and shabby walls in one of the rooms downstairs. Addy had been gone for hours and the silence gave her time to think. She needed to work up to having someone with her, after three years of self-imposed solitude, and she had to steel herself for spending time with Addy.

Addy still seemed as glamorous as ever and she'd become still more enviably beautiful the older she was, with a confidence replacing the obsessiveness of her teenage years. Roma tried not to dwell on her own feelings of inadequacy about that. It had eaten her up as a teenager, that competition and that envy. And while a tiny bit of that envy still lived in her darkest heart, many years ago Roma had come to a peace with the fact that some people were simply born beautiful and that she happened not to be one of them. Whatever miraculous mix of DNA it took to be attractive, some people had it and some didn't. She could already see it in some of the children she spotted walking with their parents at the supermarket. She'd spent a lot of time staring at other people's kids when she'd been desperate to have a baby with Tom. It wasn't to do with a hair colour or a physique but more with the mysterious combination of all those things that made a person seem confident and symmetrical and perfect. Those people stopped traffic, got the best jobs and the pay rises, got asked out and noticed. They were *seen*. They commanded attention without even knowing. People like that would never know a day when they weren't admired and gazed upon. Addy had always been one of those people.

Roma had not been one of those people.

Roma and Leo had grown up in a world in which they were judged for their intelligence and groomed to support causes their parents were passionate about, instead of anything as illusory or shallow or random as the way they looked. The Harrises were activists. They'd named Roma after Roma Mitchell, the brilliant South Australian lawyer and social justice reformer. Mitchell had graduated in law from the University of Adelaide in 1934, winning awards as the most brilliant student, and was later the first woman in Australia to be appointed a Queen's Counsel and then the first woman in Australia to be appointed a Supreme Court judge. They'd clearly believed that the bestowing of a name instilled in its recipient the same intellectual brilliance and success of its owner. Roma must have disappointed them tremendously.

She couldn't remember a year when she and Leo hadn't been dragged along to marches and rallies and demonstrations. The Harrises were the kind of family who boycotted particular brands of food because their international owners were dumping formula on

Third World countries, discouraging breastfeeding. They shopped at small supermarkets, not the corporately-owned stores, and boycotted certain petrol stations over oil spills in the world's oceans. Roma couldn't remember an issue on which they didn't have firm opinions.

Roma had felt their look of disappointment when she started to politely refuse to march for this cause or that outrage. It wasn't that she disagreed with the ideas that her parents cared so passionately about, it was simply that she was done with nailing her colours to the mast at every turn. She didn't want to end friendships because people felt differently about things than she did. Sometimes she was hungry and tired and just wanted a burger and fries without first checking the hiring practices and labour relations record of whichever fast food chain she passed on the way home.

She'd grown up around opinions and was tired of having to come up with one on every issue at a moment's notice. For Roma, things weren't black and white, now more than ever.

She had never lived up to one-tenth the promise of her namesake. She'd done well at school, but not brilliantly. She'd been at a loss as to what to do after she'd completed high school and had half-heartedly chosen an arts degree. She'd mentioned something vague to her parents about using that as a base from which to do International Studies, so she could apply for a position in the Department of Foreign Affairs, and their eyes had lit up with enthusiasm and excitement. She'd never intended to do anything more than complete her degree and find a job locally. That's how she'd met Tom, when they were both studying. He'd laughed at her jokes and wasn't into causes—the only things he was passionate about were football and cricket—and she decided that was enough. He was her first boyfriend and they married two years out of university. Tom had gone on to study a Diploma of Teaching and had become a primary school teacher. She'd been accepted into the graduate program of the public sector and had won a job in a government department. Her parents' world had been full, of causes, of politics, of opinions, of like-minded people with outrage in their hearts and determination in their souls.

Her world, from the outside a perfect world, had always been small. Home. University. Tom. Work. Her family. Tom's family.

And now, her move to Remarkable Bay had seen it shrink even smaller.

But she couldn't get lost in a little life.

Later that day, as the sun was setting in the western sky and colouring it with late evening swirls of pinks and purples, the two women sat out on the balcony, swathed in blankets, sipping their gin and tonics. Addy had done a decent grocery shop while she was out and had thrown together a meal of grilled chicken and salad while Roma showered, and Roma had scoffed it gratefully and hungrily while Addy did the dishes and cleaned up. Now, they were taking in the view, sitting in silence. They were both dressed for bed: Roma in loose-fitting pyjamas and ugg boots, and Addy in a silk kimono she'd pulled tightly around her, covering a chemise underneath. Her feet were bare, and she'd tucked them under her perfect arse for warmth.

In the distance, the bay was darkening from blue to black as the sun set, and the evening breeze had dropped. Seagulls on spindly orange legs gathered in the park across the road, as if staking out their positions for the discarded food from the next day's picnics. It was peaceful and quiet and Roma felt a swell of something warm and remotely familiar, something that felt like family. Leo had been in Sydney for years. Their parents were both dead. Tom was dead. She hadn't seen Addy in so many years and now, there were so many regrets about that she could hardly articulate them.

She leaned across the small table separating them and clinked glasses with Addy. 'This is great gin.'

'It is.' Addy sipped and then plunged two fingers into her tall glass for the slice of lemon. She put it in her mouth and sucked on it noisily.

'I see you found a lemon,' Roma noted.

'That I did.'

'And I'm glad because one can't indulge in *mother's ruin* without a slice of lemon, you know.'

Addy pulled out the rind from between her teeth, and looked perplexed. 'Mother's *what?*'

'Mother's ruin,' Roma repeated. 'That's what gin used to be called. Men could always handle their liquor, apparently, but it would do outrageous things to women.'

'Like what?' Addy laughed.

'Well, people believed that gin would lead women down the path of debauchery and hedonism. Perhaps it might even encourage them to …' Roma dropped her voice to a whisper and leaned in to Addy. 'Have sex.'

'I damn well hope so!' Addy exclaimed. 'Although I'm not liking my chances in Remarkable Bay.'

'And then,' Roma lifted her glass to the sky, 'By god and damnation, if they had sex they'd be corrupted and shamed and no better than common prostitutes. All when they should be home protecting their children and everyone else's morals.'

'Sounds exactly like my kind of drink,' Addy slurped what was left in her glass. She crunched the ice between her teeth and poured herself another with a slosh.

Roma held out her glass to Addy, who reached her fingers into the ice-filled Tupperware container on the table and tossed a couple in to Roma's glass. When she poured some more gin, it splashed up on to her fingers and she licked them slowly.

Roma shifted in her chair. They hadn't addressed the elephant in the room. Now, she was finally ready to ask.

'So, are you going to tell me the real reason you're here and what Leo told you about me?'

CHAPTER

7

Addy sighed and stared at her bright red fingernails for a moment. She knew that if she didn't tell Roma the truth, Leo would. Her bossy big brother Leo. The big brother Addy had always wanted for herself.

'It's true about the film being postponed. I really don't know if they'll ever get the money and at the moment, I couldn't give two shits, to be honest. But,' she continued, waving away the thought, 'Leo called me.'

'You said. So what did he say?'

'He's worried about you.' Addy figured paraphrasing Leo was probably better than quoting him. *He thinks you've gone nuts.*

'That's not news. He tells me that too, every Sunday when he calls.'

'You talk to him every week?'

'Yes.'

'Wow. That's such a big brother thing.'

'I know.'

'And you're lucky to have one, although I've always kind of thought of Leo as being my big brother, too. An annoying big brother, but still.'

Roma frowned. 'So he asked you to come and check up on me, huh?'

'When I called my mother to let her know I was going away, in the slim hope she'd care, she took delight in giving me the benefit of her very firm opinion. She insisted that this isolation, down here in the middle of nowhere, isn't good for you and is, quote, not a recognised part of the grieving process, unquote. And she blathered on something about you throwing yourself off a cliff.'

'There are plenty of cliffs along this part of the south coast.'

'Yeah, there are.'

'I'm so pleased everyone thinks I'm holding it together,' Roma said dryly.

Addy poked Roma with a stiff finger. 'C'mon, Romes. You know my mother. She's convinced she has some magical insight into everyone's head.'

Roma looked at Addy. 'She *is* a shrink.'

Addy scoffed. 'She's never managed to have any insight into her only child, as you very well know. So, when Leo called me, I suddenly realised there was no place on earth I'd rather be—except on a film set with Chris Hemsworth and Hugh Jackman playing strippers—than here with you in Remarkable Bay.'

'Strippers ...' Roma said wistfully.

'Now that's a movie I'd pay to see,' Addy said.

'Me too, sister.'

Sister. The word drifted over to Addy and lodged right behind her breastbone.

'Just for the record, Addy, I'm not entertaining suicidal thoughts.'

'Good to know,' Addy said, surprised to hear her own voice cracking just a little. And then she summoned up every piece of advice she'd ever given an actor on the brink of panic, a producer on the verge of drink or a director on the verge of locking herself away in a dark room and rocking back and forth until everything was over.

'You can do this, Roma. I know you're going to be okay.'

Roma looked sharply at Addy. 'Now you're sounding like your mother.'

'Ouch.' Addy sucked on a piece of ice. 'You've always been the smartest and most responsible person I know, and I trust you to be doing exactly what you need to be doing to get over Tom. Even if that means moving to Remarkable Bay. God, I don't think I've known you to do one single, frivolous thing in your whole life. Even your car is sensible.'

'It's a Subaru. It's good car.'

'The thing is, I hope you're not going to be so sensible that you don't make room for someone else in your life.'

She could see Roma stiffen. Her mouth hardened. Oh no, she'd gone too far.

Roma's voice was quiet. 'You think that'll help me get over Tom? Another man?'

'Sorry. Too soon?'

'Your question or men?'

'You're young, Roma. You could still have children if you wanted to, couldn't you? It's been three years. Have you ever thought about meeting someone else?'

The look on Roma's face told Addy she hadn't, which Addy thought was sad in a million different ways. Tom was obviously her person. Roma was one of those people who were just *good* at relationships. She'd found Tom young and they'd been so happy. Addy had seen it at their wedding, the way they'd gazed at each other, delirious and oblivious to anyone else there. They were young but no one doubted what they were doing: it had seemed right. They'd married in a beautiful and simple ceremony at a winery at McLaren Vale and they'd even written their own vows. They'd made a life together, so easily and simply that Addy had envied them. They were what happiness looked like. The house, the dog, the sensible Subaru in which they would drive off and spend weekends away wine-tasting in the Barossa or the Clare Valley. Good, regular jobs. She wondered why they hadn't had any kids, but knew better than to ask. There were lots of reasons why people didn't. Perhaps they wanted to maintain that perfect life by not having children. That was always the impression Addy had got on the rare occasions she saw them. They were always happy, just the two of them in their perfect little bubble of a life.

They'd never seemed to want Addy in it and she'd taken the hint, and stayed away. Their lives had diverged after all. Singles never quite fitted into couples, did they? Especially perfectly happy couples like Roma and Tom.

Addy had never found her person. And she'd looked.

Roma sighed. 'Have I thought of meeting someone else? No. It's too hard …'

'Losing them?' Addy said, filling in the end of the sentence when it appeared Roma couldn't.

'Yes,' Roma said quietly, looking distracted and far away. Then she seemed to snap out of her memory. She turned to Addy. 'What about you? Leo told me you were seeing some famous director or something.'

Addy suspected that if Roma had never heard of the hot young actor du jour Josh Kruger, she would never have heard of Jack Andersson, either.

'All over red rover.' She fought the urge to vomit.

'You're not together any more?'

'No. It's the business. It's hard to keep anything going. He's in Melbourne working on a TV show.'

'You okay?' Roma asked her suddenly, concern on her face. 'You look—'

'Me? I'm fine. I'm great, as a matter of fact. Look at this. The night. A bottle of gin. My cousin seven times removed.'

'I think we're four times removed.'

'Whatever we are. We're right back here in Remarkable Bay, the scene of so many teenage misadventures. Skinny-dipping off the rocks. Kissing boys in the bushes down there off the Harbour Master's Walk.'

Roma clicked her tongue. 'You may have been skinny-dipping and kissing boys. Sadly, I wasn't.'

'You were too!'

'Nuh uh. Not me.'

Addy thought about it. 'Didn't you hook up one year with that guy, the cute one with the dreadlocks?'

'That was you.'

'Oh yeah. It was me.'

'On that note, I think I'm going to bed.' Roma stood, folding her blanket over her elbow.

Addy liked it out on the balcony. The cool air was refreshing. The darkness mysterious and calming. She could disappear into it if she had to. 'I'll be in soon. I think I'll have another drink in the glamorous moonlight.'

Roma slipped the blanket around Addy's shoulders and went back inside, calling out, 'G'night.'

'Sweet dreams,' Addy whispered.

Addy hadn't wanted to tell Roma, but parts of her house smelt strange. Musty, old man strange. Even out on the balcony, with the chill breeze from the ocean sweeping up and caressing her face, it was strong, as if those musty, old man smells were slowly leeching out of the place, like the ghosts of the past, finally free.

She poured herself another gin, filling the glass with ice. She of all people shouldn't be surprised that old buildings held odours as well as secrets. She'd once tagged along with a set designer to a decrepit city hotel to assess its potential as a movie set and it was so disgusting inside she'd walked out and almost vomited. There were used condoms under the bed, a shower black with mould, and she hadn't been able to figure out how the pungent smell of urine had somehow seeped into the peeling wallpaper. Perfect for a movie about inner-city drug addicts which, funnily enough, was what they were scouting for.

Compared with that, Roma's new home was more than bearable. Oh, Addy had made a minor show of being slightly disgusted, wrinkling her nose and raising her eyebrows, because that's what people expected of her; of someone who'd met movie stars and famous directors, who went to film premieres and drank champagne and avoided the after-party drugs. Nothing but the glamorous life for Addy McNamara, right?

She stared out into the darkness and wished, for a long moment, that it would swallow her up. Thank god for dodgy financing deals, or she would be right back there in the production office tomorrow, not knowing if it was daytime or night outside, wrangling and cajoling and pulling rabbits out of hats and doing the impossible on an hourly basis: dealing with actors demanding they change hotel rooms because 'this one doesn't have the right feng shui' or another insisting on a new personal trainer because the first three hadn't helped him lose the magical ten pounds he needed; and the outrageously talented young director and arsehole who had been fucking the barely legal actress who was now going to be a huge star.

The outrageously talented director and arsehole—Jack Andersson—who had also been fucking *her*.

The gin was making her feel woozy. She poured herself another.

Addy always got lots of attention from men. She learnt just how much when she was a teenager, right down here at Remarkable Bay, the summer she looked more like a woman than a girl, that summer she'd bought her first bikini. When she'd been shipped off to spend holidays at Remarkable Bay with the Harrises, her parents had filled her purse with notes to make sure she had enough money—guilt money—and when they arrived that year, she'd headed directly to the surf shop on Ocean Street and spent it all. Halter-neck bikinis and string bikinis with delicate little ties at her hips and at her neck, in the colours she knew showed off her milky skin and her auburn hair: jades, aquas and purples. It was the perfect antidote to having become invisible at both of the homes she was shuttling between. At Remarkable Bay, on holidays for those two weeks each summer, she felt like the belle of the ball. She was far enough away from her own parents not to feel the scorching looks of their disapproval and disdain, and always able to hide from Roma and Leo's parents, she had more fun than she should have as a teenager. She liked boys. No, she loved boys, and they seemed to like her, too. She'd seen her first cock the summer she'd turned fourteen: it belonged to a surfer, the one with the half-hearted dreadlocks she'd misremembered, who, looking back, must have been about nineteen. He'd be arrested these days for what he'd tried to do.

She'd thought he was so hot and when he'd taken her hand and led her to a secluded part of the bay, over at the eastern end, and then into the dunes to a dugout hidden by the scrubby coastal plants, she'd quivered with excitement. Out of all the girls on the beach, he'd chosen her. She remembered that he'd laid out a towel, what a gentleman, and then she'd laid back on it, waiting for him to cover her with his tanned and salty body. They'd snogged for what seemed like one minute, before he'd cupped a hand inside her bikini top and over her breast. He'd moaned and she'd liked the sound of it, liked the feel of being touched that way. A second later, he'd grabbed her hand and pulled it down to his boardshorts and grunted, 'Suck me off.'

He flipped on to his back and, when he'd freed his cock from his boardshorts, it sprang up and almost lay back flat on his tanned belly. And then he reached for her, and one of his hands was on the back of her head, gripping her hair tightly, pushing her face down to his groin. She froze. Kissing was one thing. His hand on her breast was another. But choking on his dick was another thing entirely. She'd reached around and dug her nails into his hand and he pulled back.

'What?' he'd asked in a dumb-arse voice.

A fire had ignited in her belly and she remembering scrambling to her feet. 'Suck your own dick,' she'd spat at him and stormed off.

That attention from guys had been flattering for a couple of years until it turned into attention from older men, and that had just got plain creepy. She'd been more discerning then, more confident about turning away the losers and trying to choose the good ones. The law of averages meant there had to be some good ones in the mix, right?

She'd never found one who didn't just want her on their arm or in their bed because they thought she was beautiful and fuckable. And she'd enjoyed that status for a long time, through her late teens and all through her twenties.

And now, she was thirty-five and it was twenty-two year old, wide-eyed manic pixie dream girls who were fuckable. Oh, why the hell did she care? She didn't want that kind of attention from men anymore. Because she was convinced that men would look at her and *know*. Could they tell just by looking at her? Could they sense the humiliation and shame? Their attention now made her squirm and shrink further.

She'd learnt that attention from men hurt and she made an art of covering her body with loose clothing these days, not wanting anyone to see her ribs, her bony shoulders or her broken heart.

Addy shivered. The wind had picked up and she decided it was time to head inside too. She tiptoed through the quiet dark of Roma's room, went downstairs and navigated her way to the living room. Roma had tucked a sheet around the cushions, draped a blanket on top and placed two pillows at one end. Addy slipped out of her kimono and into the warmth and the protection of the cocoon.

Roma had been through so much that Addy's troubles seemed small in comparison. How could she admit to anyone that her glittering, glamorous life was as fragile as a glass bauble on a Christmas tree? It was all too shameful. She had a reputation to live up to, after all. Her life was just like that bauble: something that was lovely to look at from the outside but so fragile up close that if you squeezed too hard it would split into shards and cut you. And oh, how she'd been cut by Jack Andersson.

She'd met Jack when she'd volunteered to work for nix on his first film. He was an up-and-coming director and she was an experienced production coordinator. He needed someone to organise the production, although he hadn't known it yet, and he'd accepted her help begrudgingly. She'd only worked for nothing as a favour to an old friend, who vaguely knew Jack and had suggested he was the Next Big Thing in the film business and that she should hitch her little red wagon to him. Strategically, she knew that hooking yourself up to the Next Big Thing in the film business was smart, but practically, she'd hesitated. While artistically she believed in supporting new talent, she also believed in the principle of being able to pay her bills and, you know, eat.

But when she met Jack, she saw in an instant why people were bending over backwards to do favours for him. There was something about his ferocious energy and self-belief that was attractive as all hell. Before films, he'd been a chef, the next in a long line of a family of restaurant owners, but he'd told her that films—not food—were where his creative passions lay. It wasn't an exaggeration to say that Addy had walked into that first meeting and fallen in lust with him. That's how quick it was: instant, unplanned, combustible, from the first time their eyes met. And what was so attractive to her back then was that he needed her. He didn't know his way around a film set, not in the way she did, and it was intoxicating and powerful, the relationship they formed. Days on set. Nights fucking. He wasn't only creative in the kitchen or on set: he was creative in bed as well. And she'd loved the sex. Sex with Jack was wild and free and satisfying.

That first shoot was two weeks long and, because he'd come late to the industry, Jack Andersson was determined to grab every opportunity and squeeze the ever-loving life out of it. As he became more successful, his ego was nourished by festivals and prizes and crews and actors and actresses who were all desperate to work with him, and he loved it, got off on all that attention and success.

The bigger his reputation, the larger his personality grew, and Addy had begun to be the target of his frustrations, about why he wasn't in Hollywood yet, about why he wasn't getting the offers he believed he was worthy of.

When he began to lash out, taking out his frustrations on her, on whichever crew member happened to be on the end of the phone, she'd grown frightened and small around him. Once, during an argument, he'd thrown his mobile phone across her living room and the violent force of it had gouged a scar into the wall, a jagged reminder of his rage.

It became a spiral of violent thought and intent and he would always make excuses for it. 'I won't be so stressed when the film is over.' 'The editing is going so goddamn slow.' 'My lead actor has spent all night drinking and he looks like shit this morning. What am I going to do?' Addy didn't want to mention that his lead actor was out all night drinking because he was being bullied by his director. He couldn't seem to grasp that editing was going so slowly because he was changing his mind every damn minute.

When he wasn't throwing things, he demanded and taunted and exercised his power over her with words and with his fierce energy; demanding her loyalty, her positive critique of whatever project he was working on. He only wanted to hear her opinions when they aligned with his and humiliated her if she thought differently. After their vicious rows, he'd grab her and pull her into her bedroom and fuck her and apologise. Always in that order. He'd only ever say sorry after.

The last project they'd worked on together was a dystopian young adult movie.

The star of the dystopian young adult movie was the barely legal actress. Okay, she was more than barely legal. She was twenty-two and ethereal and had big wide eyes like a girl in a manga cartoon. She was going to be the next big thing too, you could see it in her pretty features, her dead straight and glossy hair parted in the middle that reminded every middle-aged director in town of the girls they went to school with who would never fuck them, and her quirky gorgeousness.

She shouldn't have been surprised she'd caught Jack at the wrap party. The intense workload in the industry—long days, six or seven day weeks on location, away from loved ones—led to raucous and uninhibited celebrations when projects were wrapped. Fuelled by alcohol and drugs, petty arguments were forgiven, long-running disputes were put to bed, and mildly amusing minor flirtations often became sex. Addy had seen it all before, so she should have known, should have been prepared for the sight of Jack kissing his twenty-two-year-old ingenue leading lady. Who was she kidding? It was more than kissing. Kissing implied a peck on the cheek. When Addy had wandered out from the bar, down a dark corridor on her way to the ladies, she saw it was more than a peck on the cheek. It was a full-body snog with groping thrown in.

The air had left Addy's lungs with a gigantic whoosh and her legs had stiffened. She couldn't look away and couldn't walk away. She didn't know what to do. Her judgement about confronting him had become as screwed up as he was. She was sophisticated, artistic and dramatic. She worked in the film industry, after all. She met famous actors and actresses and directors and producers all the time. Every day. She wasn't fazed by their fame or their sometimes unusual personality quirks.

So what if her lover was kissing his leading lady?

It was all that young ingenue's fault. Jack was hot and on his way to being famous and it was completely cynical but not entirely expected that women would be throwing themselves at him like this, fucking him to get a part.

When the barely legal leading lady lifted a knee and crooked it around Jack's hip and his hand reached around further and slipped inside her knickers, Addy had clenched her eyes shut. She'd tried to breathe. Was it her high heels making her knees wobble or the humiliation rising up in her gullet? Then, there was the smell of beer, hot breath in her ear and a tight grip on her arm.

'Fucker. They've been shagging like rabbits since he cast her. Sorry, Addy.'

She knew the voice. It was the sound guy who'd been flirting with her at the bar. She turned away from Jack and the ingenue and the betrayal and the humiliation and whispered, 'Let's get out of here.'

And she'd fucked the hot sound guy—whose name was Toby—in his car out the front of her house and as soon as she'd recovered from her hangover, she told Jack it was over.

Addy knew she couldn't compete with twenty-two and adoring and quirky and gorgeous. She was thirty-five and jaded, and had finally become immune to Jack's bullshit and his constant need to be the centre of attention.

There was only room for one person in her life who commanded the centre of attention, and that was her.

Addy threw her arms back above her head and stared up at the ceiling in Roma's living room. In the faint streetlight through the windows, she counted the squares in the intricate pressed metal.

One, two, three.

At the end of her relationship with Jack, she barely recognised herself anymore. Where had her fierce strength and independence gone? Oh, she knew: it had been sucked out of her by his demands and his increasingly explosive temperament. She'd shrunk, feeling herself getting smaller and smaller, until she felt brushed aside like a ball of fluff, drifted into a corner of his life. When the end finally came, when she finally ended it, Addy felt as if she'd lived through a cyclone.

Four, five, six.

Jack was in Melbourne now, in post-production on a new TV series about a serial killer. She thought it was a perfect fit for a psychopath.

Seven, eight, nine.

Jack was the reason she hadn't been able to get to Tom's funeral. Every ounce of emotional energy she'd had was poured into the unfillable well that was Jack Andersson. He had seemed like her last chance. At her age, she needed to settle down with someone, to stop the fucking around that was fun in her twenties but became something else entirely in her thirties. She couldn't keep up anymore with the young kids in the production crews: the drinking, the drugs, the dance parties. And whatever energy she had was subsumed into hiding her grief about where she was and what she'd let happen to herself. Addy couldn't be there for Roma because she was experiencing a terrible grief of her own. But she couldn't tell anyone. Hers had to remain hidden. In a fucked-up way, she had envied Roma. When your husband dies, people understand that you're sad and fragile. They expect you might disappear off the map for a while until you process your grief and the trauma of it all and, when you're ready to bounce back to life, when you've achieved that magical mystical thing called 'closure', people will be right there clapping for you as you emerge, like a beautiful butterfly unfurling from a cocoon of despair.

Addy's secrets were deep. Inside that glass bauble were feelings of humiliation and pain and regret so big she was sure they would come bursting out of her one day and she might never be able to stop the crying.

The fact was, she'd needed to escape her life as much as Roma had needed to escape hers. The timing of Leo's phone call had been serendipitous. The honest truth was she was wrung out. She'd been running on empty since she'd broken up with Jack. A week or so in Remarkable Bay wouldn't be all that bad. It would refuel her tanks. Fill her creative well. Some of the happiest times of her life had been spent down there with Roma, Leo and their parents. It represented summer and childhood and innocence and escape for all of them.

The gin had done its job. As she drifted off to sleep, Addy hoped this place could still be all those things for her now, twenty years later.

CHAPTER
8

The next morning, a warm late winter Saturday, Addy woke up with the morning sun. Her head was still a little fuzzy from the gin—make that a lot fuzzy—and she remembered with a smile what Roma had called it the night before. Mother's Ruin. Maybe it was Single Woman's Ruin, too. Whether it deserved credit or blame, she'd slept better than she had in a long, long time and felt like she'd woken with an unfamiliar energy.

Maybe it was the idea that she didn't have to go to work in the production office and wrangle people. Maybe it was something else altogether.

Addy thought on that as she slipped out of bed and pulled her silk dressing-gown around her shoulders. Maybe it was being here with Roma, thinking about what she'd been through when she'd lost Tom, that had forced Addy to rake over the coals of what she'd been through with Jack and put her own grief in a different place in her own head. A break-up was one thing, as humiliating and desperate as it had been. A death was something else entirely.

She flipped open the lid of her suitcase and dug around for her thongs. As she slipped them on her cold feet, she realised she hadn't packed the kind of clothes she would need for helping Roma with the renovation. Of course she hadn't. She'd fully expected that she might have spent last night in a bed and breakfast somewhere, not on Roma's sofa. In Roma's house. What she needed was old track pants and her Converse sneakers or stylishly worn denim jeans, fitness gear or even a glamorous-looking white business shirt that had once belonged to a lover which she could slide her arms into and knot at her slim waist. She laughed at the ridiculous thought. That was house renovating as seen in *Vogue*. She would have to borrow something from Roma, if anything fit. Addy knew she'd lost a little weight in the past six months. Roma's things would swim on her. Addy didn't like how it felt to be smaller. She didn't like the way it drew in her cheeks, sagged the skin on her face and emphasised the veins on the backs of her hands like scars. It hadn't been a planned strategy, Roma would be pleased to know. It was simply that when Addy was stressed, she forgot to eat. Her knotted stomach rejected food. And then, after, she wondered why she felt tired and listless and why her hair seemed to have lost its shine. She had to do something about that. She had to get healthy, and the enticing smell of bacon cooking drew her to the kitchen.

Two steps into the hallway and the centre plug popped out of one of her designer thongs. She kicked them off and left them just outside the kitchen door.

'Just in time,' Roma called out as Addy entered, waving a spatula with a flourish.

'That smells amazing. Can I do anything?'

'No. Just sit. You cooked dinner last night so I'm on breakfast duty.'

Addy gratefully pulled up a chair to the table and, in a flash, Roma presented a plate full of breakfast. And full meant overflowing.

'What is this?' Addy gasped. There was bacon and two fried eggs on rustic-looking toast, with a whole tomato cut in two and crisped, a side of mushrooms and wilted spinach.

'It's called breakfast.'

'I know it's breakfast but this is breakfast for two people. Make that four.'

Roma crossed her arms and frowned.

'It's what people in the real world eat when they've got a hangover.' Roma sat down and pushed her own now empty plate aside. She made a show of stealing a piece of crispy bacon and chomping on it.

'You too?' Addy muttered as she took her first bite of runny egg on toast.

'First time in a long time, but yeah. I slept like a log.'

Addy didn't answer but kept eating.

'Addy … you've lost weight since the last time I saw you.'

She shrugged her dressing-gown closer around her. 'I've been working hard. It happens to me on a film.'

'Is everything okay?'

Addy blinked and a long-buried shame rose to her throat. She swallowed hard. Roma remembered. Of course Roma remembered. She was the one who'd confronted Addy about the empty blister packs of laxatives she'd found stuffed under the bed behind Addy's suitcase, the summer they were sixteen. And when Addy had fought back, denied it, accused Roma of prying, of snooping, of being a goody-two-shoes, of being jealous of her because she was thin, Roma had resisted the insults and called Addy's mother. Dr McNamara had driven down to Remarkable Bay in her shiny black BMW and snatched Addy back to the city. Addy was never sure what her mother had been more horrified about—that her daughter was on the verge of a full-blown eating disorder, or that she hadn't seen it herself. Of course her mother hadn't seen it. She hadn't been looking and Addy had become an expert at hiding it. One thing her mother did do right was find a good therapist, and eventually, with time, she'd pulled back from the brink.

That was the last summer she and Roma spent together at Remarkable Bay. She could never have admitted it then, but Roma had saved her. She'd refused to keep Addy's secret. She'd hated Roma for a long time for revealing her secret, for humiliating her in front of her mother, for splitting open the glass bauble of her perfection. She'd felt betrayed, exposed and so, so embarrassed.

Now, she could see things in a different light. She realised just then, staring at the enormous breakfast that Roma had prepared for her, that Roma had actually saved her life. That realisation only compounded the terrible guilt she'd felt at not being there for Roma when Tom had died. Addy lowered her head to hide the flush she felt in her cheeks, slowly picked up her knife and fork, and ate some more.

Roma got the signal. She didn't push it. 'Coffee, tea or juice?'

'Coffee, thanks. With that full-fat cow's milk of yours.' Addy smiled. This really was damn good. 'Thanks for breakfast.'

'Any time.'

A moment later, there was a mug of steaming coffee on the table in front of her.

'Hey, my thongs just broke.' Addy scooped up a forkful of mushrooms and sighed when she tasted balsamic vinegar and olive oil. 'Will I have to drive in to Victor Harbor to get a new pair? A good pair, I mean?'

Roma shook her head. 'The surf shop's still here. The one down at the end of Ocean Street.'

'The same one from a million years ago?'

Roma confirmed it with a nod. 'Although I don't know what kind of business they do over the winter. Or over the summer, to be honest. You've seen what Remarkable Bay is like these days.'

Addy couldn't miss Roma's longing look at the last piece of bacon and pushed her plate across the table.

Roma snatched it up and smiled. 'I could never be a vegetarian.'

'Me neither. I'm going to shower and change and then head to the surf shop. When I get back, I'll help you.'

'See you when you get back.'

Half an hour later, Addy walked down Ocean Street, past the bakery and the pharmacy to the surf shop. It felt like entering the twilight zone. Nothing much had changed. The window looked like every surf shop in every coastal town in Australia: filled with surfboards, T-shirts and surf posters.

Addy pushed her way through the plastic strips hanging over the door. A bell tinkled and she was inside. There were more posters of strong men spinning their boards on killer waves. There was a rack of bodyboards right by the entrance, a decently stocked clothes section and a large display of Brazilian thongs next to other casual shoes, wallets and handbags. Above the counter, mounted on the wall, was a large TV playing surf videos with the sound muted.

A voice called out, 'If you need anything, give me a yell.'

She hadn't noticed the man behind the counter when she'd entered the shop. She looked over. His hands were flat on the counter top, which hunched his shoulders a little so he looked like he was shrugging, and there was a friendly smile on his tanned face. He was looking right at her. It gave her a little shimmer. The memory of a shimmer.

She pointed in the direction of the thong display. 'I think I've found what I'm looking for.'

'No worries,' he said and his eyebrows rose quickly as he lifted his jaw. He watched her, his arms crossed over his chest now, his hair surfer blond and messy, as she snaked her way through the shop. She stopped at the racks of women's clothing, flicked through the hangars as she assessed which colours might suit her, and found an ocean blue T-shirt with a scoop neck. She looped her arm through the hangar and checked out the thongs. She found her size, chose navy blue with a gold strap, and went to the counter. She placed the items on the glass. Surfer guy must have been watching her the whole time because he was still in the same position, like a stone sentinel, calm and unmoving.

'I'll take these, thanks.'

'Sure.' He removed the top from the hanger, folded it carefully, twisted the plastic tag off the thongs, and slipped them all into a big paper bag he'd pulled up from under the counter. He propped the bag upright and smiled at her. Everything he did was at a pace

Addy could only describe as chilled. In fact, everything about him looked chilled.

'You paying cash or card?' he murmured.

'Card.' Addy retrieved her purse from her handbag and did the swipe thing with the black machine on the counter.

'Receipt in the bag or …?' His big blue eyes were the same colour as the T-shirt she'd just bought.

'Yeah, in the bag is fine.' He slipped the printed receipt into the bag and pushed it across the counter.

'All yours.'

There was something about his smile that Addy wanted to bottle. She found herself needing to look at it a little longer. She hadn't been smiled at like that, with that kind of mellow, don't-give-a-shit interest, in a really long time. She grabbed the string handles of the bag and then paused, smiled, looked around the shop. 'This place hasn't changed in years.'

He straightened. 'You been here before?'

'I used to spend summers in the Bay. A long time ago. I mean, twenty years ago. And this place was always my first stop.'

'Thanks for being a regular,' he said with a grin. 'I appreciate your business.'

'You're welcome,' Addy replied with a laugh. 'I'm surprised the shop's still here, to be honest. It must be tough going running a business in Remarkable Bay.'

Surfer guy shrugged. 'Summer keeps me going. Winter's pretty dead. But I can surf every day and I live out the back, so, you know, there are worse ways to make a living.'

'Doesn't sound too bad at all.'

He paused, studied her face. 'I probably served you back then.'

'Really?'

'This used to be my parents' shop. I worked here in the summer. When they retired, I bought the business.'

'Well.' Addy thought back, wondered what he looked like back then, in the 1990s. She had a sudden horrifying thought.

'You didn't, by any chance, have dreadlocks, did you?'

He chuckled. 'Nope.'

Thank god for that.

Surfer guy shifted, crossed his arms again. 'So it's not holiday season now. What brings you back to the Bay?'

Addy looked around the shop. There were no other customers. 'My cousin bought Bayview, you know, that old place at the end of Ocean Street? She's renovating it and I'm staying with her.'

'It's good to see it being saved. It's been a dump for years.'

'Yeah, well … that's Roma for you. She likes a challenge.'

They looked at each other for a long moment. Addy really liked his eyes and his full lips and the way his gaze settled on her mouth.

'Well,' she finally said when it appeared he wasn't going to say anything more. 'Thanks for this.'

'Any time.'

As she slid a hand through the plastic strips at the front door, she turned at the sound of his voice.

'Hey, what's your name?'

Her heart thudded a little faster. 'Addy.' Then she added after a pause. 'McNamara.'

'Blake Stapleton. Welcome back.'

Addy lifted a hand and gave him a little wave. He nodded and grinned back at her.

On Sunday morning Roma and Addy had risen early and walked to the beach, where they'd wet their feet in the still-chilly waves and the cool sand. They took a round trip up to the other end of the beach, up the far steps and then back onto Ocean Street. It was about three quarters of an hour all up, just enough of a casual saunter to whet their appetites, which they were planning to sate at the bakery. Yesterday's fry-up seemed to have awakened Addy's appetite and she craved something sticky.

As they approached, someone came out of the bakery. It was Connor Stapleton. Before she could suggest to Addy that they slink away, he lifted his sunglasses, propped them on his head and smiled. No suit today, but jeans and a long-sleeved T-shirt pushed up his forearms.

'Hey Roma.' There was altogether too much enthusiasm in his voice.

'Hi, Connor.'

Roma didn't have to look at Addy to know she had questions in her eyes. Before she copped another sharp jab in the ribs, she motioned to Addy. 'Connor, this is my cousin, Addy.'

'Connor.' He held out a hand and Addy slipped hers into his big fingers.

'Pleased to meet you,' she said. 'How do you two know each other?'

Roma had lost her appetite for cake. 'Connor lives next door.'

'Oh, how lovely,' Addy said.

'With his family,' Roma clarified.

Connor smiled. 'Just my son. And meeting you solves our neighbourhood mystery.'

Roma and Addy exchanged glances.

'Angas told me he saw someone stealing lemons from the tree in our backyard on Friday.' He didn't even try to contain his grin.

Addy's hand flew to her mouth. 'Oh, shit. I didn't think anyone was home. There was no car in the driveway.'

'I was in court,' Connor said, tucking his hands into the pockets of his jeans. 'Angas must have picked that exact moment to pry his eyes away from his computer screen to see some, and I quote, "weird red-headed lady" nicking lemons.'

Addy laughed out loud and threw her head back. Roma stepped back from the bantering conversation between her cousin and her neighbour. Addy could commit a crime in broad daylight and still charm everyone. Roma still envied her mysterious skill.

'Guilty as charged, Your Honour. What was a gal to do? We were in desperate need of a gin and tonic.'

Roma looked away but turned when she felt a hand on her arm.

'How's the reno going?' Connor asked.

'Good. It's going well. Thanks.'

'It's looking wonderful,' Addy interrupted. 'You really should come over and have a look. Roma's done an amazing job with it.'

'I'd like to. I had a look through when it was on the market so it'd be great to see what you've done with it.'

'Sure,' Roma said.

'Well, it was nice to meet you, Addy. See you soon, Roma.'

It took a whole two minutes for Addy to ask. They'd gone into the shop and while Roma studied the display, Addy leaned over and whispered in Roma's ear.

'So?' she demanded.

'So what?' But she knew what the *so* was all about.

'When were you going to tell me about *Connor*?'

'There's nothing to tell. He's my neighbour. And he's the man you stole lemons from. I can't believe you did that. That is mortifying. I thought you'd bought them when you did the grocery shopping.'

'Oh, come on, Romes. There were so many that half the crop is on the ground. I knew he wouldn't mind. He seems quite lovely. What do you know about him?'

'Not much.'

'Well, we know he's a single man. He said it himself. Rather directly, if you remember, that there's just him and his son. He looks the right side of forty. And he mentioned something about being in court? I hope he's a lawyer or a magistrate or something and not a criminal or traffic offender.'

They placed their orders and, a few minutes later, walked out of the bakery carrying a bag each.

Roma shrugged. 'I don't know what Connor does for a living. I didn't ask.'

Addy pulled Roma to a stop in the middle of Ocean Street. 'Can you tell me why you have no curiosity about the lovely looking man who lives next door and can't seem to keep his eyes off you?'

Roma continued walking. 'Stop being so dramatic. This isn't a movie. There's no meet-cute happening here. He lives next door, that's all.'

'Really? You didn't see it? The way he looked at you?'

'You've been working in the movies too long. He was just being nice.'

Roma would never admit it to Addy, but she had seen it, had felt it, but desperately wished she hadn't.

Addy slipped an arm through Roma's as they walked. 'I think he was being more than nice to you. Pity for me. He's rather nice looking.'

'Go for it, Addy. He's all yours.'

Addy chuckled. 'Oh, I don't think so.'

As Bayview came into view, Addy tugged Roma towards the stretch of lawn across the road and they sat on the grass and ate their sticky buns, their legs kicked out in front of them. A flock of demanding seagulls landed noisily, and waited expectantly. Roma thought about her dog, Charlie. The only time he ever sat still was when food was being dangled in front of his nose. She'd lost him two years after Tom; the disobedient golden retriever had slept on her bed every night after Tom died.

'So,' Addy said, brushing crumbs from her jeans onto the grass. 'What do we do now we're exercised, fed and watered? Give me a job, damn it.'

Roma studied her. 'You really want something to do?'

'Of course I do.'

Roma thought on it. 'The cupboard downstairs at the end of the hallway, on the left by the laundry. I've been too scared to unlock it. I had this horrible thought that all the smells in the house were emanating from something inside. Do you want to have a look and see what's in there?'

Addy screwed up her nose. 'If there are any dead rats, I'm checking in to the nearest motel.'

Roma's work continued. When they arrived home, she changed into her painting gear and got back to work on her bedroom. Yesterday's coat had dried well and now it was time for the second.

She cranked up her favourite songs, picked up her brush and began cutting in the corners for the second coat.

Half an hour later, just as she was about to pick up the paint roller and really start to transform the room, her music cut out mid-song. She turned to see Addy across the room holding something in her hands, something that looked like an old book. She was coughing, and seemed to be standing in a cloud of dust.

'What's that?' Roma asked her from across the room.

Addy walked across the drop sheets, looking down to make sure she didn't trip. 'It was in the cupboard you asked me to clean out. The damn thing was painted shut with about ten different colours of paint, but I finally managed to pry it open with a chisel from your toolbox. I may accidentally have chipped the frame while doing it but it's open. And—good news—no rats. A few too many daddy-long-legs for my liking, but nothing a kiloton of insect spray couldn't deal with. So, when I got the door open I found this. It had slipped down the back of one of the bottom shelves and got wedged.'

Roma put her roller on its tray at her feet and stepped over it to Addy to take a closer look. She wiped the dust and spider webs from the cover to reveal embossed gold lettering.

'It's a guest book,' Roma said. 'What on earth was that doing in the cupboard?' She pressed her fingers to the cover, felt it cool and worn under the layer of dust obscuring the letters on the front.

'It looks like leather,' Addy noted. She blew some more dust away with a quick exhalation of breath and carefully opened the heavy cover. There on the first page, handwritten in delicate and intricate cursive, were the words:

Welcome to Bayview. 1934.

'Bayview,' Roma said, moving closer to Addy so she could see it closer. 'This used to be a guesthouse back in the day. That's why there are so many bedrooms.' She felt an excitement growing within her. 'Turn the page. Let's see who stayed here.'

'What if it was someone famous? C'mon, smartypants,' Addy teased. 'Who was alive in 1934?'

Roma thought for half a moment. 'Bradman. Dame Nellie Melba. Roy Rene. Squizzy Taylor.'

'Okay. I know one of those people.' Addy gently turned over the frontispiece and flicked through the book. There was page after page of names and addresses and dates on heavy paper. Roma skimmed them, making out the names of suburbs and towns she knew: North Adelaide. Kensington. Gilberton. Mt Gambier. Mt Compass. Lyndoch.

Addy flipped back to the first page. 'This is incredible. It's in such great condition. It must have been stuffed in that cupboard decades ago.'

Roma ran a finger down the list of names. 'Wait a minute. Look at this. It's… oh my god. Mr and Mrs Charles Allen. December 27th, 1934. Are they, could it be, our great-great-grandparents?' When she deciphered the name underneath it, she laughed in delight. 'Look at this. "Miss Ruby Allen". My great-grandmother!'

Addy giggled in giddy excitement, too. 'There she is. Miss Adeline Allen. My great-grandmother. Hell, I wish my parents had chosen Adeline instead of Adelaide. How could they do that to a girl growing up in Adelaide, huh?'

Roma didn't lift her eyes from the list of names. 'Oh stop. It's a beautiful name.'

Addy nudged Roma with her shoulder good-naturedly. She leaned over and traced an index finger over her great-grandmother's name. 'She should have been an actress with a name like that, don't you think? "The winner of the Best Actress Oscar is Adeline Allen". I don't think she was anything. Just a mother and a housewife.'

They sank to the floor, leaning their backs against the wall, staring at the names of the two women they'd never met; the two women who were sisters, who linked them right there and then, by blood, more than eighty years later.

'Did you know they stayed here back then?' Addy asked.

'I know that Charles and Henrietta started the tradition of summer holidays down here at Remarkable Bay. They were quite well to do, apparently, and they could afford to come down to the south coast to escape the city summers. But I had no idea they stayed here at Bayview.' Roma felt a swell of sadness battle with her excitement at the discovery. 'My mum and dad would have loved this.'

'It's amazing it survived intact.'

'The handwriting is incredible,' Roma said. 'So neat. Considering they would have used those old-fashioned nibs and ink bottles.'

'That means no emojis, right?'

Roma poked Addy in the ribs and they laughed heartily while she continued down the list. '"Mr and Mrs Frank Whitelock and family".'

Addy laughed and pronounced theatrically, '"Miss Gertrude and Miss Wilhelmina Smythe". Gertie and Willie. Spinsters, obviously. With names like that I'm not surprised. Poor things.'

'There were a lot of them after the First World War,' Roma added soberly. 'Spinsters, I mean. And widows.'

'Oh god. Of course there were.' Addy stilled. 'Wait a minute, Roma. Look at this. There's another Allen here.'

They peered closer, trying to read the smudged last name crammed at the very bottom of the page.

'Miss Celia Allen?' Addy tried to decipher the scrappy handwriting.

'No, it's not Celia. It's Clara. Miss Clara Allen,' Roma said slowly. The handwriting looked rushed, cramped at the margin, and the ink of the name 'Clara' had faded before there was a scratch and then a dark splodge where the surname had been dashed off. Whoever had written it had done so in a rush.

'This is so strange.' Roma was confused. 'Miss Clara Allen. And on the same page right here as Ruby and Adeline. I've only ever heard of the two Allen sisters. Your great-grandmother and mine. Ruby and Adeline.'

Addy looked over at Roma with wide eyes. 'Then who the hell is Clara Allen?'

CHAPTER
9

Remarkable Bay, 1934

Miss Ruby Allen, the eldest of the three Miss Allens of North Adelaide, stopped abruptly at the front gate of the beachside guesthouse in Remarkable Bay, her mother in front of her and her two sisters behind. At one end of the street the ocean beckoned, sparkling blue. In front, in the near distance, was the bay, its protected position making it the perfect place for bathing and walking and enjoying the fresh air. Today, the wind came along with the bright sunshine and Ruby slapped a hand to the top of her head to keep her delicate straw hat firmly in place. The last thing she wanted was for it to be picked up by the ocean breeze and swept out to sea. She'd bought it especially for this holiday and had guarded it carefully on her lap during the four-hour train journey and then the comparatively short half-hour taxi trip to the grandest guesthouse on all of Ocean Street.

'Welcome back to Bayview!' Bayview's proprietress, Mrs Nightingale, greeted them at the gate with a proud and friendly smile.

'Why, Mrs Nightingale,' Mrs Allen answered. 'We are delighted to be back for the summer once again.'

'And, as always, we're honoured to have you.' Mrs Nightingale, wiped her hands on the crisp white apron tied around her waist. Her ruddy cheeks and grey bun were so familiar to Ruby. Every year, the woman looked a little older, a little greyer, a little rounder. But her smile and her warm greeting hadn't aged at all.

'Hello, Mrs Nightingale.'

'Miss Ruby,' she exclaimed. 'Look at you.' She turned to Mrs Allen when she spoke. 'I see you have all your daughters with you once again?'

Ruby tried not to frown. She was fully aware of the subtext of the question. *Yes, we are all here,* she wanted to declare. Not one of us is yet married, although it wouldn't be long.

'Yes, all the girls are with me. We're all in need of some sea air. It's been so dreadfully hot up in Adelaide these past weeks.'

'Will Mr Allen be joining you this year?'

'Just after New Year's, as a matter of fact. Girls, hurry please and come in from the sun.'

Ruby glanced behind her. Her younger sister, Adeline, was proudly smoothing the skirt of her new summer travelling suit. Behind her was Clara, the youngest Miss Allen, who stood a way back with her head bowed. Ruby wasn't sure why she'd imagined her sisters would get on any better here in Remarkable Bay on holidays than they did at home in Adelaide, but she was disappointed their differing temperaments were already so obviously on display. Four weeks by the seaside always seemed like a wonderful idea when they were up in Adelaide and the summer heat was already blazing by early December. The thought of escaping the city for a sojourn on the south coast, where it was cooler by a few degrees and where the zephyr blew in throughout the afternoon and cooled everyone and everything, always made Ruby happy.

But now, standing on the street in the heat, with the wind trying to peel her straw hat from her head, she believed she might come to regret her initial enthusiasm. At least in Adelaide, back in their elegant city home on Buxton Street, Ruby could escape to her own room and her own peace. Here, she would be sharing with Adeline and Clara, and would therefore be a witness to their personality conflicts. It was a familiar routine: Adeline would taunt and Clara would bite back. In her head, she was already hatching a plan to slip off on her own, to feel the sand between her toes, to find her solitude. Silence, Ruby Allen had discovered, was a rare commodity with two younger sisters.

'When can we go bathing?' Adeline called out from behind Ruby. She'd turned to look across Ocean Street, past the croquet lawns and the neatly manicured hedge, to the curve of the bay in the distance. 'I can't wait to try out my new swimsuit. I'm sure it will cause a scandal,' she teased.

'You know Father won't let you wear it,' Ruby added wearily. She'd been hearing about the swimsuit all the way from Adelaide. The whole train journey had been filled with nothing but fashion and romance. Adeline had persuaded their mother to buy similar suits for all her daughters earlier that year, at the very fancy John Martin store on Rundle Street in Adelaide, but Ruby had been nervous about them ever since. Last summer, they'd all worn knitted, navy blue costumes, the kind that sagged and bagged when wet, but which provided respectable coverage from neck to knee. Their new swimming costumes were a generation on in just twelve months: backless bodices with matching shorts, barely disguised by an over-skirt. Adeline had seen them in the new magazine, the *Women's Weekly*, and had been immediately taken with how modern—and how Hollywood—they looked.

'You'll get a tan,' Clara added in a quiet voice.

'Oh, phooey,' Adeline said to the street.

'And even worse than a tan, you'll get freckles,' Ruby added.

'More than I already have?' Adeline tugged off her hat. She tossed her red curls over her shoulder and poked out her tongue at her youngest sister. Clara looked away. It was a familiar dynamic: at twenty-two Ruby was respectful and obedient, the perfect eldest sister. Adeline was flamboyant and audacious, always on the look-out for attention; and Clara, dearest Clara, would rather read a book than talk to anyone. It was going to be a long and trying summer.

'Girls!' Their mother called insistently and the Allen girls fell into line.

'Feel that cooling breeze,' Mrs Nightingale announced as they entered the Bayview Guest House. 'Isn't it refreshing? It will do you the world of good to take it in during your stay.' She inhaled enthusiastically and ushered them inside.

The sisters waited while their mother chatted politely with Mrs Nightingale, who fussed over a drawer at the reception counter before pulling out a set of keys.

'You never know what might happen this summer,' Adeline whispered to Clara. 'You might even find a husband.'

Ruby looked over her shoulder. Clara was blushing furiously. Her gaze dropped to her T-bar shoes.

'Adeline. For goodness sake, stop teasing. Clara is only just eighteen. She'll have plenty of time to think of that.'

Adeline huffed at Ruby and looked away.

'Here you are, Mrs Allen. I trust you'll enjoy your stay. All the usual activities are on offer this year. There are services on Sundays, of course, and we've been blessed with a new minister at St Andrew's. I believe he's organising picnics for the young people on Saturdays at Inman Valley. And then we have our annual tennis and croquet tournaments against the guests of the Sunnybrae Guest House. You'd better get practising, girls! We are delighted to have a new tearoom, the Orange Grove, further down Ocean Street, right between the chemist shop and the salon.' Mrs Nightingale clapped her hands together and almost bounced on the spot. When her grey bun had settled back into place on top of her head, she looked at the girls in turn. 'And of course, there's bathing.'

Adeline's ears pricked up. 'Tell me, Mrs Nightingale, are the men swimming topless down here this year? We've seen it in the magazines. It's all the rage in the south of France, you know.'

A silence fell on the party. Mrs Allen glared at Adeline.

Mrs Nightingale's lips pinched together in disgust. 'I'm sorry to say they are. So shameless. I can't think of anything more horrid than a man's hairy chest.' She shook the thought away. 'I hope the Miss Allens aren't exposed to any such thing during your stay. Come now, but before you go up to your rooms, would you care to sign the guest book? We've a new one this year and we'd be honoured if you would record your arrival.'

'Why, certainly,' Mrs Allen responded proudly and walked to the small polished wooden table in the hallway. She picked up a pen, dipped it in the crystal inkwell positioned next to the book and wrote with a flourish, *Mr and Mrs Charles Allen*.

'Come, girls,' she turned and beckoned to her daughters, 'I believe you're old enough to sign your own names this year.' Ruby and Adeline followed their mother and wrote their own names underneath, but Clara had been pushed aside by a bustling Mrs Nightingale, who'd spotted some arriving guests.

'Oh,' she cried. 'Mr and Mrs Whitelock. How delighted we are to have you back at Bayview. I hope 1934 has been kind to you.'

As the Whitelocks chatted amiably with Mrs Nightingale, she was distracted again by the arrival of two older women dressed head to toe in black. Ruby beckoned to Clara, who was trying to hurry past her sisters.

Ruby reached for Clara's arm and held her back. 'The guest book. You didn't sign it.'

Clara looked up at Ruby, her brown eyes flat, her normally rosy cheeks pale. 'It's just a silly book.'

'Please, Clara. Sign your name there so we're all together.' Ruby came close to whisper in her sister's ear. 'This might be the last summer.'

Clara understood her sister's meaning and nodded. She waited for other guests to finish writing their names and then picked up the pen and started. The nib scratched on the page. It had run out of ink. She hurriedly jabbed the pen into the inkwell and finished her name with a scribble.

'There. Happy?'

Ruby looked down. She was terribly disappointed that the Whitelocks and the Smythes had slipped in before Clara's name appeared. On this page, she would forever be separated from her youngest, most sensitive sister. She felt a pang of regret, of sadness about that, that their last summer would be recorded this way.

She made a point of looking closely at the page. 'Five out of ten for penmanship, Miss Allen.' Clara managed a thin smile before turning and heading down the hallway to the stairs.

Ruby took one last look at the guest book and her name written there, the ink still wet and shining. As insufferable as this summer would be, she thought about the fact that it may well be the last time she signed her name here as a Miss Allen.

She had four weeks to agree to marry Edwin Stuart.

Within the hour, every suitcase and bag belonging to the women of the Allen family had been unloaded from the taxi, carried up the stairs by the young local boy wearing a flat cap who worked for Mrs Nightingale, and deposited into the two rooms they'd booked for their summer. The girls' room was plain and simple, with three single beds, each with stiff white sheets and pale blue woollen blankets, and a dressing table of dark wood with a hinged mirror atop it. It held a porcelain wash bowl and a jug filled with fresh water, which they used to freshen up as they changed out of their travelling clothes into something more suitable for the holiday climate. There was one wardrobe to share between them, and they'd battled over hanging space for their day dresses, their summer suits, their evening gowns and their sportswear. Adeline had already tried on her new swimsuit, a racy emerald green to match her eyes, and had paraded around the room as if she were on the Cote d'Azur with Fred Astaire on her arm. Ruby had laughed at Adeline's antics. Clara had sunk her nose further into her book. Ruby wasn't so sure about her own swimsuit, in a slightly more demure navy polka dot pattern with thin white straps and white piping, so it remained in her suitcase.

After the excitement of the unpacking and the fashion parade had passed, Ruby found herself alone in their room. Her parents always took the grandest room upstairs, the huge room with double doors that opened out to the balcony, which they would have for their exclusive use during their stay. The sisters' room was next to that. Its tall sash window looked out over the yard of the neighbour's house, a low, flat stone cottage with a shining silver roof. The window was positioned perfectly to capture the sea breezes so the room would cool down at night. As the eldest sister, Ruby had the authority to claim the bed in the best position, the one right under the window, and was resting on it with her beloved copy of *Jane Eyre* when Adeline burst back into the room and flopped on her bed.

'Mrs Nightingale says afternoon tea will be at four. I'm famished. She does the best sponge cake this side of Adelaide and I'm simply bursting for a piece. Aren't you, Ruby?'

'I'd quite like a cup of tea.' Ruby lifted her gaze from the pages. 'I'll have to change first. Have you seen Clara?'

'Oh, I don't know where she is. She ran off somewhere almost as soon as we arrived. She's such a bore lately.' Adeline threw open the wardrobe door and pulled out a different dress, held it against her lithe frame. 'What do you think of this dress, Ruby?'

Afternoon tea was an elaborate spread in Bayview's front reception room. The large windows, topped and tailed by squares of dusky rose stained glass, overlooked the croquet lawn and, in the distance, the sparkling and restorative waters of Remarkable Bay. Mrs Allen, Adeline and Ruby had changed out of their travelling clothes into more formal dresses; their mother had thrown a spotted scarf around her neck with her cameo sitting neatly below the smallest bit of décolletage on show, and she held her short white gloves. Stockings and T-bar sandals completed her seaside elegance. Ruby felt much more modern: she and Adeline had chosen cotton dresses with short sleeves, modest collars and cinched-in waists. They wore sun hats like their mother but had left their gloves in their room. It was a small decadence but it was summer after all. Ruby glanced at Adeline. Her neckline was a little lower than Ruby's, her cheeks a little more rouged and her hat just the slightest bit more decorative. She was allowed these flamboyances because she was engaged.

When they appeared at the doorway to the reception room, Mrs Nightingale fluttered over, tapping her fingertips together.

'Good afternoon, ladies. I've saved our best table for you. If you would follow me.'

Each table was covered with a white linen tablecloth and silver flatware gleamed in the light. Mrs Nightingale directed them to a table surrounded by elegant high-backed chairs right in front of the window. Ruby waited for her mother to sit, and then pulled out a chair opposite her. Adeline chose the seat with the best view of the street—or rather, the best seat from which to be seen—and immediately pulled a silver compact from her clutch purse and checked her lipstick.

Mrs Nightingale stood solicitously at Mrs Allen's side and waited while she and her daughters settled.

'We're not seeing Miss Clara for tea this afternoon?' Mrs Nightingale looked at each of them in turn.

Ruby glanced at the empty chair and when she saw Adeline's red lips part with words on the edge of them, she blurted, 'A headache, I'm afraid.'

'Poor Miss Clara,' Mrs Nightingale tutted. 'To have journeyed all this way and be ill. Never mind. There will be more days and evenings' entertainment for her, no doubt. Now, shall I bring you a selection of today's offerings? We have sponge cake, Banbury cakes, Bakewell tarts and some delicious shortbread, made with butter delivered daily from the local farms. Everything is fresh as a daisy and made right here at Bayview.'

'That all sounds delicious,' Ruby said politely. Mrs Nightingale prided herself on her good table. 'Thank you, Mrs Nightingale.'

Adeline was sitting straight-backed in her chair, clutching her purse in her lap, staring out the window, when Ruby kicked her under the table. Adeline glared at her before finding her manners. 'Why thank you, Mrs Nightingale. You do make the best tea on the south coast. Oh, and Mrs Nightingale?'

'Yes, Adeline?'

'Would you happen to have the latest edition of *The Advertiser*?'

'Since when do you read the paper?' Ruby said out of the corner of her mouth.

'I don't believe it's arrived yet,' Mrs Nightingale said. 'As soon as it does, I'll make sure you see it.'

She bustled off happily, in her element, cheered by a full house for summer. Ruby supposed there had been lean years during the Great Depression, not only for Bayview, but for the whole of Remarkable Bay and each of the holiday towns along the south coast. They'd heard rumours in their circles that some families had lost everything, but the Allens had remained immune from the misfortunes many had faced. They had never stopped coming to Remarkable Bay.

Adeline leaned in and hissed. 'There's no need to kick me, Ruby. I'll have a bruise on my leg now. People might think I've been playing cricket or something just as ghastly. I can't have a bruise when James gets here.'

'What will your fiancé care about a bruise?' Ruby asked. 'And what do you want with the newspaper?'

Addy lifted her chin. 'As a matter of fact, I wanted to see if Lady Kitty has mentioned us. It would make my friends so envious if we were to get a mention.'

Ruby could think of nothing less important than a mention in Lady Kitty's column, 'Around the Bridge Table', which listed all the holiday comings and goings—who in Adelaide society was going to Victor Harbor or Melbourne or London.

'Girls,' Mrs Allen hushed with a quick glance from side to side to see if anyone had overheard. 'Goodness me, can we stop the bickering? And Ruby, what did you say about Clara? She didn't mention anything to me about a headache. Where is she? I don't know what I'm going to do with that child.'

Ruby searched for an excuse for her sister. She didn't want Clara to get into trouble. 'Perhaps it's a little hot for her today. I'm sure she'll be fine after a lie down.'

'I didn't see her lying down in our room,' Adeline said with her chin lifted haughtily in the air. Ruby desperately wanted to kick her under the table again—much harder this time—but found another distraction in the form of familiar faces entering the room.

Their mother had noticed them, too. 'Mrs Cameron. Susanna. How lovely to see you. Are you staying here at Bayview?'

'Mrs Allen. Girls. Delighted to see you. We have rooms in Victor Harbor, at Linger Longer, but we've heard so much about the afternoon tea here we simply couldn't resist stopping in.'

'You won't be disappointed,' Mrs Allen said, and the way she puffed out her ample chest made Ruby think that her mother seemed to be personally taking the credit for everyone else's hard labours in the kitchen.

The Camerons were acquaintances from Mrs Allen's gardening club and they'd appeared in the nick of time. When Mrs Nightingale returned with a pot of tea and a china plate of biscuits, the Camerons joined the Allen's table and made chitchat about the season, the tennis tournament, the condition of the croquet lawn and, happily for Adeline, her wedding to James Stuart in a few months' time.

The mere mention of the wedding perked her up no end and soon she was engaged in animated conversation with Susanna about gowns and music and where she and James might honeymoon. 'Victor Harbor is one option, and it's very popular, but we may go into the Adelaide Hills. James's family has a cottage there, which they may allow us to use. It could still be rather warm in April, so it might be cooler up there, don't you think?'

Ruby allowed herself to slip out of the conversation, taking her tea slowly, nibbling delicately on a Banbury cake. The room was full now and there were many conversations happening all round her. Snatches of them floated to her: reunions, reminiscences, remonstrations and polite laughter. With another more searching look, Ruby realised the room seemed to be full of women, all sipping tea delicately from Royal Albert tea cups, their backs upright, their hats just so, their dresses perfect for afternoon tea.

'Are you looking forward to being a bridesmaid at your sister's wedding, Ruby?'

Ruby brought her attention back to the table to see that her mother and the Camerons were staring at her. Adeline was wide-eyed, clearly waiting for an answer in which Ruby would say that it was undoubtedly going to be the ultimate honour of her twenty-two years to be the bridesmaid at her younger sister's nuptials.

This time, Adeline kicked her.

'I … I beg your pardon?' Ruby stammered.

'Adeline's wedding,' Mrs Allen said. 'Mrs Cameron was asking if you're excited about being a bridesmaid.'

'Oh, yes,' she smiled and tried to mean it. 'Adeline has such marvellous taste. I can't wait to see what she'll want me to wear.'

Adeline beamed, completely missing the irony in her sister's tone.

'And of course,' Mrs Allen added with a proud expression, 'Ruby will also be a bride before too long. She has a fiancé, who happens to be Adeline's fiancé James's brother. Edwin Stuart. Two sisters are to marry two brothers. Our two families are going to be linked in such a happy way. We are truly blessed.'

Ruby wanted the earth to crack open so she could hide in its fissure. 'Mother. You know we're not …'

'What a delight,' Mrs Cameron said. 'It seems 1935 will be a momentous year for the Allen family.'

'Yes,' was all Ruby managed to say. All eyes were on her and she fought the strong urge to squirm—or vomit. She wasn't sure. She picked up her Banbury cake and bit off a huge chunk. It caught in her throat and it made her cough loudly and repeatedly. Others in the room looked over as she made a spectacle of herself. She pressed a hand to her chest and tried desperately to breathe.

'Ruby,' Mrs Allen said with a pat on her daughter's shoulder. 'For goodness sake, take a sip of tea.'

Ruby clutched at her cup and swallowed the sweet liquid. She didn't want to talk about weddings or Edwin.

'Perhaps I need some air,' she spluttered. 'If it's all right with you, mother?'

'Why yes, off you go.' Mrs Allen turned her attention back to the Camerons, and Ruby grabbed her bag from her lap and headed out to the door.

Ruby walked up Ocean Street, until she was sure she was out of view of the prying eyes in the tearoom, and stopped, drawing up deep breaths. She let her gaze drift to the end of the street, past the stone houses on the right side—each yard carefully contained behind a white picket fence, each planted with red rhododendrons, whose flowers looked like puckered lips ready to be kissed—to the dip at the end. The sand of the street gave way to the cliff tops and a vast expanse of blue ocean, white caps dancing in the distance, and a hint of cloud in the bright sky. That's where she wanted to be, her feet buried in the sand, the breezes clearing her head of the thoughts that were crowding in on her, choking her.

She turned back, and breathed a sigh of relief when she found the path which she remembered led down to the cool waters of Remarkable Bay. She was careful of slipping on the loose ground and slowly made her way down the winding track as it looped around to the left and then down the steep wooden stairs to the beach.

She slipped off her sandals and dug her toes into the cool sand.

She needed to be alone, to quell her anger: at Adeline, at her mother, at Clara.

And at the situation she had found herself in.

She hadn't wanted her mother to mention Edwin. She supposed it couldn't be helped: Mrs Allen's life revolved around her husband, her children, her relations, her garden and the house. Whatever happened within that small sphere became her highest priority. And marrying off her daughters to the right men from the right families was most important of all.

It was her mother's dearest wish—and her father's clear instruction—that she should marry Edwin Stuart. Their fathers were longstanding business acquaintances and their mothers had spoken of nothing else since Edwin had called on Ruby one wet Sunday afternoon and asked to be introduced to her parents. Her father had afterwards made it abundantly clear that she was twenty-two years old now and, having been educated at the best schools (an education Ruby believed to have been entirely wasted if the object of her study had purely been to find a husband), it was now time for her to create a household of her own. And the thought that two of the Allen girls would marry two of the Stuart boys was simply too delicious not to encourage.

Edwin had proposed two weeks before, in the lead-up to the excitement of Christmas. She'd hadn't been blind to the fact that it was coming, in the same way lightning follows thunder, but she hadn't said yes right away. She hadn't wanted him to propose and, the longer they'd courted, the more certain she had become of that. So, she'd bought time and promised him an answer when she returned from Remarkable Bay.

She had only agreed to see Edwin because he was James's brother and it was easier than admitting she hadn't found anyone to love. It wasn't that he was objectionable. He was, in fact, a terribly nice chap. Her father found him agreeable and her mother was satisfied that he came from a prosperous family, the right kind of family. And of course there was James and Adeline's engagement, which had only made Ruby feel more trapped. The problem was that she didn't love Edwin. She could never love him—and the burden of that secret was like ballast around her neck.

She ran to the water and gasped in delight when the rippling waves splashed her ankles. She wished she could scoop her hands full and splash her face too, but someone might see and she might wet the hem of her dress and then she'd have to explain it to her mother and the recriminations would be tiresome.

Ruby held her purse and her shoes by their straps in her right hand and with her left, clamped her straw hat on her head. She lifted her face to the warm afternoon sun and closed her eyes against the brightness. She wanted to wish all these dilemmas away, to have them float out to sea until they reached the South Pole. She knew how important this summer holiday was. It could well be the last one she would spend as a young woman with her sisters. After that, it was expected that the burdens of an adult life would be hers as well: a husband, children, a house, her relations, her garden and her charity work.

It's what young women in her set did.

She stilled, let the water lap at her feet, wave after wave, and matched her breaths to the rhythm of the current.

Her solitude was over. She must get back. She had to find Clara.

CHAPTER
10

It didn't take long for Ruby to find her youngest sister. Clara hadn't strayed far. A cursory search of the large backyard at Bayview revealed that Clara was in the far right hand corner talking to the chickens. Clara adored anything with wings. She'd settled herself on a low stool, next to the sizeable and abundant vegetable patch, taking advantage of the shade of a tree to protect herself from the sun and to hide. Ruby walked down the path which divided the yard and called her sister's name. Clara looked up, her eyes swimming with tears.

Ruby quickened her step and, when she reached her, slipped an arm around her shoulder. Her youngest sister sobbed, her shoulders heaving and shaking.

'There, there,' Ruby said, patting her mousy brown hair. 'Whatever is the matter, Clara?'

Clara didn't say a word but clung to her sister so tight that Ruby almost lost her balance. She gripped the cotton of Ruby's dress and pressed her mouth and nose into it to stifle the sound of her sobs. Ruby felt herself stiffen. She was scared into wordlessness now. Clara was usually a quiet and contained person. At just eighteen, she held herself neatly together like a piece of embroidery; she had never been prone to wild displays like Adeline. She preferred her own company, and had always seemed to love these beach holidays. They would often lose her for hours and would later discover she'd been roaming the walking trails along the cliff tops, or through the coastal bushes, stopping to admire the finches and sea birds, the kites and the pelicans which soared overhead on the updrafts. Sometimes she sketched them in a little notepad she kept tucked in her pocket. She was as gentle a creature as the birds she loved.

Ruby knelt down at Clara's side. 'Clara, has something happened?'

And when Clara met Ruby's eyes, Ruby knew the answer. Her face was pale and streaked with tears. Her eyes, red and swollen, were frightened.

'Please don't tell mother. Or Adeline. Please don't breathe a word.'

'Of course I won't. Will you tell me what it is?'

Clara shook her head furiously. 'I can't, Ruby. I can't tell you.' And she pushed herself off the stool and ran towards the house, her straw hat flying off her head and landing on the path.

Ruby picked it up and took Clara's place on the stool. She watched the chickens scratching in the dirt, clawing and pecking at what looked like potato peelings and corn husks. She knew her mother would be wondering where she was but had to settle the panicked racing of her heart before she went back inside.

Without thinking, Ruby nibbled at a fingernail before swiftly pulling it with her teeth. What on earth was wrong with Clara? Had her heart been broken? Was there a beau she was missing, someone secret in Adelaide, someone so precious to her heart that the idea of being away from him for four weeks had upset her so?

Ruby settled her breathing. No, it was more than that. This was more than an upset. The look she had seen in Clara's eyes resembled sheer terror. She turned her back on the clucking chickens and steeled herself to go back inside to her mother and sister and pretend that nothing at all had happened.

* * *

The Allens had no plans for the evening, which Ruby was greatly relieved about. They'd changed for a late supper and enjoyed Mrs Nightingale's cold cuts and potato salad and then honeycomb pudding for sweets, although none of it was delicious enough to tempt Clara to eat more than a mouthful.

She had reappeared for dinner, although she hadn't changed into a suitable dress which irked their mother, and picked at the offerings on her plate. Ruby had been anxious to distract her mother and Adeline from Clara's low mood, so had regaled them with the details of an item she'd read in the most recent *Women's Weekly* about girl cricketers and their first international cricket match between Australia and England. The idea so appalled Mrs Allen, who along with most Australians had been enraptured with the feats of Don Bradman's triple century at Headingly just six months before, that she had talked of nothing else for fifteen whole minutes, enabling Ruby to take the stairs up to their rooms without saying another word before wishing her mother a good night.

Once they were in bed, Ruby tried to shut out Adeline's complaints about the enforced early bedtime and how excited she was about seeing James, and eventually her two younger sisters drifted off to sleep. The sound of the waves from the bay below was somehow louder at night time, providing a soothing lullaby.

But still Ruby lay awake, restless, her mind racing in a hundred different directions. She pulled the blanket up to her chin, guarding against the cool of the night, and then pushed it back, hot and bothered. What was wrong with Clara? She wasn't frivolous or dramatic, so this change in her behaviour flooded Ruby with concern. The tears and fear couldn't be about a young man, could it? She resolved that in the morning she would demand to know the truth, believing that a problem shared was a problem halved.

Ruby turned on her side to look out the window to the night sky, trying to find a star to wish on. Her big-sisterly instinct came naturally, but she also fretted that any advice she might have for Clara—if indeed she did have a simple broken heart—would be less than useless. After all, what did Ruby know of love? She'd never had a sweetheart and had definitely never been in love, and her thoughts of Clara's suffering only reminded her of that sad fact. She'd been trying so hard to love Edwin, but had never looked at him and felt anything other than a brotherly sort of friendliness. He was handsome enough, she supposed, and courteous. He had a quiet humour about him and loved the cricket, which impressed her parents. He was the opposite of his brother: James was charming and tremendously handsome, with a boisterous wit and the ability to make friends with absolutely everyone he met. He and Adeline were, in that respect, a perfect match. Edwin and Ruby were the older, more settled siblings and perhaps that's why their families had decided they would suit one another. He had good prospects in his father's business—as Ruby's mother reminded her frequently—and it would be more than enough to sustain a wife and a family. Recent history had reminded everyone how important that security was.

Ruby knew what she was supposed to do and how she was supposed to feel, but she found herself not caring if more than a week went by without a visit from Edwin. And the few times he'd reached for her hand while they'd been walking in the park near her parents' house, she'd only let him because it was what was expected of two young people who were courting.

Ruby pulled her pillow over her ears, trying to block out the thick sound of Adeline's heavy breathing. Her sister was loud even in slumber. It was no wonder she was sleeping like a baby: Adeline the beautiful didn't have a worry in the world. She was as pretty as a picture and charming and everything Adeline did brought a shine to their father's eyes. To him, she was unutterably delightful. Her engagement to one of Adelaide's most eligible young men had only rendered her more favoured. James Stuart came from a good and prosperous family. He worked in the family's stock business too, which had interests in cattle properties in the mid-north and the fortune that went along with that. He was strapping and manly, with dark hair and a rakish smile, and Adeline seemed smitten from the first moment she had laid eyes on him. He'd romanced her with wildflowers and invitations to West's Coffee Palace on Hindley Street, which was so exotic she'd squealed, and had quickly proposed to her.

Ruby had seen for herself how enamoured Adeline was with James. She giggled girlishly at the mere mention of his name and when she came home after spending time with him her cheeks were so flushed that Ruby could only imagine they'd been kissing by the front gate.

Ruby pressed a cool finger to her lips. What would real kissing be like? When she was younger, she'd watched Rudolph Valentino films at the Mayfair Theatre in Rundle Street. *The Son of the Sheik*, co-starring Vilma Bánky, had been one of her favourites. She'd watched in fascinated delight, imagining how kissing must feel: passionate and romantic, wild and lustful. She sighed into the darkness of the room. Edwin was in the habit of pressing his thin lips to her cheek, chaste and discreet. He didn't even look her in the eyes after, as though he was embarrassed. Perhaps that was what real love looked like, she thought. Discreet. Courteous. Respectful. The movies were make-believe, after all. Especially Rudolph Valentino. He wasn't even a sheik—he was Italian.

Was she wrong to want to be properly kissed by someone? As she lay in the dark, Ruby wrestled with the knowledge that Adeline would be gone soon, and so might she be.

This would be the last summer of the three Miss Allens.

They might be as different as night and day, as the city and the coast, but they were sisters, after all. As she finally drifted off to sleep, Ruby resolved to talk to Clara and get to the bottom of what was wrong. And, she acknowledged, she definitely needed to be more charitable to Adeline.

The next morning, the Allens met for breakfast at precisely eight o'clock. The breakfast room was large and long, with eight square tables arranged precisely in two rows of four. On one wall, a breakfast-room cabinet with leadlight windows caught the light and gleamed. The two tall windows opposite were wide open and the sheer net curtains billowed in the sea breeze, cooling the already warm room. Mrs Allen chose porridge with honey despite the forecast for a hot day. Adeline nibbled on a boiled egg, shaking salt on top of it like snow. Ruby slathered home-made bread with a pat of butter so fresh there were beads of moisture in it and topped it with deliciously sweet apricot jam. Clara nibbled on a piece of toast and had tea with no milk. When their mother announced plans for a walk along Ocean Street, Clara pleaded a headache. Ruby suggested she should stay and see to her sister. Adeline scoffed but after a swift kick in the shins under the table and a wide-eyed rebuke from Ruby, she reluctantly acquiesced to the excursion and Mrs Allen and her middle daughter headed off.

Ruby saw Clara up the stairs to their room and watched her as she undressed; in slow motion, as though in a trance. Ruby slipped Clara's cotton dress on a hanger, put it back in the wardrobe and slipped her shoes under the bed. When Clara climbed between the covers in her slip, Ruby tucked her in and sat by her side. Her sister was pale and unfamiliar dark circles shadowed her eyes.

'Shall I ask mother to get the doctor for you, Clara?' Ruby stroked her sister's forehead. She was clammy and sweating.

Clara's eyes had fluttered shut but sprang wide open at Ruby's suggestion. And there it was again, the look of horror which had worried Ruby the day before. 'No! Please. Leave me alone. I need to lie down, that's all. Perhaps it was something I ate.' Her voice trailed off weakly.

'How can that be? You've barely touched any food since we arrived yesterday. Please, Clara. You must tell me … is there someone special you're missing? Is there a boy?'

Clara stared up at her sister, stony-faced now, her cheeks tear-streaked. 'No, Ruby. And please don't ask me again.'

Ruby reluctantly left Clara alone. She found her worn copy of *Jane Eyre* and went downstairs to the front parlour to read it undisturbed. The book had been a gift from their aunt Jane, Mrs Allen's oldest sister. She'd lost her husband in the war and had never remarried, but had remained in Sydney where they'd lived. Ruby had always liked her: there was something independent and mysterious about Aunt Jane. She dressed flamboyantly and had a rich, plum-cake voice which meant everything she uttered had an air of authority. Mrs Allen thought Sydney had ruined her, with its wild ways and modern attitudes, but Ruby had always wanted to be like her. She hadn't seemed to have suffered from being a tragic childless widow, as her mother always described her.

Holding her book in her hands, turning the thin pages, Ruby wondered if the very act of reading the book her aunt had given her might help her absorb some of her wild independence. She looked about the room and huffed. Such wild independence, indeed: she was on holiday with her family and sitting inside reading when the sun was shining and there were no doubt adventures to be had out-of-doors. While it was tempting to get out into the fresh air herself—she felt as if she'd been cooped up for weeks instead of days—she'd decided it was probably best she stayed close in case Clara needed her and, if their mother returned and found Clara had been left on her own, she might well call the doctor herself.

Ruby was happy to have found a calm and peaceful haven in the guest house, which was normally bustling with people. There were a number of settees in the room, upholstered in bold floral patterns, with round high tables positioned at each end. In the far corner of the room, a blue-and-white Chinoiserie vase filled with apple-green fern fronds sat on its own pedestal. There was a dark wood phonograph in one corner and a low table with a stack of records on it, but no music was being played this morning.

She found a comfortable position in the overstuffed armchair and opened her book.

And promptly closed it again. She couldn't concentrate on it today. There seemed to be too much going on outside in Remarkable Bay and she suppressed the urge to explore it. The sun was shining warm and the breeze was slight, and judging by the thwack and occasional cheers, croquet was being played on the lawns across Ocean Street. There was fierce practising underway for the competition with Sunnybrae, the other large guesthouse in Remarkable Bay. The annual event was a serious contest with a silver cup awarded to the winner. For three years straight, the Morrison family from Sunnybrae, via Adelaide, had been instrumental in the house's victory, but this past winter one of the young sons had died of strep throat, and another had joined the army, so the Bayview crowd believed they might be in with a chance.

Ruby sighed. She hated croquet. And tennis. It was the only thing she loathed about summers at Remarkable Bay: the organised sport. Maybe it was all because of Adeline, who was altogether too competitive. Ruby suspected Adeline loved the attention she received when she won more than the actual winning—and win she did. Often. No doubt she would be instrumental in the Bayview Guest House Croquet Team 1934.

Ruby laid her head on the back of the armchair and looked upwards. The parlour's ceiling was made up of intricate squares painted a dazzling white. Curlicues and lilies decorated each one, alongside leaves and swirls and flowers that looked to be proteas.

'Hello?'

She startled at the voice, which had come from the direction of the reception desk, situated on the other side of the hallway. She waited for Mrs Nightingale or one of the kitchen girls to come, but a minute passed with no response.

'Coo-ee.' It was a male voice, deep, but with a chuckle, the kind that had to belong to a young man.

There was still no response from Mrs Nightingale. Ruby wondered where the older woman could be at this time of the morning. Usually, she would be clucking over the young women who worked at the house: ensuring the breakfast dishes were done and stacked away; that preparations were underway for that day's hot lunch and that evening's supper; and that bathrooms were cleaned and surfaces were dusted and polished. It was about this time every day that the scents of cakes and biscuits baking wafted up the stairwell into the upstairs rooms, rumbling everyone's stomachs as they imagined what delights awaited them for afternoon tea and dessert later that night. Ruby lifted her book from her lap and stood. She smoothed down her white cotton day dress and went to investigate. She'd been right. A young man was standing at the reception desk. A very tall young man, looking left and right over his broad shoulders. When her movement caught his eye, his hand flew to the brim of his flat cap, and he tugged it off in a deft move, exposing chestnut brown hair which he quickly patted down with his other hand.

'Good morning,' he said quickly.

'Good morning,' Ruby replied.

'I'm sorry to bother, but I'm looking for Mrs Nightingale. I went around the back as I normally do, but she's not to be seen, so I thought I'd check here.'

Ruby's hand went to the nape of her neck, where her short and relatively new bob haircut exposed the skin. It prickled and she pressed her fingers to the warm skin there. 'She doesn't appear to be here.' She glanced to the reception desk and then behind her to the hallway. 'In fact, no one seems to be here. Except for me.'

'That's pretty lucky for me, I'd say.' The young man raised an eyebrow and grinned.

Ruby found herself smiling in return. 'It's rather unfortunate, as it turns out. I'm not sure I can help you with anything.'

'I take it you're a guest here?' He took just the slightest step towards her. His blue eyes were trained on her and she warmed at the clear intensity of his gaze. Her pulse quickened. She felt hot. It was strangely thrilling to be looked upon this way by a total stranger.

'Yes. I'm here with my family.'

'Are you in Remarkable Bay for the whole summer?'

'A mere four weeks, I'm afraid. We return to Adelaide at the end of January.'

'Four weeks.' His grin became something more and its transformation had Ruby feeling unsteady on her feet. 'That's just enough time to see all there is to see in Remarkable Bay, I believe.'

'I believe it is.'

Neither of them spoke for a moment. Ruby knew she should find Mrs Nightingale so this young man could conduct his business and be on his way. She could judge by the smudges of dirt on his white shirt, which was rolled up into cuffs at the elbow, and his dirt-covered working boots that he wasn't a prospective guest. His skin was the colour of honey and without even touching it she could feel the warmth and strength radiating from his forearms. *He looks like Rudolph Valentino,* she thought.

She found some words. 'I find Remarkable Bay to be a nice respite from the city's summer heat.'

'It definitely is,' he said, his eyes fixed firmly on hers. She could see the muscles moving in his strong jaw, cleanly shaven. 'There's nothing better than a dip in the bay to wash off the city blues,' he added. 'Do you swim?'

'Yes I do. A little.'

'You should be careful of the rips out there in the bay. It looks calm but if you swim out too far, they might drag you away to the South Pole. And that would be a tragedy.'

Ruby laughed. 'I'll be safe in the shallows, I can assure you.'

He looked at his feet and then up to Ruby's face. She shivered at the realisation there was a blush in his cheeks and a new shine in his eyes, which were the most remarkable shade of aqua blue.

Ruby's fingers gripped tight on her leather-bound Brontë. She could feel her breasts rising and falling with her deep breaths.

He shook his head, as if he'd been hypnotised by a snake charmer and had suddenly remembered where he was. 'I have milk for Mrs Nightingale. And butter.'

'You do?' Ruby said.

'They're from my family's farm. We supply both Bayview and Sunnybrae.'

'Oh.' Ruby thought back to breakfast and the lavish way she'd spread her toast. It was with butter delivered by this young man, from his farm. She could taste its delicious creaminess all over again.

'I'll go ahead and make my deliveries.' He played with his flat cap, running his fingers along the stiff brim as he held it against his stomach. 'Would you be so kind as to tell Mrs Nightingale that I've been by?'

Ruby looked him up and down. He was dressed like a farm hand but he certainly didn't sound like one. 'She'll probably guess when she sees the milk.'

He smiled. 'Yes. She probably will.'

'And I shall think of you when I eat my toast at breakfast tomorrow morning,' Ruby said, feeling brave and flirtatious.

His chin lifted and a look of delight crossed his face, creasing the corners of his eyes. 'I apologise for my manners. I didn't introduce myself.' He held out a big hand. 'Cain Stapleton. I'm very pleased to meet you.'

'Ruby Allen.' She reached out and put her hand in his.

'Wishing you a good day, Miss Allen,' he said, 'And a very pleasant four weeks in Remarkable Bay.'

She nodded mutely as he walked down the path to his truck, whistling a song she'd heard on the radio.

When she looked down at her fingers, she could see her hand was shaking.

CHAPTER
11

2016

Roma and Addy sat at the kitchen table, carefully poring over the pages of the dusty guest book. It was set out in landscape format, about thirty centimetres high and sixty wide, and there were pages and pages of names, beginning with the Allens in December 1934 right at the top of the first page.

'This really is incredible,' Addy said.

'All these names,' Roma replied. 'All this history. I still can't believe our great-grandmothers were here.'

'They probably were never right *here*,' Addy noted. 'Not in the kitchen. There would have been servants, you know. To bring them their cups of tea and their fancy cakes. I remember my mother telling me once about her grandmother, that there were live-in staff when she was a child. The war changed everything, apparently, much to my mother's disappointment. After that, people didn't have big parties and fancy functions at home anymore. She would love to have live-in staff to cater to her every whim. To cook and to clean and arrange dinner parties and fetch her dry-cleaning.' A shadow crossed Addy's face.

'Can't see a downside myself,' Roma said. 'Although having people living in your house all the time, knowing your secrets? Being there every time you went to the toilet or were pre-menstrual? How could you ever spend a day binge-watching DVDs in your track pants if you had people working in your house? Nope. I couldn't do it.'

Roma pointed to a name on the page of the guest book. 'Who were all these people? And what do you think happened to them?' To think that Bayview, left unloved for so long, had once been a welcoming place for so many people made Roma happier than she had been in a very long time. Had some of them gone off to fight in World War II?

'If these walls could talk, huh?'

'Maybe they'd be able to explain the weird smell upstairs,' Addy said with a poker face. 'Do you think people fell in love in this house? Took honeymoons? Maybe had sex with people they shouldn't?'

Roma flicked back to the first page and ran her index finger over the name that intrigued her. 'Probably all of the above. I get the feeling the good old days weren't always quite so good. What baffles me is … no one in our family has ever mentioned a Clara before.' Roma peered down at the faded cursive. She placed her coffee cup away from the book once she'd had another sip, careful not to spill anything on it.

Addy quickly gulped in a lungful of air, turned her head and sneezed. Her red hair bounced. 'Sorry.' She sniffed. 'It's the dust.'

'Bless you,' Roma said, distractedly.

'Thank you.' Addy found a tissue in her pocket and blew her nose. 'It's not that unusual a name. There were probably loads of Allens back then. The name could be as common as muck. Like Wang in China or O'Reilly in Ireland. Maybe …' she waved a hand in the air while she pondered a solution. 'Maybe there were other Allens staying at Bayview who aren't related to *our* Allens? Or maybe they were distant cousins they didn't like?'

Addy and Roma shared a smile at the knowledge that might have been them.

'But look at the date. All these Allens arrived on the same day— December 27, 1934.'

'But her name isn't with the other Allens,' Addy pointed out. 'There are all these other people in between.'

'True.' Roma studied the names again: the Whitelocks. The Smythes.

In the living room, a mobile phone rang. Addy stood. 'That's me. I'll go grab it.'

Roma closed the book. If her parents were still alive, she could have asked them. Clara Allen would have been her mother's great-aunt but Roma had never heard the name before. And even if there had been any family paperwork or old photos that Roma's grand-parents on the Allen side might have had stored away, everything had been lost in the Ash Wednesday bushfires of 1983, when their home in the Adelaide Hills had been razed into nothing but grey ash and twisted sheets of roofing iron. They'd evacuated with only the clothes they were wearing and their kelpie, Bessie.

Maybe Leo would remember something, some old family story, a name from the past. Roma pondered if she should chase up some cousins, if she knew their names. They hadn't been one of those families who stayed tight. When people became grandparents, they created new dynasties and new extended families. Roma barely knew her own aunts and uncles, much less their children—except Addy, of course. Would Ruby and Adeline be disappointed to know that their descendants barely knew each other? Would they have imagined it would be any different? Would they be disappointed to know their memory and their names and reputation hadn't been carried on forever? That their stories had died with them?

Her thoughts turned to her own family. What did she really know about her own parents? If she had questions now that she was older, it was too late to ask. A sadness overwhelmed her at the idea that she would not pass on her great-grandmother Ruby's DNA to a child. The line had stopped with her. She was almost too old now to ever have children to pass on her stories to, no matter how much she'd burned with desire for a family of her own. Her brother Leo was three years older—thirty-eight—and kids didn't look likely in his future, either, so her stories would die with her. Would she even be a footnote in any other family's history? Who would remember her? And who would remember Tom now that he was dead?

Time passes, people change. Stories are only important to the people who live them.

Which brought her back to the guest book. Who was the mysterious Clara Allen?

Roma took her coffee cup to the sink and rinsed it, set it on the draining rack. She'd have to think about Clara later. She had painting to do.

In the living room, her temporary bedroom, Addy had missed Leo's call. She found her phone—tossed on to the floor earlier that day—and saw his name. There were others too. One from Jack and one from her mother. There was only one of them she wanted to talk to.

She made the call. 'Hi, Leo the Lion.'

'Hey, Addy.'

'What's up with you?'

'Just touching base to see how she is.'

Addy sat on the sofa, looking around the room as she talked in a low voice in case Roma overheard anything. 'She's good. Better than I thought, actually. Wait until you see this place. It's actually pretty spectacular and she's already made a start on cleaning up and painting. I'm going to stay for a while and help her.'

'You? Really?'

'Yes, me.'

'I'm sure you two will have some interesting things to say to each other after all this time.' Leo chuckled. 'Thanks again for going down there. I feel much better knowing she's not on her own.'

'It works for me too. Hey,' Addy added almost as an afterthought. 'We found something.'

'A dead possum?'

'No. An old guest book from 1934. It was jammed down the back of an old built-in cupboard in the laundry. And guess what? It turns out our great-grandmothers stayed right here in this house in the thirties. Ruby and Adeline Allen.'

'In Bayview?'

'Yeah. Their names are right there in the guest book. But there's a name we didn't recognise. Alongside Adeline and Ruby was the name Clara Allen. Do you know if she's a relation? Have you ever heard anyone in the family mention her?'

There was silence down the line while Leo mulled over the question. 'No, I don't think so. Clara Allen,' he repeated. 'Adeline and Ruby were the only sisters I've ever heard of. They grew up in that big house on Buxton Street. The one that was sold off after World War II when everything went pear-shaped for the family.'

'I can ask my mother but I've never heard of her, either.' Addy shrugged. 'Maybe she was a nobody.'

'Aren't we all?' Leo laughed.

'It seemed to perk Roma up a bit, finding the book, seeing the names there.'

'I'm glad something has. Listen, thanks again, Addy. Ring me with an update in the next few days, huh?'

'I will,' Addy said.

'I'll get it,' Addy called when she heard a knock on the front door later that afternoon. Roma was pouring them a drink and that was a task too important to be interrupted. Addy was surprised to see that it was the guy who lived next door. Connor. The one who'd been making Hollywood eyes at Roma. Addy couldn't hold back her smile.

'Why, hello there.'

'Hey,' he said. 'I'm Connor. From next door.'

'I remember.' She looked him up and down. He was holding a hessian bag in his hand, bulging and heavy.

'Oh, what do you have there? Are they lemons?' Addy clasped a hand to her mouth. 'I apologise again. That was so wrong of me.'

'Don't worry about it,' he smiled and looked past her. 'Is Roma in, by any chance?'

'She certainly is.' Addy led Connor down the hallway. When they reached the kitchen, Addy stopped and announced, 'Well, look who it is, Roma. It's Connor from next door.'

Roma was at the sink shaking ice cubes out of a tray and when she glanced over her shoulder, Addy saw it: the flicker of interest she'd been denying. Pity her cousin wasn't wearing something a little more attractive. She'd been painting all day and had just stepped out of the shower. Her dark hair was piled up on top of her head in a loose knot, her face was clean and pale, and only Roma would choose a blue dressing-gown with fluffy white clouds on it.

'Hi, Connor,' Roma said with a sigh.

'I'm sorry. I didn't mean to interrupt anything.'

Addy watched the two of them stare at each other and couldn't stand it. She gave Connor a gentle push forward. 'Your timing is perfect. I'll go fetch the gin.' She spun on her heels and left them alone.

Roma scooped up the ice cubes and dumped them in a bowl, before wiping her hands on a tea towel. She tucked it on the handle of the oven door and turned around to face Connor.

'I can see my timing sucks,' he said with a grin as he placed a bag on the floor by his feet. 'You're already in your PJs.'

Roma chuckled and glanced down, found the tie on her dressing-gown and began twisting it around her fingers. 'Well, you know, I was covered in paint half an hour ago. It felt good to get clean.'

'Nice socks,' he said, leaning against the doorjamb, his arms crossed, one hip cocked.

She lifted the front of her fleece gown just slightly to reveal her bright red socks. 'It's the latest look in Paris, you know. Remarkable Bay chic.' She felt the heat in her cheeks and wished it away.

'Whatever it's called, you're rocking it.'

Roma chuckled. 'You're a liar.'

He smiled warmly at her, his blue eyes shining. 'So. How's the renovation going?'

Roma sighed, crossed her arms around her. 'Really well. I've discovered muscles I never knew I had and grown blisters in places I didn't think possible.'

He laughed, a deep chuckle that floated across to her. 'You've taken on a big job, that's for sure.'

Roma shrugged. 'I've got time. And Addy's staying to help me for a little while.'

'A problem shared is a problem halved,' Connor said. 'My grandmother used to say that all the time. I think it was her way of getting into everyone else's business. But I'm not here to talk about my grandmother. I brought you these.' He bent and picked up the bag and walked slowly towards her, as if wary of startling her. 'Maybe these will help with the aches and pains. Lemons. For your gin. Please take them. I've got loads in the backyard.'

Roma stepped forward and took the bag from his hand. 'Thank you so much. That's very kind of you.'

Connor dropped his chin and shoved his hands into the front pockets of his jeans. 'I thought it was my neighbourly duty to prevent the repeat of a break and enter, theft and possession of stolen property.'

'Are you a cop?' Roma heard the slightest hint of panic in her raised voice and felt like an idiot.

'No, a lawyer.'

Connor Stapleton didn't look like any lawyer she'd ever met. When Tom's hit-and-run case had gone to court, all the Crown's lawyers looked like they were barely out of law school and already exhausted. Connor was older and there was sense of looseness about him that was hard to define. She couldn't seem to imagine him arguing vociferously in court: he looked like he would never get angry about anything. Maybe it was being a father. Maybe it was Remarkable Bay. She hoped it was the latter. That maybe the Bay would do for her what it seemed to have done for Connor.

Except she'd have to try that theory out again tomorrow because having Connor Stapleton in her kitchen was not helping her relax one bit.

'She's kind of spontaneous, our Addy.' Roma put the bag of lemons on the sink, opened a tall cupboard and found a large wooden bowl. She set it on the counter top and one by one, arranged the lemons in it. All to distract herself from Connor's aqua-blue eyes. She didn't have to be looking at him to know he was watching her.

'You're cousins, right?'

'Distant cousins. We never did actually figure out how many times removed but our great-grandmothers were sisters.'

'That explains it. You look alike, actually.'

Roma was so taken aback by the idea that she looked anything like Addy that she was sure her mouth fell wide open. There was no way they could look alike. Addy was petite, auburn-haired and thin as a rake. Addy's idea of changing for the evening was to slip into a pair of black yoga pants and a figure-hugging T-shirt with a pashmina around her shoulders. Roma was tall, dark-haired (almost black if you didn't count the grey) and she was carrying a few too many pounds. And in her dressing-gown and bright red socks she looked a little like she'd given up on fashion entirely. 'Addy and me? I don't think so.'

Connor grinned. 'Yeah, you do.' He came closer. His eyes darted to her mouth for a moment. Then back up to her eyes, studying her intently. 'There's something in the eyes. The shape of your mouth, maybe.'

Roma finished piling the lemons in the bowl, folded up the bag and handed it back to him. He tucked it under his elbow.

'Thanks.'

Roma sighed. He seemed like a nice man. He'd welcomed her to Remarkable Bay, he'd brought lemons and he was here. It was the least she could do. 'Would you like a wedge of one of your lemons in one of my G and Ts?'

Connor thought about it.

'I'd love one. And a tour of the house, if you don't mind.'

'I don't mind at all. Follow me.'

Fifteen minutes later, Roma and Connor were on the balcony outside her bedroom. Connor was leaning over the railing, admiring the view.

Roma sat down in one of the wicker chairs which had become her favourite place in the house and Connor turned at the creaky noise her move made. His face, lit by the moon and the faint street lights, was soft and kind and lovely. She looked at the slice of Connor's lemon in her glass.

'You know,' he started, 'I've looked at Remarkable Bay a million times from the street and from my house. But this? This is spectacular.' Connor watched her, waiting for a reaction to his conversation starter. Roma hesitated. She pulled the sides of her dressing-gown over her legs, covering her flannelette pyjama pants.

'It's amazing,' she replied. 'Even though it can get a little windy when it's blowing, I love it. The real estate agent promised me I'll be able to see the whales in the Bay from up here in winter. I think I got here too late this year.'

'It's a beautiful sight when they're out there calving. No doubt about that. Although it was a quiet season this winter. It seems the only newbie in town has been you.'

Roma still hadn't got around to replacing the globe in the light above them—it was probably 997th on the list of things she still had to do—so Connor's face was half in shadow and half in light, creating interesting and dramatic angles at his jaw when he smiled.

'So this is your bedroom?' Connor cocked his head to the French doors they'd walked through a moment before.

Roma nodded. 'Yes. I mean, it will be when it's finished. I don't want to move in until it's just right. There's still a bit of work to do.'

'It's huge.'

'That's why I like it. I'm guessing it must have been a living room in the past because of the balcony and the view. I have this image in my head that back in the day people would sit out here with their cups of tea and watch people playing croquet across the road, over there on the lawn.'

'It's cricket now,' Connor said as he looked out.

'Pardon?'

'The kids use the old wooden pickets as stumps and it's six and out if they hit the ball down the Harbor Master's Walk to the beach.'

'Does your son play cricket?'

Connor chuckled. 'On his Xbox, yeah. So, have you done this before, renovated a house?' He leant back against the railing.

'God, no. I lived in a modern house up in Adelaide with a security system, loads of built-in storage and a courtyard garden and I was two blocks from three very decent coffee shops.'

'So why give up all that for the cosmopolitan stylings of Remarkable Bay?'

Roma thought long and hard on her answer. It seemed everyone who knew her was obsessed by it and perplexed at her explanation. Leo. Addy. Tom's family. Her friends at work. She'd been asking herself the same question since she'd signed on the dotted line, since Bayview had officially become hers.

She went for the simple answer, one that made as much sense to others as anything else she could cobble together. 'I needed to leave the city.'

Connor's eyes widened. 'In trouble with the law or something? If you ever get into trouble, I can offer passably good legal representation.'

Roma took a long gulp of her gin and then held the cool glass in her hands. Deciding. Debating. She looked up and met his warm eyes, and wondered how long they would shine down on her with interest rather than pity if she told him.

She tried to smile. 'I had one of those moments. You know, what am I doing with my life and all that, blah blah blah.'

'I can relate. Had one of those myself a few years ago, when Angas's mother and I got divorced. There I was, twenty-seven years old with a five-year-old kid I saw half the time. And the other half? I didn't know what the hell I was doing.'

So Connor was divorced. Not a widower. Roma clamped her lips closed and waited to see if there was more to his story that he was willing to share.

Connor sipped his drink and the ice cubes tinkled against the glass. It was such a lovely sound in the quiet of the night. 'After it was all official, she—my ex-wife Cathryn—got this great job in Sydney and I decided to move back here, to make sure Angas did some of his growing up down on the south coast. I wanted him to learn how to surf, that kind of thing.'

'You're a surfer?' Roma asked.

'Yeah,' he grinned. 'You?'

She felt herself smiling at the memory, so sweet and familiar. 'My family used to spend our summer holidays down here at Remarkable Bay. I took lessons one summer. I got pretty good, actually, but then we stopped coming and I gave up and I haven't surfed in years.'

'You've got to get back out there. The town may be a little tired these days but the waves haven't changed a bit.'

'But I have. I reckon my centre of gravity is in a totally different place these days. I'll probably trip over carrying the board down the beach.'

'Bullshit,' he smiled. 'You're never too old. It's just like riding a bike. You just pick smaller waves, that's all. Look at me.' Connor held his arms wide. 'I don't do the big waves anymore. I can't compete with the crazy young dudes.'

Roma stood and went over to the balcony railing next to him, looked out on to the reserve. The conversation had changed and she wanted to know more. 'Angas's mother didn't want him to live with her in Sydney?'

'She did, but it wouldn't have worked out with her job. She was always more ambitious than me and her job's pretty intense,' Connor chuckled, 'although that's probably obvious given she's in Sydney and I'm in Remarkable Bay. And Sydney's no place for a kid with one parent, I reckon. Angas flies up every couple of months and Cathryn comes to Adelaide when she can. They stay with her parents, his grandparents. It works. Or should I say that we've made it work. We always wanted to do the right thing by Angas. We never wanted him to suffer because we couldn't stay married to each other. And anyway, families look all kinds of ways these days, right?'

Connor was right. Things had changed. Nowadays, people created their own families, moulded them to shape their own circumstances. Friendships made families. Love made families. Blood didn't mean anything if you didn't have more in common than that.

She wanted to know more about Connor and in the dark, in the cool of a Remarkable Bay evening, she felt brave enough to ask. 'So, are you from here originally? You said something about moving back.'

'I grew up close by, on a dairy farm about four clicks away. My folks sold it years ago and retired to Victor Harbor, when they finally realised that, despite generations of history, I didn't want to take it over. It's bloody hard work and the prices for milk are shit these days. Sorry. Agri-politics. My two younger brothers didn't want it either. One's in London anyway, so it was down to me and I couldn't do it. But there's something about this place, isn't there? I've always thought of the Bay as my backyard. The beach in one direction and the low hills in the other. The big skies. I wanted to make sure Angas had a taste of this life. The pace of things down here, without constant connection to all the social media that gives kids weird ideas about the world.' He laughed and then sighed. 'But what happens? We got the NBN last year and now he's as connected in his bedroom in sleepy old Remarkable Bay as he would have been up in Adelaide.'

'Does he hate it? Living here? I guess Remarkable Bay is pretty slow for a teenager.' She remembered how Addy had described it: a pimple on the backside of a coast in the middle of nowhere.

'Slow? What are you talking about? He saw a crime being committed the other day. In his own backyard, no less.'

Roma covered her eyes with her fingers to hide her embarrassment. 'I could kill Addy.'

Connor rested a reassuring hand on her arm. Roma stilled, looked at his fingers. There was a layer of flannelette and another of blue fleece with clouds between his hand and her skin but she felt it.

'Don't worry about it. Really. I've got more fruit than I know what to do with.' And then his hand was gone. 'And Angas? Yeah, he has a whine every now and then, but he's got good mates at school. I get to spend more time with him down here than if I was working up in the city. I only work four days a week so I get to hang around with him on Fridays after school. We go for a surf. Make dinner together, that kind of stuff. He'll be gone before too long. I mean, he's fifteen already. If he decides to take a gap year after high school and go travelling, he'll be gone anyway and then if he goes to uni? He'll really leave. It's pretty pathetic but I'm trying to hang on to my kid for as long as I can.'

'That's not pathetic. It's nice,' Roma said. 'You two seem pretty close.'

'Yeah. I'm sure he'll look back on all this one day with fondness.' Connor rolled his eyes. 'Now, I'm just a gigantic pain in his arse.'

'All parents are to their kids, aren't they?'

'It's our job. To drive our kids crazy.' Connor upended his drink and finished it, put it on the low table between the two chairs. 'Well. Thanks for the gin and tonic. I'd better get back.'

'You're welcome. Thanks again for the lemons.'

When she moved to follow him through the French doors, he held up a hand. 'You don't have to see me out. I know the way. I'll see you, Roma.'

'See you, Connor.'

'Hey.' He stopped, turned, looked at her with a curious look on his face and a question in his narrowed eyes. 'Roma's a pretty unusual name for someone who's not Italian. Are you named after—?'

'Yes,' she said abruptly. 'I am.'

He nodded his respect. 'She was an amazing lawyer. Amongst a whole lot of other things.'

'She was.'

'Your parents wanted you to be a lawyer, right?'

'Yep.'

'And you're not?'

'Nope.'

Connor chuckled as he left, his rangy steps creating long strides on the hallway floorboards. A moment later, when she heard the front door close, she leaned over the railing to watch him leave.

When he reached the front gate, he stopped and turned to look up to her.

'Sweet dreams,' he said. She'd picked him as near on forty, but right there, looking up at her the way he was, she saw someone with a boyish excitement about life.

'Night, Connor.'

Roma flopped on one of her wicker chairs, trying to figure out what had just happened. She'd felt something unfamiliar with Connor, something new and alien and scary. Feeling that connection with him, noticing the way he'd looked at her, touched her arm, brought a maelstrom of emotions to the surface.

She closed her eyes.

It had been three years since the police had knocked on her door, three years since she'd buried Tom. They say grief steals your memory and part of that was true for Roma. Some things she had no recollection of at all. Were there two police officers at her door that night? All she remembered was a blur of black uniforms against the dark of the night street behind them. What had she been doing when they'd knocked? The whole day, and days after, were gone.

But the pain and the shock of it were right there in her head every morning when she woke.

She'd waited to feel better, waited in the house they'd lived in, in the bed they'd shared, for some sense of resolution to develop in her heart about moving on. For the clichéd 'closure'. As if she could close the door on the past even if she'd wanted to.

People talked about closure as if it were a point in time. 'I'm so glad you can have some closure.' What exactly was supposed to close over? The hurt? Her heart?

She'd waited for the tears to stop. Waited for her energy to return. It hadn't happened like that. Quite the opposite, in fact. One day, eventually, she grew sick of the waiting. Sick of waiting for the heaviness of her grief to suddenly lighten, to thin out and stretch so she could see through it.

The enormous emotion she'd been struggling with since Tom's death that sat like a stone in the pit of her stomach was something she was too scared to name. And tonight, spending time with Connor, brought it vividly back to life.

But was it grief or was it guilt?

CHAPTER
12

1934

'Of course you're disappointed that Edwin can't be here.' Mrs Myrtle Stuart took a china plate from the large table in the middle of the downstairs reception room at Bayview and filled it with biscuits, a freshly baked scone and a generous slice of Mrs Nightingale's cinnamon cake.

'I beg your pardon?' Ruby hadn't been paying attention to her prospective mother-in-law, too distracted by the people streaming into the room. It was afternoon tea and the aromas of freshly baked cakes and tea had people following their noses to the display. There were some people Ruby recognised. There were the Smythes, both in sombre black, and the Whitelocks. The poor Whitelocks, as Mrs Allen had referred to them since they'd tragically lost their six-year-old boy, their only child, to whooping cough. They'd continued to holiday at Remarkable Bay despite their loss, each year looking sadder than the last. Mrs Whitelock was a forlorn-looking woman, and her husband was constantly by her side, solicitous and equally as heartbroken. Following them were a youngish couple with a babe in arms, and then Adeline flounced in. The first thing she did was to search the room to determine who was looking at her, and her expression quickly changed from anticipation to disappointment when she realised no one was.

'Oh, look at that,' Mrs Stuart remarked. 'Your sister has arrived. Isn't she a beautiful young girl?'

'Yes, she is.' The only thing to do was agree, for it was objectively true. Adeline was a jewel. From her head to her toes, she was a picture of young Australian womanhood. Blessed with auburn hair, which looked golden in some light, she glowed. Her figure was petite and she seemed to glide when she walked. Her eyes were a slate blue and her facial features were perfectly symmetrical. A delicately arched brow with the finest eyelashes, a pert nose and the sweetest cupid's bow lips created a package that people crossed the street to look at.

To Ruby's dismay, Adeline's looks were not shared with her sisters. Ruby herself was tall and slender, with no curves to speak of. She'd always thought her nose was slightly too big, and when she'd had her hair trimmed into the very fashionable bob she'd longed for, it only seemed to make her nose appear larger. Her eyes were rather squinty when she smiled and her lips were thin. Clara still looked like a young girl, with her hair pulled back into a simple plait. She had wayward eyebrows and deep brown eyes, and there was a natural quirk in the shape of her lips which made her appear to be snarling most of the time. Adeline had certainly inherited the best from both parents. Ruby and Clara had to share the best of what remained.

Being blessed with looks brought so many of life's advantages to Adeline with seemingly little effort on her part and Roma envied her that.

The Allen sisters hadn't spent much time together so far this holiday and Ruby was not particularly sad about it. Adeline's head was full of marriage and her future husband, which didn't leave much time for her sisters and activities with her family. Even though she was two years younger than Ruby, Adeline acted as if she had out-grown her older sister. She had already moved on, had already taken that step into her new life. Her fixation with her fiancé and her wedding had become tiresome and annoying, as it reminded Ruby too much of Edwin and her own impending decision. One she was still hesitating over.

Mrs Stuart looked down her nose at Ruby, clearly frustrated with her inability to pay attention.

'I was saying, dear girl, that this holiday must be dreadfully sad for you, not having Edwin here with us. You two young lovebirds could have had so much fun down here at Remarkable Bay. Think of it! Bathing, tennis, croquet, picnics.'

'Yes. It's a great pity,' Ruby answered politely, turning her atten-tion to a batch of fresh scones one of Mrs Nightingale's kitchen girls had placed on the end of the table.

'I know he was very disappointed that his father insisted he stay in town, but there is some ongoing business at the office. I never bother with the details myself, but I'm sure it is important. This will all be your concern once you're married, of course.'

'Yes.' Ruby spooned a dollop of glistening strawberry jam on to the side of her own plate, guessing that the frustrated colour in her cheeks would be about the same shade of red. She didn't want to talk about Edwin. She didn't want to think about Edwin. She was more than relieved when Mrs Stuart bustled away to sit down with the Whitelocks before all the seats in the room were taken. It was no surprise it was so busy. Mrs Nightingale's reputation preceded her up and down the south coast.

'No cream on that scone today?'

'Pardon?' Ruby shivered at the familiar voice and slowly looked up from her plate.

'The cream. It really is rather good. I should know. I milked the cow myself.'

'Mr Stapleton.' Ruby could barely get the words out without stammering. Her hand trembled instead and her spoon tinkled against the china plate she was holding.

'Miss Allen. I'm very happy to see you here today.'

Ruby took a surreptitious glance around the room. Her mother had her back to them. Adeline was too busy chatting to someone about her wedding, no doubt; Mrs Stuart was deep in conversation; and Clara had remained upstairs, despite much pleading to come down for a cup of tea.

It felt safe to talk to Cain. 'Are you here for afternoon tea?' She looked him up and down. He wasn't dressed for a delivery, but was wearing a tweed suit, a crisp white shirt and a brown tie. His brown hair was smoothed back and there was no flat cap on his head today.

He smiled. 'One should never say no when Mrs Nightingale invites you to afternoon tea. She's the best baker this side of Victor Harbor. Have you tried her lemon slice?'

'No,' Ruby said, careful not to look at him too long before averting her eyes, for fear they were being watched. People did like to gossip.

'You must. Let me get you a piece.' Cain moved around the table and selected a small square, picking it up with a pair of ornate silver tongs. He placed it on his plate and returned to Ruby.

'Here,' he said, proffering his plate to her. 'You should taste this.'

She reached for it and took a small bite, smiling as the lemony tang exploded in her mouth. 'It is delicious.'

'I told you it was. You should trust me, Miss Allen.'

Ruby felt playful. 'Why should I trust you? We've only just met. I don't know anything about you to help inform my judgement about your character.'

Cain nodded thoughtfully, rubbed his chin. 'That is very true. What would you need to know to find me trustworthy?'

Ruby took a deep breath. 'Your middle name.'

'My middle name is a measure of my trustworthiness?'

'I won't know that until I find out what it is.'

'It's William. I'm Cain William Stapleton. It's after my father and each of my four brothers have it as their middle name, too. Not very original, I'm afraid, but we believe in tradition in my family. Does that help?'

'Mmm,' Ruby said. She thought about it and finished off the lemon slice. It truly was delectable. 'Tradition can be a good thing.'

'What else would you like to know about me?' he asked, careful to avert his gaze to the food on the table so he wasn't seen staring at her. She liked that he had to.

She grinned. 'Do you like milking cows, Mr Stapleton?'

He turned back to her with a grin. 'Not in the slightest. Thank goodness I won't be doing it forever.'

'You won't?'

'I have plans that don't entirely revolve around Remarkable Bay.'

'Really? And what are they?'

Cain raised an eyebrow and lowered his voice as he leaned in. 'Meet me at the beach tomorrow at two o'clock and I'll tell you.'

Ruby looked at him blankly. She didn't think before the word, 'Yes,' slipped from her lips.

'Are there any more scones?' Her mother was suddenly by her side, but she was distracted by the food and all her attention was on the display on the table. Ruby waited a moment before she glanced back to Cain, but he had discreetly disappeared.

Ruby pulled herself together, but kept her eyes on her plate in case her blush was obvious. 'Yes, mother. Look. A whole plateful. Try some of this cream on them. I hear it's delicious.'

Later that night, once they'd taken an after-dinner walk up and down Ocean Street and then endured an interminable evening filled with card games and backgammon, entertainments which Mrs Allen found diverting but which bored her daughters to tears, the three Miss Allens had taken a final cup of tea and were in bed. It was a clear night out, with little wind, and it was cool enough to pull the blankets up to their chins. Clara had slipped into bed as soon as she'd washed her face, silent and sullen. Ruby had slowly removed the remains of her lipstick, brushed her hair with trembling hands, feeling a faraway flutter in her stomach, before she got into bed. Adeline, however, took an age. She undressed carefully, checked three times that there was enough room in the cupboard for her dress to hang without being creased, a move which shoved Clara's and Ruby's frocks together like troops on a train. Finally, after sighing loudly and singing the chorus of a show tune—badly—she noisily got into bed.

Ruby had opened the curtains wide to let in the moonlight and the sea breeze. She could smell the salt in the air and all she could think about was the beach tomorrow.

And Cain William Stapleton.

She couldn't stop to think about her actions, that she'd agreed to meet a young man when she was, for all intents and purposes, spoken for. Ruby couldn't explain this wildness that had overcome her; this reckless indifference to all that she had left behind at home. Remarkable Bay somehow felt like another world, where different rules applied, where she could take this chance to explore the attentions of a lovely young man with the kindest eyes she'd ever seen.

'Ruby?'

'Yes?'

'Do you miss Edwin?' Adeline asked dreamily.

Ruby held in a nervous breath, not sure where Adeline's question was leading. Surely she couldn't have seen Cain that afternoon. Adeline wasn't the smartest of girls, and Ruby relaxed a little in that knowledge. Adeline was far too self-obsessed to even guess what was going on with her older sister. What Adeline missed in intelligence, she made up for with the uncanny ability to capitalise on her beauty. In Ruby's experience, beautiful girls didn't have to concern themselves with being smart. Everything Adeline said was charming because she laughed so attractively as she was voicing her opinions; and the sad things became incomprehensibly tragic as her eyes glistened with unshed tears. If she was getting lost in a conversation, she would easily distract with a batting of her eyelids, and a demure glance downwards which drew attention to her full, lipstick-red lips. Adeline had a way of flattering people that completely disarmed them, taking the anger out of their words and rendering them almost helpless in the face of her charm.

Ruby settled her nerves by reminding herself that Adeline wasn't really after an answer; she merely wanted to talk about how much she was missing James.

'Of course I miss Edwin,' Ruby answered as she crossed her fingers under the blankets. It was a sin to lie, she knew that, and the weight of her guilt started to get heavy on her chest, making her pulse quicken and her palms sweat.

Adeline turned to Ruby, the bedsprings squeaking under her as she moved. Her face was pale and almost innocent-looking in the dark. 'I don't know how you can bear it, not seeing him for all these weeks. I miss James dreadfully and we've only been separated a mere few days. I can barely sleep for knowing he's to arrive tomorrow.' There was another dramatic sigh. 'I can't wait to be married, Ruby. Can you?'

Ruby bit her lip so she didn't tell another lie. 'I can tell *you* can't.'

'Clara?' Adeline called out. 'We're talking about getting married. Don't you want to be married one day?'

'Sshhh, she's only eighteen. Leave her alone,' Ruby said in an admonishing tone. And she was a young eighteen: more interested in her birds and nature than any boy. Ruby tried to remember if Clara had ever been dreamy-eyed over anyone in their circle. She couldn't come up with a single name, which made her behaviour since they'd arrived at Remarkable Bay even more troubling.

'No. I'm never getting married. Not ever,' Clara hissed.

Adeline met Ruby's eyes, shocked. And then she asked, 'Why ever not?'

Clara refused to answer. She turned to face the wall and pulled her blankets over her head to put a full stop on her involvement in the conversation.

'Wait until you're older. You'll meet a lovely young man and you will have forgotten all about being so young and independent,' Adeline chided. 'What else will you do with your life if you aren't married?' The idea was clearly unthinkable to Adeline. What else was there to do? A young woman in their circle didn't go out to work. Other women worked: the women and girls who made up their household staff, spinster teachers, perhaps nurses, and accommodating and solicitous women like Mrs Nightingale. Ruby could hear the clear meaning in Adeline's words: they were the Allen sisters. Things were expected of them.

Adeline's words repeated over and over in Ruby's ears. *You'll meet a lovely young man.*

'I can't wait until next April. Being married on the first Saturday in April has a lovely ring to it, don't you think? I saw a beautiful gown when I was out shopping with mother before we came down here to Remarkable Bay and I can't wait to go back to Adelaide and see if it fits. It should. It's wonderful, Ruby. It's the whitest of white silk with long trumpet sleeves and there's a veil that will go perfectly with it. Oh, Ruby. I can't wait to be James's wife.' She paused and lowered her voice. 'In every way.'

Ruby squeezed her eyes shut tightly. 'Adeline. Please. Don't talk about that.'

Adeline looked shocked. 'Why ever not? It's what married men and women do.' Ruby wanted to block her ears so she didn't have to hear the excitement in her sister's voice.

'Ruby … can I ask you something? How does it feel when you kiss Edwin? Do you like it? Do you feel it everywhere? Do you feel that you want more than his lips on you?'

Not once, ever, Ruby realised with heart-wrenching sadness. Edwin had only ever held her hand and kissed her on the cheek. She suddenly felt uncomfortable and hot at the realisation that she wanted Cain to kiss her and touch her. 'I don't want to talk about this with you, Adeline.'

'Please, Ruby,' her sister pleaded with a quiet seriousness in her voice. 'You know I can't talk about this with mother or anyone else. But I feel things when I'm with James. That's why I love him so much. He makes me feel …' At a loss for words now, Adeline turned on to her back and stared at the ceiling. 'We almost did, once, you know.'

Ruby wanted to hush her sister. She knew what she meant and she couldn't even think the word, much less say it out loud. But she was curious.

'What was it like?' she finally whispered across the room.

'It felt ... well, James didn't want to stop. He's very strong. He ... he must love me very much because he ... well, he took some persuading. But I had to be firm with him, to tell him we had to wait until we're married. And our wedding night? It will be the most important night of my life. I love him so much, Ruby. I want to ... to share everything with him. As man and wife, do you know what I mean?'

Ruby knew what she meant. 'It won't be long, Adeline. April isn't really that far away, you know.'

As Ruby drifted off to sleep, she dreamt of Cain and the idea of his mouth on hers and all the complicated possibilities of tomorrow.

CHAPTER
13

It was Saturday, just after morning tea, and Adeline was bouncing around the walls of the sisters' guesthouse bedroom. Ruby and Clara were sitting on the ends of their beds, trying to read and ignore her, in case the attention excited her even more, but Adeline wouldn't be tamed. She paced up and down, then sat at the dresser and checked her hair for the fifth time, reapplied her lipstick, powdered her face, inspected her array of dresses in the wardrobe and finally pulled her suitcase out from under her bed, rummaging through it to find her new swimsuit. She leapt to her feet and held it up to her shoulders so it draped flatteringly, and she kicked a leg forward the way she'd seen actresses pose in magazine photos. The suit was emerald green and sported thin white shoulder straps with a matching belt. 'Ruby, Ruby. What do you think? Isn't it splendid!'

Ruby didn't look up from *Jane Eyre*. 'It surely is.'

'Clara? What do you think?'

Clara ignored her and then emphasised how bored she was with the conversation by turning on the bed so she was facing the wall.

Adeline scoffed. 'I knew there was no point in asking you what you think, Clara. Honestly,' she flopped down on the bed next to her youngest sister. 'For someone so young, you are the saddest sack I've ever seen. We're on holiday. The sun is shining. What on earth do you have to be miserable about?' She poked Clara's shoulder and Clara whipped her arm away.

'I myself have every reason to be perfectly happy. James is arriving in about two hours. My darling James ...' Adeline skipped to her bed and fell backwards on to it. She lay, sighing loudly, staring up at the ceiling and clutching her new swimsuit to her slim frame.

'He'll no doubt be calling on me as soon as he arrives. And we shall leave you two and head down to the bay, hand in hand, to swim and who knows what else. Oh, I've missed him so much!'

Clara tossed her book violently onto her bed, leapt to her feet and slammed the door behind her. They heard her footsteps stomping down the hallway and then fading.

Ruby looked up from her Brontë. Worry gnawed at her.

'What did I say?' Adeline asked with genuine concern, her bottom lip beginning a sad little tremble as she searched her older sister's eyes for an answer. 'Aren't I allowed to be a little excited about my fiancé coming?'

Ruby sighed. 'Of course you are.'

'Whatever is the matter with that girl? Honestly, she's becoming such a bore. I don't know how on earth she thinks she'll ever find a husband with that permanent scowl on her face. It'll give her the most unattractive wrinkles. She needs to grow up.'

Ruby stood. 'Perhaps she needs some sun, as do I.' She picked up her hat from the dresser, checked her watch. It was almost two o'clock. Her heart felt light at the idea that she was about to leave behind her squabbling sisters and see Cain.

'Say hello to James for me.'

Ruby crossed Ocean Street, clutching in one hand the straw hat she should probably put on her head instead of carrying, and passed a croquet match in progress on the lawns opposite Bayview. She made her way across the park to the Harbour Master's Walk which led down to the beach. It was a grand kind of walkway: there was a low stone fence on either side with regularly placed columns at intervals, resembling a bridge, until it sloped down to meet the dirt track past the Norfolk Island pines and then the steep section to the beach. Once she reached the clean white stretch of sand, which curved around in an arc to another clump of pines at the far end, she slipped off her sandals and dug her feet into the warmth. She challenged herself to walk the length of it, so she could think, or perhaps not think.

The beach was busy. Children were huddled in groups in what appeared to be a sandcastle-building competition, and down at the water's edge, couples holding hands were standing ankle-deep, playfully splashing each other with water and squealing. She picked up her pace when she spotted a section towards the far end in which there was no one. It took a good five minutes before Ruby dropped to the sand, kicked her legs out in front of her and closed her eyes in sheer relief at being alone.

Ruby wondered what it was that had her feeling so uncomfortable about the thought of Adeline and James's happy and excited reunion. Would she be that excited if Edwin were to arrive in Remarkable Bay? The truth was, she wouldn't. She knew he was working on a project of some kind or another at his father's business, a burden James didn't seem to face even though he worked in the business too. She had said all the right things to his face about missing him and being anxious for her return to Adelaide, but she'd secretly been looking forward to this break from him. She needed to decide her own feelings about marrying him, and she needed to do that in peace. The trouble was, the more she thought, the more confused she was, not less. It was expected she would marry and have a family of her own.

Was that all she was destined for?

Ruby lay back on the sand and threw her arms back above her head. The warmth of the sand seeped through her simple cotton dress into her back and the backs of her legs. Her hat was on the sand next to her, not on her face as her mother had reminded her. Ruby decided she could do with some colour in her complexion, some hint that she was still young, with energy to burn, with a life yet to live. Her mother would warn her against wrinkles and, god forbid, freckles. Adeline would tell her she needed a healthy glow. She closed her eyes against the light and tried not to think about Clara and Adeline and James and Edwin. And her mother's hopes and her father's expectations and oh, especially what he was going to say when he saw his daughters' new swimsuits.

'Miss Allen?'

Ruby blinked her eyes open and the blazing sun was so intense she squeezed them shut again immediately. She didn't have to ask who the interloper was, nor was she frightened by the interruption. She knew that voice and recognised the shiver at the back of her neck when she heard it. She covered her eyes with her hand and slowly opened them, bringing him into vivid view right in front of her.

'Mr Stapleton.'

And then she felt, rather than saw, him take his place beside her on the sand. When her eyes had become accustomed to the sunshine once again, she looked over at him and her breath left her in a giant whoosh. He wasn't wearing a bathing suit. Instead, he looked like he'd stepped out of the pages of a Hollywood magazine. His swimming trunks were tight and black. Mrs Nightingale's words were ringing in her ears: *I can't think of anything more horrid than a man's hairy chest.* There was nothing horrid about what she was seeing at all. Cain was so close she could almost feel his chest rising and falling as he breathed, and he'd splayed his legs out in front, his hands behind him, half-buried in the sand. He was golden.

'Did you fall asleep? You look sunburnt.' Cain peered closer at her face. His bright, aqua-blue eyes were smiling and open.

'No, I don't think I did.' A hand flew to Ruby's cheek. She felt flushed and hot. Perhaps she had overdone the sun.

'You're not swimming today?'

'No.'

'That's a shame.'

He looked her up and down, from the white collar on her day dress which dipped down modestly on her décolletage, to the thin belt at her waist, to the hem, sitting just below her knees.

'What about you? I thought you'd be working. Don't those cows of yours stop for no man?'

He narrowed his eyes at her, curious. 'What do you know about cows?'

Ruby shrugged. 'A little.' She'd read about cows. She'd never actually seen one herself.

'They need milking twice a day, it's true, but lucky for me I have a few hours in the afternoon to come down here and swim.'

Ruby thought on how lucky it was for her too, but didn't say it.

He turned to her quickly. 'Miss Allen, look!' She followed his pointed finger out to the waves and spotted two young men standing up in the water. Each was balancing on a long wooden plank that stretched forwards and backwards beneath their feet, and they were magically moving towards the beach.

'What on earth …' She sprang to her feet to get a better look. She'd read about surfing but hadn't seen it down here at Remarkable Bay before.

Cain stood next to her. Ruby realised just how close when his arm brushed against her shoulder.

'They're friends of mine from university. It looks like tremendous fun, doesn't it?'

She was taken aback. 'You go to university?'

'Yes,' he said, not shifting his eyes from the water. 'I'm home for the summer holidays to help my father on the farm.' And then he turned his attention to her, a tease in his eyes. His voice dropped lower. 'Did you think I was a simple farmhand?'

Ruby felt emboldened by his flirtation and looked him up and down, delaying her gaze on his chest. It was smooth and covered in a fine film of sand. 'I wouldn't mind if you were. I don't care about those things.'

'You don't?' He looked as if he didn't believe her.

'No, I don't. I like to judge people on what they do, on their character, not their name or their position in society or the family they were born into.'

Ruby hesitated, trying to remember who she was and what was expected of her. And what exactly was that? She was a Miss Allen of the Allens of North Adelaide. She'd been to a smart ladies' college and was properly educated. She moved in the right circles and was intelligent and well-read. But all that meant nothing in the face of who everyone thought she should be: the responsible older sister who should care for her sisters more than herself. The dutiful daughter who should marry Edwin because he'd offered and because he was from a proper family and because she was a young woman with no other destiny than that.

Cain turned to Ruby and took a step closer. 'Miss Allen?'

She glanced around. The beach near them was deserted. She craned her neck to look in his eyes. 'Yes, Mr Stapleton?'

'Would you like to meet me for a swim tomorrow afternoon, same time, right here in this spot?'

Ruby hesitated. Things were changing for women, weren't they? It was the thirties, after all. And she was still young, just twenty-two, and the fact that she'd never been kissed and had had no romantic adventures of her own gnawed at her the way she would gnaw at a hangnail if she didn't say yes right this instant.

She was going to say yes to the handsome young man and she was going to wear her new swimsuit. It may have been a small rebellion, but it was a rebellion nevertheless.

'Yes. I think I would.' Ruby hesitated for a moment, remembering the effect of his touch on her the first time they'd shaken hands. She'd remembered it every night since, while she lay in bed fighting sleep, in her dreams, over breakfast as she buttered her toast with Mr Stapleton's butter.

She decided to be bold. She reached out for his hand and he took hers. He didn't let go in a hurry.

'I'll see you tomorrow,' she said. 'Two o'clock.'

He nodded. 'I'll see you then, Miss Allen.'

'Please. Call me Ruby.'

He moved closer and pulled their joined hands towards him. 'Ruby. Call me Cain.'

Her knuckles brushed against his muscled stomach. 'Cain,' she repeated.

When they let go of each other's fingers, Cain dipped his head to her and then jogged across the beach back into the water to join his university friends on their surfboards. Ruby picked up her book and her hat and floated back to Bayview.

She took the long way along the waterline, stopping to observe the view, splashing her feet in the waves and letting them sink a little into the wet sand. She was oblivious to the activity around her. There could have been a hundred hairy chests on show and she would not have noticed any of them. All she could think about was tomorrow and Cain. The lovely, golden Cain Stapleton who had flirted with her twice now, and she'd found herself flirting back. It felt daring and delicious and yes, she had to admit it, a small betrayal of Edwin. If he'd been here, there was no way on earth she would have agreed to meet Cain again.

But Edwin wasn't.

It was meeting for a swim, nothing else. Perhaps that's what these weeks at Remarkable Bay were to be about: her last chance at freedom before the strictures of the life she was expected to have closed in all around her, like the corsets women had eschewed a decade before.

Ruby started up the gentle incline of the Harbour Master's Walk and spotted Adeline and James coming towards her. Her sister had an arm slipped through her fiancé's, and he strode along confidently, wearing a cream linen suit and a straw hat at a jaunty angle, as if he was setting off for a spot of tennis. He clearly fancied himself as some kind of Australian Clark Gable. All that was missing was the rakish moustache.

'Here she is! My wandering soon-to-be sister-in-law. I wondered where we might find you.'

'Hello, James,' Ruby called, and she fought the nerves which flushed her cheeks and twisted her stomach. Seeing Edwin's brother,

when she'd just been talking to Cain, was unsettling to say the least.
'I see you arrived safely.'

James kissed Ruby on each cheek. 'I did but god knows that train journey is a bore. The only thing that got me through the ghastly thing was knowing that my Adeline was at the other end.'

Adeline slipped her arms around James and hugged him from the side. 'Darling, you are a gorgeous man.'

'Edwin sends his regards, by the way,' James said, looking over Ruby's shoulder.

'Thank you.'

'He had me carry a letter for you. It's quite thick. Lots of pages. He must have poured out his heart in it,' James smirked. He glanced sideways at Adeline before remarking, 'All that passion.'

Adeline giggled. 'I left it on your bed, Ruby.' Then she gazed adoringly at James, as if the mere fact that he'd carried a letter in his breast pocket rendered him heroic.

'Why, thank you,' Ruby said, her fingers tightly entwined around each other. 'I shall read it when I get back. I'm heading back to Bay-view now.'

'We're taking a walk on the beach and then we're going to the Orange Grove Tea Rooms. I can't wait to show off this darling man to all the young ladies there. They'll be so frightfully jealous, don't you think, Ruby?'

'Yes, of course they will be.' And for the first time in a long while, Ruby didn't feel that mortifying pang of envy at seeing Adeline so happy, and seeing so blatantly what she didn't have with Edwin.

'I hope they are, my darling,' James said and kissed Adeline on the forehead. 'There's nothing like another woman's attention to keep a fiancée on her toes.'

'You have no need to worry about that, Mr James Stuart,' Adeline said, gazing up into his eyes. 'I would fight to my last breath for you.'

'And that makes me the luckiest man on earth.'

Ruby turned away and resumed her walk. 'I'm heading back. I shall see you both later, I expect.'

CHAPTER
14

Ruby remembered reading earlier that summer in the *Women's Weekly* that young women in Sydney drank beer, smoked cigarettes and exposed their legs by wearing shorts. She sighed at the unfairness of it all. Sydney was one thing; Adelaide was quite another altogether. In 1934 in the City of Churches women didn't even wear shorts playing tennis, for goodness sake. Adelaide's metropolitan beaches continued to be patrolled by inspectors who kept a stern and censorial eye on anyone indulging in mixed bathing and, God forbid, men in swimming trunks who disobeyed the No Topless Bathing Orders.

That kind of rigid moral panic seemed to fade the further they got from Adelaide and things were a little looser on the beaches of the south coast, which explained why Adeline thought they could get away with wearing the modern swimsuits they'd bought earlier that year especially for this holiday. Adeline had somehow convinced their mother to purchase three for her daughters. Ruby had no idea how she'd accomplished such a feat, but it was a sign of her sister's powers of persuasion that Ruby was now wearing such a suit.

She was crouching down and then standing on tiptoe to see herself in the small hinged mirror sitting on top of the dresser in their guest room at Bayview. Edwin's letter lay on the dark wood, unopened. James had been right: the envelope was bulging, which made Ruby even less inclined to read it. It was probably full of promises and plans for their future, where they would live, how many children they would have, his latest thoughts of promotion at the office and a vague idea about setting himself up in his own wine exporting business, with the backing of his father.

Edwin's plans—and her family's plans for her—could wait.

Ruby Allen had plans all of her own.

She dipped in front of the mirror. The navy suit was quite lovely. The top was rather like a brassiere, with two thin black straps over her shoulders with a matching belt. When she turned and looked back over her shoulder, she realised quite how far it dipped down in the back, almost to the curve of her waist. The bottom half fitted as tight as a girdle around her hips and the demure over-skirt hid the curves at the tops of her thighs. She felt young and modern in it. Free and rebellious. Wistfully, she wished she had a tan to complete the look, but her pale skin just didn't seem to become golden no matter what she did. She would pink up and then burn, unfortunately, because a tan had become quite fashionable lately. Apparently all the Sydney women were doing it: baking and bronzing in the Australian sun to acquire just the right kind of healthy glow.

Their mother was always reminding her daughters about freckles and wrinkles, so Ruby aimed for the middle ground and doffed her floppy hat to complete the outfit. Just as Ruby was arranging the curls of her bob underneath the brim, the door closed quietly.

It was Clara. She leant back against the closed door, her eyes wide, hands tucked into her cotton dress. 'You're not actually going to wear that thing, are you?'

'"It's all the rage on the French Riviera,"' Ruby said with dramatic flair, her arms stretched out to her sides. 'Or so Adeline says. What do you think? Tell me honestly.'

Clara studied Ruby's long legs, the curve of her hips and the swell of her breasts encased tightly and provocatively in the new suit. 'Father is going to be apoplectic.'

Ruby sighed. She knew Clara was right. Her sister was a quiet, circumspect sort of girl, which was perhaps understandable given that she'd grown up in Adeline's shadow. That reserve made her a keen observer of people and their habits. She wasn't a huge conversationalist and always preferred to sit in the quiet corner of the drawing room at home, sketching or reading, but she would follow every nuance in the conversation being conducted around her. Good listeners had many secrets. She knew that their father, steeped in the morality of Victorian England, even though he was born eight thousand miles away, would never approve. He took enormous pride in being from a pioneering Adelaide family that enjoyed middle-class respectability. And respectable men such as he were more concerned with the Freemasons, the Anglican Church and his positions on various charity boards more than he was ever concerned with the activities of his daughters.

Except, of course, when it became time for them to marry. He heartily approved of Adeline's engagement to James and had decided without consulting her that Edwin would make her a perfect husband. All those things whirled around in Ruby's head. And thoughts of Edwin, her father and then, secretly and thrillingly, Cain Stapleton made her suddenly cross and stubborn. 'Well, father's not here, is he?'

Then she stopped before she blurted out the words that would give her away. *And neither is Edwin.*

'This is our summer holiday, Clara, and I don't want to walk around town looking like a widow from the war or a member of the Woman's Christian Temperance Union,' she huffed. 'I'm young. Or I was last time I looked.'

Clara walked to her sister, took her hands. Ruby's heart lurched when she saw the expression on her sister's face. It was a sad resignation. 'You look wonderful, Ruby,' she said quietly. 'Go and swim and have some fun.'

A surge of guilt flooded her. Adeline was off with James and she was about to meet Cain. What was Clara to do? She knew how upset her sister had been and she was going to leave her alone? She studied Clara's face. She still looked pale.

'You don't want to swim? You're going to look wonderful in your swimsuit. Why don't you come with me?'

Clara let go of Ruby's hands and went to her bed. She lay down and turned away from Ruby to face the wall. 'I won't be swimming these holidays.'

'Oh, come on, Clara,' Ruby pleaded. 'You can't stay cooped up in this room.'

There was no answer from Clara. She lay still, her thin shoulders rising and falling in a sigh. Ruby didn't want to push and she didn't want to fight. She checked her watch. It was almost time.

'If that's what you want,' she said finally.

When Clara didn't answer, Ruby slipped on a light cardigan and a pair of loose silk trousers: another new purchase for their holiday. Some called them beach pyjamas, which Ruby thought slightly ridiculous, but they were comfortable and modern and wearing them made her feel as if she were in St Tropez rather than Remarkable Bay. She closed the door quietly behind her, leaving Clara to rest—or to stew—and went downstairs.

The beach at Remarkable Bay was a blaze of colour. A rainbow of umbrellas dotted the sand and groups of young children were gathered around deep holes, digging out spades full for their sandcastles. Picnic blankets decorated the scene and there were clusters of young women in the new bathers sunning themselves in the baking sun, their legs spread out in front of them, big floppy hats on their heads.

Ruby sauntered through the crowd, stopping to chat with some of the other guests from Bayview, until she eventually made her way to the other end of the bay, where a young Norfolk Island pine had been planted in the bare sand hills just that year. This was the spot Cain had suggested they should meet and as she slowed to look around, setting her towel on the sand, she spotted a man emerging from the water. Her heart leapt into her throat when she realised it was Cain. He jogged up the sand to her, his body glistening with tiny grains of sand caught in the fine hairs at his chest. He was wearing his black swimming trunks and the first thought to pop into Ruby's head was: he'd never get away with that at Glenelg. And thank goodness for that.

'Miss Allen,' Cain said with a beaming smile as he approached her.

She looked him up and down and propped her hands on her hips. 'I thought you agreed to call me Ruby?'

'Ruby,' he said slowly and deliberately and she decided she liked the sound of it on his lips. No one had ever said her name that way before. She knew in that instant that she would be hearing it in her dreams for the rest of her life.

'Hello, Cain.' Ruby stood nervously near him. She placed a hand atop her head to keep the wind from blowing off her hat and glanced out to the water.

'I hope you're hungry,' he said. 'I have some bread in a basket right over there, with some butter I churned myself this morning.'

'From your own cows?' Ruby laughed.

'The very ones. And I have some sweet strawberries, fresh from my mother's garden.'

The mention of food had Ruby's stomach growling. She didn't care now about missing Mrs Nightingale's afternoon tea of scones with fresh cream and strawberry jam. This would be a hundred times better, sitting on the beach with Cain Stapleton and feasting on bread and butter.

'It sounds delicious.'

'And.' He stopped and was he blushing? 'These are for you.' He took a step towards her and proffered a small bunch of white carnations.

Her nerves began to jangle. 'You brought me flowers?'

'Yes. Although they're not very fancy. I'm sorry they're not roses.'

'Oh no,' Ruby said, and without thinking about it placed a reassuring hand on his bare arm. Her heart skipped at the feel of his skin, warm and strong. 'I love carnations. They're my favourite flower.'

'I'll remember that,' Cain said with a warm smile. 'Do you want to eat first or swim?'

'Swim, definitely,' Ruby replied. At that moment, it seemed like the most marvellous thing in the world to do on a hot day in Remarkable Bay. Although she wouldn't have minded if he watched her, Cain discreetly looked away while Ruby slipped off her beach pyjamas and her hat.

'Let's go.' Ruby ran towards the water, the sand hot on her toes, and when the first wave lapped against her feet she squealed. 'It's so cold!' She looked back to see where Cain was. He hadn't followed her, but was standing by the basket filled with food and flowers, staring at her. He hadn't taken a step.

Ruby shielded her face with her hand. 'You coming in?' She was suddenly nervous, wondering if perhaps he'd changed his mind. But his smile told her he hadn't. He took slow steps towards her at first, and then picked up his pace, and when he reached her he grinned wildly and ran out into the waist-high water, extending his arms in front of his body and diving into a wave like a sleek dolphin. Ruby laughed and laughed, watching the waves, wondering where he would bob up, and then gasped when he appeared with a splash right in front of her.

'You scared me,' she giggled, and splashed him. The water sprayed up in an arc across his chest and his mouth and he spluttered and came closer.

'I should dunk you for that,' he said, mock-seriously.

'You wouldn't dare,' she said, lifting her chin in dramatic defiance. She met his eyes, so blue, so breathtaking, as blue as the water itself. The droplets of water on his chest caught the sun and sparkled like diamonds. He looked like an ancient Greek hero. Poseidon, perhaps. God of all of the seas.

He looked down at her, his breath erratic, his chest rising and falling. 'I would.'

This time, Ruby took a step closer and Cain's eyes drifted down to her breasts and her new swimsuit.

'And if you did, I would exact my revenge, Cain William Stapleton.'

'Sounds interesting. How might you do that, Ruby Allen?'

'Like this!' And quick as a flash, Ruby ducked down under the water and pulled one of Cain's legs out from under him. He toppled backwards and then he too was underwater, and the sand had clouded up like fog and she couldn't see where he was, but she quickly felt two firm hands on her waist, and then she was above the water line, breathing hard and laughing all at the same time.

'I see you play dirty,' he said with a smirk.

'A lady has to defend herself these days, you know.' Ruby brushed off his grip and swam out further, liking this game, until she was just deep enough that she could stand with the water lapping at her shoulders. A part of her knew she should be thinking of Edwin, but she didn't want to.

Cain swam to her side, ducked under the water and then flicked his head back, and brushed his hair off his forehead. They floated in silence for a while. With no one else in the water, they were alone at this end of the beach. The crowd of people was at the western end of the bay, where there were public facilities and organised activities.

'You said you were a university student?'

'Yes,' he answered. 'And I hope to be again soon.'

'You didn't like studying?'

'No, it wasn't that, at all.'

Ruby had loved school; had loved filling her mind with new ideas and history and facts to challenge everything she knew about the world around her. She'd excelled at French and History and had loathed Latin. It had been four years since she'd completed her secondary schooling at the finest ladies' college in the state and, although she'd been dux of her school, her father hadn't thought it necessary that she attend university. Although some women had already been studying at the university and doing brilliantly, her father didn't believe it was a place for a young woman like Ruby. He thought it would turn her into a bluestocking.

Ruby not only missed the learning, but the routine of it, and the camaraderie of being with her friends. Her life had become small: filled with church activities, outings with her mother and sisters, tennis on Saturdays (which she loathed), gardening and reading. Most of the time she felt as if she was growing up in a Jane Austen novel. It may have been 1934, but her parents still held firmly on to the morality and mores of another era altogether. The only daily excitement had been the arrival of the postman.

Oh, how she envied Cain. 'Why haven't you finished?'

He moved his arms in the water between them; it created a rippling wave which cooled her shoulders. 'I really loved university and I loved living up in Adelaide at the residential college. But things got tough a few years ago. Not just for my family, but for everyone. My father had a few labourers on the farm, local lads, but he had to let them go. I was cheap, you see. So I deferred my studies and came home four years ago. Lucky for me, things have picked up and I'm going back in February.'

'What were you studying?'

'Science. Agriculture, specifically. I always wanted to learn everything I could and then come back to the farm, so I could put into practice everything I'd learnt. It's a hard life running a dairy farm. I thought I might be able to change things for the better. Make life easier for my father. And my mother, of course.'

'How does your father feel about that? New ideas. You changing things.' She knew exactly how her father would feel.

Cain smiled, pleased with himself. 'He's proud of me. My mother, too. I've talked about it with them and they think my ideas could really work. If we had a bigger herd, we could produce more, but only if we invested in generators for milking machines. We're still milking seventy cows by hand, morning and night.'

Ruby glanced at his shoulders. She now understood why he was so strong. 'Your parents sound like lovely people.'

He looked at her for a long while. 'They are. So. What about you, Miss Ruby Allen? What fills your days?'

She rolled her eyes. 'Not university, that's for certain. My father made sure of that. I'm ...' She hesitated. She didn't want to tell him about Edwin. What would he think of a young woman who was almost engaged to one man to speaking so intimately with another?

'My parents want me to be married and have children. What point is there in an education if that's my future?'

Cain looked incredulous. 'That's rather old-fashioned thinking, if you don't mind me saying.'

Ruby looked down into the water. They were barely moving and it was so clear she could see Cain's body, the black smudge of his trunks, his long legs, his hands, flowing back and forth in the water between them. He was so close that if he moved six inches towards her they would be touching. The thought alone made her catch her breath.

'Yes. Well. That's my father.'

'Ruby. Is there something I should know?'

'What do you mean?'

'Do they have anyone particular in mind for you to marry?'

Ruby couldn't hide the truth. 'Yes. The son of a business acquaintance of my father's. The brother of my sister's fiancé.'

A dark look shadowed Cain's face. He didn't speak for a long moment. 'Are you telling me you're engaged, Ruby?'

Her heart thudded. 'No, no, I'm not,' she protested. Looking at Cain, she was more confused than ever. 'I'm in a terrible position. He has asked but I have not given him an answer. I'm down here for the summer to decide what to do. There is so much expected of me but I don't know if I can be the daughter my parents want me to be. Dutiful. Good. Obedient.'

'What's his name, this man you're supposed to marry?'

Ruby shook her head slowly, regretting that she was even talking about him to Cain. 'Edwin Stuart. He's in Adelaide, working. This is supposed to be my last summer …' She waited, scared of the words on her lips.

Cain's smile had disappeared and Ruby closed her eyes. When she flickered them open a moment later, his hands were on her waist again, not lifting her up this time but pulling her closer. And she willingly took that step into his arms, her feet finding his half-buried in the sand so she stood on them, giving her a little height to meet his mouth. She pressed her wet hands on to his warm chest, excited and scared by the strength of the muscles under his taut skin, the feel of his heart pounding under her fingertips.

'Ruby,' he murmured. 'Tell me you're not in love with someone else.'

She shook her head adamantly. Droplets of water sprayed against his chest. 'I'm not.'

And she leant up and pressed her lips to his. Ruby Allen, the oldest sister, the good girl, was claiming that first kiss she had dreamt about. When her warm lips met Cain's, his hands moved around her back, deliciously touching the bare skin revealed by her new swimsuit, and she splayed her hands on his chest. Cain tilted his head to one side and she opened her lips tentatively, inexperienced but curious, and he deepened the kiss. Something hummed all over her body, and a trembling earthquake rose from her toes to the top of her head. At the top of her thighs, there was an explosion of sensation so unfamiliar and so thrilling that Ruby couldn't breathe.

When she finally pulled her lips from his, she whispered, 'Cain.' His name, that's all it was. So simple. One syllable. But it was a declaration of something far more.

'Miss Ruby Allen …' Cain rested his forehead on hers and breathed deep. 'Please tell me we can see each other again?'

'Yes. I do want to see you again.'

'What are you doing for New Year's Eve?'

Ruby tried to get her thoughts in order. What had been the plan? 'We're going into Victor Harbor. My mother has a bridge party with people down from Adelaide. My sisters and I are supposed to be going to the Wonderview with Adeline's fiancé. For the dance.'

'And he's Edwin's brother?'

Ruby nodded. 'James and his family are at Sunnybrae.'

Cain narrowed his eyes. 'I deliver milk there, too. I think I saw him today. Tall chap, dark hair. Likes a white suit?'

'Yes, that's him.'

'And he's engaged to your sister, did you say?'

'Yes. They're marrying in April.'

Cain thought a moment. 'Does your sister have blonde hair? Rather tall?'

Ruby was confused. 'No, not at all. Adeline's petite and has auburn hair.'

His expression grew serious. 'Oh. Forgive me. I must have mixed her up with someone else. Tomorrow night. If I saw you at the Wonderview and asked you to dance, would you dance with me, Miss Ruby Allen?'

Ruby's heart felt light, her lips still tingled from his kiss and she wondered if she would ever feel as happy as she did at this moment. 'Why yes, I believe I would, Mr Cain Stapleton.'

CHAPTER 15

'Oh Ruby, look!'

Adeline slipped an arm through Ruby's and Ruby could feel her sister shake with excitement. She couldn't deny that a thrill coursed through her as well. 'There must be thousands of people here. How wonderful!'

The party had taken the train from Remarkable Bay and, three stops later, they'd disembarked the crowded carriage on Railway Terrace and followed the throng of people making their way to the centre of the New Year's Eve festivities. The main street of Victor Harbor, stretching from the grassed reserve at one end with the causeway and the water and Granite Island beyond it to the centre of the town, was a chattering, laughing party. The road had been closed to traffic for the night and it was now crowded with people in all their evening finery, coming and going to parties and guesthouses and the hotels along the foreshore. Young and old, widows walking arm-in-arm in their dour black outfits, to pretty young things in their silks and organzas. One daring young woman sauntered past wearing shorts, and Mrs Allen gasped. 'Is she playing tennis at this hour?'

'It's apparently quite the fashion now,' Ruby said, barely concealing her smile.

'And no stockings? What is the world coming to?' Mrs Allen shook her head in disbelief, which ruffled the fox fur stole around her neck.

The street was a sea of hats and bustling groups of people walking in this direction and that, coming and going from the Wonderview and the other dance halls in the town.

Mrs Allen moved to speak quietly in Ruby's ear. 'I do wish Clara had come,' she said, her face grim. 'She's become rather a sullen young thing and no matter what I say, she doesn't want to leave her room. I'm sure your father will have words with her when he arrives from town. She needs some fresh air. She's becoming paler and paler with every day that passes. Do you know what the bother is with her, Ruby?'

Ruby was torn. It felt disloyal not to tell her mother that she'd seen Clara crying by the chook shed, that Clara had begged her not to breathe a word to anyone. It pained Ruby to lie but she felt she had no choice. 'Not a clue, mother,' she managed and hoped it sounded breezy, as if Clara's tantrums were of no concern to her in the slightest. And then she hurriedly changed the subject, the guilt pressing down on her. 'Shall we go and deliver you to your bridge game?'

'Yes, do. But Ruby,' she paused and looked about her. 'Please keep an eye on Adeline. You know how … excitable she is.' Ruby understood what her mother meant, that no good could possibly come of Adeline drinking too much champagne.

'Of course I will, Mother,' Ruby told her. 'I'll be the damp squib at her side the whole night.' And the guilt that had been weighing down on her like a stone became a boulder of granite like those on the small island off the coast. When had she become the kind of person who told lies, who hid the truth? When had she become the kind of person to lie to her mother? How on earth could she tell her that, no, she couldn't keep watch over Adeline because she was planning to run away herself? When had she become this frivolous person?

When had she become Adeline?

Ruby knew when. It was the day her parents told her about Edwin. She'd lied from the very first, from the first slice of sponge cake served on delicate Royal Albert china in the front parlour back on Buxton Street. When she'd smiled at Edwin and pretended to her family—and his— that she could ever consider marrying him.

Ruby, Adeline and James pushed through the crowds and deposited Mrs Allen at the private residence of some Adelaide friends, the Miltons, for a rather more subdued New Year's Eve celebration. After politely declining Mrs Milton's offer of a cup of fruit punch, the young threesome made their way to the Wonderview, where a table was booked in James's name. It only took them a few minutes to walk there, despite the crowds, and when they reached the building, it looked grand in the moonlight. Its name, spelled out in white on the facade, was lit from below. It seemed hundreds of people were milling about outside and Ruby nervously clutched her purse, filled with apprehension and excitement, on the look-out for Cain. Every young man in a hat drew her quick attention, until she felt if she darted a glance one more time she might dislocate her neck.

'He will come,' she whispered to herself. 'I know he will.'

It wasn't perhaps in the most salubrious part of the town, not with the Victor Harbor Power Generator Station next door, but the atmosphere more than made up for its location. Inside, past the maroon leather cinema seats, the open area in front of the screen was edged with tables, each featuring a tall vase with white gladioli spikes in each, surrounded by delicate ferns. Pink and blue balloons were tied on every available upright post, and the orchestra was huddled at one side around the Duo Concerto, a strange mix of piano and pipe organ that had become all the rage in modern picture theatres.

The musicians were halfway through a popular tune that Ruby recognised from the radio and unable to contain her excitement at everything—at the music, at the dancing, at seeing Cain, at the idea of being held in his arms and dancing with him—she squeezed Adeline's arm.

The sisters looked at each other and laughed excitedly.

'How wonderful,' Ruby said on a sigh.

'It is, Ruby. And I don't believe you'll have any trouble finding someone to dance with tonight. I think your card might be rather full. Look at all these young men!'

The room was indeed full of handsome young men dressed to the nines. It seemed that many of their acquaintances from Adelaide were in Victor Harbor for the celebrations. There were a few faces she recognised from the tennis club and from church, but Ruby only had one young man on her mind. She glanced quickly at the crowd but couldn't see him, which only made the nervous anticipation rise up in her throat. She swallowed it away. She was going to have fun tonight. She'd never been surer of anything.

As they walked down to the front of the ballroom, taking the steps between the row of picture-theatre seats, Adeline leaned into James. They were walking in front of Ruby and she could see Adeline's shining eyes.

'We're going to have a marvellous night, aren't we?' James glanced at her for half a second before casting his gaze about the room. He was wearing the white suit he favoured and a striped pale blue tie. 'Of course we will. I predict there will be dancing till dawn.'

Adeline looked back over her shoulder at Ruby and winked. 'You don't mind terribly being Ruby's chaperone as well, do you?'

James doffed his hat gallantly and Ruby laughed. 'Not at all.' He stopped and turned back to Ruby. 'It's just a pity that Clara didn't feel well enough to come. I know she's young but I'm sure she would have loved all this.'

Ruby was surprised at his analysis of her youngest sister. James clearly had no idea at all about Clara. She would have hated all this noise and loud music and raucous laughter. She much preferred the company of her books.

'Phooey to her,' Adeline said a wave of a gloved hand. 'She couldn't be convinced and besides, she's been a melancholy thing our whole holiday. And as much as she's attempted to make us all equally as miserable, I won't buy into it. See if I care if she's stuck at Bayview tonight playing cards with Mrs Nightingale.' When she'd discovered Clara would be staying back, Mrs Nightingale had promised Mrs Allen she would make sure Clara had a slice of sponge cake and a glass of cordial when the year turned over, so she wouldn't have to see in 1935 on her own.

'Adeline,' Ruby cautioned, although she didn't quite know why she was worrying about anyone overhearing their conversation. They'd had to shout to be heard above the laughter and the calling out and the other conversations all around them. 'Don't be unkind.'

No matter how hard they'd tried, Clara had been determined to remain at Bayview. It had been a wet and windy afternoon, and those in the Bayview and Sunnybrae Guest Houses had gathered at afternoon tea earlier that day (during which they'd eaten Mrs Nightingale's most delicious coconut sponge layer cake and honey drops) to make contingency plans in case the weather had really set it. The discussion made Ruby nervous: she could think of nothing else but meeting Cain at the dance. She'd thought of nothing else since but the kiss they'd shared on the beach. She wanted more of his lips and his arms about her; she wanted to feel the warm strength of him enveloping her. She wanted everything about Cain Stapleton.

While Clara had seemed relieved that the evening's plans were about to be thrown into turmoil, Adeline had been beside herself at the thought of a cancellation. She'd brought with her to Remarkable Bay a new evening gown that she'd been desperate to wear—a white velvet frock, cut in a deep 'v' at the front with a big black velvet bow—and, more importantly, she was desperate to show off her dashing new fiancé.

Luckily, the rain and wind of the day had eased off and although the streets were still damp, the air was refreshingly cool, a respite from the heat of the past few days, when the north winds had blown down to the south coast and crisped everything and everyone.

'I'm determined to have fun tonight.' Adeline lifted her chin and looked away from Ruby haughtily. 'I have the handsomest man in the world on my arm and we're going to dance all night, aren't we, James?'

'Of course we are, darling.' James leaned down to kiss Adeline on the cheek and when she nestled into his embrace, Ruby noticed he seemed more intent on seeing who was watching him than returning Adeline's affection. When he glanced at her, his heavy-lidded gaze and intense stare made Ruby look away. She couldn't fight the sudden feeling that he took pleasure in making her feel uncomfortable.

'Oh, sorry Miss.' A young man rushing down the stairs towards the tables and the music had bumped her shoulder and Ruby stumbled, almost losing her footing on the edge of the carpeted step. He stopped, reached for her arm to steady her. 'Are you all right?' He was tall and quite thin under his too-big suit, with a ruddy complexion and apologetic eyes. His shoes had been lovingly polished but Ruby could see they were almost worn through at the toe.

'Listen here …' James started, puffing out his chest and moving protectively between Ruby and the young man.

The young man with the too-big suit stepped back, his hands raised in acquiescence. 'I didn't mean nothing by it, honestly. It's the party, that's all. Everyone's a little excited.'

'James, really. I'm all right.' Ruby smiled at the young man and shook her head slightly to show James she didn't want or need his protection. 'No offence taken. It seems everyone here tonight is already in a party mood. Happy New Year.'

'And to all of you,' the young man said before scampering down the stairs, two at a time, towards the dancing.

Ruby hoped so much that it would be a happy new year. As they made their way to their table, she reflected on the past week in Remarkable Bay. It felt as if so much had happened and she couldn't shake the feeling that tonight was going to be more than the beginning of a new year. She'd worn her favourite evening gown, wanting to look lovely tonight. The amethyst-coloured silk dress hugged her figure and then kicked out at the bottom with narrow pleats. The satin waistband sat low on her hip and curved around her back, a large rosette decorating it at the point where it dipped low. She'd had to be careful the entire journey over not to sit back on the train's leather seats in case she squashed it. Her outfit was finished with a simple pale green cloche hat with a spray of delicate feathers. She felt rather pretty in it. Perhaps even beautiful.

As Ruby took her seat and watched James and Adeline twirling on the dance floor, the frills on her sister's gown swirling at her knees, her delight at her good fortune evident in the smile on her beautiful face, Ruby knotted her fingers together and waited for Cain.

'Ruby? Ruby, is that you?'

Ruby tore her gaze from the steps to the man standing in front of her. And when she realised who it was, she felt sick.

CHAPTER
16

'Harold,' Ruby finally spluttered.

Edwin's best friend, the lanky and haughty Harold Mortimer, looked Ruby up and down. They played doubles together at the tennis club and had gone to school together. And now, here he was, a potential witness to her betrayal. Her heart fell into the pit of her stomach. How could she have thought that amongst all these people she might remain anonymous? How did she imagine she could get away with being secretive and clandestine? Was everything about to be ruined? What if he'd happened upon her talking to Cain and went back to Adelaide and told Edwin?

A thousand fears darted through her mind but she tried not to settle on any of them. Perhaps she was safe. She hadn't seen Cain yet, after all.

'Hello, Ruby. What on earth are you doing here?' She'd met Harold a number of times and he'd never seemed to like her. He worked in his family's insurance company and believed himself to be rather important. Ruby decided that the New Year's Eve celebrations hadn't miraculously rendered him any more amiable.

'I'm ...' Ruby opened her mouth to speak but no words came. 'Edwin's in Adelaide, unfortunately, so I've come along with my sister Adeline and her fiancé, James.'

'Oh, yes, Stuart,' Harold said, swiping imaginary lint off his suit lapel. His lip curled. 'Edwin will be relieved to know you're being chaperoned.' Harold looked down his nose at her. 'Although I don't know what Edwin would think about you being here in this crowd, even with your sister and his brother.'

Ruby's heart pounded in quiet fury. Why on earth was it any of his business what she was doing on her family holiday? And then it struck her. Her guilt about what she was doing behind Edwin's back struck her like a sledgehammer.

She stood up quickly. She felt dizzy and a little sick and needed some air. The music seemed to get louder and it was thudding a jazz rhythm between her ears. She held a hand out to him. 'Happy new year, Harold. May 1935 bring you many blessings.'

'Oh, right. And to you.' Harold looked slightly annoyed which made his next question even more incomprehensible. 'Would you like to dance? Edwin would throttle me if he knew I'd left you sitting here like a shag on a rock.'

She wanted to scream *no* with every fibre of her being, but nodded with a polite smile.

And that's where she was, standing in the middle of the crowded dance floor with Harold's arm about her, pulling her rather too close for her liking, when Cain arrived.

Ruby's heart leapt into her throat when he caught her eye and suddenly there was no band and no dancing and no crowd around her and no other man holding her close. All she could hear was her racing heart in her ears and all she could see was him. In a suit tonight, dark navy with a blue-and-white tie, with a waistcoat underneath his jacket and a white carnation tucked into the buttonhole in his lapel. She adored that little touch, that reminder to her of the flowers he'd given her on the beach. That something special just for her.

She lifted a hand to wave at him and then the music crashed back to life, louder than ever. As he began to weave his way through the crowd, she was half-thrilled, half-terrified that he was on his way over to interrupt Harold and ask for a dance for himself. When she shook her head just the slightest, he stopped on the edge of the dance floor, right by the singer from the orchestra, who was crooning into the microphone, his slicked-back black hair and his pencil moustache gleaming in the overhead lights.

Without a word, Cain understood. He waited.

And Ruby made small talk with Harold, while scouring the dance floor for Adeline and James, until the song ended.

When applause erupted all around them, Ruby lifted her hand from Harold's shoulder. 'Thank you, Harold. You saved me from a night sitting at our table all by myself.'

'My pleasure, Ruby,' he replied, although he hadn't lifted his hand from her waist.

'I must go to the ...'

'Of course.'

She slipped out of Harold's embrace and turned, squeezing her way through the crowd, hoping now she didn't see Adeline and James so she wouldn't have to explain. She made a beeline for their table, fetching her purse and coat from her chair, and then hurriedly made her way up the stairs, through the foyer and out the double glass doors to the fresh air and what felt like freedom.

She crossed the road to the park and gulped the cool, fresh air as she pressed herself back against the rough bark of a tree and waited in the dark.

'Please follow me,' she whispered into the breeze.

And he was there, crossing the street, looking from one side to the other on the look-out for energetic young men on motorcycles, and jogged over to her.

And her heart leapt when she saw him. In a moment he was standing in front of her and his hand found hers. He pulled her closer until their bodies were almost touching.

'Cain,' she murmured.

'Miss Ruby Allen,' Cain said as he leaned in to kiss her cheek, slowly and softly.

Every part of her body trembled. 'I'm sorry about what happened in there. I didn't want you to come over and talk to me. Not amongst those people.'

'You didn't?'

'No,' she said, almost breathless.

Cain stilled. 'You mean you didn't want me to be seen by anyone from your set from Adelaide, I suppose?'

She nodded. 'Yes. Oh, but it's not what you think. That man I was dancing with is Edwin's best friend and he's rather awful and I simply know he'll tell Edwin everything. And if he were to have seen us dancing … '

Cain moved closer to her, gripped her hand tighter. 'And what would have happened then? Do you think he might have noticed the way I look at you?' His voice dropped lower, huskier. 'Do you think he might have realised how very fond of you I am?'

Ruby held her breath. 'I was afraid he would see the exact same thing on my face, which would rather give the game away, don't you think?'

'Are you saying you like me, Ruby Allen?'

'Yes. I like you, Cain Stapleton.' Ruby slipped her arms around Cain's waist and he pressed her hard against the tree, its rough bark hard against her back, but all she could feel was his warm lips on hers, kissing her softly and gently, his strength and his body all around her.

Their lips parted.

'Don't marry him, Ruby,' Cain implored.

'I don't want to, I've never wanted to. Especially now.' Ruby grabbed the lapels of his coat and pulled him closer.

He rested his forehead on hers. 'This is the beginning, you know that? Tonight and tomorrow morning. 1935 will be our year.'

'I hope so, Cain. But there are some things I have to tell my family first. And Edwin.'

He looked at her as if he understood. 'And I want to tell mine. They'll like you very much, Ruby. My parents and all my brothers. I know they will.'

They smiled at each other, breathing the same air, thinking of a future together.

'I don't want to go back in there,' Ruby said. 'Not without you.'

He tugged on her hand and they began to walk. 'Follow me.'

They made their way back across the crowded street, Cain gripping Ruby's hand firmly so they wouldn't be separated, and turned down a small alleyway between two cottages. It seemed like a secret short cut as there was no one else on the dim cobblestoned path, and they slowed their pace. Ruby held fast to Cain's hand and with her other held on to his arm. This felt like a thrilling adventure: her and Cain heading off to who knew where, and she wanted to remember every moment of it.

'Where are we going?' she whispered to him, still nervously afraid they might be seen by someone she knew.

'We're nearly there.'

They reached the end of the cobbled laneway and turned right, crossing Railway Terrace and the train line and then, a few moments later, they were at the grassed reserve that curved around the beach. Wooden seats had been placed periodically so people could sit and enjoy the view out to Granite Island and the Bluff, and Cain and Ruby stopped when they reached the bench furthest from the noise of the celebrations. Cain waited while Ruby sat first. She smoothed her dress and pulled her coat about her against the chill evening wind.

He simply stood there, his arms loose at his sides, looking at her, his aqua eyes filled with something so warm and tender it brought tears to hers.

'Are you going to sit down?' she teased.

'The view's better from here.' And then he grinned and it shot a bolt of lightning through her.

'I need someone to keep me warm.' Ruby felt a sudden flush of heat in her cheeks. She wasn't sure what had overcome her. She'd never been this flirtatious with anyone.

'Ruby ...' he started and then shook his head as if he couldn't believe his luck. 'You look so pretty. I wish we could go right back there to the Wonderview and dance all night. I want to take you in my arms and twirl you around that dance floor and show off to every other bloke in the place.'

She patted the bench next to her and he came to sit beside her, one arm around the back of the bench, one leg crossed towards her. She laid her head on his shoulder and he gathered her in closer, and Ruby knew that this was the place she was meant to be. This was happiness. In the arms of this man, a man she had chosen, not someone who had been chosen for her.

'Cain, you were right about what you said before, about me not wanting Harold to see us together, but it's not for the reason you think.' She paused, wanting to get this right. She looked into his lovely blue eyes. 'I'm not embarrassed about you. But I have to do the right thing by Edwin. It's so complicated, with Adeline and James engaged and our fathers working together. Our families are already tied up with each other in too many ways to count. Edwin has to hear it from me—no one else—that I'm never going to be his wife. I have to be the one to tell him that I don't love him.'

Ruby knew she could be strong. She was a young woman and in a few hours it was going to be 1935 and things were changing for women, after all. She wasn't the only one who hoped they were. She'd read the *Women's Weekly* from cover to cover and knew girls and women were making their places in the world fuelled by their own ambitions, not those of their families. She could be strong: after she'd told Edwin, she would tell her parents she wasn't going to marry Edwin, and then she would introduce them to Cain Stapleton, son of a dairy farmer of Remarkable Bay, who was studying science at the University of Adelaide. Surely he would be respectable enough for them?

It had to be. She had made her choice.

'Are you certain?' Cain's arm around her shoulder tightened, squeezing her closer.

'More certain of it than anything. When we return to Adelaide after our summer holiday, I'll tell him and then we'll be free.' She pressed a hand to his chest, right about where his heart was, and she could feel it racing under her palm.

This was what love was, she knew that now.

'Each day will seem like a year until then, Ruby.' He ran a knuckle down her cheek and then kissed her tenderly. She already loved his touch. 'I'll be leaving the farm and going up to Adelaide in February. I'll be moving back into my old digs at the residential college in North Adelaide, near the scoreboard end at Adelaide Oval. It's a damn good place to be when the cricket's on, I can tell you. Every time someone hits a four, you can hear the crowd roar. And when Bradman plays? Well, you can hear the whole of Adelaide clapping. You live near there, don't you?'

Ruby realised home was ten minutes away from there, on foot. Cain would be that close. 'Yes, on Buxton Street.'

Cain looked at her in disbelief. 'All those years ago, when I was studying. We were so close. I can't believe that. Do you think we ever passed each other on the street?'

'It's a funny thought, isn't it?' Ruby sighed.

Cain paused. 'What do you think your parents say about me, Ruby?'

She snuggled closer into his arms. Her confidence drained. He was right to ask and his question revealed he was perhaps more realistic about what Ruby was planning than she was.

'It's almost 1935,' Ruby said, wanting to sound tough, if not for him then for herself. 'Young women can do things their own way now, don't you know.'

Cain stroked her hair. 'Although that's perhaps not as easy as you think, sweetheart.'

She grabbed his lapel and there it was, the white carnation. He slipped it out of his buttonhole and gave it to her. She lifted the flower from Cain's fingers and held it to her nose. It had no scent of its own, she knew that, but it smelt of Cain's soap and that was the best kind of perfume.

'I'll be studying for a couple of years at least.'

'I know.'

'And then I may have to go and work in the country.'

'I can wait,' she said confidently and he kissed her again, hungry this time, his hands gripping her shoulders, his tongue exploring her mouth, and Ruby didn't need to think about Rudolph Valentino any more.

They sat in silence, knowing more words weren't necessary, and gradually soft music drifted in their direction. Behind them, The Anchorage Guest House seemed to be having a party of its own. It carried on the wind and Cain began to whistle along with the tune.

'Do you know this song?'

She cocked her head and listened. 'No, what is it?'

'"Let's Fall in Love".' And when Cain kissed her again, and they held each other in the moonlight with the Eddy Duchin song playing softly in the background, Ruby knew beyond a doubt that she already had.

She startled at an enormous, echoing sound and clutched Cain.

'That's the cannon being fired at Warland Reserve,' he said with a chuckle.

'It scared the life out of me,' Ruby gasped. They could hear the distant cheers of the crowd in the centre of Victor Harbor.

'And the ceremonial firing of the cannon means it's gone midnight. Happy New Year, Ruby.'

'Happy New Year, Cain. 1935 holds so much promise, don't you think?'

Nothing could put a dampener on Ruby's happy feelings as she headed up the Bayview stairs to her room. After the cannon had fired at midnight, Cain had seen her back to the Wonderview before slipping out of sight. Ruby had found Adeline and James, who were still dancing wildly, and they made their way back to Railway Terrace to board the late train back to Remarkable Bay. Their mother had made her way back earlier with Mrs Stuart. Deliciously, Cain had never been far from her the whole trip back. She sensed his presence at the train station, and when she turned, he was there, two people behind her, jammed in the crowd. And then on the train, Ruby and Adeline managed to find seats. James stood next to Adeline, holding the overhead strap, and there was Cain, next to him but one. They shared secret glances the whole way back to Remarkable Bay.

When they got off the train, Cain brushed past her and his fingers lingered on hers for just a moment. Oh, she was in love. She knew she was. She could still feel the tingling in her fingertips as she climbed the stairs and reached for the door of the room she shared with Adeline and Clara. Adeline was still outside, sitting on the lawns across the road talking with James, so she was alone. She knew she would have to be as quiet as a mouse so as not to wake Clara.

Her youngest sister was sound asleep and Ruby snuck into bed, feeling aglow from the inside.

She had found it. She had found him. She had found love with Cain Stapleton and that made her the luckiest young woman in the world.

The next morning, on the very first day of 1935, Ruby washed in the bathroom at the end of the hallway and came back to her room to dress for breakfast. She pulled out the upholstered stool and sat at the dresser, while Clara slept and Adeline fussed and bothered about which frock she should wear.

She was glancing around for her hairbrush, pushing away Clara's straw hat and Adeline's slip, when she saw Edwin's letter. She'd forgotten all about it.

She still hadn't read it. Now she knew she must. She owed him that much. When she slowly opened the envelope, she could see there were perhaps six pages of his neat, small handwriting. She took a deep breath.

'Is that Edwin's letter you're reading?' Adeline looked over her shoulder and Ruby flipped the pages face down on to the dresser.

'Go away.'

'Are you only just reading it now? James gave it to you days ago.'

Ruby scrambled for an excuse. 'Of course I've already read it. I'm … I'm missing him, that's all so I thought I'd read it again. If you'll leave me in peace, that is.'

Ruby's obfuscation worked and Adeline changed the subject.

'What are you doing today? I'm heading over to Sunnybrae for breakfast with James and his parents. They'll officially be my in-laws soon. I can hardly believe it.'

'Yes. I'm off to …'

Ruby stopped. She'd made plans to meet Cain again at the beach that afternoon at two. She looked down at Edwin's letter, then tossed it on the dresser. What was she doing? What kind of person was she to be caught between two men? Both loved her but she only loved one and that meant one of them was going to be hurt. She put her head in her hands and tried to think about what to do and how on earth she was going to do it.

She would read Edwin's letter and then she would discuss it with Cain today.

'I'm going to have breakfast and then read for a little while. No big plans. I'm a little tired from last night, actually.'

Adeline sidled up to Ruby and sat on the edge of the dresser. 'Where exactly did you disappear to last night? James and I were looking for you all over when the clock struck midnight and we all linked arms and sang "Auld Lang Syne".'

Ruby caught her sister's reflection in the oval mirror and saw the deceit in her own expression. She hoped Adeline was too distracted to notice. 'I caught up with some friends from Adelaide. Remember Harold, Edwin's friend from the tennis club? He was there and we danced for a while.'

'Mmm,' she replied. 'I don't know anyone who'd want to dance with Harold, but beggars can't be choosers, can they, Ruby? Anyhow, I'm off. I'm desperate for a cup of tea.' When she flounced past Clara's bed, she slapped her hand on the mattress. 'Wake up, sleepyhead. Please tell me you're going to do something today other than stay cooped up in this room being miserable.'

An arm emerged from the blankets, smacking Adeline's hand away.

Adeline took her purse and slipped her straw hat on her auburn curls. '*Au revoir, deux soeur.*'

Ruby nodded her goodbye and then slowly picked up Edwin's letter. She took a deep breath and began to read it.

My dearest Ruby …

* * *

Twenty minutes later, Ruby was downstairs at breakfast, eating to distract herself. She had porridge and then eggs, sunny side up, and toast with thickly spread butter. She stopped to think about Cain while she was eating the butter from his very own cows.

There were a few too many sore heads that morning and many of the guests were still sleeping, so she had a table to herself. She needed to think, to plan her way out of marrying Edwin. Because he seemed quite determined to marry her. His letter had implored her to say yes and it set out all the reasons why she should agree to be his wife. With every sentence, she'd felt sicker and sicker. He'd listed off a series of transactions. How successful his father's firm was and how secure his position therefore was. While he didn't hint at the size of his salary, he indicated it would continue to increase until one day he would be managing the firm. Ruby wasn't quite sure where that left his older brother James in the scheme of things. There would be a house, he wrote, a gift from his parents to them once they were wed. A bluestone cottage in Norwood, just east of the city. There had been tenants in it who would be removed as soon as they had set a date. There were lots of rooms for children and for help, nannies and a cook if she wanted one.

How on earth could he know her at all if he thought these things were important to her? He was promising her security and the continuation of the life she was already living. That was not the life she wanted. She wanted laughter and adventure and love.

In all that he'd written, he hadn't mentioned love once.

I know you are down at Remarkable Bay to consider your options. I would expect nothing else of someone so sensible as you. I hope you will come to the conclusion that we are very much suited to each other, and I'm certain that we will have a happy and settled future together.

When she'd finished reading, she'd screwed the pages into a tight ball and stuffed it at the bottom of her suitcase.

Now she stared at the toast she'd covered with Cain's butter.

She was more determined than ever to tell her mother the truth.

She wanted Cain Stapleton, not Edwin Stuart. No matter what it would cost her.

Ruby went back upstairs to find her mother, but there was no answer, so she returned to the room she shared with her sisters. When she turned the knob and pushed, it knocked against something and wouldn't open all the way. She tried with a little more force and it gave another couple of inches.

When she squeezed her head through the gap she saw something on the floor. The curtains were drawn and it was dark. It took Ruby a confused moment to realise what it was.

Clara.

Her sister was lying on the floor, crumpled, her knees pulled up against her chest. Ruby had been forcing the door against one of her shoes.

'Clara!' Ruby gasped and flicked on the overhead light before falling to her knees. There was little response from her sister. Ruby smoothed her hand over Clara's forehead and could feel in an instant that she was clammy and hot. Her full lips were almost bloodless and sweat was trickling down the sides of her face. 'Good god, Clara. What's happened? Did you fall and strike your head? Why are you on the floor?'

And a sinking, suffocating sense of dread almost bowled Ruby over.

She could not keep this secret any longer. She struggled to her feet, but she was shaking so much she was barely able to stand. She leant back against the door and gripped the doorknob. Her own breath was shallow and quick. 'I'm fetching Mother. You need a doctor.'

Clara moaned and sucked in a deep breath. Then she shot up and reached for the silver bucket beside her and dry-retched into it. Ruby didn't need to look inside to know that Clara had nothing left to bring up.

'Please, Ruby.' Clara shook her head weakly. 'Don't.'

'I must tell her, Clara. Look at you. I can't keep this secret any longer.'

Clara burst into violent tears and the shock of seeing her this way scared Ruby.

'Please, Ruby,' Clara begged, her voice an aching sob. The sound of it cut Ruby to the core and she began to feel frightened. 'Tell me what to do.'

'I don't understand. What to do about what?' Ruby pleaded, pushing the damp hair back from Clara's forehead, fighting the sensible urge to go and find their mother.

Clara placed a hand across her belly and looked up at her sister with weeping, red eyes. 'The baby.'

CHAPTER
17

2016

Roma had Bayview all to herself for the weekend.

Addy had driven up to Adelaide to pick up a few things from home and then have lunch with some of her friends from the film world. Roma couldn't blame her. Addy had been down in Remarkable Bay for three weeks now, and she could understand that Addy needed to get together with people who knew what best boys and gaffers actually were. Addy still hadn't heard anything further about the finance for the film she'd been working on, so her stay was becoming more open-ended than they'd both originally thought. But Roma didn't mind at all. They'd settled into a comfortable routine with each other. During the day, they worked on the house to really loud music. Room by room, they were making their way through the upstairs and only had Roma's bedroom and the long hallway to go. Its ceilings were high and there was lots of ladder shuffling, but Roma was in no rush. And, once she was swept up in the rhythm of their work, Addy had seemed to relax. She didn't feel the jittery need to talk quite so much and—shock horror—one day she hadn't even put on any lipstick before lifting a paint brush.

Roma was growing to like Addy's company more than she thought she would, and it was the simple things. The silent sharing of a coffee in the mornings. The unspoken way they knew how to clean up together after dinner—Addy would wash and Roma would dry. The witty conversations at night in front of something fluffy on TV, especially the home renovation programs.

'When did the paint dry?' Addy would call out at a miraculous room transformation that seemed to happen in a commercial break and Roma would laugh uproariously.

Those were the things she'd missed living alone.

It was September now and spring had done its typically South Australian thing and thrown up a series of days with temperatures in the mid-thirties. Today was one of them and Roma decided it might be time for her first swim of the season, so she'd slipped on her bathers, thrown on a light dress, found a wide-brimmed straw hat and slathered herself in sunscreen, before toeing into her thongs and doing a last-minute search for her keys.

She had to laugh at this routine. Since when had going for a swim turned into a military operation? Since skin cancer, that's when. Although she had dark hair, not auburn like Addy, Roma's skin was pale and would burn to a crisp unless she was slathered in SPF50. She'd been cautious her whole life, not just because her mother had sung the 'Slip, Slop, Slap' song to her when she was a child, but because her father had paid for a lifetime of playing tennis by having to endure annual visits to the dermatologist so he could have numerous pre-cancerous growths burnt off his nose and arms.

Roma locked the front door behind her and set out to cross the road to take the Harbour Master's Walk to the water. She looked left and right to check for traffic—a city habit she knew she would probably never break—and as she did, something in the distance caught her eye. An A-frame advertising board was set out on the footpath further down Ocean Street. Roma decided to investigate so she turned left instead of crossing the road. It was warm, the sun was on her back and she didn't mind taking the long way round before she hit the water. As she approached, the lettering on the sign came into clearer focus. It was positioned on the footpath in front of the old, vacant shop. The sign said *Open For Business* in white chalk on a blackboard, and as Roma got closer, she could hear the relaxing sounds of world music floating out through the open door. Fresh lettering on the window said *Remarkable Bay Pilates Studio* and when Roma looked through the window and into the shop, she saw a woman inside, wearing loose navy shorts and a bright orange singlet top, her legs and arms bare and toned. She was rolling up yoga mats and storing them in an open shelving unit when she looked up and smiled.

'Hey,' she called out and waved.

'Hello.' Roma stood at the open door and looked around. The old shop was a rectangular shape and where she expected it to be long and dark, there was bright sunlight streaming down in the middle. The polished wooden floors gleamed and the walls were a soothing pale green. It seemed that Roma wasn't the only one who'd been renovating in Remarkable Bay. The woman standing with her hands propped on her hips had a friendly face, and an open, warm and welcoming smile. Roma thought she had the perfect coun-tenance for the owner of a business in which people might enter worried about the flexibility of their wobbling thighs. There was something fresh and reassuring about her.

'Come on in.'

Roma pushed aside her hesitation. She had been the new person in town not long before and someone had welcomed her. Connor, specifically, had welcomed her. She was suddenly determined to get this small-town thing right. Paying it forward wasn't so hard, right? She stepped inside and was immediately struck by the cool-ness and the scent of lavender. Roma had become accustomed to the still vaguely musty smell of Bayview so it was a pleasant surprise to smell something fresh and floral. She made a mental note to text Addy and ask her to buy some candles while she was up in Adelaide.

The woman approached and held out her hand. 'Hey. I'm Keira Kozlowski. Welcome to the Remarkable Bay Pilates Studio.'

'Roma Harris.' They shook hands warmly and Roma could feel the strength in Keira's fingers. Maybe Pilates worked after all. 'This place looks great,' Roma said. 'Smells great, too. Did you do all the work?'

Keira shook her head. 'It was all done when I leased it. Isn't it a beautiful space? I think it was going to be a bookshop or something, which is why it was painted this relaxing shade of fashionable green but whoever it was changed their mind. Lucky for me, huh?' She played with her high ponytail as she spoke, twisting her plain brown hair around and around into a knot. Roma had to stop herself from staring at her cheekbones. She figured they were about the same age, give or take a year. Keira was definitely in her thirties.

'I heard a rumour this was going to be a Pilates studio but I thought it might have been nothing more than small-town gossip.'

'Ooh, I'm the subject of gossip already? I'm not sure if I should be flattered or not.' Keira smiled happily. 'On the other hand, maybe that'll help me drum up some business. I had been hoping to move down here in July to set things up over winter, but it didn't work out. I got stuck in Sydney and ...' she waved a hand and looked sheepish. 'You so don't want to hear my life story. But,' she threw her hands up in the air and smiled genuinely, 'I'm here now.'

'Did you say you're from Sydney?'

Keira nodded and her ponytail bobbed from side to side. 'Born and bred, although I've lived all over and travelled a fair bit. My parents tell me I'm a bit of a gypsy. So, Roma, tell me all about Remarkable Bay. You know, who's who in the zoo and all that.'

Roma smiled at the idea that she was a local. 'Don't look at me. I've only been in the Bay for a month.'

Keira laughed. 'So you've probably had the same question as me. Everyone's poked their head in and once the polite introductions are out of the way, they've all looked at me sideways and asked, "Why Remarkable Bay?"'

'I've had that question a few times myself.' Roma started to add up in her head all the people who'd thought she'd gone mad when she told them of her plan to leave Adelaide and buy Bayview. Not that they'd used that word exactly—mad. It was too loaded where Roma was concerned, too close to the bone. People didn't even joke because they clearly thought she had slipped over the edge. Leo had kept asking her if she didn't just need a holiday. Her colleagues in the lunch room at work had been perplexed, not quite believing that someone would give up a permanent job ('In this economic climate?' her line manager had gasped) to do what, no one was sure, exactly. It had only been a month, and she would have to go back to work eventually, but so far, moving to Remarkable Bay had felt like the best decision she'd ever made. Tom's parents had been angry with her, believing somehow that leaving Adelaide meant she was leaving Tom's memory behind. They should have known, better than anyone else, that memories don't leave you. They follow you around like your own personal cloud, blocking out the sun every now and then, making you feel cold even on a warm night.

Roma was curious. 'So what do you tell people when they ask?'

Keira shrugged. 'I came here once on holidays with my family and I always remembered it. There's something about this place ...' Then she shrugged her shoulders. 'Who am I kidding? It's a total mystery to me that when I could have moved to any beach town in New South Wales, where the weather is way warmer, I chose this place instead. Maybe it's the name. Maybe the romantic in me is hoping something remarkable might happen to me in Remarkable Bay.'

Roma's laugh echoed in the empty space.

'Or maybe some*one* remarkable might happen ...' Keira waved as though pushing the thought away. 'Like I've improved my chances by coming to a town as small as this.'

'You're single?'

Keira nodded. 'You know, I'm a twenty-first century woman and I don't need a man, but having one would be kinda nice.'

Roma wanted to wish her luck, but she didn't believe in luck. It was a humorous juxtaposition that she had come this far to avoid life's entanglements at the same time Keira had arrived hoping to find one. Keira glanced quickly at Roma's left hand, trying not to be obvious. Roma noticed but didn't mind. There hadn't been a ring there for two years.

'Did you move down here with a significant other?'

'No,' she sighed. 'And I'm not looking for significant, either.'

'Go you.' Keira cocked her head to the side. 'Hey, you don't have kids by any chance, do you?'

'No, sorry.' Roma fought the memory, swallowed the pain. Her little black cloud hovered. She and Tom had been arguing about having a family the night he died.

Keira must have seen the change in expression on Roma's face. 'Oh god, sorry. I wasn't trying to be nosy. Some people have kids and no partner, right? I was hoping to connect with a mothers and babies group down here, that's all. I thought I might be able to get some baby exercise classes up and running.'

'Babies need to do exercises?' Roma asked incredulously. Add that to the list of things she didn't know about children.

'It's for the mums, really. I used to run classes like that in Sydney at the studio I managed and the mums loved having the chance to get together and talk and have coffee after. You know, mum bonding stuff.'

Roma smiled. 'You might have more luck in the Bay if you do strength for seniors.'

'Hey,' Keira's face lit up. 'That's a great idea. "Strength for Seniors".'

'You could ask at the bakery if they'll let you put a sign in the window. And maybe the pharmacy, too. Between those two places, you'll capture every senior in town.'

'Thanks.'

'Well. Good luck with everything,' Roma said. 'It was nice to meet you.'

'It's really nice to meet you. Do you do Pilates?'

Roma hesitated. She didn't want to appear rude, especially to someone who seemed so nice and who had moved to a small town halfway across the country with the hope of setting herself up in business.

'I'll be honest with you, Keira. Organised activities aren't really my thing.'

Keira laughed. 'Please. No pressure. We've all got our thing. What's yours? What do you get up to in this little town, huh?'

'I've been renovating my house just up the road.'

Keira's eyes widened. 'You're the one with the place next to Connor's?'

A wave of disappointment swamped her. Maybe Keira had already run into the someone she'd been hoping to meet. Of course Connor had been by. Wasn't he unofficial president of the non-existent Remarkable Bay Welcoming Committee? Clearly he did the same to every new person in town. Or was that every new woman in town?

Roma felt ridiculous. She had no reason or no right to be jealous. She didn't want to think about Connor—or any man—that way, not any more. But, no matter how hard she'd tried, little ideas had been creeping into her head late at night. The memory of his smile. His lemons. And, most of all, his kindness.

She tried to concentrate on Keira's question instead of going over her conversation with Connor on her balcony the night he'd brought her lemons. She shook herself out of the memory. 'Yes, that's my place. The big, old dilapidated two-storey one up at the end of Ocean Street.'

'Wow. The renovator's delight. Connor came by yesterday and told me about all the work you've done. I'd love to get a look inside one day.'

Roma smiled. 'I'd love to show you.'

After Roma and Keira had pulled out their smartphones and exchanged contact details, Roma back-tracked up Ocean Street and made her way down the sandy track to the warm sand and clear waters of Remarkable Bay. She was hot now and sweating from the walk in the thirty-five degree sun and as soon as she hit the sand, she flicked off her dress, tossed it on to her beach bag and ran into the cool water. She gasped in shock as a small wave hit her stomach and then decided to bite the bullet and dived under the next one. The curved and protected bay didn't have the surfing and body-boarding waves that some of the other beaches up along the coast had, but the gentler waves had made it an ideal beach for holiday-makers with young families for almost a century. There were rips further out, but Roma never ventured out that far: periodic shark sightings made her cautious.

Roma floated on her back for a while, looking back up at the brilliant blue southern sky while she cooled down and watched the seagulls swoop and float above her. She thought about Keira, and how nice it might be to have another youngish person in the Bay to hang out with. One who didn't know her tragic story. While she'd loved having Addy to stay, she wouldn't stay forever: as soon as the delayed film was green-lit, she'd be gone with a farewell jangle of her bracelets.

And Connor? She didn't know what to think about Connor.

She'd missed having friends. She'd always been somewhat of an introvert, but Tom's death had been the catalyst for a three year shut-in. Part of her plan had been to escape from the demands of friendships she couldn't reciprocate; but Addy's arrival, and meeting Connor and now Keira had her revisiting that plan. Would she and Keira become friends now they'd taken that first step? Friendship was about proximity and a couple of shared interests, wasn't it? They were proximate, there was no doubt about that. As for shared interests? Pilates wasn't going to be it, so she might have to work on that one.

When she'd cooled down enough to begin feeling a chill, Roma swam back to the shallows and walked back up the beach, looking up past the shoreline and to the town beyond. It was only a little blip on the map these days. You couldn't see much from down here: the church spire, a mobile phone tower and Bayview's balcony visible above the shrubs in the reserve. She hadn't felt lucky in a long, long time, but something about this beach, her house and Remarkable Bay was conspiring to make her feel just the slightest bit … content.

She planted her feet in the warm sand near her towel and her bag and pulled her shoulder-length hair to one side, twisting it into a knot to squeeze out the sea water. She reached down for her straw hat and plonked it on her head, breathing in the air and the salt and the day.

'Buster!'

A tiny, decrepit dog ambled towards her and began sniffing her feet. It was a straggly old thing, some kind of terrier, and its thin coat was almost completely grey. Connor was coming up the beach after it. She recognised his long legs and his rangy stride. And when Buster let out a squeaky little bark, she recognised it as the same one she'd heard over her side fence.

'Watch out,' Connor called. 'She's vicious.'

Roma looked down. Buster was sitting on her left foot and squinting into the wind. 'I can see that.'

And then Connor was standing near her, a red leash in one hand and a baseball cap in the other. He was wearing shorts and a loose T-shirt and that smile that had a way of reaching right inside her.

'Your dog is a girl and you called her Buster?'

Connor shrugged with a grin. 'Angas chose it when he was four years old. Could've been worse. He lobbied hard for SpongeBob SquarePants before I exerted my authority as a parent and ruled it out of order.'

'Buster's definitely better,' Roma said with a smile.

Connor looked out to the water, and then back at Roma. 'Looks like you've been out for a swim.'

'Yep.'

He looked around. 'Watch out, people will think you're a local if you're swimming in September without a wetsuit.'

'I don't have one. Not really sure if I need one.'

'If you change your mind, go and see Blake at the surf shop. Tell him I sent you.'

'You on commission or something?'

'He's my cousin. And a friend as well. You have to work real hard in a small place like Remarkable Bay not to be friends. It's the kind of place where people just keep running into each other.'

'So it seems.'

He shook his head in disbelief. 'The woman is fierce,' Connor said with an appreciative chuckle. 'Willing to go into the water when it's eighteen degrees out there *and* tackle marauding dogs.'

They laughed and looked down at Buster. The dog was safe ground. She really was the mangiest thing Roma had ever seen. Her golden retriever Charlie had been about eight times the size with a shaggy golden coat. Her dog had always stared at her as if she was the love of his life and became her companion and protector after Tom had died. Roma realised she hadn't patted another dog since Charlie. There was a sudden lump in her throat and welling tears. She leant down and scratched Buster's ear. The dog reacted by rolling over on to her back and looking up at Roma pleadingly.

'How's the painting going?' Connor finally asked.

'Good,' Roma said, suddenly self-conscious. She grabbed her towel from the sand and wrapped it around her shoulders.

'And how's Addy? Keeping out of trouble?'

'She's gone up to Adelaide this weekend, seeing some friends. She'll be back on Monday.'

'I'd better tell Angas so he can stand down from guard duty.'

Roma felt her cheeks heat. 'You're never going to let us forget that, are you?'

'And give up on the fun of teasing you about it? No, Your Honour.'

'Hey. I met Keira just now. From the Pilates studio. She said she'd met you already.'

'I stopped by yesterday to introduce myself. She tried to sell me classes.'

She regarded him, tried to judge if there was any interest in his eyes for Keira. 'She seems nice.'

'Yeah. She's pretty game to be starting a business like that here in the Bay. But, you know, we like people who come here and shake things up a little.' Connor lifted his sunglasses and pushed them back on his hair. 'I was wondering. I'm throwing some curry together tonight for Angas and me. I have to fill him up with rice or he'll eat two-minute noodles all night. Seeing you're on your own tonight … do you want to come over for a bowl?'

Roma bit the inside of her cheek. Oh no. Connor had interpreted her comment about Addy's absence as an invitation. She could have kicked herself. She didn't want a pity curry. She shouldn't want to say yes to a meal with Connor and his son, the mysterious Angas.

But she couldn't say yes. She wasn't ready for this, for changing gears.

Not yet.

'Thanks, Connor. But … I can't tonight.'

Connor slid his glasses back into place. He looked up the beach and then bent down to scoop up Buster.

'Sorry,' Roma added. 'It's just that …' She stopped. She couldn't explain to him the reasons why.

'Can I ask one thing? Are you saying no for tonight … or for any night?'

'Connor, I'm sorry.' And then her voice trailed off because she couldn't say what she really needed to say. I can't drag you in to my mess, my hurt, my grief. You look like a happy man. You don't need to share my pain.

'I understand. See you, Roma.' He lifted a hand, waved, and turned. She watched him walking back up the deserted beach, looking as lonely as she felt.

CHAPTER
18

Addy lifted an empty suitcase on to her bed, flipped open the lid and then searched the clothes in her wardrobe to find something to take back to Remarkable Bay. She lifted a hanger and stared at one of the ten little black dresses she owned. This one was a favourite: high and demure at the neckline, it suggested thinking. But its micro-mini hemline screamed dancing. She loved that dress. Correction: she used to love that dress. The last time she'd worn it was to the wrap party for Jack's film. The night she'd found him with the ingenue. The night she'd finally found some kind of inner strength and decided to leave him.

She tugged the dress from its hanger and tossed it on the floor, then fought the urge to stomp on it with delirious glee. Instead, she found jeans and T-shirts, a couple of little skirts, something warm to throw around her shoulders for evenings on the balcony, some other casual clothes. Her favourite mohair cardigan. She dug out a multi-coloured maxi dress with skinny straps and packed that. The one-piece swimsuit she liked to swim in. Sandals. Slip-on shoes.

Her Converse sneakers. A couple of books, biographies of actors that she'd been meaning to read.

Well, maybe just a few hair products.

When her phone vibrated, she lightened, thinking it might be Roma. Addy was surprised to realise she'd been missing her.

She glanced at the display. Her heart sank when she saw it wasn't Roma.

'Hi, Mum.'

'Where have you been?' Her mother's voice was tight and harried and Addy knew what that meant; that she was between patients and someone had run late and her whole day's schedule was now out and she didn't like to keep people waiting and she had a board meeting to go to and blah blah blah.

Addy tried not to feel the tightness in her chest. 'Have you been trying to call me?'

'No. I thought you were still working on that film. In the middle of nowhere. With no reception.'

Addy winced. She may have accidently on purpose mentioned to her mother that she would be out of phone range during the shoot.

'No, I'm not. The film—'

Dr McNamara interrupted as she always did. 'Are you home now?'

Home was an abstract concept to Addy at the moment. Looking around her bedroom, she tried not to see Jack in her bed, his clothes strewn all over the floor; his phone and laptop charger plugged into the power board where hers had been; and film magazines all over her bedside table. When he'd been there he'd physically sucked up every available amount of space. He was the kind of person who wasn't happy unless everything was all about him. She was so glad he was out of her life.

'Addy. Did you hear me? Are you home?'

'Yes,' she replied distractedly.

Was she home? This didn't feel like home anymore. It felt like the place The Woman Formerly Known As Addy McNamara used to live.

'How's everything with you, Mum?'

'I'm calling about that French film festival that's on next week. Could you get me some tickets to the screening on Wednesday night? I've forgotten the name of the film. Something from Syria. About the refugees. Poor things.'

Addy pinched the bridge of her nose and her head began to pound. 'Sure.'

'Send them to the office.'

'Sure.' And then Addy remembered what she'd meant to ask her mother. 'Mum, have you ever heard of a Clara—'

'Must go. I have a patient.'

'Allen?' Addy stopped when she realised her mother had already disconnected the call. And that was it. No goodbye. No 'I love you'. Nothing.

Addy tossed her phone on the bed and sat down. She rested her hands on her knees and watched them clench into tight fists. Her fists said everything she couldn't and she closed her eyes against the anger she saw in the protruding veins and faint freckles on the backs of her hands. And then, she was ten years old, inspecting her new summer freckles, and her jeans were stonewashed and baggy, instead of skinny. She wasn't wearing black suede ankle boots but white ankle socks with a lace trim and brand new white canvas sneakers, tied tightly around her little feet with bright pink laces in elaborate bows. She'd run home from school and pulled the outfit together, a practice run for her eleventh birthday party the next weekend at the local bowling alley, and had waited and waited until her mother got home to see what she thought.

Her mother had walked into the house and gone straight to her study. When Addy had knocked on the door, she'd answered, 'Not now,' and the fashion parade was over. Addy didn't get to have her birthday party that year and two weeks later, Addy was sent down to Remarkable Bay to spend the holidays with Roma and Leo and their parents. When summer was over, she was delivered back to her mother in one house and her father in another. She'd never felt at home in either place.

Addy straightened her back, flexed her fingers and sucked in a deep breath. She looked down at the contents of her suitcase. She didn't need costumes for Remarkable Bay. She didn't need little black dresses or high heels or jewellery or hair products.

And her old life?

Maybe she should throw that on the floor and stomp on it, too.

Roma had put on weight during the past three years. She'd always been of a normal build, neither rake thin nor too curvy, and she'd pretty much stayed that way for as long as she could remember. Sure, she'd gone through phases where she wanted to be slimmer, but had never been so obsessed with getting there that she'd put in much effort to achieve it. There were half-hearted attempts to give up wine for a week or three and chocolate for a month at a time. Those measures worked with varying degrees of success. Tom had always liked to walk after dinner, and she'd joined him most nights, enjoying the quiet time together where they got into a rhythm and talked about what had happened during their work days. When they adopted Charlie, it was a good excuse to walk him. Maybe it was that exercise that had kept things under control back then. Whatever it had been, she'd been happy with her body. She'd always quite liked her breasts, medium size but not so big that she couldn't sleep on her stomach, and her height. At five foot eight in the old money, she was tall enough to see over most people's heads at concerts (if she wore heels) and not too tall that she could never get trousers to fit her.

After Tom's death, Roma hadn't forgotten to eat. Once she'd emerged from the fog and the early days' thick-headedness and anguish, she waited for her appetite to crash, for her sense of taste to disappear, figuring it was one of the stages of grief she would go through. But it never happened. Instead of her senses being dulled, everything had become *more*. She became hyper-alert and over-anxious. Every screeching of a car tyre was an accident. Every passing ambulance was on its way to a crash. It seemed the news

was filled with more and more stories of the rising road toll, shoot-
ings, disease, tragedies, and in the end she didn't turn it on. Every
time Charlie barked she became more anxious that her neighbours
would complain about her neglecting him, so she brought him
inside and he slept on her bed, where he continued to sleep every
night until he died too. At work, she began to triple check everything: her timesheets, her files. How long she had for lunch. How
long the walk to her car park was. Food became tastier and alcohol
more stupefying, so she'd over-indulged in both. For years.

Now, she was eight kilos heavier than she had been the day the
police had knocked on her door with the news. She felt protected
by the weight, cushioned, literally and metaphorically. Perhaps she
liked it because it would turn people off; she knew men wouldn't
look twice at her when her thighs wobbled and her stomach was
anything other than flat. It comforted her to sit on her sofa at night,
bingeing on a TV series, a glass of wine in one hand and a box of
chocolates in the other. She didn't feel uncomfortable in her new
life because of her bigger body: she felt uncomfortable in her new
life because she'd been tossed in the air like a rag doll and landed in
a broken, crumpled mess.

But her new body had begun to ache. In the mornings now, she
woke up hurting rather than rested. There was a grinding in her
hip that radiated pain all the way down past her knee to her toes,
and she decided that probably wasn't good for a thirty-five-year-old
woman. There was a bonus in living at the beach which meant she
could walk along the Bay, from end to end every day. But it only
took fifteen minutes or so, and she sauntered distractedly in a way
that didn't even raise a sweat.

She knew it was time to do something slightly more serious. But
she needed to start slowly. So Roma decided she would try one of
Keira's Pilates classes tomorrow night. Addy was still away and it
would give Roma something to do in the evening. She also wanted
to encourage a new business in Remarkable Bay, which meant she
might be able to make more friends who weren't Connor.

Connor. She'd put up a wall where he was concerned, but that didn't stop him being generous and kind. That morning, a bag of lemons had appeared on her front doorstep.

That afternoon, she made lemon slice with his lemons and ate the whole tray of it herself.

Which is why, despite everything she knew about herself, Keira's Pilates class was suddenly looking like a good idea.

CHAPTER
19

'I'm back!' Addy's voice echoed up the stairwell and into Roma's bedroom. It was just past ten and Roma had dragged all the drop sheets into the adjacent room and swept the floor. Under the musty old carpet and the stained underfelt under that, she'd discovered floorboards which matched those in the hallway: a hundred years of footsteps and sunshine had worn them honey-coloured and wonderful.

'Good,' Roma called down. 'You're just in time to help me get my mattress on to the bedframe.'

The big front room with the balcony was tonight going to officially become Roma's bedroom. The painting was complete and the room looked fresh and clean, with warm white walls. Roma didn't want colour in her bedroom: she wanted a blank canvas. She wanted to start afresh in the most intimate of spaces. Her shared bedroom with Tom had always been dishevelled. She was tidy, he wasn't, and she'd been worn down over the years, inured to his clothes on the floor and his books tossed like used tissues by the side of his bed. She'd been determined not to clean up after him and hadn't; she'd nagged at him instead and that hadn't worked either. So she'd come to a kind of truce; a domestic blindness when it came to his untidiness. Six months after he'd died, Roma had found an old sock wedged between the bedhead and the mattress. She'd tugged it out and when she'd realised that the grey clump in her hand wasn't a dust bunny, she'd fallen onto the bed and stared at it. But at that stage she'd already cleaned out his clothes. She knew he wasn't coming back, and on one terrible day she'd emptied his drawers, thrown half of his things away and donated the rest. Their CDs were separated into his and hers piles and they'd been donated, too. What was the point in keeping them? Or his books? His stacks of magazines in the bathroom? His half-deflated football covered in fallen leaves under the back veranda or his old bike with the flat front tyre?

This new room was an important step. Finishing it really did feel like the beginning of the rest of her life.

When an image of Connor flashed through her mind—Connor, not Tom—she blinked it away with a guilty throb at her temples.

Addy rounded the door, rushed over and threw her arms around Roma.

'Hello,' Roma said, guarded.

'I'm so glad to be back, you have no idea.'

Roma had never been hugged so tight in her life and she fought the urge to push Addy away. Instead, she relaxed, let herself be held. Let herself enjoy it. The surprise of it was that Addy seemed to need the hug as well.

'I can tell.'

'And I have a surprise,' Addy finally said when she'd let go. 'Well, two surprises actually.'

'You do?'

'I won't have to sleep in your living room anymore because I bought a mattress and it's being delivered today.'

'You didn't need to buy a bed, Addy. I was going to get around to it eventually.'

Addy looked at her shoes. 'The thing is …'

Roma saw uncertainty in Addy's expression. She looked vulnerable, small for a change. She seemed to have shrunk in the days she'd been away in Adelaide and when Roma looked closely, she realised Addy wasn't wearing any make-up. She wasn't sure she'd seen her bare-faced since Addy had discovered mascara.

Roma regarded her face. 'You all right?'

Addy swept up her hair and twisted it around itself into a bun on top of her head. 'Of course! I'm fabulous, as always. The thing is … Adelaide feels so boring when there's no work on and nothing will start before at least mid-January and I really like your house. I really like being back in Remarkable Bay. I was wondering if I could lay claim to one of the rooms upstairs. Maybe Bayview could be my home away from home. Officially.'

This all seemed like a bolt out of the blue to Roma, who'd thought Addy was down in Remarkable Bay solely to keep an eye on *her*, the grieving widow. 'Really? You'd want to stay here?'

Addy nodded and when she quickly turned away to look out to the balcony, Roma could have sworn there were tears in her eyes. For once, Roma felt like the tough one.

'I really would,' she said to the window.

'Well then. Of course you can stay.'

'Really?'

'Really.'

Addy wore a sad smile. 'It'll be just like old times, won't it?'

Roma wondered which old times Addy was referring to. Which particular part of their history was she trying to relive?

Addy turned, wrapped her arms around herself as if giving herself a hug and sighed deeply. All her dramatic pretence disappeared when she said, simply, 'Thanks, Roma.'

They went downstairs to the kitchen for a coffee and a catch up. Roma didn't mention anything to Addy about Connor. There was nothing to tell, really. So he'd asked her over for dinner? It was hardly a date. It was a friendly invitation between neighbours and she'd said no. She didn't want to have to hash over her reasons for declining, not to Addy, not to anyone.

As it was, Addy asked about the house, where Roma was up to. The coffee seemed to do the trick, because Addy was bright-eyed once again, full of tales from her film friends, the latest Hollywood flop and rumours about a famous director who might be coming to the Adelaide Hills to shoot a drama about a man whose wife had been murdered.

'Oh, great,' Roma said. 'Imagine being that poor actress. "Guess what Mum and Dad? I got a role in a movie! I'm playing a naked, dead body."'

Addy waved a hand. 'Believe me, actresses would donate a kidney if it meant they got to work with Helmut Sprang, even if they're killed off in the first three minutes.'

'For once I'd like to see a murder mystery open with a shot of a naked dead bloke. Just saying,' Roma said over her coffee.

'Oh, Roma,' Addy sighed. 'Welcome to my world.'

They sipped their coffees and ate pieces of lemon slice Roma had arranged neatly on a china plate.

'Oh, I have some news. I haven't told you about the new shop. It's opened and it's a Pilates studio and there's a woman running it.'

'Really?'

Roma nodded while she chewed. 'Her name's Keira Kozlowski and she's from Sydney.'

Addy thought on it. 'It doesn't sound like the most practical business decision, but hey, what do I know? Why Remarkable Bay?'

Roma smiled. 'We could ask ourselves the exact same question, Addy.'

'True. What's she like?'

'She seems really nice. Friendly. Don't hate me, but I've booked us in for lessons.'

Addy's face registered her shock. 'Oh, you haven't.'

'Yes I have. I know what it's like to be the new person in town. And okay, I admit, I took pity on her. You know I hate organised exercise more than almost anybody I know, but I need to do something for my health and she's new in town and if people like us don't take her classes, who will?'

Addy propped her chin in a hand and sighed. 'Roma Harris. You're a chip off the old block. Still out to save the world. One person at a time.'

Roma was taken aback by Addy's observation. 'What do you mean?'

Addy reached across the table and patted Roma's hand. 'It's not an insult, Romes. It's just what you do. What you've always done. You parents were the same. I haven't forgotten that you did it for me, all those years ago.'

Neither said a word. Roma knew what Addy meant, about how she'd found the laxatives. How she'd told her parents and Addy had got into trouble. How their friendship had severed over it.

'I never said thank you.' Addy looked over at Roma with shining eyes.

'It's all right.'

'No, it wasn't all right. I was lost and confused and I couldn't seem to get myself out of the rabbit hole. I don't know what would have happened if you hadn't stepped up and done the right thing. No matter what I said back then, it was the right thing, Roma. Thank you.'

Addy wrapped her fingers around Roma's and she held on tight.

Later, they went upstairs to move furniture and it wasn't long before Roma's bed was in place. She and Addy had moved in a chest of drawers, her standing lamp and a bedside table, and placed a small lamp on it. They'd laid out a rectangular rug in shades of deep burgundy at the end of the bed, which looked right at home on the honeyed floorboards, and then Roma nailed holes in the walls for a couple of her favourite pictures.

They stood back and admired the fresh white new sheets on the bed and pillowcases on the pillows. Roma thought it looked like a room at a health spa. She had to pinch herself that this room was all hers.

'Well,' she said, looking around, taking it all in.

Addy raised her hand for a high five. 'Woo hoo.'

'Woo-bloody-hoo,' Roma corrected. She felt exhausted but exhilarated with it. She was standing in her new bedroom. A new bedroom just for her. The only memories in this room were the ones in her head.

This room would be hers and hers alone. Maybe for the rest of her life.

This really did feel like changing gears, she thought. One move at a time down the road on the rest of her life.

Finally.

Keira Kozlowski was a bitch.

Ten minutes into the Pilates class, Addy McNamara had already made up her mind about the new girl in town. Well, the other new girl in town. When Addy had agreed the day before to go with Roma to the class, she'd been feeling all soppy and emotional about being back in Remarkable Bay and far away from all her troubles at home. She screwed up her nose and tightened her pelvic floor at the same time, which was a remarkable feat of concentration. Something about this place was making her soft in the head.

She tried to hold the plank position—propped on her elbows and her toes with nothing but her non-existent abs to hold her up—but every muscle in her body began to wobble. With a loud sigh, she flopped stomach first on to the very thin rubber mat stretched out underneath her in Keira's Pilates studio. Oh, who was she kidding? Addy huffed as she felt the tension in her stomach. This wasn't a studio—it was a torture chamber.

She turned her head towards Roma, who was trying desperately to maintain the same pose. 'I can't do this,' she mumbled. 'I'm so not twenty-two anymore.'

With a loud exhale, Roma collapsed to the floor too. 'Ouch.' She crossed her eyes and laughed. 'That's what I said after my first lesson.'

'You mean you've come back for more?'

'It's only my second,' Roma whispered. 'Three is looking highly doubtful.'

'Come on, you two,' Keira called from the front of the room, clapping her hands twice in quick succession. Her voice bounced around the mostly empty space. There was only the three of them: instructor and two reluctant pupils.

'You might be skinny, Addy, but you don't have much muscle strength.'

'Do so,' she pouted into the mat.

'This is all about your core strength, ladies. If you are strong here,' Keira held a flat palm to her stomach, 'You'll stand up stronger, prevent lower back pain and fight stress incontinence.'

'We're thirty-five, not fifty,' Addy said snarkily.

'So am I.' Keira appeared above her, looming like a drill sergeant— or one of those reality TV show trainers—her hands on her hips and her brows furrowed. Addy suddenly felt a little nervous.

'But you do this for a living which is obviously why you have abs of steel. I'm only doing it as a favour to Roma.'

'Addy!' Roma exclaimed, pulling her head up from the mat and widening her eyes.

'Well, it's true. I'd much rather be watching a movie.'

'She works in the film industry,' Roma explained.

'Really? How exciting.' Keira walked over to them and sat crosslegged on the floor. She propped her chin in her hands 'Are you a producer or a director? Or an actress?'

Addy rolled on to her back and stared up at the ceiling. 'I work in the production side of things.'

'Sounds important. Do you get your name in the credits?'

'All the time.' She had to admit, that never got old. Her friends still got a kick out of seeing her real name up in lights—Adelaide McNamara. She'd insisted on it because it looked bigger on the screen than Addy and she wanted everyone to notice. Her mother never had, not once mentioned she'd seen her name in the credits on a movie she'd worked on. Then again, Dr McNamara didn't go to see the kind of films Addy worked on. They had to be subtitled or about something *important* and *meaningful* to be worthy of her attention. Her mother didn't do frivolous. She had never done fun. Maybe that was why Addy had always run headlong into both and damn the consequences.

'Wow,' Keira said. 'That is totally cool.'

'It is cool. Loads of hard work but hey, it's pretty glamorous, I must admit,' she lied.

There was movement on the mat next to her. Roma pulled herself up to a sitting position. Addy laughed as Roma tried to cross her legs and then gave up.

'How long have you been a queen of torture, Keira?'

'A couple of years. I was an environmental scientist before that, but the grant funding for the research project I was working on was cut by some dumb-arse politician in Canberra and I was out of work.'

'You're a scientist?' Roma said, and Addy thought Roma probably didn't realise she sounded stunned.

'Yep. Most people see the lycra and think I'm an airhead.'

'No, I didn't—'

Keira shrugged. 'Yes you did, but that's okay. In my other job, I'm Dr Kozlowski.'

Addy decided Keira Kozlowski wasn't a bitch after all.

Keira slapped her hands on her knees. 'I take it you two have had enough for tonight?'

'I think I've had enough for the rest of my life,' Addy mumbled with a smile at Keira.

Keira sprang to her feet. 'Thanks for coming. Sorry there weren't more people in the class. I've tried really hard to drum up some numbers. Everyone I spoke to was really nice, smiled, took my pamphlet and said they'd think about it. But in the end, it's just you two.'

Roma got to her feet and stretched her arms above her head. 'It'll get better. You'll see. Not that I know much about small towns, but I think it probably takes time for people to warm up to newcomers.'

'Not to you,' Addy said with a sly smile. 'If Connor is anything to go by.'

'Well, well, well,' Keira grinned. 'I'm not going anywhere for a while, so I'll see how it goes.'

Roma and Addy picked up their drink bottles, swigged noisily, and then shrugged on their long-sleeved tops for the short walk home.

'See you,' Roma said.

'Bye,' Addy called. 'I'm aching already.'

Keira turned to them, looking sad, forlorn and happy all at once. 'See you next time.'

The next morning, Roma woke, stretched out her tired abs, gulped down water from the bottle on her bedside table to soothe her wine hangover and went downstairs to the kitchen. She cut her latest batch of lemon slice into neat, square pieces and placed them into a vintage plastic container, carefully placing a layer of baking paper between each layer. Her grandmother—her mother's mother—used to make it and had taught Roma when she was still small enough to need a footstool to reach the kitchen bench. 'Lemon slice is the perfect thing,' her grandmother had said while Roma pushed her rolling pin over the plastic bag filled with milk arrowroot biscuits, trying to use all the muscles she had to transform it into crumbs. 'It's all mixing and no cooking, which makes it very safe for a little girl like you.'

When her grandmother died, Roma asked for the long shallow aluminium tin they'd made slice in, and her collection of Tupperware. In the fifteen years since then, Roma had added to her collection by scouring second-hand shops and garage sales. She had the pale yellows and blues and pinks of the sixties, and then the rich yellows, mission browns, orange and green variations of the seventies. She had the lettuce crispers and the celery containers; the deep, vaguely wedge-shaped container that she learnt years after was for storing Christmas hams; and a brilliant triangular-shaped shallow piece that would have been just the right shape and size to fill with a slice of apple pie if one was making someone's lunch. She didn't bake apple pie and she'd never made anyone's lunch in her life but she liked the container anyway.

The lemon slice she'd just sliced and packed neatly was a present for Connor. Despite her rejection of his offer of dinner, his lemons had been arriving with great regularity. She would discover them perhaps every second day sitting on the front door mat when she went out to check her mail, and it had taken her a while to work out how to thank him. Finally, she'd decided how. Tart and lemony with a condensed milk and biscuit crumb base, she'd added a sprinkling of coconut, although the coconut was a controversial addition that she wasn't sure her grandmother would have approved of. She'd also made preserved lemons, lemon meringue pie, lemon marmalade and lemon cake. There were lots of lemons.

She really needed to stop making so much food. And she really needed to stop avoiding Connor.

Roma picked up the Tupperware and made sure the lid was snapped shut, and in the minute it took her to leave her front yard and knock on his door, she debated over what to say. When she raised a hand to knock on his door, she had nothing. She entertained the thought of leaving the container on his front doorstep. It was, after all, sealed, safe from local dogs and Buster, if she ever wandered into the front yard. But leaving it wouldn't be very neighbourly, so she knocked on the heavy wooden door and prepared herself to be friendly: she dug up a smile and some words to say.

The door opened wide and someone grunted.

'Yeah?' A lanky teenager, wearing boardshorts and a singlet top, blinked at her. His hair was long and hung over his forehead, and his tanned cheeks bore a smattering of acne. She couldn't see enough of his face to judge if he looked like his father but he certainly had his height.

She experienced a strange sensation: relief mixed with a tinge of disappointment. 'You're Angas, right?'

'Yeah.' He yawned and waited.

Roma thrust the Tupperware container forward. 'I made some lemon slice. For your father. To say thanks for all the lemons.'

Angas moved in slow motion, hesitating before taking the container from her. It was either still too early for a teenager or he'd been watching too many horror movies featuring suspicious Halloween treats. 'Uh ... cheers,' he said sleepily and then shut the door. Roma stood for a moment, her mouth open on a question she wouldn't get to ask: 'Is your dad here?'

A moment later, as she rounded her front gate, she allowed herself to feel nothing but relief. Wasn't this what she wanted? Wasn't her plan to land in Remarkable Bay and be simply unremarkable, so she might continue to be invisible, to hide, to remain buried in her grief?

She wasn't sure if that had been such a great idea after all.

CHAPTER
20

Three lessons in, Addy stopped complaining about Keira's Pilates classes. For three weeks in a row, she and Roma had diligently appeared at five pm on Wednesdays and Saturdays, and held themselves in painful positions for the sake of their health and their apparently deteriorating pelvic floor muscles.

Roma endured the lessons stoically, Addy thought. She pushed Addy so they arrived early, tried her hardest to contort and hold herself in the positions Keira suggested and then even helped to clear up afterwards. It was all so typically Roma. Addy didn't believe she'd ever heard her complain about anything, even when Tom had died so tragically. She'd borne it all stoically, quietly, internally. Addy didn't know how she did it.

There was another routine they'd slipped into. After each class, the three women would head to the quiet pub in Ocean Street for a bite to eat and a couple of glasses of wine. They wouldn't even bother to change out of their T-shirts and leggings. The place wasn't that fancy. It was simple pub fare: schnitzels and salt-and-pepper squid and roast of the day. Addy suspected that the salad bar consisted of food liberated entirely from tins; and the house wine was from a cask. Three single women living large in Remarkable Bay, Addy thought ruefully as she looked at the menu. The food didn't matter. The company was what counted, and these girls' night out dinners were beginning to be important to Addy. And to Roma, too, she could tell, even without Roma saying so.

The three women put their mobile phones and their purses at the centre of the table.

'My turn to order. What are you having?' Addy looked up from the menu.

'I'll have the salt-and-pepper squid,' Roma announced and, anticipating the response, continued. 'I know, I know. Same as last week and the week before. Which probably means I'm boring. But it probably comes pre-prepared from the freezer and they can't bugger up the deep-frying, can they?'

'Schnitzel for me.' Keira handed her menu to Addy. 'With lots of gravy. And mashed potatoes, please.'

Addy looked their Pilates instructor up and down. 'Really? You eat that and you still look like that?'

'I run ten kilometres a day. That's why I look like this.'

Addy rolled her eyes. 'Show off.' When she ordered and returned to the table carrying three glasses of wines, Roma and Keira looked deep in conversation. Addy was happy for Roma that she looked to have made a friend and swallowed the slight jealousy she felt. When her film resumed production, she'd have to leave, she knew that. She reminded herself that it would be good for Roma not to be on her own. Leo had been excited about the news of a new friend, too. 'Takes a load off your shoulders,' he'd said to Addy when she'd called him a few days before. And Addy had to stop and think about what he'd said. Roma wasn't a load on anyone's shoulders. She wasn't a burden. Had never been. She was the least burdensome person she'd ever met. She had always carried her own secrets around on her shoulders without a complaint.

'It's really old,' Roma was telling Keira.

'What's really old?' Addy sat and took a sip of her white wine with a grimace. It really was terrible.

Roma looked up and reached for her glass. 'I was just telling Keira about the guest book we found and the mystery of the Allen sisters.'

Addy twitched her nose. 'It made me sneeze.'

'There's a mystery?' Keira leaned in closer.

Ruby nodded. 'Yes. There are two Miss Allens we know about. Ruby and Adeline.'

'What lovely names,' Keira said, propping her chin in her hand.

'Ruby is my great-grandmother,' Roma said.

'And Adeline is mine,' Addy noted. 'And yes, before you ask, I was kind of named after her, although my mother thought Adeline sounded positively pre-historic so I was named Adelaide instead. So I'm Adelaide from Adelaide.'

'It's a beautiful name,' Keira said.

'I think Adelaide was named after Queen Adelaide,' Roma explained, 'So technically you're named after a queen, which suits the Little Miss Drama Queen perfectly, I reckon.'

Addy poked her tongue out at Roma with a laugh. 'I bet Queen Adelaide didn't get dragged to Pilates.' And then she giggled at a memory. 'Remember those Little Men books? When we were kids, Roma decided I was Little Miss Drama Queen. So I dubbed her Little Miss Practical.'

'God, those nicknames stuck for years.' Roma laughed.

'So these two women from the thirties. Ruby is yours,' she pointed to Roma, 'And Adeline is yours?'

Roma and Addy nodded.

'So what's the mystery?'

Roma leaned in. 'The mystery is about another name we found in the guest book. A Miss Clara Allen.'

'Same last name,' Keira noted.

'But we've never heard of her before,' Addy explained.

'We don't know anyone with that name in our family. So we've been wondering who she was. If she was a relative, or if it was just some coincidence that a woman with the same name as our great-grandmothers arrived to stay at Bayview on the exact same day in 1934.'

'How fascinating,' Keira said, her eyes darting back and forth between the two women as she watched their banter. 'It's not an unusual name like mine. If I meet a Kozlowski, we're usually related. Allen was probably pretty common back then, right? When every name in Australia was Anglo. You would have hardly even met an Italian or a Greek here in the '30s.'

Roma pondered. 'True.'

'It's amazing you have these long connections with Remarkable Bay.'

Addy answered. 'We weren't born here. We're from Adelaide but Roma and her family, and her family before that, used to come down for summer holidays. I'm an only child and when my parents separated, I used to stay and hang out with Roma and Leo, her brother. They were the best holidays.'

'I came here on holiday once, too,' Keira said. She looked to the ceiling as she worked something out in her head. 'I think I was fifteen so maybe it was 1995? Let me think. What song was I listening to that summer?'

'You remember the songs you were listening to twenty years ago?'

'Of course! Hang on. Yep. It was my summer of Silverchair. I thought those boys from Newcastle, with the flannies and the shyness and the long hair, were amazing. They were all over Triple J back then.'

Addy raised a hand and turned away. 'Stop. You came all the way to Remarkable Bay for a holiday when you lived in Sydney? What about Bondi and Bronte and Tamarama?' Addy asked, incredulous. 'Or Noosa or Byron Bay?'

Keira snorted. 'That wasn't my part of town. I don't know why Mum and Dad decided to come to South Australia. My grandmother had just died, my Oma, and, I don't know. We were all so sad.'

'We probably walked past you on the beach,' Roma said, sipping her wine.

'Or at least in the bakery,' Addy said.

'You would have remembered Addy,' Roma said. 'She would have elbowed past you to get to the head of the queue.'

'Me? I never ate cakes,' Addy said, and twinkled her eyes to tell Roma it was just a joke.

'Funny, isn't it?' Keira said thoughtfully. 'The twists and turns of your life. If my grandmother hadn't died then, if we hadn't come here, if I hadn't loved it, I might not be sitting here with you right now drinking this really bad house wine.'

'It really is terrible,' Roma admitted, pulling a face.

'Shocking,' Addy agreed.

'It'll do,' Keira said.

'So, Keira. What's your rental place like?' Roma asked.

She shrugged. 'It's a fibro shack, a long walk from the bay. It's draughty. The paint on the outside is peeling and the hot water heater is so rusty it looks like it might die any minute, but it's fine. I was a little surprised when I looked online before I came to find there's not a lot to rent in the Bay, in any decent condition anyway.'

'Will you buy something, do you think?'

Keira shrugged her answer. 'I don't know. It all depends. I'll see if the Pilates studio works out. Or maybe things'll change in Canberra and science might be popular again and we'll get some funding for the research I do. I kind of go with the flow, after everything I've been through. Too much can change in your life these days to want to put roots down somewhere for good. I didn't really feel settled in Sydney, and I grew up there. The same with Canberra.' She paused a little, swallowed nervously. 'So, if Remarkable Bay doesn't work out, I'm heading to Perth.'

'I've never been to Canberra,' Addy said, not wanting to let that hint go.

'I'm never going back,' Keira shuddered.

'Didn't like it? I hear it's very clean.'

'It's a lovely place to live. I just didn't like who I left behind.'

Addy and Roma looked at each other.

'A man?' Addy asked quietly, curiously.

Keira chuckled. 'Yeah, a man. You thought I meant a woman?'

'Well, you never know. Not judging.'

'Definitely not judging,' Roma confirmed.

Keira smiled sadly. 'It was a guy. A guy who worked as an adviser to the politician who cut the funding to the research program I was working on.'

'Bastard,' Addy said.

'Luddite,' Roma added for emphasis. 'Had you been together very long?'

'Two years. The sex was still great but we broke up on principle. Turns out he didn't have any.'

Roma raised her glass. 'Excellent reason.'

'Are your parents still in Sydney?'

Keira shook her head. 'They sold up and moved to Coffs Harbour when they retired earlier this year. So you see, I couldn't even run home to my teenage bedroom. I had to find somewhere else altogether.'

'My old bedroom became a home office about two minutes after I moved out,' Addy said.

'So, this family connection through your great-grandmothers. Is that why you bought Bayview, Roma?'

'Funnily enough, I didn't know they'd stayed in the house until we found the guest book. There's just something about Remarkable Bay I've always loved. You wouldn't know it now, but it used to be a really fancy beachside town. It was apparently quite the thing right up to the 1930s for the well-to-do people of South Australia to head to the beach for the summer. Breathe the ozone, and all that.'

'Ozone?' Addy chuckled. 'Isn't that stuff poisonous?'

'No. It's in the air all around us,' Keira said. 'Oxygen is O_2, and Ozone is O_3 with 50 per cent more oxygen in each molecule. People used to think it would cure diseases and ailments. Restore your energy, that kind of thing.'

'Handy to have a scientist around,' Roma smiled. 'But things changed. During the war, people didn't come and later, everyone had cars and it was all day trips and weekends after that and guesthouses like Bayview kind of died. And once the roads got better and petrol was cheap, people starting building their own holiday homes or staying in fancy motels. No one wanted to stay in a musty old guesthouse anymore. There were others here in the Bay, Sunnybrae and Ocean View, but they were knocked down years ago, sold off for land value.'

'So both of you have this connection to Bayview,' Keira said. 'That's incredible. And weird.'

Roma's eyes lit up. 'I know. We never stayed at Bayview when I came down with my family and Addy. It was horrible in those years. It became some kind of squat or something. We used to cross the street to avoid it. The street out in front was full of Holden Commodores blaring loud music and the place smelt like dope.'

'Schnitzel with extra gravy?' A young man appeared at the table, nervously balancing a plate in his hand. His white shirt, at least two sizes too big, was billowing out the back of his black trousers and there was a dribble of gravy down the front of it where a tie might have been.

'Here, thanks,' Keira said, moving her cutlery aside to make space for the piece of crumbed deliciousness that seemed to cover half the plate.

Roma looked at the young man. 'Angas?'

'Yeah?' He looked at her through his floppy fringe.

Roma smiled up at him, a hand flew to her chest. 'I'm Roma. From next door.'

'Oh. Hi,' he answered as he placed the plate in front of Keira. Within about two seconds, she was digging in and moaning her delight.

'I brought you the lemon slice. Remember?'

'Right. Thanks. Yeah. It was good.'

From the corner of her eye, Roma could see Addy drop her gaze to the table. This was going to be fun.

'And this is my cousin Addy. She's the one who stole the lemons from your backyard.'

Addy groaned. 'God, Roma. Why don't you announce it to the whole place?'

'And I'm Keira.' Keira held up a hand for Angas to shake.

Angas shook her hand quickly and then withdrew his. 'Uh ...
I'll go get the other meals.' He scurried away from the table like a
frightened rabbit.

'You are terrible, Roma,' Addy said with a laugh, lifting her glass
for another sip. 'That poor boy. He's barely out of short pants and
you've gone and got him totally shit scared of women.'

They laughed uproariously, only halting when Angas returned
with the other two meals, and then launched into loud laughter
once again. And in that moment, Roma felt it. It was as real as
if someone were standing beside her pricking her with a pin. She
turned to the bar. Connor was there, perched on a tall stool, cra-
dling a beer. He smiled and waved at her. How long had he been
there?

She gave him the smallest nod, hoping it escaped the notice of
Addy and Keira.

Apparently not.

'Hey, Connor.' Keira was calling out across the dining room.
'Come say hello.'

Roma wanted to shrink under the table. Of course Keira and
Connor had already met. He was the one who'd told Keira about
Bayview.

A moment later he was pulling up a chair next to her.

'Hey,' he said, nodding to Addy and Roma.

'You're not eating?' Keira noted. He placed his beer on the table
in front of him.

'Nah, I ate at home. I just came down for a sneaky beer.' He
chuckled. 'I came to give Angas some moral support, to tell the
truth. It's his first shift.'

'He's doing great,' Addy said, lifting her chin. 'He even remembered our meals.'

'Don't let on that I told you, but he's incredibly nervous. It's his
first job.'

Connor glanced over his shoulder to the two-way door that separated the dining area from the kitchen and then let his gaze return to

his beer. When he chuckled to himself and ran his fingers through his hair, Roma realised that the son wasn't the only one who was nervous. The proud father sitting at the table was equally so.

'He's tall,' Roma said and then felt like an idiot.

'He clearly gets that from his father.' Addy had stopped eating her schnitzel and was staring at Roma with wide eyes.

Connor shifted in his seat, leaned back. 'Noses run in our family, too.'

Roma laughed and he turned to her, smiling quickly.

He upended his beer. 'I'd better go. The kid will die of shame if I stay too long.'

'Bye, Connor,' Keira said, shoving a forkful of mashed potato into her mouth. 'You really should come to one of my Pilates classes.'

'When hell freezes over,' he said with a warm smile as he pushed in his chair.

'See you round, Connor,' Addy said but she was grinning at Roma as she said it.

'I'll see you, Roma.'

She looked up and smiled at him then darted her eyes away. He hadn't mentioned a word about the lemon slice. Perhaps he was hurt by her rejection and was now rejecting her in turn. She sighed. This was why she couldn't do this with Connor. She didn't know the rules anymore. She'd been with Tom almost half her life and didn't know how to navigate around men anymore, if she ever really had. It was a game of manners, of give and take, that she wasn't sure she still knew how to play.

Roma nodded and lowered her eyes to her salt-and-pepper squid before watching his long-legged stride as he walked away.

Addy leaned across and speared a piece of squid from Roma's plate and popped it in her mouth. 'He's a lovely man.'

'Yes, he is,' Roma replied.

Addy leaned close to Keira, nudged her with an elbow. 'Did you see the way they look at each other?'

'I noticed,' Keira said. 'She's all he could talk about the first time I met him. What's stopping you, Roma?'

Roma felt the familiar tightening in her chest and her throat. 'I'm not interested.'

'In men or in Connor?' Keira asked innocently but her words cut Roma to the quick.

Roma tensed. The words came out uncensored, painful. 'My husband died three years ago.'

Keira was silent for a moment, then, 'Oh, shit.'

Roma couldn't explain why, at that moment, she needed to tell the truth. She normally gave people a simple answer, a trite answer, which went something like, 'I wanted a sea change. I love this part of the coast. Who can resist that view?' But with Addy and Keira, she felt she didn't need to pretend anymore.

Roma felt the familiar pinpricks stinging the backs of her eyes. She let out a deep sigh. 'I came to Remarkable Bay because I needed to find somewhere with no traffic lights.'

Keira's eyebrows knotted together. 'You colourblind or something?'

'My husband—Tom—was waiting at the traffic lights one street from home and a drunk driver ran a red light. Hit him.'

'Oh fuck,' Keira whispered. 'That is awful.'

'I heard the sirens and I just sat there on the couch watching TV. I thought it was someone else. You always think it's someone else, you see.'

'How could you have known, Roma?' Addy whispered.

Three years had passed. She could talk about it now. She needed to talk about it. There were things on the tip of her tongue she hadn't told anybody. Not Leo. Not her shrink. Not anyone. And when the words tumbled from her lips, she didn't see the laminate wooden table or the old wine glasses. She didn't see the daggy swirling purple-and-orange carpet of the pub or the terrible comb-over on the head of the oldest barman in Australia. She could feel her lips and her tongue and the pressure of her short and rough fingernails on the inside of her palm as she spoke. There was a stray hair on her cheek. It felt like a burr scratching her skin and she brushed it away.

'At first, I started to avoid that intersection. For months afterwards, every time I drove through it I would freeze up when I saw the paint markings on the road, you know, where the police had marked out the scene with spray paint? And then I'd get to work and be like a zombie for an hour while I tried to pull myself together. When I walked past with our dog, Charlie, there were still tiny shards of orange plastic in the gutter—for months after— and I always wondered if they were from Tom's car or … the other guy's. So, I found another way to get to work and I did that, even though it took ten minutes longer. And when that didn't work anymore, I found ways to avoid traffic lights altogether.'

'You lived in Adelaide and you managed to avoid traffic lights?' Keira asked softly.

'It was a skill, believe me. And then one day, when it took me an hour to get home instead of the fifteen minutes it used to, I began to understand something was wrong.'

'There was something wrong,' Addy hissed. 'Your husband was killed by an inconsiderate, drunk arsehole.'

Roma lowered her eyes.

'Sorry, Romes.'

Roma breathed deep and long. 'The longer it took me to get work, the less time I had for anything else. And it kind of took over my life for a while. The longer I was in the car, the less time I was at home having to face all the memories. So I thought I'd find a place without traffic lights.'

'Remarkable Bay doesn't even have a roundabout,' Keira noted.

'Exactly,' Addy said.

'You seem way too young to be a widow. I mean, we're the same age and I've never even been married,' Keira said.

'Me neither,' said Addy.

'There are lots of reasons people are alone at our age. Death. Divorce.'

'Bad choices,' Addy mentioned but didn't elaborate. 'Careers.'

'Being on your own isn't so bad,' Roma said. 'It was horrible. It's still horrible sometimes. But I'm better off on my own, I think.'

'That's why she moved down here,' Addy explained to Keira. 'To be by herself.'

Keira chuckled. 'Well, that didn't work out so well, did it? You seem to have made a whole lot of new friends here in Remarkable Bay.'

Keira was right. Roma lifted her wine glass for a toast. 'Here's to new friends.'

When they got home, Addy saw she had a missed call from Jack. She'd put her phone on silent during the Pilates class and had forgotten to switch it back, so she only saw it when she was getting ready for bed.

And there was a message, too. She brushed her teeth, filled her glass of water from the bathroom tap, smoothed moisturiser onto her face, her arms and legs, before she listened to it. She should have deleted it, just as she'd tried to delete him from her life. She'd had a great evening with Roma and Keira. She shouldn't have listened to it.

But she retrieved the message.

'Babe.' Then a pause.

'How dare you call me babe,' Addy muttered through gritted teeth, feeling pinpricks at the back of her neck.

'Hey. Listen. Ads. I know I fucked things up. I need you. I need *you.*'

He sounded drunk, his words were slurred, but it was the closest thing to an apology she'd ever had from him. And he always had to be pissed before he'd ever been contrite.

'I'm sorry. I'm so, so fucking sorry.'

Addy put the phone down on the bed next to her because her hands were shaking.

'It was just sex with her. That's all. It was just fucking. It wasn't the same as what we have. Where are you? I'm still in Melbourne and this TV show is fucked up. I need you. I need you.'

She didn't want to hear it. She wanted to scream. *Leave me alone. Don't you ever come near me again or I'll …* what would she do?

What had she done? She'd run, that's what. That was Addy's modus operandi. Her fight–or–flight response was firmly in flight mode. She flew so fast it was as if she had wings. And here was Jack, trying to drag her back down to earth.

'I need you to come and fix things on the show. We're delayed by two weeks as it is. Pick up the goddamn call. Call me back, Addy.'

She stopped. Jabbed the screen to end the call and then deleted it.

She went downstairs in the semi-dark, found the tonic water and the bottle of gin in the kitchen, and poured herself a huge one. Half and half. No ice.

It was the only way she could calm her racing mind and the humiliation rising once again in her throat so she could fall into fitful sleep.

The next day, Roma and Addy drove to a salvage yard in the next town and scoured through tin sheds filled with rows and rows of old furniture. There were wardrobes and dressers from the fifties; terrible 1970s pine laminate TV cupboards; and loads of Scandinavian DIY furniture, seemingly abandoned almost as soon as it had been assembled.

Roma thought the excursion would excite Addy's eye for design, since she'd offered to help Roma with renovating Bayview. She'd been a big help at the house so far, getting stuck into the painting with as much gusto as Roma had herself. She'd cleaned windows and scrubbed floors, loaded rubbish into the skip that had been delivered to the backyard for the paint tins and the rolls of musty old carpet, and had done her fair share of cooking and dishwashing. She was a long way from the glamorous film world she was used to, but had seemed to have fitted right in. To Roma's house and Roma's new life. When she was young, during those summers at Remarkable Bay, Roma used to pretend Addy was her sister. It had been a long time since she'd imagined Addy in that role again, but the idea was starting to take hold in her heart.

But today, she'd seemed distracted the whole afternoon. While Roma fossicked around, Addy sat on a dusty old Art Deco upholstered sofa and stared into the distance. When Roma found a stand-alone bar with sparkling sixties gold explosions on its top, she called to Addy, 'Come and look at this. It's incredible.'

But Addy either hadn't heard Roma or had ignored her.

Something was up, but Addy wasn't revealing anything, so Roma half-heartedly chose a few items: four cane chairs for the balcony; another rug for one of the bedrooms; a couple of occasional tables and a sofa setting in moss green. Bayview was a big house and the furniture she'd brought with her from her old home in Adelaide hadn't filled half of it.

Once Roma had paid and arranged for the items to be delivered the next day, she found Addy in the china section, picking up and examining old crockery. Addy looked like she was in a trance, her attention far away from the salvage yard, from Roma, even from Remarkable Bay.

'Are you okay, Addy?'

Addy slowly placed a teacup on the shelf in front of her. 'Fine.' Roma could see through her attempt at a happy smile. 'You finished? Did you find anything?'

'A few things. Let's go.'

On the way back to Remarkable Bay, Roma was so lost in her thoughts about Addy that she almost missed turning into Ocean Street from the main road. She screeched to a halt, flicked on her indicator and reflexively thrust her left arm towards Addy to make sure she hadn't jolted forward in her seat.

'You okay?' Roma asked.

'Sure.' Addy stared straight ahead through the car window.

Roma narrowed her gaze. 'You're a million miles away.'

There was nothing more from Addy. Roma waited for an old Falcon towing a caravan to pass before she slowly took the turn

'Hey,' she said, the video shop on her right giving her an idea about what might cheer Addy up. 'Feel like a movie marathon tonight? I was thinking something rom com.'

Addy didn't answer. She was bent over, digging in her handbag and brought her phone out to read the display. When she did, her face became ashen.

'You okay? What is it?'

'Stop the car.' Addy clasped a hand on Roma's arm, gripping hard.

Roma checked her mirrors and pulled over outside Keira's Pilates studio. She studied Addy's face. Addy was jabbing at the screen, violently, rhythmically. Then she tossed her phone back in her handbag at her feet.

'Who was that?'

'Nobody.' Addy ran her hands over her face, breathing hard. 'It's nothing. I'll see you at home. I need some air.'

Addy unclipped her seatbelt and opened the door.

'Where are you going?' Roma called out, feeling worried now.

Addy slipped out of the car and just as she was about to slam the door, she bent down and looked at Roma through the open window before turning her head towards the surf shop. Now Roma knew. All afternoon, Addy had been thinking about Connor's cousin. The surf shop guy. What was supposed to be a fun girls afternoon had been something that had got in the way of a hook up.

Roma slipped her sunglasses back on, sighed.

'I'll be home later.'

'Sure. Whatever.' Roma drove the short distance up the street, swung her car around and pulled up out front of Bayview. She cut the engine and sat for a while, trying to understand what had just happened.

The old Addy was back. The old Addy who dumped Roma whenever a guy came along. Roma closed her eyes, fighting familiar emotions from so long ago. And suddenly Roma wasn't a thirty-five-year-old widow anymore; she was fifteen years old again, resentful, jealous, annoyed, alone. She was the girl left behind when Addy had gone down to the beach to meet guys when they were teens. She was the huffily disappointed fifteen year old who went to surfing lessons on her own because Addy hadn't wanted to smudge her mascara by getting her face wet. She was the sad and guilty sixteen year old who'd had to tell her parents about Addy's eating disorder. Once again, Addy was having all the fun and Roma was the moral police.

Disappointment pricked behind her eyes. She scolded herself at how ridiculous it was to be feeling this way, but she couldn't seem to stop those emotions from resurfacing. She dragged herself inside, took the stairs in a slow and tired climb, and moved in slow motion to her bed. The pillow was soft under her head and she pulled a rug over herself before turning on her side, drawing her knees up to her chest. It was one step forward, two steps back, even after all this time. When she felt down, everything came back to her in an eddy of grief. Thoughts of Tom, of Addy, of her dead parents, of all the friends she'd alienated and who'd not known how to cope with her grief, swirled and spun in her head. Snatches of conversation came back to her, things she'd said to other people, hurtful things that had been said to her face and behind her back. She'd come down to Remarkable Bay to avoid it all and be alone.

Things with Addy weren't working out, after all. Roma didn't want to look back, and that's what having Addy to stay was doing to her. There was only one thing to do.

Before she drifted off to sleep, Roma resolved to ask Addy to leave.

Addy checked her reflection in the glass window of the surf shop and then pushed through the plastic strips hanging over the door and went inside.

She shimmied a little when she saw Blake at the counter. He was studying something spread out on it. As she approached, she saw it was the local paper. So he was a man who kept up with current events, she thought. Roma might appreciate that, but Addy couldn't have cared less. All she needed to know about surfer dude Blake was whether he wanted sex. She didn't need hearts and flowers or any of that bullshit. She didn't believe in happy ever afters or soul mates— her own family and a succession of men had ruined that for her.

She was only after what every man she'd ever known had been after: sex.

He looked up. 'Hey.'

'Hey.' Addy lowered her gaze to his lips for a half a second. She'd added an extra sway to her hips as she'd crossed the shop to the counter and when she reached it, she looked up at him and tucked her hair behind her ears.

'What can I help you with today?' He closed the paper with a rustle and stood taller.

She glanced down at his well-built chest. *Come in, spinner.*

'Funny you should ask.' Addy placed her palms flat on the counter and leaned over. She made a point of glancing at the watches and jewellery in the cabinet, visible through the glass top.

'You looking for a new watch?'

She flicked her gaze up to meet his. 'No. I'm not after a watch. I'm looking for some fun tonight.'

Blake's eyebrows raised for just a flicker and he slipped his thumbs through the belt loops on his jeans.

Reeling you in, buddy.

He cleared his throat. 'And you think I can help you with that.' She liked the way he said it, like it wasn't a question.

'Uh huh.' Addy bit her bottom lip.

Blake shifted his weight, raised his chin and looked at her through narrowed eyes. 'What if I'm with someone?'

'I don't care if you are, but are you?'

He smiled, just. 'No.'

'Then there's no problem, is there?'

He moved, put his palms flat on the glass cabinet and leaned in to her, over her. Addy tilted her head back.

'What if I'm not interested?'

'I don't think that's an issue here, right?'

He chuckled. 'No.'

She looked at his mouth once more. 'So, Blake Stapleton. You want to show a new girl in town a little fun?'

When Roma roused, still curled on her side on her bed, she heard the shower running. There was something not quite right with the plumbing and the pipes shuddered and shook whenever the hot water was on, echoing through the house. She guessed Addy was back. A glance at her mobile revealed it was six o'clock. She'd been asleep for three hours and now she was hungry, still cross, feeling on edge. She hadn't forgotten her resolution to ask Addy to leave, in fact she was more certain of it than before. She was just a little nervous about telling her, that was all. After everything she'd been through, she needed a real friend, not a fair-weather one. She couldn't be left behind again. Addy had to go before Roma would miss her too much.

She went downstairs to the kitchen, opened the fridge and studied the Tupperware containers of leftovers, trying to decide if she was hungry or not. Addy strolled in, her shoes sounding on the floor. She didn't say a word.

Roma looked over the door. Addy was dressed to kill, the lost look from earlier that afternoon gone, covered over with make-up and attitude. Her mask firmly back in place. She looked like she was about to attend an opening night. Her lips were full and red and her cheeks were ever so subtly rouged so as not to clash with her auburn hair, which was swept over one shoulder, exposing her pale neck and a long silver thread earring was dangling there, catching the light. Her perfume was something musky and sexy; her loose maxi dress sunk low on her décolletage and billowed around her lithe legs. She'd gone to a lot of trouble for a fuck, Roma noted.

'What do you think?' Addy asked, preening in her reflection in the glass doors to the backyard.

'You look great.' Roma closed the fridge door with a little more force than was necessary, and turned to the sink.

'What's the matter? Are you all right?'

Roma took a deep breath, felt her fists tightening into balls of anger, ready to punch something or someone although she'd never come close to it in her entire life.

'Roma?' Heels on the floor, closer.

Roma spun around. 'You look gorgeous. As you always do.'

'Don't be like that,' Addy said nervously tucking her hair behind her ear. 'Are you sure this is okay? It's still a little cool out. You think I'll be cold?'

Roma's hands found her hips. 'You know you look fantastic. Why bother asking me?' And then something happened. Something unexpected. Her years of frustration with Addy's attention-seeking behaviour bubbled up and came out of her mouth in an angry spit of words. 'I take it you're all sorted for tonight then. Your fuck is all organised, is it?'

Addy startled. 'Yes, I—'. She stopped, shrinking back from Roma, taking small, hesitant steps, her hands raising in a defensive posture in front of her body, as if to quiet Roma, to calm her.

'So tell me something, Addy.'

Addy stared at her, her face pale now, her rouged cheeks looking like toffee apples against her white skin.

'Why do you pretend to care what I think? Haven't you ever thought how that makes me feel?'

'I don't know what you're talking about,' Addy stepped backwards.

'Yes you do. Look at you. You've always been beautiful. Just a little bit skinny. Just a little bit tall. I bet you've never gained a pound in your whole life or had a cold sore. Even your freckles are cute. You've always had men lusting after you. You've always been that girl. You're perfect.'

Addy's voice was thin. 'No one's perfect, Roma.'

'Please.' Anger welled inside Roma. 'You have a fabulous job surrounded by famous and beautiful people. You look like that. You want sex so you go and proposition some guy in a surf shop and guess what? You're about to get laid. What could possibly be wrong with your life?'

'You have no idea …'

'Don't pretend to be coy, Addy. You've been this person your whole life. Here I was, thinking you might have changed, that you might have grown up. Apparently, I was wrong. Tell me. What's it like to get out of bed each day and be the fabulous Addy McNamara? How on earth have you coped slumming it down here in the pimple on the backside of the earth with me?'

Addy stiffened. She lowered her eyes and turned to go.

'Have fun,' Roma called after her, not even bothering to hide the sarcasm. 'Say hello to Blake for me. If you can remember his name, that is.'

Addy didn't hear that last retort. She'd run out of the kitchen and out the front door. Roma winced as it slammed.

She sat at the table. She was the one who'd lost a husband. She was the one who'd left her old life behind to find a new one, a shinier one. A happier one. Yet she seemed to be stuck, jammed right back in the old battles in her head with Addy. Being around her meant those old emotions floated to the surface like scum on a pond. Why did she hope Addy might have changed? Hadn't she shown her what she was really like all those years ago?

Addy had dumped her as soon as she'd had a better offer. She was off to her lover.

A lover. Roma had never had a lover. She'd had a boyfriend, then a fiancé, then a husband, and they were all the same man. And then she was a widow.

She thought about Connor. Tried not to.

Roma tidied the kitchen table, stacked the pile of magazines neatly, trimmed the wick in the candle in the centre of the kitchen table, refilled the water in the vase sitting next to it.

A widow at thirty-five.

It wasn't fair.

Was there going to be more to her life than this?

A big, old lonely house with her in it, rattling around with a head full of ghosts?

Connor.

He was there again. She still hadn't had a word of thanks from him about the lemon slice she'd left. Maybe he wasn't as nice as he'd first appeared to be. Perhaps his friendliness and kindness had all been an act. Or perhaps she'd pushed him away too. She seemed to be really good at that.

She'd just go next door and ask for her container back, she decided. That would be a start. Or, rather, a finish. And after that, she might ring Keira to see if she fancied coming over for the movie marathon she'd been planning to have with Addy.

She didn't need Addy. Never had.

* * *

Roma pulled a light cardigan around her shoulders and pulled the front door closed behind her as she left. She was slowly letting go of her city instincts and didn't lock it. This visit to Connor wouldn't take long. She turned to the street and pulled up in surprise.

Connor was standing at the front gate, holding her Tupperware.

'Hey,' he said, holding the container towards her. 'I was just bringing this back.' The moon was rising and the stars were already bright in the sky behind him.

'Oh.' Roma sighed. She was embarrassed at the quiver in her voice. She was still upset from the argument with Addy, still tense and shivery.

'Is everything all right?' He came to her, his face full of concern, and he gently touched her hand.

She pulled it away from his. 'I'm fine.'

He dipped down to study her face. 'You sure?'

'I'm sure.' She managed a smile but it didn't feel real.

'Is this yours by any chance?'

'Yes.' She took the Tupperware from him and clutched it against her stomach.

Connor was close now, close enough that she could see his smile in the dark. He always seemed to be on the verge of laughter; that just-heard-a-funny-joke kind of smile made him seem perpetually happy. She, on the other hand, seemed to be on the verge of tears.

'I'm no detective, but I take it there was something in it?' he asked.

'Yes,' Roma answered. 'It was full of lemon slice, actually.'

'Damn that kid.' Connor made a show of looking angry. 'I didn't know you'd dropped it round until I found it just now shoved under his bed. Right there in the space between his stinky socks and something I can only guess was a cheese sandwich about three months ago. Sorry about that. It may need the high pressure hose treatment.'

'Thanks for bringing it back.'

'Shit,' he laughed, ruefully. 'I didn't even get a single piece.'

Roma felt herself unwinding. His smile could do that to her. 'I guess I should be flattered that he liked it enough not to share it.'

'You should be. His food of choice is a meat pie.'

A gust of wind picked up, pulled Roma's hair from behind her ear. She tucked it back, smoothing it. She shyly met his gaze and then looked down at her feet.

'I'm sorry. You look like you were about to head off somewhere.'

'I was … just looking for some fresh air.'

She swallowed the emotion in her throat, her anger and envy. So she was stupidly jealous of Addy for going after what she wanted. What was to stop her from doing the same? 'I needed to get out of the house for a while. I've been cooped up too long.' The stammer in her voice was there but she felt a strength behind it now. And then she said, quietly and purposefully, 'To tell the truth, I was on my way to see you.'

Connor looked taller somehow. 'You were?'

She nodded.

Connor's chest rose and fell on a sigh. He ran a hand through his hair, studied her for a moment. 'Well, funny thing is, I was heading over to invite you to my place. I happen to have plenty of fresh air over there.'

'I'd love to come,' Roma said.

'Wait a minute. You haven't heard my condition.'

'There's a condition?'

Connor nodded. 'Got any more of that slice?'

Roma felt a big whoosh of relief. 'I may just have a secret stash.'

'I'll go open a bottle of wine,' Connor said. 'Meet you at my place in five minutes.'

CHAPTER 21

1935

In their room at the Bayview Guest House, Ruby stood over Clara's sweating, shivering, pale form. Clara's words were thumping and echoing in her head.

The baby. Tell me what to do about the baby.

What baby? Clara was the baby. Four years older, Ruby had mothered her youngest sister. Dressed her when she was a child. Plaited her hair, read to her. Taught her how to read, in fact. She'd been at her side every day and night when it was feared she had polio. Horrid days and horrifying nights.

Clara must be hallucinating. Ruby collected herself, knelt down and pressed the inside of her wrist to Clara's forehead. Clara flinched.

'Clara …,' Ruby whispered. 'There's no baby. Why are you saying such things?'

Clara turned to her. Pale. Horrified. Ruby could see the truth in her sister's eyes.

'There is a baby, Ruby. I can feel it. I'm not a silly girl. I'm not a stupid girl.'

Clara reached for her sister's hand and pressed it to her belly. As soon as Ruby felt the swell and then—oh, my—the kick, she knew her sister wasn't lying. Ruby had felt a baby move before: their cousin Amelia had a baby last year and they'd taken turns to press their hands to her stomach to feel the little kicks and the movements.

Ruby knew Clara was telling the horrifying truth.

A truth which was too big for the both of them.

'I have to get mother,' Ruby blurted out as she struggled to stand, the weight of Clara's revelation already making her unsteady on her feet. She so desperately wanted to know, but couldn't ask: Who was the father? Who had done this to her baby sister? She pressed her hand to her own stomach, and swallowed against the roiling turmoil in it.

Clara began to sob.

'Clara, I don't know what else to do. I have to get her.'

And the look in Clara's eyes as she slowly nodded was heartbreaking. It was grim resignation and the deepest despair.

Ruby's desperate search for her mother came to a sudden halt in the downstairs reception room. She was playing canasta with Mrs Stuart and Adeline and James. From across the room, Ruby could see the game held little interest for the two lovebirds, who were playfully nudging each other and sharing a hand. Her mother and Mrs Stuart were studying their own, discarding cards and picking up from the deck, chatting quietly.

Ruby was torn. She suddenly didn't know what to say or how to say it. She knew this must remain a secret. She was well aware of the shame of it. She must not give away a hint or a suggestion that anything was the matter. Not in front of a reception room full of strangers. And most especially not in front of James and his mother. Ruby crossed the room as quietly and calmly as she could, weaving around tables, and nodding and smiling politely to the other guests. When she reached her mother's side, she dragged in a deep breath to steady her racing heart and her growing panic.

'Hello, everyone.'

James shot to his feet. 'Why, hello there, Ruby. Let me find you a chair.' There was a spare at the next table and he shifted his own to one side and made room for her. She simply nodded her thanks and sat. She smoothed down her dress and folded her hands in her lap, willing them to settle.

'Where have you been, Ruby?' Adeline asked huffily. 'Why must I be forced to stay indoors and play this interminable game of cards when you are free to do whatever you choose?'

'Come, Adeline,' James said with a smile at Ruby. 'You're only saying that because we're losing. And rather badly I might add.'

'Oh, phooey.' Adeline laid her cards on the table and sat back in her chair. She looked about the room as if she suspected something far more entertaining was happening somewhere else.

'Enjoy it while it lasts,' Mrs Stuart announced. 'Once you're married, things will change forever for you, my dear.'

'They certainly will,' Mrs Allen said. 'You'll be entertaining at home, not gallivanting around the city like young lovebirds.'

The idea seemed to shock Adeline. She sat upright, gazing in turn at the two women. 'Why should I stop going out just because I'm married?'

Mrs Stuart leaned in. She wore small round metal-rimmed glasses and Ruby decided she had the most enormous bosom she'd ever seen. She had a deep voice, rich as Christmas cake, which commanded attention.

'Because, Adeline, that's what married women do. James will have his work and the club and his business entertaining. You will have a household to establish and staff to employ. I'm sure you'll find yourself busy enough with church and charity activities and tennis perhaps, if you're sporting.' She stopped, laid her cards flat on the table. 'Are you sporting, dear girl?'

'Not in the slightest,' Adeline replied with a measure of pride.

'Hopelessly uncoordinated,' James added with a wink.

'In that case, there will be clubs and charity work and your garden. And, if you are blessed, and I know you will be, there will be children.'

Adeline looked doe-eyed as she turned her gaze to James. 'May our sons look exactly like my darling James.'

James reached for Adeline's hand and kissed the back of it. 'And may our daughters look exactly like their mother: petite and ravishing, with the prettiest red hair in the world.'

Mrs Stuart regarded her son over the rim of her glasses. 'I know James will make his family proud. I've always thought so. Not only is he handsome and clever but he'll be a wonderful father.'

'Oh mother,' he said slyly. 'Are you trying to make me blush in front of my future in-laws?' He winked at Ruby. She looked down at her hands.

Adeline laughed and blushed, looking as if her heart might be about to burst. If only she knew, Ruby thought. If only she could sense that in the room almost above them, their sister was in agonies of her own. Ruby felt confused and sick. Something was dragging the three Miss Allens in competing directions and it ached to know it. Ruby began to fidget, twisting her fingers around each other until they turned white.

'If motherhood is God's greatest blessing,' Mrs Allen added with a sly glance at each of her two daughters, 'becoming a grandmother oneself must be the next greatest.' The upcoming weddings of her daughters had been all she could talk about that year, and at each engagement party and wedding they attended, she seemed to judge each woman's success as a mother by the marriageability of her daughters.

'It certainly is,' Mrs Stuart replied.

Ruby let herself feel some hope for Clara's situation. This talk of children and motherhood, the sanctity of it, surely must mean that ... but her sinking chilled heart told her otherwise.

'There is such a sense of history about one's children having children of their own, isn't there?' Mrs Allen asked Mrs Stuart.

Mrs Stuart laid a card in the middle of the table. 'I do agree.'

'And, as we both know,' she shared a knowing smile with Mrs Stuart, 'our families will be blessed with not one, but two weddings next year,' Mrs Allen boasted. 'We expect Ruby and Edwin to set a date when we're back in Adelaide, after the summer has passed. The Allens shall be the talk of the town. Two daughters married in the one year to such handsome young men from such a good family.'

All four sets of eyes turned to Ruby and her escalating heartbeat was suddenly thudding in her ears. She felt dreadful. Every nerve ending shocked. She felt the heat rise up her décolletage, colour her cheeks and goosebump into her hair. Under the table, she gripped the starched white linen tablecloth and scrunched it in her hands.

'We ...' She lifted a hand to her forehead and felt it clammy and hot.

'What is the matter, Ruby?' Her mother narrowed her eyes at her daughter across the table. 'You don't look well.'

James leaned closer too, his shoulder bumping hers. 'You look rather ill, Ruby. Can I fetch you a glass of water? Or a cup of tea?'

'No. Thank you.' Ruby hadn't set out to create a ruse so she could distract her mother and take her upstairs to Clara but now she had one. Perhaps it was the weight of the secret she was keeping that was making her ill. With guilt. With dread. With panic.

'A headache,' she managed.

Mrs Allen piled her cards and set them on the table. 'Won't you excuse us? I think I'll see Ruby upstairs for a powder and a rest.'

'Of course.' James got to his feet, as gallant as ever, and Mrs Allen and Ruby said their goodbyes to James's mother.

Ruby couldn't manage a word until they were upstairs and safely out of earshot of any of the other guests. Looking around the empty hallway, gripping the doorknob to the room she shared with Adeline and Clara, Ruby struggled to speak.

Her mother bustled to her side. 'Well, open the door, child. Are you frozen on the spot?'

'It's not me, mother. It's Clara.'

Ruby blinked, squeezed her eyes closed, trying to find the words. She knew this moment would be the end of everything she knew. Everything that was safe and respectable and *good* about her family was about to be ruined. Ruby knew that motherhood would not be a blessing for Clara. It would be a curse, a stain which the whole family and the whole world would try to erase. She knew that because she'd seen it happen. In their very household, no less. She was fully aware of the shame and disgrace that would descend on their family if such news were to be known. One of the girls who had worked in their kitchen had got 'into trouble' a year before and had been let go so quickly she barely had time to untie her apron. The words that had been used about Molly—only sixteen years old—were cruel and Ruby remembered with shame that she had used some of them herself. Harridan. Slut. The epithets had been whispered in the bedroom with her sisters. Molly disappeared off the face of the earth and her name was never mentioned again.

Surely Clara was different to Molly. She was a respectable girl from a good family. There was a difference. Who knew what kind of family Molly had come from, or even if she had a family? Clara was not like her. In any respect. Things would surely be different for a girl like Clara.

Tears welled in Ruby's eyes and a sob caught in her throat. She wanted to beg her mother to be kind, to understand, to love Clara as much as she did.

'Before we go in, Mother,' she managed in the quietest whisper. 'Remember she is your daughter. And my sister, and that we love her.'

Mrs Allen's face lost all colour. She pushed Ruby aside and went into the bedroom to see Clara.

Ruby desperately wanted to burst through the closed door and comfort her sister, fight for her, defend her. But she knew her place and waited in the hallway with her ear pressed to the door. There was silence for a long while and then a burst of loud sobbing, quickly muffled. Each hair on Ruby's body goosebumped. Then there was nothing. Not a raised voice, nor a shout. It felt like an hour but what must have only been three minutes later, her mother emerged and closed the door quietly behind her. She didn't seem surprised to see Ruby waiting.

'Mother, what—'

Mrs Allen showed Ruby her palm, silencing her, although Ruby didn't need the gesture to be rendered speechless. In that moment, she barely recognised her mother. Her nostrils flared, her eyes were cold and hard. She looked like a stranger and Ruby felt a spoke of fear spear her heart.

'Follow me,' she commanded and Ruby did as she was told. When they were inside her parents' room, Mrs Allen found a fresh handkerchief on the dresser and blotted her brow. It was only in the privacy of her room that she let the tears well and soften her eyes.

Ruby waited. The French doors were open and the sheer curtains billowed and beckoned. There were chairs on the balcony outside and a small table. Ruby wanted to go outside, to breathe some fresh air, but she waited. Her mother finally turned to her.

'Oh, Mother,' Ruby gasped and reached for her hand.

Mrs Allen allowed a brief moment of comfort to her daughter before pulling her hand away. And then her reserve was back, the flint in her eyes once more. Her voice was hard and dripping with anger. 'How long have you known this shameful secret of your sisters, Ruby?'

Ruby took a step back, stumbled, as if she'd been slapped with her mother's open hand instead of with her words.

'She only told me today,' she stammered, more scared now. She resolved in that terrifying moment not to reveal her suspicions that she'd known something was wrong with Clara. She had never suspected it to be this. Never this. Never in her worst fears would it be this. 'Immediately before I went downstairs to find you.'

Mrs Allen paced the room, her shoes sounding rhythmically on the floorboards. From outside the open window, the happy noises from a croquet match across the road on the lawns could be heard, the thwack of a ball, laughter and applause. That was another world now.

'What's to be done, Mother?'

'I shall call your father directly.' She crossed the room and reached for Ruby. Ruby wanted to cry at the thought that her mother was going to comfort her with a hug. She wanted it. She needed the reassurance that everything was going to be all right, that they would look after Clara. Instead, Ruby felt hard fingers digging in to her arms. Mrs Allen glared directly into her daughter's crying eyes.

'Listen to me, Ruby,' she hissed. 'You are not to say a word about this to anyone. Not a single word. Especially to Adeline. Do you understand?'

'What's going to happen to Clara?'

'This will be dealt with. That is all you need to know.'

'But downstairs you said … you told Mrs Stuart that mother-hood is God's greatest blessing. That you would be proud to be a grandmother.'

'Not like this, you stupid girl.' Mrs Allen's hands dropped to her sides and her chin lowered. When she turned away from Ruby, she said in a quiet voice.

'Please leave, Ruby.'

'Mother …'

'Do as I say.'

Ruby quietly shuffled out and when she closed the door to her mother's room, she stood in the hallway, pressed her back to the wall, wanting to disappear. She felt lost, trapped, caught between her mother and her sister, not knowing if either wanted her comfort and knowing they were in no place to console her. She couldn't bear to see the disgust in her mother's eyes and the distress in Clara's. Without even thinking, Ruby headed to the door at the other end of the hallway, to the stairs down the outside of the house, and pushed it open. The bright sun had her blinking as she stepped outside on to the landing and she moved quickly, hoping not to be seen, taking the stairs two by two as she ran down them, almost tripping at one point as she half missed a step. She stumbled, grabbed the rail with both hands to steady herself but didn't stop, kept going, kept running across the road, past the croquet game, to the Harbour

Master's Walk and down to the sand and the water and the wind
and the solitude of her tears.

Charles Allen arrived in Remarkable Bay on 2 January, as previously
arranged. Any change of plans would have alerted the suspicious
and the curious and everything had to appear as normal as possible.
He'd summoned a taxi cab up in Adelaide, boarded the train at the
Adelaide Railway Station, disembarked four hours later in Victor
Harbor and caught another taxi cab to Remarkable Bay. All in all,
it was an exhausting day.

Ruby would normally have been pleased to see her father, as
would her sisters, but now, in these circumstances, she was afraid.
Their father was a quiet, conservative man. Ruby liked to talk books
with him. Adeline would make him laugh and Clara would share
the discovery of a bird she had never seen before. He was tall, with
a thick moustache and wore wire-rimmed reading glasses he always
seemed to be losing, and Ruby believed she'd never seen him wear
anything but the three-piece suit he favoured.

She was watching from the bedroom window when he arrived,
her heart heavy with trepidation. Adeline was with James, something their mother had encouraged her to do, while Clara sat calmly
on her bed on the other side of the room. She hadn't said a word to
Ruby since the talk with their mother. Ruby thought she might be
in some kind of trance. She sat staring blank-eyed and expression-
less. Perhaps it was nervous shock.

Their father alighted from the taxi and paid the driver. While
his bags were carried inside, Charles looked around, across to the
croquet lawns, then peered up to the end of Ocean Street where the
road met the blue of the ocean in the distance. She heard him greet
Mrs Nightingale and then there were footsteps, heavy leather on
the stairs and in the hallway outside their room.

The door opened and he came inside, ducking his head so he
didn't hit it on the doorframe. He didn't look either of his daughters directly in the eye. Both of them sat rigid, suddenly afraid
to speak.

'Clara, come with me to see your mother.'

Where were the hellos? Where were the smiles for his daughters?

Ruby watched Clara go wordlessly. Once the door was closed quietly behind them, Ruby picked up her Brontë and tried to distract herself in the pages while she waited, but the words swam in confusing patterns. Ten minutes later, Clara came back into the room, white-faced. A ghost. Ruby watched her, shuffling as if she were sleepwalking.

'Clara?'

She knelt down by her bed and reached under it for her suitcase, lifting it on to the bed, flipping open its lid.

'What's going on?' Ruby demanded, her heart palpitating so hard her chest ached. 'What did father say? And what are you doing with your suitcase?'

'I'm to leave.' Clara's voice was flat and quiet.

'What do you mean, leave? We're not due back in Adelaide until the end of January. You don't have to leave now.'

'I'm being sent away, Ruby.'

Ruby felt as if all the air had been squeezed from her lungs. She lowered herself on Clara's bed. 'Where?'

'Father's organised everything. There have been telephone calls. I'm to go back to Adelaide tomorrow. And then I'll be on the next train to Sydney.'

'Sydney?' Ruby gasped.

'Yes. Where I shall wait out my shame, so this humiliating stain on our family and its character can be erased and then forgotten.'

Ruby knew they weren't Clara's words. Or her mother's. They were most definitely their father's. He was a respectable man at the head of a respectable family and the idea of having a daughter with a child out of wedlock would be intolerable to him. How had she even possibly entertained a tiny hope that they would rally around Clara? Ruby had heard the Sunday sermons during which the Allen family had stood solemnly in church together, the priest piously clucking his tongue at the moral failings of young women who found themselves in such circumstances. There was a sanctity to marriage, and the superiority of sex within these bounds. Ruby had heard it all. Those women who found themselves pregnant already had some kind of moral inferiority; they had committed the mortal sin of failing in their responsibility to say *no*. Ruby had heard it about Molly, too, the young kitchen girl and, to her shame, she'd believed it then, she'd repeated those words to her sisters.

'Oh, Clara,' Ruby whispered and her hand flew to her mouth to stop the sobs.

Clara's voice was flat and emotionless. 'I'm to go and stay with Aunt Jane until …'

A small sense of relief fluttered through Ruby. Yes. Aunt Jane! Their delightful, independent and mysterious Aunt Jane, the tragic, childless widow, as she was frequently described by their mother, who was as flamboyant and full of character as the city of Sydney itself. Modern in thought and attitude, she had never come back to Adelaide once she'd left after the War. Aunt Jane, who their mother had always believed had been ruined by Sydney's wild ways and modern attitudes, had clearly not been ruined enough that they wouldn't send Clara to her.

Ruby suddenly felt hope where there had been none. Surely, Aunt Jane wouldn't judge Clara. She would look after her as if she were her own daughter, Ruby knew that in her heart. Clara would be safe with her.

'Aunt Jane? That's a relief, isn't it?'

'Yes.' Clara's voice was quiet, dazed. The words were falling from her lips but she was telling someone else's story. 'Father says I'm fortunate to have in her someone who *understands*. If it wasn't for her, it would have been a home for unmarried mothers in Melbourne. Under a different name, of course. Nothing to taint the Allen name. Either way, I'm being sent far away from all those who know us. I'm to go and hide until the baby is born.'

Ruby was certain that Clara hadn't realised it, but she'd pressed a hand to her gently swollen stomach and looked down at the connection she was making with the baby she would never call her own.

'What about the baby?' Ruby whispered.

'He says I must ...' her voice faltered and tears spilled down her cheeks. '... that I must have been chosen by God to give the baby to a childless couple.'

'Oh, Clara.'

Ruby's heart broke.

She felt the hurt for her sister deep inside. 'And once the baby is born ... you'll come home? By winter, perhaps? You'll definitely be back for Christmas, won't you?'

Ruby knew that would mean Clara would miss Adeline's wedding to James in April.

Clara went to the wardrobe, took out her clothes that were hanging there and slipped them off the wooden hangers. They were simple dresses, the patterns and fabrics of a girl, and she placed them in the suitcase on top of her shoes. She patted them down and then reached for something buried at the bottom. When she tugged it out, Ruby saw it was her new swimsuit. Clara tossed it in to Ruby's lap.

'Take this. I won't be needing it.'

Ruby could hardly bear to touch it. She folded the pink polka dotted outfit and placed it on the bed next to her. Then she quickly turned and found her Brontë on her small bedside table. She handed it to Clara.

'Here. Take it. Think of me.'

'I can't. It's your favourite.'

'Please.' Ruby leaned over and pressed her hand over Clara's. 'I love you more than I've loved any book.'

Tears filled Clara's eyes as she put the book in her suitcase. 'Thank you.'

The next morning, Mr Allen sat in the downstairs reception room, reading *The Advertiser*, burying himself in articles about the latest bank clearances and the opening of the wheat markets in London. Mrs Allen and Adeline had walked to Sunnybrae for morning tea with the Stuarts, and Ruby alone was given the task of accompanying Clara to Victor Harbor to meet the Adelaide train.

Their father had told Mrs Nightingale that Clara was going to Melbourne to undertake ornithological studies and the older woman clucked her approval, wide-eyed at the opportunities afforded to the well-bred young ladies of Adelaide. There had been no debate about what was to happen to Clara. Ruby knew her mother would not have said a word when her father was handing down his decision about Clara's future. He wasn't a judge but his word was like a verdict that could never be appealed. The word of men—and fathers in particular—was law. It was not to be gainsaid, questioned or doubted. There were polite goodbyes to Clara in the privacy of her parents' room—again, Ruby had been barred—and Clara had emerged holding a small, red leather purse, filled with coins. She was to change trains once she reached Adelaide and head directly to Sydney.

They travelled by taxicab and were delivered to the train station in Victor Harbor about forty minutes later. They were early: there was barely anyone there yet to meet the train and although there was still plenty of time to cross the road to the Hope Tearooms for tea and cake, Clara had declined. If she was honest with herself, Ruby had no appetite either. They found a bench in the shade of the railway station's platform and stared at the track forlornly.

Ruby held Clara's hand. Her sister was about to leave. This might be their last chance to discuss what had happened, before history would be rewritten and it would never be spoken of again, like Uncle Clem's shell shock after the Great War or their old neighbour Mr Mitchell's secret gambling habit. There was a question she was still desperate to ask.

There were topics about which there would never be dinner party discussion, Ruby was beginning to understand. Character faults were overlooked, if you came from the right kind of family, and were hidden. She glanced down at Clara's small hand in hers. How was it possible that she was carrying a child? She seemed so small, still, so young. Her interests were birds, not young men. How could this have happened?

'Clara?'

'Yes?' Clara didn't look at her sister. She continued staring at the tracks, the Norfolk Island pines beyond and then the haze of blue, blue ocean in the distance.

'Will you tell me …' And then she wasn't quite sure how to ask. Clara pulled her hand from Ruby's.

'Will you tell me who it was? Who is the father of your child?'

CHAPTER

22

2016

Roma opened Connor's front door and went inside. Loud music blared from the end of the house, and as she walked towards it, past the two rooms on either side of the long hallway, she called out, loud enough to be heard over the music, 'Hello?'

Then there was silence and Connor appeared at the end of the hallway, framed by the doorway. Buster appeared too, quivering at his feet, making a sound that barely passed as a bark.

'Hey,' he called. 'Down here.'

Roma passed Angas's room—she could tell it was his by the shooting sounds and dramatic music from behind the door—and then emerged into a huge room which seemed to run the width of the back of the house. The kitchen was at one side while the other was configured as a living area. Sand-coloured sofas were positioned opposite each other and Buster's small dog bed took pride of place in the middle. A large wall-mounted TV occupied one wall and big windows overlooked the backyard. The floors were polished concrete and the kitchen … oh, the kitchen. The walls were a mushroom colour, taupe rather than pink, and there were lots of white cupboards in a bank on one wall and a long island bench parallel to it, with a gleaming inset sink. A huge stainless-steel fridge was set into the cabinetry.

'This is nice,' she managed. 'Really nice.'

'Thanks,' Connor said with a warm smile. He looked so at home in this small beachside stone cottage. He was dressed in jeans and a warm jumper, its sleeves pushed up his arms a little. He held a glass of wine in his hand and, without breaking his smile, he popped an olive into his mouth, throwing it up into the air in what seemed like a practised party trick. There was something different about his face and then Roma realised that he was wearing glasses, light brown frames that caught the colour of his hair and his eyes. All this detail had escaped her when they'd met on the footpath just now. That's was probably because she'd been trying not to look at him.

She was looking at him now.

'This room makes my kitchen look a million years old instead of a mere forty.'

Connor chuckled, popped another olive into his mouth. 'I've seen your kitchen so I know you're not exaggerating.'

'It's on my list of things to do, but I wanted to live in it for a while first, so I could get a feel for how the house works and what I want to do.' Roma glanced around Connor's living area. 'I like what you've done here with these big doors, the way it opens up the room to the back yard. And all this storage.'

'Don't open any of the cupboards. It's a disaster behind those closed doors,' Connor said.

'My kitchen is okay and perfectly usable, but I have to admit to missing a dishwasher.' Roma rolled her eyes at how that sounded. 'First world problems, right?'

'Hey, don't be so hard on yourself. We all want the creature comforts, don't we? Those little things that make your little slice of the world feel like home?'

'I guess we do,' she said.

'Nothing wrong with that.'

'No,' she smiled distractedly. Her own little slice of home. Roma hadn't felt that way about her house back in Adelaide. It had been a practical house, that was all. One with good resale value, as Tom had always liked to remind her. They'd got it at auction for a good price, and it was in an up-and-coming suburb, close enough to the city that she could catch the tram to work if she wanted to and Tom could cycle the winding bike track to his job. He'd done his research and had determined the house would appreciate in value and enable them to trade up in no time. All it needed was a lick of paint, a kitchen renovation and some TLC. They'd done the painting and the kitchen but there wasn't much tender loving care in that house. Tom had gone back to university to study and the rest of the renovation slowed. They never had traded up. They'd become too comfortable in its plain and undemanding location. Roma had been reluctant to move away from the convenience of the tram line, and they'd never needed a house with more bedrooms because they'd never had the children Roma imagined they would, that would have necessitated a nursery and then a third bedroom and, perhaps later, a teenagers' retreat. They stayed in that house, taking no risks, and settled in. And Roma had existed in that world until that world had imploded around her.

Was that what had drawn her to Bayview? The chance to find that little slice of the world that was the place of her heart?

'All I know, Roma, is that taking on Bayview was incredibly brave.'

Brave? She'd never thought of herself that way. Addy certainly wouldn't think that, nor Leo. Unless crazy-brave fell under that general description, which Roma sincerely doubted.

She changed the subject. 'When did you do all this work?'

'You mean the kitchen? It was only finished this past summer, which is why it still looks brand new. I'm pleased to say that Angas hasn't managed to do any major damage. Although, having said that, a month after the new dishwasher was installed he tripped backwards over it, went arse over tit and dented the lid. I had to get the whole thing replaced.'

Roma laughed. 'How is that even possible?'

Connor smiled back at her. 'I think he'd just gone through puberty that morning and he still wasn't sure what to do with all those long arms and legs. Being a teenager is a shocker, right?'

Roma had to agree. She wouldn't go back there for anything.

Connor took a step closer, nodded at the container Roma had in her hands. 'I don't mean to be presumptuous, but is that what I think it is?'

She'd been holding her Tupperware like a shield, pressed against her stomach.

'Yes. Lemon slice, as promised.' She handed it over.

'Thank you from the bottom of my stomach.' He lifted the lid and held the container up to his nose. 'Oh my god. I'm having some now.' He popped a whole piece into his mouth and chewed it languorously, all the while smiling at her.

'So, Roma, tell me. What would go best with your incredible lemon slice? A white or a red?'

'A sauvignon blanc, of course. If you have it.'

Connor opened the gleaming stainless fridge and produced a bottle from one of the finest wineries in the Adelaide Hills. She watched him while he took a gleaming glass from an overhead cupboard, poured hers and topped his up. He rounded the island bench and handed the wine to her. He was so close she could smell soap and the beach, and when he looked down at her she felt that twinkle in his eyes like a heat lamp.

'Cheers, big ears,' he said.

'To lemon slice.'

'To lemon slice,' Connor chuckled and clinked glasses with her.

Roma and Connor had moved outside and were sitting in two canvas chairs on the wooden deck which ran the length of the back of the house, looking out over the backyard. The space was as big as Bayview's. There was a big lawn, freshly mowed, and then a neat line of fruit trees along the back fence, one of which she could see was the lemon. Connor had carried the wine in a silver bucket full of ice and put it on the deck between them, and Roma had brought out the rest of the slice.

She took in the view and tried to relax in Connor's company. She listened to the distant waves and the wind whisper all around them. It was a lovely spot, not as nice a view as her balcony, but lovely and calm and secluded all the same. As she sat in silence, Connor ate. She tried not to count, but he didn't say a word until he'd devoured six pieces of her lemon slice.

When he was done, he slumped back in his chair, his eyes to the sky, and patted his flat stomach. 'That is unbelievable.'

Roma felt a strange rush of pride. 'Thanks.'

Connor turned his head to her and looked at her with raised eyebrows and a grin. 'No. You don't understand. When I say unbelievable, I mean un-fucking-believable. Better than my mother's and she learnt from her mother who passed the recipe down from her mother and her mother before her. I mean better-than-the-bakery unbelievable.'

He lifted his glass of wine and reached it over to Roma, his gaze never leaving hers as he paid her this tribute. She clinked glasses with him.

'No wonder Angas ate the whole lot,' he said. 'And I'm sorry it took me two days to realise what you'd done for us.'

'Don't worry about it.' Roma felt lightheaded and happy.

'I would have thanked you sooner had I'd known.'

'Your thanks just then was pretty good.' Roma cocked her head to the house. 'He doesn't say much, does he?'

'Angas? Nope.' Connor looked back to the house and thought for a while, his brows furrowed. 'I try not to worry about all the time he spends in his room. It wasn't what I did when I was a kid but, you know, that was last century, as he continually reminds me. You know,' Connor grinned, 'when I found your container under his bed and asked him where the hell it had come from, he muttered something about "the old lady next door".'

'When I was fourteen I thought anyone over twenty-five was *old*.' Roma chuckled. 'I suppose to him I am ancient.'

Connor sat up a little in his chair. 'How old is ancient?'

'I'm thirty-five.'

'Ah, you're a spring chicken.'

'And you?'

'Thirty-nine. I'm about to hit the Big Four-oh.'

'How does that feel? Are you freaking out about that?'

'In a weird way, no. I've felt old since about the time Angas was born. There's something about becoming a parent which takes you from cool to middle-aged overnight, I reckon, no matter how hard you fight it.'

Roma looked into her glass, swirled the wine around. 'I've heard that.'

'You don't have any kids?'

Roma looked into her wine. 'What about Angas? Is he an only child?'

'Yes, he is. His mother and I separated when he was two years old and neither of us have had any more kids with anyone else, so it's just him. Well, him and Buster. Sometimes I think it would have been better for him to have had a brother or a sister. He might not have been so lonely when he was a little kid, all that.' Connor shrugged off the thought. 'Ah, parent guilt. It's a killer. It keeps you awake at night. It makes you doubt everything you do and it gives you grey hair.'

Roma couldn't help but look at his hair.

He leaned towards her. 'Now you're checking out my grey hair, aren't you?'

She laughed and felt shy suddenly but didn't look away. She made an exaggerated point of inspecting his temples, his forehead and his hairline. 'I can't see any.' And then her gaze drifted, bravely, to his gleaming blue eyes and his mouth, his lips full, slightly parted.

He waited while she took in every detail. 'Good answer.'

'Although … it is getting dark,' she teased. When his smile grew warmer, she realised he seemed to like it. She liked it too, this banter, this getting to know Connor, this slow revealing of herself. 'Do you want Angas to be a lawyer, like you?'

'You think that would be a bad idea, right?'

'No. It's just that I think kids should choose their own path in life. It's hard enough out there in the big wide world without trying to live up to anyone else's expectations. Especially your parents'. It's up to him, isn't it?'

He looked at her, clear-eyed. 'I agree with you. Angas can be whatever he wants to be. And at this point in time, he seems to think that his future lies in getting rich from posting videos to YouTube.'

'Is that even a thing?'

'Apparently it is a thing. Honestly, as long as he doesn't end up being a client of mine, it's all good. My folks hoped I'd take over the dairy farm one day but once they got the hint that my interests lay elsewhere, they never pushed. They let me find my own way in the world, make my own decisions about what I wanted to do. That's the kind of father I'm trying to be.'

Roma remembered her own parents. She was sure they were disappointed that she hadn't aimed higher, studying law or social work at university so she could go off and save the world, one downtrodden individual or community at a time, but they'd never told her so exactly. When she and Tom had announced their engagement, they'd sat her down without him, and asked her if she was sure. She'd told them that she was, that she loved Tom and she was choosing this life with him. Perhaps she should have listened to them more. Maybe they should have tried harder to chip her out of her comfort zone, to assuage her fears, to broaden her horizons, to challenge her. Then she felt guilty for thinking they had any blame to share for her decisions. She'd been an adult when she'd accepted Tom's proposal. When she'd chosen that life.

Connor picked up the wine bottle and Roma pushed those thoughts aside. She held her glass to him for a refill and he topped up his, too.

'Sorry. All I've done tonight is talk about Angas.'

'Don't be sorry. I asked.'

'So what's Addy up to tonight?'

'She's got a date.' Roma tried not to sound cynical.

Connor sat up. 'It's not with Blake, is it?'

'How did you know?'

'He told me about this hot redhead who came into his shop and since there's only one hot redhead in this town, I did my lawyer thing and put two and two together.' He looked at Roma intently. 'He's a good guy, you know. Do you know what they're doing? It better not be dinner at the pub.'

'I don't know where they're going. I just didn't really want to be there if they came back to Bayview. I didn't want to be a cock-blocker.'

Connor laughed so hard he almost choked. When he stopped and had wiped the tears from his eyes, he leaned towards Roma. His gaze dropped to her lips and she felt her heart, slamming in her chest. Something she hadn't ever felt in her life.

'I can't believe you just said that.' He was still grinning.

'Why? You don't think I know what it means?'

'No. It's not that. It's just not what I ever expected you to say. You seem to have this wall around you, this reserve. The one I've been trying to crack since we first met.' He gazed at her: her eyes, her cheeks which she was sure were flushed, her lips where he lingered for a moment longer. 'You're a bit of a mystery, Roma.'

A mystery? She knew part of what he'd said was true. She had created a mask to hide behind. *You're always smiling*, someone had told her once, an acquaintance of not very long standing. *You're always so happy.* She was clearly good at the pretending. If only people knew what was behind that mask. Things much too hard to ever say out loud to anyone. Secrets she worked over in the middle of the night, when she tangled herself in the sheets and kept herself awake. There were things she'd never told anyone, least of all Tom. Because those deep, dark secrets were the truth about her life. A life unfulfilled and empty. They were about her failures as a daughter, as a person, a woman and a wife. If she'd been so unhappy, why had she stayed with Tom for so long? Why had she put herself through that intense misery? And she'd wanted to scream at him sometimes, too. Why don't you leave? What are we doing to each other?

Yes, she was a mystery. Even to herself. 'Listen, Connor. Things have happened in my life ...' She trailed off, unsure of how the story would feel if she told it out loud.

He leaned forward, rested a hand on hers. It was warm and reassuring, which she hadn't expected. 'I'm sorry to hear that. I really am.' He waited a moment before asking, 'Is that why you came to Remarkable Bay? Were you looking for a fresh start or something?'

Roma took a deep breath and then a sip of wine to calm the racing of her heart. 'Something like that.'

'If you want to talk about it, I'm a good listener, you know.'

Connor waited while she considered what else to say, if anything. And when Roma didn't elaborate or explain, he took another piece of lemon slice from the container and bit into it.

'I get the fresh start thing. That's what I did when Angas's mother and I divorced ten years ago. Shit. I've just realised that. Ten years ago last month.' He settled back into his chair, holding his glass of wine on his denim-clad thigh and looking at her. He was serious now, looking a little like he was about to mount a prosecution for the defence in court.

'Okay, this is me,' he started. 'I'm a small-town lawyer with no ambition to do anything else and I love my kid to bits, which you might have guessed already.'

'That's obvious. And nice,' she said quietly. The breeze picked up to a gust and rustled the leaves in the fruit trees, which sounded like faint applause from a distant open-air concert. She could smell the lemony tang of her slice and the salt in the air from the beach not far away. And she was aware of his presence, of being with him, talking intimately like this about things that were real and important.

'My parents drive me nuts but that's normal,' he continued. 'My two brothers are idiots and I'm an idiot when I'm with them. I've never smoked and I like to surf. Even when it's eight degrees out there and the wind whips up straight from Antarctica. I drink, as you can see.'

'Nothing wrong with that,' Roma added, raising her glass.

'I don't reckon there is. I tell myself I'm supporting the local wine industry.' Connor laughed and sipped his wine. 'I've been around the block a time or two. Most people at my age have. I've been sad as hell and there are times when I've drunk a little too much, but no more or no less than any divorced father who wonders what the hell's going to happen to his kid in the carve-up of a marriage. But I got over it. I bounced back. I've had a couple of relationships since the divorce, nothing serious though. One woman couldn't stand Angas and the other one tried too hard and Angas ended up hating her, so that was never going to work.'

Connor studied her face and Roma knew he was trying to find a reaction in her eyes to his openness, his honesty. His case. He was mounting a case for himself, giving her the facts about him so she could judge him. He was wanting her to decide if he was someone she wanted to spend more time with. She still didn't know. She still wasn't sure. Her courage and her fear tussled with each other.

'You bounced back,' she said. 'That's admirable.'

'That's all you can do, right? Especially with a kid. You put them first and wait until they've grown a bit and you keep in the back of your mind that one day, when you're ready, the right person might move in to the house next door to you.'

Connor reached for her hand, his palm upwards, his big hand waiting for her.

She didn't move.

'Roma,' he said low and quiet. 'Put your hand in mine.'

She waited. Considered.

'Come on. See how it fits.'

And she held her breath and waited until she'd run out of excuses not to do what he asked. She put her hand in the warmth of his grasp and his big hand slowly closed around hers. Something inside her shifted. The wind got louder in her ears, or perhaps that was her heartbeat.

Her hand fit just right in his.

'You make me laugh, Roma,' he said. 'And you're beautiful.' He leaned across the arm of his chair, his body closer to her now, and tugged her hand just a little so she moved closer, too. 'But none of that would have mattered if that lemon slice had been mediocre.'

She laughed nervously. 'There's something about your lemons.'

'There's something about you.'

She held his hand tighter, fought the fear of saying it out loud. He'd said she was brave. Was she?

Roma took a shuddering breath. 'I was married for a long time but my husband died three years ago in a car accident. We had a dog called Charlie who slept on my bed every night for two years until he died, too. One day I realised I couldn't do that life anymore so I sold up and came down here to Remarkable Bay to find myself another one.'

Connor's eyes were soft as he pulled her hand to him. He pressed his lips to the back of her hand. And then they sat in the fading evening light, hand in hand, not saying another word for a long time.

CHAPTER
23

Addy didn't know why she'd laboured over what to wear. Within five minutes of arriving at Blake's shop, they walked through a back door to his house, and without a word having been spoken, she was naked and lying flat on her back on her bed with Blake between her legs. It was exactly what she'd wanted. A man, an orgasm and diversion. She gasped and gripped the sheets as she came.

God, it felt good. It took her out of her head, made her feel like someone else. She'd been around actors long enough to have picked up some tips about pretending, although she'd had a pretty good handle on it before then. But she didn't need to pretend how good it felt.

One hot minute. That's all it had taken to get from the space where they should have been saying hello to this. When they'd walked through to his house, Blake had pushed her up against the living room wall and looked at her before kissing her hard and fast and so hot she wanted to fuck him right there on the shag pile rug. No words. Not even her name. He knew somehow that she didn't need it. She wanted sex, not romance. A fuck, not a future, and she'd picked well.

They made it to his bed and stripped each other, fast. He'd urged her back on the sheets and she went willingly, thrillingly, marvelling at how fast it was happening, how little she'd had to explain. And then he'd used his tongue and his mouth on her and she'd squeezed her eyes shut to savour her orgasm, its ripples and quakes and, a minute after hearing the ripping of a condom wrapper, she felt him lower himself on top of her. Instinctively she spread her legs and cradled him into her.

When Addy looked at his bedside clock, it was ten past nine.

Blake was on top of her, all around her, breathing hard, waiting until his heartbeat slowed. It took a moment before he propped himself up on his elbows and looked at her. He took in her mouth, her cheeks, the curve of her jaw, her nose. And when he slowly came closer and kissed her, his lips were soft. It was so unexpected and tender that she froze.

She only wanted sex. She pushed her hands against his chest.

'What?' he said, his voice gruff.

'I need to get up.'

He didn't argue or protest but rolled off her. Addy sat up and her feet hit the floor. She felt his hand on her back, warm and strong and calm. She closed her eyes, thinking about how his hands had felt when they were roaming her body, exploring her, pleasuring her.

'Where you going?' he asked, his voice croaky, his fingers tracing a sensual trail on her hip.

'I'm going home.' In a jolt, her fight with Roma was back in her head, every line of dialogue crisp and clear, as if she were listening to it through headphones in an editing booth. The place she was living wasn't her home. It was Roma's. Once again in her life, she'd been an interloper in Roma's life. She took in a deep breath to stop herself from crying about Roma's accusations, and the sudden realisation that was making her chest constrict. She'd done it again. She used sex to distract, to dissemble, to remind herself that her body was desirable, that she was wanted by men. That she had some worth.

And what had she done? She'd shat in her own nest. She was so far from having a home now it was laughable and, judging by their fight, she guessed she might not be welcome at Bayview one minute longer.

Blake was gazing at her as if her hesitation meant she was changing her mind about wanting to stay. She hadn't changed her mind. She was now more adamant than ever.

'I'm going,' she said dryly as she walked to the door. She found her maxi dress on the floor and slipped it over her head. She should go. She needed to go. With one last look at Blake, she found herself unable to move. How could he look so relaxed when she felt as jittery as an Oscar nominee on awards night? Half his body was covered with blankets, but his chest was bare and his feet were hanging over the end of the mattress, his toes pointing to the ceiling. He hadn't moved, but was watching her glowering at him, a sly grin on his lips.

'Tell me something, Addy.' He drawled her name slow and sexy. 'By the way, is that short for something?'

'Yes.'

'What?'

'Adelaide.'

'You're kidding.'

'No.' If he ever met her mother he would understand. She pulled herself up. What the hell was she talking about? He was never going to meet her mother. She hadn't dared introduce any of the men who had been in her life to her parents, together or apart. If they'd spent one minute in Dr McNamara's company they might imagine Addy was just like her and run. 'I've really got to go,' she repeated.

Blake narrowed his eyes at her. 'You a vegetarian?'

'That was your question? You want to know if I'm a vegetarian?'

Addy was used to unusual questions in the production office. *What time does the sun come up? Can you make sure there are no clouds tomorrow? Can you find me a hotel room with good feng shui? I will only eat coconut paleo balls while I'm acting. And only with organic coconut. I will not have any pretty extras on set. Will you get rid of that blonde one with the legs immediately?*

'Yep.'

'No,' she answered, flummoxed into answering. 'I'm not.'

'Good.'

'Why is that good?'

'Because I'm cooking you dinner tomorrow night.'

'No, you're not.'

'Yes, I am. You do eat, right?' He looked her up and down, and she didn't like the scrutiny.

'Look, Blake. You don't have to bullshit me and I'm not into playing games. I'm a big girl and this was just a fuck. You got lucky. Get over yourself.'

He grinned, still so effortlessly sexy that she wanted to slap his face.

'And,' she continued, 'I'm not interested.'

'In games or in bullshit?'

She noticed he hadn't thrown himself into the mix. 'You don't need to cook me dinner or buy me wine or chocolates or flowers.'

He shrugged. 'What time's good for you?'

She rolled her eyes. 'How about never?'

'Seven o'clock.'

'I said no.'

He got out of bed. Stretched. Addy shivered. She was around beautiful people all the time but there was something about this man, something that she'd felt during sex but couldn't define. He walked to her, his beautiful surf-toned body moving slowly, each muscle doing its job in a perfect rhythm, but didn't touch her. After what they'd just shared, not touching him was torture.

'No,' she repeated.

Blake reached for a strand of her hair and twirled it around his finger. She looked at his body, all flat planes and a shadow of chest hair, and then craned her neck to look into his eyes, to challenge him.

'I'm. Cooking. You. Dinner.' Each word was punctuated by a tender kiss. Her forehead. Her left cheek. Her right. Then her mouth. Addy didn't want to like it or need it.

'We don't have to eat. This is just fucking, remember?'

He slid an arm around her waist, then he smoothed his other hand down her belly, along one thigh, inching up the fabric of her dress until he hit skin. Then he pressed his palm against her, and found her sweet spot with his long fingers.

'Oh, damn,' she moaned, her knees buckling. She was still tender and throbbing from the last time and so ready for another go round she was almost there.

'You want this?' he whispered against her cheek, his fingers moving slow, then faster, soft then hard.

'Yes … yes.' Addy lifted her arms around his neck and held on, letting him take all her weight.

'Then come to dinner.'

She managed to say, 'Okay, okay, you win.'

'It's not a fight, Addy,' he whispered into her ear.

It always was for her. Always.

Roma and Connor had moved inside when the mosquitoes had begun to buzz around them like tiny invisible stealth bombers and they'd opened another bottle of wine. Angas had remained sequestered away, gaming in his room, although he'd emerged for food at one point, during which Connor had roused on him for not saying hello and he'd reluctantly waved as he'd carried packets of cheese crackers back to his room. Connor had warned him off what remained of the lemon slice and if Angas cared that she was in his house, he didn't show it.

They'd sat on the sofa and talked for hours, laughing gently at each other's jokes, sharing and debating their passion (him) and loathing (her) for Scandinavian crime dramas.

'All that snow!' she'd laughed.

'Great scripts!' he'd answered. 'And a female prime minister.'

When Roma finally checked her watch, it was midnight. They went to the kitchen and Connor returned her now-empty Tupperware container. Slowly, they ambled to the front door. Connor reached around her to open it, and she opened the screen door and moved out on to the veranda.

'Thanks,' she said. 'I enjoyed tonight.'

Connor followed her to the front gate. 'Me too.'

Then he was next to her. His arm bumped her shoulder as he took her hand. She let him.

'Look at that sky.'

Above them, the Milky Way sparkled like a million Christmas lights strung from one end of the sky to the other.

'It's so beautiful,' she sighed, squeezing his hand, her way of thanking Connor for getting her to look upwards and outwards.

She wanted to kiss him, knew he wanted to kiss her, but she let go of his hand. She couldn't take that step yet. When Roma was on the footpath, she turned back to him, smiled.

'I'll wait,' he said, his expression serious now, his normally twinkling eyes sober despite the wine and the night and the stars.

'Connor—'

'I'll wait.'

As Roma slipped into bed ten minutes later, she realised she wanted him to.

CHAPTER
24

1935

During the return journey to Remarkable Bay from the train station at Victor Harbor, Ruby tried not to feel like her heart was breaking. As the dry and barren landscape passed her by from the smudged windows of the taxi, she wished her final moments with Clara had been happier ones.

The train from Adelaide had chugged in to the station, causing much excitement. People had come to meet their family and friends and the all-important post which came on the train every day, and once the large crowd of new tourists had dispersed, there were only a few passengers left on the platform making the return journey to Adelaide. It was still the height of the summer season, after all, and there were still many more weeks of fresh sea breezes and sunny days to capture the attention of holiday-makers. Clara was going against the tide, it seemed.

They'd stood together on the platform, Clara clutching her suitcase in her hands, Ruby trying not to make a scene by crying.

'You'll write, of course,' she said, trying for matter-of-fact.

'Yes,' Clara had nodded, her eyes swimming with unacknowledged tears.

'Please send my best regards to Aunt Jane. Be sure to show her the Brontë, how well-thumbed the pages are. Tell her it's my favourite book in the whole world.'

'I will.'

When the conductor had called, 'All aboard,' Clara shrank back from Ruby. 'Don't cry, Ruby. People will see. They'll talk.'

'I won't,' Ruby managed. She had to be strong for them both. For the three of them: for Clara, for herself and for the baby. But the unanswered question still burned, the one Clara had shaken off earlier with a steely glare and a quivering bottom lip.

'Are you sure you won't tell me? Who … who …' Ruby couldn't say the word *baby* out loud in case anyone heard. 'Who is responsible?' she had whispered.

'Don't ever ask me again. And don't hug me.'

'Please, Clara. I'm allowed to say goodbye, surely?'

'Don't make a scene,' Clara hissed, her voice a fierce whisper, and she turned and climbed the steps into the carriage.

Ruby squeezed her purse to her chest and willed herself not to cry. She walked down the platform, standing on her tiptoes to find Clara, and spotted her through a window. She called her name and waved frantically. The whistle sounded and the train began to move, huge clouds of white smoke billowing into the air, as if clouds had fallen from the sky and created their own storm right there on the platform, with Clara and Ruby at its epicentre.

Clara didn't look back at her sister. Her gaze was stoically ahead, to her future, however mysterious and unknown it might be.

Ruby managed to compose herself until she arrived back at Bayview. When she walked through the front door, Mrs Nightingale appeared seemingly out of nowhere.

'Ruby, there's a message for you. You know I pride myself in dealing promptly with all letters and telegrams, so I've been waiting here to give it to you.'

She looked down at the envelope. Her name was written across it in a neat hand and she hoped for a moment that it might be a farewell letter from Clara, full of things she hadn't been able to say to Ruby's face, perhaps holding a clue to the unanswered question. But she knew Clara's writing, and this wasn't hers.

'Thank you, Mrs Nightingale,' Ruby said, trying her best to summon a grateful smile. 'I'll head up to my room to read it.'

The proprietress nodded her head in thanks and bustled back to the kitchen.

Ruby's feet felt like lead. She bypassed the reception room, not tempted at all by the radio or the happy chatter, and made her way upstairs. She had to be strong for Clara. She was now the keeper of her secret. She still had managed not to cry when she opened the door to her room and found it thankfully empty. The sheets and blankets on Clara's bed had already been stripped off for washing and the striped grey-and-white cotton ticking of the mattress reminded Ruby of prison bars.

She didn't cry until she'd ripped open the crisp white envelope and seen the note addressed to her in handwriting she wasn't familiar with.

Meet me at the Harbour Master's Walk at 10pm.

It was from Cain.

That's when the tears came and wouldn't stop, as relentless as a winter storm, so fierce they squeezed her heart dry and scorched her throat. She threw herself down on her bed and covered her head with her feather pillow to stifle the sounds of her agony at everything that had happened. Her poor sister. Her dear sister. All she could see was the final look on Clara's face: the haunted despair.

How could her mother and father have done this to Clara? How could they have treated her so cruelly? Nothing would ever be the same in the Allen family, Ruby knew it with absolute clarity, felt it in the darkest depths of her heart.

And as she lay there, clutching the note from Cain, she also knew in the darkest depths of her heart that these terrible circumstances had forced her hand. She now had no choice but to marry Edwin Stuart and forget all about Cain Stapleton from Remarkable Bay.

And she had to tell him tonight.

At ten minutes to ten, Ruby crept out of her room and took the outside stairs. She supposed the sparse and heavy wooden steps had been constructed for safety, so that people could flee down them in case of fire. It was dim down the side laneway when she jumped the final step on to the dirt below. She smoothed down her dress, pulled her cloche hat lower down over her face and crossed the road.

The Harbour Master's Walk seemed ominous tonight. She'd walked the little pathway that led from the croquet lawns down to the bay a hundred times or more in all the years she and her family had come to Remarkable Bay for the summer. It had been Clara's favourite thing to do: to take the trail and search for birds in the coastal shrubs. There were robins and kingfishers and thrushes and dotterels and snipes. She'd often shown Ruby her sketches when she was younger, the pretty little drawings she'd compiled in one notebook after another, but after Adeline had teased her about her hobby, called her silly and girlish, Clara had kept her drawings hidden.

Clara had been taught to keep secrets.

There was no one about in Remarkable Bay at this time of night, for which Ruby was grateful. The only light was from the waxing half-moon, which was just bright enough for Ruby not to trip on the stone gutter as she crossed through the hedge and scuttled across the lawn. When she reached the sign, etched in wood and painted in white so it was bright in the dark, she hid herself in the shrubs and waited.

She reached inside her pocket and pulled out Cain's note. His handwriting was lovely: neat and even. This was all she had ever had of him and she would have to give it back. She simply couldn't take the risk of it being discovered in her things and with Adeline as a sister, there was every likelihood of that. Adeline's curiosity had no scruples: she seemed not to have soaked up anything from their mother or father, from school or church, about decorum. How was it then that Clara, careful, innocent Clara, had been the one to find herself in trouble?

All Ruby knew, as she waited in the dark for Cain, the sea breeze in her hair and the smell of the beach all around her, was that she didn't have the courage to say yes to him. Her fierce determination to choose her own life, her own fate, was yesterday's foolishness. She could bring no more scandal or ridicule to her family. After Clara's situation, she would never have her father's permission to break her engagement to Edwin. Twenty-four hours ago, she was in the mind not to care if she had his approval or not. Was it only three days ago that she and Cain had held hands in Victor Harbor and made promises about a future? Everything had seemed possible when she was with Cain, smart, handsome, caring Cain. But her world had flipped on its axis. One sister's scandal could be covered up. But questions about the behaviour of the oldest sister would lead to questions about the youngest and Ruby knew, even if she hated them, that there were rules. She had a duty to her family now, as the eldest, to do what was expected of her. She could not cause a scandal by breaking what everyone assumed was an engagement. And Adeline's engagement to Edwin's brother made things even more complicated. Could she make a decision that would ruin Adeline's life too? Wasn't the ruination of one sister in the family more than anyone could bear?

She couldn't do it. She wasn't strong enough, she knew that now. Clara had been the strong one, keeping her secrets, shielding the truth and stoically accepting her fate. Ruby had been off on a frivolous lark, carried away by ideas and emotions that she had no right to feel. Until the circumstances of the past two days had forced her to grow up, to be plunged into the adult world she merely imagined she had been on the cusp of before.

There were footsteps on the path. Ruby looked up. 'Cain?'

'Ruby?'

She recognised his suit by the gleaming white pocket kerchief. He'd worn it at the dance on New Year's Eve and it made her heart ache that he'd dressed up for her in his best suit.

'Hello, Cain.'

He reached for her, grasped her elbows in his warm hands and pulled her close. She wanted to kiss him but couldn't lose her nerve. When she detected a spicy aftershave, she tried to remember Clara's face. When she quivered at his touch, she tried to remember Edwin. And then she felt nauseous and weak-kneed and she wanted to sink into his embrace, into the comfort of his arms, into the promise of a world and a life far, far away from what was happening in her own.

'I'm so glad you came. I wasn't sure if you'd receive my note. I thought Mrs Nightingale might open it herself and that I'd be meeting her here tonight instead of you.' He laughed quietly and stopped when she didn't join in on his joke.

She felt her head pound and she held on to his arms, tight. 'Cain ...'

'What is it, Ruby?'

'Can we sit down?'

'Of course.' He took her hand and led her down the trail to a clearing. A weather-worn wooden bench was situated off to one side of the path. He guided her to sit down and then paced before her.

'Ruby, there's something I need to say to you.'

'Cain, I—'

'Please, Ruby.' He implored her to listen and she owed him that, she knew. Her heart thudded and her hands felt suddenly hot and then cold and then hot again.

'You're the loveliest girl I've ever met and I meant what I said to you on New Year's Eve. This year holds so much promise. The past few years have been hard ones for my family and for me, but I get the feeling 1935 is going to be a good year. I'm back at university which means I have decent prospects and after you and your family return to Adelaide at the end of your holidays, we can be together again.'

Ruby held a hand to her mouth to stop the words coming out: *no no no no*.

Cain tugged off his hat and knelt down before her. When he reached into the breast pocket of his suit jacket, she tried not to look. She couldn't touch him, but she couldn't will herself to keep her hand away. This was going to be the last time she saw Cain. She needed to remember what love felt like. The touch of his hand. The warm press of his lips. The adoration in his eyes.

He unwrapped something from a white handkerchief. 'This is my grandmother's wedding ring. I told my parents about you, Ruby, and they gave this to me to give to you. Miss Ruby Allen, will you marry me?'

Ruby leaned forward and clutched his hand with hers, so hard he made a play of flinching. 'Ouch,' he said and searched her face in the moonlight, waiting for an answer. When there wasn't one, he edged closer and continued in a nervous rush. 'I know we won't be able to get married until I finish university, but we can be engaged, Ruby. It's only two years. I'd like to go and talk to your father and ask his permission. And until we marry, we can spend as much time as possible together. We can go to the picture theatre and dances at the Town Hall and take walks in the Botanic Gardens and play tennis. We can be together, Ruby, from today and forever, if you'll say yes.'

Ruby had never before wondered what the worst day in her life might feel like. Now she knew she was in it. Her head swirled and her stomach roiled. The waves in the bay below seemed suddenly explosively loud, battering her ears with their rhythm. Her heartbeat seemed to be breaking her ribs it was that painful.

'Ruby?'

'Cain,' she managed through her quivering lips. 'Dear Cain.' And she managed to say the words she'd been dreading. 'I can't marry you.'

Cain was so shocked he fell backwards and he stayed there, his legs splayed out in the dirt, his chin on his chest.

'Please, Cain. Let me explain.'

What could she tell him? Not the truth, never the truth.

'I've … I've been foolish and I let myself get carried away down here at Remarkable Bay. With you.' She squeezed her eyes closed so she didn't have to see Cain's stricken expression. 'I have obligations that I recklessly … foolishly tried to ignore. It was only today, when I received your note, that I was reminded that I am engaged to someone else. I can't possibly cause any hurt and disgrace to my family by breaking that arrangement.'

'I don't understand, Ruby. You said … you told me you don't love him.'

'I shouldn't have said those things. It was wrong of me. I've been so selfish.'

His voice was low now, ragged. 'Are you saying that you don't love me, Ruby?'

How could she break his heart? Hadn't she seen enough broken hearts in the past two days to last a lifetime? It would be easy to lie, to tell him she didn't love him. But she couldn't bring herself to. 'Please come and sit with me.'

He got up from the ground and sat on the bench next to her. The warm strength of his thigh pressed against hers and her heart shrank at knowing this was the last time. She reached for his hand, ran her fingers across each one of his, savouring the calloused fingertips and the tough pads on the fleshy part of his palm.

'I won't ever lie about that, Cain. About loving you. Please believe that I do love you. As I believe you do love me.' She wrapped her small hands around one of his large ones, tried to soak in their warmth and strength for what she had to say. 'This can't be, that's all.'

He was silent for a long while. He had every right to be angry with her. 'I understand. A farmer's son would never do for a Miss Allen.' The hurt dripped from every syllable.

'No, that's not it. Please believe me,' Ruby pleaded. 'A farmer's son would never do for my *father*,' she whispered. 'There is a big difference. An insurmountable difference.' She leaned her head on Cain's shoulder and he took her weight, slipping an arm around her and drawing her in close. 'I've been reminded, as if I didn't know it already, that daughters must bend to the will of their fathers. I have no other choice.'

'I'll talk to him,' Cain said, his back straightening. 'Once he meets me, he'll understand that I'm a good man, that I have prospects, that I will be able to look after his daughter one day. Surely, if he met me, he would see for himself how much I love you.'

Ruby shook and clung to him. 'You can't. It's hopeless, Cain.'

It was a long time before Cain spoke as they both waited for the hard truth to sink in. 'Can we continue to meet, here, until you go home?'

Ruby shook her head and looked up to the face of the man she truly loved. 'No.'

His eyes flashed dark and there was a twitch in his clean-shaven jaw. 'So this is the last night we'll ever see each other?'

'Yes.' She reached for his face, cupped his cheek and urged him closer. 'Please kiss me. One last time. I want to remember this always. This moment with you.'

And he did. He kissed her fiercely and desperately. Ruby didn't want to let him go, but it lasted only a moment and then he tore himself from her grasp.

He stood. She saw him drag his forearm across his face and heard him sniff. Her eyes filled with tears and she sobbed. He looked down at her, and she could see he was torn, but he held himself still. He tucked the ring back in his breast pocket.

'I'm so sorry, Cain. You can't know how sorry I am.'

'Goodbye, Ruby.' His words sounded final but he didn't move.

'I'll never be able to say it again but listen to me. I do truly love you.'

He put his hat on and disappeared into the dark.

Later that night, after Ruby had climbed back up the stairs, her legs a dead weight under her, and removed the piece of tree branch she'd slipped in the door so it would remain slightly ajar from the outside, she lay in the cool sheets of her bed and felt frozen. Adeline was breathing noisily across the room, having not even woken when Ruby had tiptoed back inside. She'd kicked off her shoes and slipped noiselessly under the covers in her dress, struggling to comprehend everything that had happened. She felt ten years older than when she'd arrived in Remarkable Bay with her mother and her sisters. Her whole world had turned in on itself and everything she knew to be true was a lie. Clara was pregnant to a man whose name she wouldn't reveal and their parents had treated their youngest daughter as a pariah. How could they have betrayed Clara in such a way? How could they have put status and reputation and church before family? Did they not love Clara? Ruby had always believed she and her sisters were loved by their mother and father but now she doubted even that. Their actions had made the ground beneath Ruby's own life less certain. She had always believed she would have her parents' support but now feared their actions if she'd gone ahead and broken off her engagement to Edwin. They had tossed one daughter on to the scrapheap, instead of holding her close and loving her, despite her predicament.

How could they? Ruby felt betrayed. Deceived. Cheated.

And that realisation would change her young life forever.

CHAPTER
25

2016

When things got complicated and hard and awful, Addy McNamara ran.

She'd been running for twenty years, since her parents had split and she'd been sent to stay with Roma's family at Remarkable Bay that first summer. Since then, she'd felt as if she was living on a fault line, one foot on either side of a precarious and rumbling split. There hadn't been solid ground under Addy's feet for a very long time. She'd been dislocated, pulled between her parents, dragged from house to house, from life to life, a witness to their fucked-up relationships with each other and with other people. School had been the same: one didn't fit so she was shunted to another, and another year of isolation and dislocation and navigating the schoolyard cliques of girls, so she didn't try. She gave them all the proverbial finger and slept with their boyfriends instead. And that set her apart, so she fought harder to be different, to stand out from the crowd, to show them she didn't give a rat's arse about what they thought. She'd created a world in which she believed that something new and better was always just over the horizon. That's why working in the film industry suited her: it was sporadic, short-lived, with intense highs for a couple of months and then, when she fell, no one was around to see her shatter.

If she kept moving, kept obfuscating, no one would see the real her, full of mistakes and regrets and imperfections. She'd spent a lifetime papering over hers, the fact that she wasn't smart or particularly clever. She knew she was too demanding of people's attention, but couldn't find a way to define why. Maybe because it stopped her disappearing. Maybe because if she stood still long enough, people would see her truth: how sad and lonely and broken she really was. If people looked at her, laughed with her, marvelled at how attractive and glistening she was, they wouldn't be tempted to dig deeper, to get to know her, because they would find out that's all she was. As brittle as old film stock, full of perforations and discolouration.

People liked her better when she was this Addy, the beautiful, sexual, flirtatious creature she'd created out of the shell of a scared, forgotten schoolgirl. And sex was part of reminding herself who she was. She needed the attention of men to help her feel anchored in this persona. When a man was fucking her, she knew who she was. She didn't have to be the real Addy. She'd started to be the real Addy with Jack Andersson. She'd let her mask slip, had believed he wanted her for more than sex, that she was his muse, his inspiration, the wind beneath his wings and all that crap. And he'd looked inside her, seen that crack in her and had pushed through, picking at her weaknesses, her failings and her insecurities.

She couldn't let that happen again or she would crack for good. Her mask was firmly back in place. Roma's condescension had helped her keep it there. She had learnt to accept that this was who she was, that this was the way she navigated the world. Some people, like Roma, thought deeply about things and were *good* people. Addy had never thought of herself as *good*.

She'd stayed in Remarkable Bay too long already. She would have to leave before Roma asked her to go.

She would have one more night with Blake Stapleton, a farewell fuck. A last hurrah.

The day after her argument with Roma, Addy walked out the front door at ten minutes past seven. She'd managed to keep her distance from Roma the whole day and had been thinking about her perfect distraction. There wasn't much conversation with Blake. It was just sex. No justifications, no explanations. And if he wanted to cook her dinner first? She would think of it as foreplay.

She knocked on the shop door and a minute later Blake answered. His T-shirt said 'Remarkable Bay Surf Shop' in retro lettering and below it there was a 1970s style bikini-clad girl with long hair holding a surfboard on her head.

'Blake.' Addy shifted her weight on to her left hip, dipped her head to the side. This was who she was. Addy McNamara could cock a hip and get men wanting her. A look down their bodies and they wanted to fuck her. And a lick of her lips and they were right there, doing exactly what she needed them to do.

This was who she was.

'Addy.'

He stepped back and she went in, following him through the shop, past the counter to the rear door she knew led to his house. She hadn't noticed any of this detail last night, having been too busy fucking, but the room was light and blue with high white ceilings and comfortable-looking dark leather sofas. A tall bookcase on one wall was crammed with novels, and there was a large TV on a cupboard in front of the fireplace. It was neat. Tidy. A high pile of surf magazines teetered on the low coffee table and Addy could smell something good. Something delicious.

'Your weren't kidding about cooking.' She sauntered over and put her handbag down on the kitchen table. She could smell peanuts and chilli and freshly cooked rice.

Blake went to the stove and turned off one of the burners. 'Indonesian spinach and pumpkin curry.'

'Oh wow,' Addy murmured.

Blake opened the fridge. 'Wine?'

Addy shook her head. On second thoughts, she didn't want this kind of foreplay. This was already feeling too much like a date, during which there might be actual talking.

She lifted the front of her dress, inching it up in her fingers. Blake's eyes drifted to her thighs. She watched the look on his face, the serious, hot, distracted look, the flare in his nostrils when he realised what she was doing, the dark flash in his eyes when she raised her dress far enough that he could see she was naked under it.

He slammed the fridge shut, crossed the kitchen in long strides and slammed her with a kiss.

Later, they were in his bed. Blake had reheated the curry and brought their bowls into bed. With pillows propped behind them, and one of her coltish legs draped over Blake's, they feasted on the delicious food.

'You should be a chef,' she murmured as she scooped a forkful of rice into her mouth.

He looked sceptical. 'Because of this? It's just a curry. It takes half an hour.'

'It's incredible.'

He looked sideways at her. 'You don't cook, do you?'

Addy shook her head.

'Pathetic,' he said with a low growl. He dug into his curry hungrily.

'It's not a life skill I value. I can get food anywhere at any time of the day or night. Well, at least I can when I'm up in Adelaide. And you know, even when I'm not, if I play my cards right, I can always get someone to cook for me.' She jiggled her leg against Blake's and he laughed.

'I bet you can.' He turned his attention from devouring his curry to devouring her with his eyes instead. 'Someone like you would never go hungry.'

Addy tried not to flinch. *Someone like her*. Why should she be surprised that he'd guessed that about her? Wasn't that who she'd shown him she was? She liked sex and she liked men and she'd revealed to him just how much an hour before. After he'd kissed her, crossed the room with that long-legged stride and enveloped her in his arms and with his body, he'd carried her ... yes, *carried* her ... to his bed. She'd fallen back on it and he'd pulled off her dress, his eyes never leaving hers, and then stripped naked himself and had loved her with his strong body and his hands and his tongue and she'd given back as much as she'd got. Long strokes, him in her mouth, loving how he groaned when he came, and then how he kissed her right after and slid into her, so fast and slick that she let go of needing to control, to control the sex, and let herself feel how good it was instead of pretending that it was hot. More than once in her past she'd had to resort to imitating Meg Ryan's famous scene in *When Harry Met Sally* to make men feel good and get herself out quick, but there had been no need to pretend with Blake.

'How long have you had the shop?' Addy asked.

'Ten years.'

'You like it? The retail thing?'

'Yep.'

'Ever thought of doing anything else?' *Keep asking him questions so he won't ask you any.*

'Nope,' Blake answered between mouthfuls.

'Did you ever want to leave Remarkable Bay?'

He waited. 'What makes you think I never left?'

'You said that ...' Addy fumbled. She studied the chunks of creamy golden pumpkin in the bowl she was holding. Why was she asking him so many questions? This was just sex, right? She didn't need to know his backstory, his history, his shoe size or anything else about him.

'I was up in Adelaide, first in school, then university, then working in a firm. I hated it.'

'You hated the city?'

'It's too far from the surf.'

'And you hated the firm? Are you an accountant or something?'

He shook his head ruefully. 'I was a lawyer.'

'Like Connor,' Addy noted.

'We're cousins. We went through uni at the same time. Even worked in the same firm. We still have fights about which one of us hated it the most. We used to meet at the pub after work and cry into our beers.'

Addy doubted that very much. 'So you both came back to the Bay.'

'I was first. My folks decided to sell up the shop so I bought it.'

'They still alive, your parents?'

'Nope.' He hesitated, looked into her eyes. 'Yours?'

'Yeah. I don't see them much.'

And then she saw it in his eyes. The don't-get-involved-with-a-woman-who-comes-from-a-screwed-up-family expression. Which was exactly the look she wanted to see. Drive him away now, she started to tell herself, before things flip and you don't want him to go.

'How does that go for a girl not to see her mother?'

Addy settled back into her pillow and drew her knees up. 'If you knew my mother you'd understand why I don't see her much.'

Blake finished his bowl and set it on the floor by the side of his bed. He turned back to her.

'Why are you here in Remarkable Bay?'

Lying came so naturally that it scared her sometimes. 'For Roma. She's been through a lot.'

'So I hear.'

'Did Connor tell you?'

'We need to talk about something when we're hanging off our boards for hours waiting for a wave.'

'I guess.'

Blake leaned across and ran a slow finger down Addy's cheek, her neck, over the curve of her breast and her nipple and then down to her belly button. She held her breath and let the sparks fly all over her body.

'How long you down in the Bay for?' he asked quietly.

'Not long,' she managed. 'I'm going back to Adelaide this week.'

She was leaving Roma, leaving the only happy place she'd had for more years than she could count, for what?

'What do you do?' he asked.

'I work in the film industry.'

His raised his eyebrows in surprise. 'You like the bright lights, huh?'

'I'm good at it. Organising people and things. Wrangling crews and equipment and schedules and budgets. It's a skill.'

'I get that. So when does the next film start?'

'I'm not sure.'

Blake took her bowl from her hands and she heard the clatter as he reached over and put it on top of his on the floor. Then, he turned back to her, reached an arm around her and pulled her close. She felt enveloped by him, not just by his strength. This seemed easy, Addy thought, to be with him. He must have been hiding something because she was acutely aware of the lack of drama, of tension, of anxiety. She hadn't known men like Blake. Either all they wanted to do was talk, be propped up emotionally, psychologically stroked, or they didn't want to talk, just fuck.

This thing with Blake seemed like it fell somewhere in between.

'If you play your cards right, I'll cook for you some more before you go,' he said, cupping her small breast with his big hand.

Addy felt the shimmer, reached out to grab it. 'A girl's gotta eat.'

Roma was waiting for Addy in the kitchen, sitting at the table nursing a lukewarm coffee. It was late, almost midnight. She'd restlessly tried to watch some TV but had switched it off, unable to concentrate on the plot. She needed to talk to Addy and figured this was the only time to do it. Addy had made herself scarce during the day, and had avoided Roma tonight by going to Blake's. Roma wondered if it was, in part, some kind of *fuck you* to Roma about what she'd said. About Addy and men. About Addy and sex. About how easy it was for her to get it, as if she was judging her.

She needed to tell Addy she had to pack up her things and go back to Adelaide.

The front door opened and then closed quietly with a clicking of the lock, and then there were footsteps down the hallway. Roma breathed deep and gripped her coffee cup with both hands, willing the final bit of warmth to seep through to her fingers.

When the light flicked on, she heard Addy gasp. 'Fuck. You scared the crap out of me.'

Addy was carrying her shoes in one hand. Her long, flowing dress was swamped by the navy hoodie she was wearing which almost reached her knees. The sleeves were so long they covered her hands and she looked tiny and fragile.

'Sorry,' Roma said. 'I didn't mean to scare you.'

'What are you doing sitting here in the dark?' Addy's voice was cautious.

Roma summoned her strength. That was something having Addy around had taught her. She wasn't going to bullshit any more. 'I've been waiting here to talk to you. To say sorry about what I said to you and that ...' Roma tried to get the words right in her head, to articulate why she was doing this, why she was kicking Addy out. 'I appreciate that you came down here to see how I'm going, Addy, but—'

'I'm leaving.'

Addy had interjected so fast Roma barely heard what she'd said. 'Pardon?'

Addy flicked her hair over one shoulder and crossed the room to the fridge. She took out the jug of water, took a glass from the high cupboard and filled it to the brim. She drank the whole thing down with barely a gulp.

'I said I'm leaving. I'm going back to Adelaide tomorrow. Thanks for letting me stay.' She put her glass in the sink then turned to look at Roma with an expression that was unreadable.

'You're welcome.'

'I'll be sure to call Leo when I get back and tell him you're doing great.'

There was silence in the room. In the quiet dark outside, not a sound. Inside, the faint ticking of the clock on the kitchen wall steadied Roma's heartbeat.

'What about Blake?'

'What about him?' Addy asked, the harshness of her tone scraping against Roma.

'Are you coming back down here to see him again?'

'Why would I do that?'

The two women, feeling more distant from each other than they ever had in their lives, stared at each other from opposite sides of the kitchen.

'Have you ever been in love, Addy?'

'What?'

'I asked you if you've ever been in love.'

'I've slept with lots of men, Roma.'

'Have you loved any of them?

'I don't have to love them to fuck them. This isn't the fifties, you know.'

'No, it's not.'

Addy walked across the room, past Roma, to the door. She hesitated and turned back. 'I don't need love, Roma.' Her voice broke on the words. 'It fucks you up in a million different ways.'

Addy had walked halfway up the stairs before Roma could tell Addy she agreed with her.

CHAPTER
26

1935

The north wind was blasting Remarkable Bay on the day of the annual croquet tournament between the guests of the Bayview and Sunnybrae guesthouses. It swept down from the open farmland behind the town and curled its tentacles around everyone and everything on the dry croquet lawn on Ocean Street. Ruby could have sworn the grass was greener yesterday; this morning it appeared to be browning before her eyes, crunching underfoot as she walked across to the starting stake at one end of the rectangular playing field.

That morning when Ruby had come down to breakfast, she had hoped to hear an announcement that the game might be at least postponed or cancelled altogether. One glance outside revealed how fierce the winds still were, the same that had lashed the town all night, making sleep impossible. Ruby had hardly slept, tangling herself in the sheets, her mind racing with a million thoughts of things she couldn't change but couldn't forget.

When Ruby had asked if the game might be off, Mrs Nightingale looked at her as if she'd lost her senses.

'Why on earth would we cancel the Cup?'

Ruby pushed her empty breakfast plate away. 'Because of the heat and that nasty wind.'

'Goodness, no. Especially not now that I've organised a replacement for young Jack Dougall. He was going to be our fourth team member, as you know, but he's upstairs in bed.'

'What happened to him?'

'He's so terribly sunburnt. He looks like a lobster. His mother told me he spent all day yesterday down there on the beach ...' She stopped, leaned closer. 'All day. Topless bathing, Ruby.' Mrs Nightingale didn't put much effort into hiding her disgust, as if one bare chest might turn Remarkable Bay into a modern-day Sodom.

'The poor thing,' Ruby said.

'His mother is this very minute applying the sunburn lotion I made up this morning. Milk, cream, lemon juice, a pinch of powdered alum and some sugar. I hope it brings the poor boy some relief.'

'I'm sure it will.'

'I'll see you at ten o'clock then with your sister? Across the road on the croquet lawn?'

'Yes, Mrs Nightingale, of course.' Ruby tried to summon some enthusiasm for the tournament. Clearly, it was very important to the woman. 'I hope we bring the Cup home for Bayview this year.'

'You're good girl, Ruby.' She leaned forward and lowered her voice. 'And here's a tip from the groundsman. He tells me it's a fast lawn today.'

'Oh, that's good news indeed,' Ruby added, unclear of the difference it would make to the game.

Mrs Nightingale bustled away to refresh someone's pot of tea and Ruby had steeled herself for the competition.

Two hours later, after she'd laid down and read a few quick pages of her book, a glance out the window revealed that the wind seemed worse. There was not a speck of relief in the dry air and it seemed to whistle about her ears as she crossed Ocean Street for the game. She looked ahead to her playing partners, who had already gathered at one end of the lawn, and Ruby desperately tried to come up with a reason to quit and retreat into the cool living rooms of Bayview for tea. She felt hot from head to toe, from her cloche hat, which was making her hair damp with perspiration, to her close-fitting cotton knee-length white skirt. Socks and flat shoes completed her outfit and made her feel even hotter.

Adeline had left before her, after primping and fussing over her outfit, and was already with James, leaning on the handle of her mallet, flirting with him. The propriety of fraternising with the opposition didn't seem to concern her. She wore white too, from head to toe, which made her auburn hair seem burnished gold, and she somehow managed to look crisp and unbothered. Ruby wasn't sure how her sister did it, although she had so little to be bothered about it shouldn't have been a surprise to Ruby. Her life was about to begin, wasn't it? She was to be James's wife within a few months. She was not troubled by Clara's pregnancy and banishment; of their parents' cruel treatment; and Ruby hadn't breathed a word to her about meeting Cain, let alone falling in love with him. Life had always been easy for Adeline Allen, and there was nothing to suggest that this charmed life wouldn't continue.

They really were a handsome pair, her sister and her soon-to-be brother-in-law. It was as if they captured all the beauty in the world in their forms. Perhaps that's why they seemed fated to be together, the sartorial and charming James and the glamorous and delightful Adeline. Soon, they would begin their glittering life together and give glamorous parties and take holidays to London and Paris on a P&O liner. Ruby was sure Adeline would have all of life's advantages. The trifling matter of them being on opposite teams today—James was captaining Sunnybrae's team for the third year running—didn't bother her in the slightest. Ruby had the distinct feeling Adeline might throw the game so her fiancé could be the victor. James Stuart was a striking sight in his white linen suit and his panama hat. The three other young men making up his team were all handsome too, and Ruby wondered if that was the criteria for selection or if it had happened by chance.

Adeline tore her gaze away from James. 'Where have you been, Ruby? Hurry on so we can get this over with.'

Ruby stood by her sister's side and spoke under her breath. 'Believe me when I say that I would rather be back at Bayview with a cool glass of water and a book. This wasn't my idea, if you remember. It was mother and father's.'

'You can forfeit if you like,' James said, smiling. 'Which would mean Sunnybrae would keep the Cup.'

'There's no honour in winning like that now, is there?' Ruby replied.

James raised an eyebrow. 'There's only winning, Ruby.'

They all turned at the sound of Mrs Nightingale's voice.

'I have some more lemonade for you all.' She was carrying a wooden tray in her hands with a tall glass jug and four glasses and caught herself once, stopping to right her load.

'Watch out, aunt.' The young woman walking just behind Mrs Nightingale skipped to her side to steady the glasses.

'Thank you, Edith. Such a good girl. This is my niece on my brother's side. Edith Robinson.'

Polite hellos were exchanged and Edith smiled politely before lowering her gaze.

Mrs Nightingale's cheeks were flushed and sweat beaded on her brow and upper lip. Poor Mrs Nightingale, Ruby thought. For the first time in all the years they had been coming to Remarkable Bay, Ruby saw how hard she toiled so her guests could have a relaxing holiday. She was up and about from first light, and she switched off the lights and locked the front door at night. She checked every pot of tea was just the right temperature and Ruby guessed she pulled the trays of scones out of the oven herself. All day, seven days a week during the holiday season, she managed the activities of Bayview, its guests and its kitchen and laundry, with attention to detail and great pride.

And now Mrs Nightingale was out in the heat bringing refreshments to her guests so they didn't faint. She really was a kind woman and Ruby realised, to her shame, that she'd never appreciated it before today. She was beginning to become aware of many things she'd never paid attention to before, as if she'd finally opened her eyes into the bright light and seen the world for what it truly was.

'Oh, you poor things,' the older woman clucked. 'Here. Have a glass of lemonade. I don't want you all to succumb before you've returned the Croquet Cup to Bayview. It's been a long time since we surrendered it and it's high time we brought it back to the mantel, don't you think?'

Ruby went to the woman and took the tray from her. 'Why, thank you so much, Mrs Nightingale. This is very considerate of you.'

'What are you doing?' she asked, flabbergasted.

'We're all braving the heat for the good of Bayview, aren't we? So we're all suffering equally. Why don't I hold the tray while you pour?'

'Why, that's very kind of you, Ruby.' Mrs Nightingale lifted the jug and filled each of the four glasses. Ruby thought how thirst-quenching they looked, with slices of lemon and mint swirling in each glass. She was already thirsty, the wind having dried her mouth in the five minutes she'd been outside. They each took a glass and sipped it thankfully while they waited for the two extra players. Bayview's team comprised a reluctant Ruby, a very reluctant Adeline and Edith, who was a strapping young woman with a wide smile. Ruby had seen her once or twice, when she'd looked into the kitchen at Bayview. Edith had been rolling dough on the big wooden table in the centre of the kitchen, her sleeves pushed up her arms, and singing quietly to herself, something that sounded like a lullaby. They made three players and they were still waiting for the sunburnt Jack Dougall's replacement.

'Oh, here he is!' Mrs Nightingale looked past Adeline and Ruby and squealed in girlish delight. 'I have a very good feeling about this match, ladies. A very good feeling indeed.'

Ruby lifted a hand to hold her recalcitrant hat on her head and turned to look.

Something in Ruby sparked and tensed. Cain was striding towards them, wearing white trousers and a white shirt, its sleeves turned up neatly to his elbows. Ruby would know his long-legged lope anywhere.

'Hello, Cain,' Mrs Nightingale called out.

Although Ruby had imagined his face a thousand times, she hadn't seen Cain since the evening at the Harbour Master's Walk when he'd dropped to one knee and proposed to her. It had been two weeks since the night she'd hurt him so terribly and herself, too. She knew she would regret her decision until she took her last breath. She had believed she would never see him again and yet there he was. This would be her last chance to savour every word, every look, every smile. They would have to last a lifetime.

Cain doffed his hat. 'Hello, Mrs Nightingale.' His voice was quiet and serious.

The older woman fluttered to him with a glass of lemonade. 'Thank you so very much for coming to rescue us today, Cain. We would have had to forfeit the game—and the Cup—if you hadn't been such a gentlemen.' She turned to Ruby and winked. 'He's a lovely young man, is our Cain Stapleton. Didn't hesitate when I told him yesterday that we needed a fourth team member.'

'You've been very good to my family over the years. It's the least I could do. Even if I don't know the rules.'

'It's easy,' Edith said. 'We're playing two games, with two teams of two. The object is to hit our balls through the six hoops in order and then finish by slamming the ball into the centre peg.'

'I can do that,' he said. 'Is that for me?' Cain asked, nodding to the glass of lemonade Mrs Nightingale had forgotten to give him.

'Of course. Here you are.'

Cain took the glass from her hand and lifted it to his lips, drinking slowly, his head back, exposing the tanned strength of his neck to the sun, until the glass was empty.

Ruby tried not to look, tried not to feel the quiver inside at the sight of him, but couldn't draw her eyes away. He didn't give the glass back to Mrs Nightingale, but walked to Ruby and placed it on the tray. She held her breath as he approached.

There was the quickest of glances but his lovely aqua eyes were cold, his mouth unsmiling. 'Hello, Miss Allen,' he said, almost under his breath. Despite what he'd said to Mrs Nightingale, he didn't appear to be happy about being called in to save the day for Bayview.

'Hello, Mr Stapleton,' she replied, her voice as breathy as she felt.

And then Mrs Nightingale was beside her. 'Do you two lovely young people know each other? My heavens. How did I not know that? Isn't it wonderful of Cain to step in when we need him so desperately?'

Ruby looked at her feet. 'Yes. It's very kind.' I would expect nothing less from a man like Cain, she wanted to say. For so many reasons, she held her tongue.

'Well, well, well. Who's this ring-in?' James approached and turned his attention to Cain. He stood to the side, holding his croquet mallet like a cane in one hand, with Adeline glued to his other side.

'This is Cain Stapleton,' Ruby said, before Mrs Nightingale could make another fuss.

Ruby watched the way James eyed Cain up and down, studying his height and the strength in his shoulders, before extending a hand and shaking Cain's in a reluctant greeting. James was clearly judging his competition and believed his team might come up wanting. 'I've seen your face before. Have we met?'

Cain looked at James directly. 'Yes, I think we have. I deliver milk to Sunnybrae.'

'Right. Yes, that must be it,' he replied, his tone suddenly cold. 'Listen, old chap. I do believe you're wearing cricket whites. Not sure they're suited to the croquet courts of Remarkable Bay or to our friendly competition. I'd hate for you to be disqualified on a technicality.'

Cain looked over the lawn to the bay, glistening blue, the horizon hazy in the distance and the heat. 'Whites are whites, I would have thought.'

Adeline nudged James. 'Oh, James, don't be such a fuddy-duddy. I'm sure you're going to win, so what does it matter? Can't we just start so we can get this game over with?'

Ruby noted Mrs Nightingale's crestfallen expression and interrupted before Adeline could be any ruder.

'It's because of the heat, Mrs Nightingale. That's what my sister means. She feels it much more than we do, what with her pale complexion.'

Cain gave Ruby a quick, knowing glance before holding out his hand to Adeline. 'Miss Allen, I'm Cain Stapleton. Pleased to meet you.'

Adeline looked at him distractedly, her hand extended. 'And you.' They shook politely and then Cain's hand dropped to his side, forming a fist.

Ruby watched the awareness flare in his eyes, and it was only the slightest glance her way that revealed he understood her connection. This was her sister, Adeline, who was about to marry James Stuart. Edwin's brother. She wanted to cry for him and for herself, too. The ties that bound her to her world were real to him now, on stark display on the croquet lawn of Remarkable Bay, and that hurt her more than words could ever explain. He had come face-to-face with her future, and the people who would populate it, and Cain, dearest Cain, had kept his chin held high and his pride intact. She found herself loving him even more.

'Let's begin this game then, shall we, before we all fry?' James rearranged his panama hat and his team mates materialised around him like a Roman phalanx. 'A coin toss all right with you, Stapleton?'

Cain reviewed his team. Ruby, Adeline and Edith.

'We're ready,' Ruby said.

Cain called, 'Heads,' as James threw a sixpence in the air. They watched it spin and flip and then land on the yellowing lawn. It landed tails.

'Tails it is,' James announced.

Adeline cheered as if they just won a Test against England with one ball to spare. Ruby thought it particularly disloyal.

'I believe we'll start,' James announced, 'Harry, you and I will be the first team and we'll take the blue and the black.'

'I'll go in the first team,' Edith said. Adeline was quickly by her side. 'And so will I. The sooner I can sit down the better.'

Ruby and Cain held back while the first game got underway. James played the first ball and it sailed through the hoop and down the court. The players walked off after it which left Cain and Ruby alone at the starting stake.

'How are you, Cain?' Ruby finally asked.

'I'm very well, thank you, Miss Allen.' He was following the play. Edith had just struck the ball and it had careened out of bounds.

'Are you familiar with the game?'

'Not one bit. Only the toffs play croquet.' Ruby heard what he meant. 'I like to swing a cricket bat, myself.'

'I'm only doing this for Mrs Nightingale. She's been so good to us over the years and this Cup seems to be very important to her.'

Ruby avoided Cain's eyes by studying Adeline's attempt at a roquet. She missed the ball and seemed to have hit her foot instead, although not with much force judging by her giggles. James had dropped to one knee to inspect the damage more closely.

'It is important,' Cain said quietly. 'Her husband set up the competition as a novelty for guests before he went off to the war. He died in 1917, at Pozieres, and since then, Mrs Nightingale has run this place on her own. Even when times were very tough, she always took our milk. She almost single-handedly keeps the butcher going, not to mention the grocer.'

People were indeed more than they appeared. Ruby was learning that now. She'd never thought enough of Mrs Nightingale to find out anything about her. Ruby turned to Cain. 'So that's why you agreed to play with our team today.'

He looked at her a long time before answering. 'Yes. For Mrs Nightingale.'

She had no right to hope he was playing to see her. It wasn't fair to think it. It wasn't right to wish for that to be the case. Her heart wept at the realisation of all that she'd lost.

Adeline seemed to have recovered and was limping after her ball. 'Where's your other sister?' Cain asked.

Ruby swallowed the lump in her throat. 'She's had to leave us, I'm afraid. She took up an excellent opportunity to study in Melbourne. Ornithology.'

'Congratulations to her. But I thought your father didn't approve of study for girls?'

Ruby obfuscated. 'When it comes to the youngest daughters, I do believe they can get away with anything.'

James was in play now and he seemed to be taking the whole game rather seriously, judging by his slow deliberation of the trajectory of his ball. He leaned down, eyed the court, and then stood, front on, holding the mallet like a pendulum between his legs, swinging it back and forth in practice before he lowered it and whacked the ball hard and fast. It rocketed along the grass and slipped through a hoop without touching the sides. Traitorously, Adeline applauded.

'So it's his brother you are to marry.'

Ruby took a deep breath, hoping it would help the word slip out without it scratching her throat. 'Yes.'

'Is he—your fiancé— anything like his brother?'

Ruby shook her head. Edwin was nothing like James, in looks or in temperament, in achievement or ambition. 'No.'

'I'm glad to hear it.' Ruby was confused at the disdain in his tone. 'For whatever faults you may see, James does love my sister.'

'I would concede that.'

Ruby's curiosity was piqued. 'Why have you taken this set against James? You don't know him at all.'

Cain looked at her. 'Edwin isn't here for me to hate, so I'll hate his brother instead.'

Ruby let his words sink in. 'I can't believe you could ever hate anybody. It's not in your nature, Cain. I know that about you already.'

Cain leaned close so he could be sure no one else would hear. 'I do hate him and his brother and I always will. Because he will have you, Ruby. The life you will create with him will be the life we should have had. Can't you understand that? If I can't love you, I will forever hate the man who does.'

Ruby held on to her mallet, pressed it into the ground for some purchase to stop herself from toppling over. He'd had two weeks to think of what to say, about how to react, to find the words to hurt her. He'd been very successful. She felt his anger and his hurt.

'You can't mean that, Cain. All this talk of hate.' She couldn't name her greatest fear, that it wasn't Edwin he really hated but her. For what she'd done to him. For loving him when she wasn't free to. How could she live with herself?

'This is the world you've chosen over me, is it? The croquet and tea parties and someone else's freshly squeezed lemonade delivered to you on platters, and families like them.'

Ruby felt the tears stinging her eyes, rising up once again at the knowledge that there was so much she couldn't say. She would have to let Cain believe the worst of her if that was what it took to protect Clara and to protect her family.

'Is this why you agreed to play on Bayview's team, Cain? So you could turn up and tell me all the things you really feel? About how much you hate me and my family?'

Cain's fingers clenched tight around his mallet, his knuckles whitening. 'You know that's not true, Ruby. I could never hate you. I've told you the truth once about how I feel and I can't say it again, for my own sake.'

There was a loud crack in front of them. A blue ball had hit the closest stake and landed with a thud near Ruby's foot.

'One home, one to go,' James announced with a smirk as he positioned himself next to Ruby. Out of the corner of her eye, she saw Cain take a deep breath in, and straighten his spine.

'Well done, Stuart.'

'Why, thank you. How do you think you'll fare with him as your partner, Ruby?' James nodded to Cain.

She pressed her lips together for a moment so she could get her scrambled thoughts in order. 'I think we'll make a perfect team, James.'

And she walked up the court to cheer Adeline home.

CHAPTER
27

The trunks and suitcases belonging to the Allen family had been packed for hours and had been waiting out by the front fence in neat rows in the blazing January sun.

As the two Miss Allens and their sombre parents waited on Ocean Street for their taxi driver to pull over and load everything, Ruby was determined that no one would see her tears.

Five Allens had arrived and only four were returning early to their outwardly comfortable Adelaide life. Where was Clara? Ruby had thought about her sister with an ever-increasing sense of dread. She must have reached Sydney by now, of course she must have. It had been two weeks since Ruby had escorted her youngest sister to Victor Harbor to take the train back to Adelaide. It had only been two weeks but it felt like an eternity. She'd had to bear the entire secret burden of what her parents had done to her younger sister, smuggling Clara away as if she were a criminal. Every day since she'd left, Ruby had waited for a letter, a note, something to indicate Clara had arrived in Sydney and was safely with Aunt Jane. Every day, she was disappointed by Mrs

Nightingale's news that nothing had come down in the post on the Adelaide train.

If Ruby was racked, Adeline was clueless; believing without question the lie that Clara had taken up an opportunity in Melbourne to study. She had been too completely lovesick about James anyway to pay Clara any more attention in her absence than she'd done in her presence. She'd spent little time at Bayview in their final two weeks in Remarkable Bay. Adeline was preparing for her life as Mrs James Stuart, and had spent more time with her future in-laws than her own family. Ruby had been relieved at her absence. It meant she had their bedroom to herself during the day, and didn't have to hide her tears over Clara or Cain. She hadn't had the energy to do much of anything other than to go over and over everything that had happened during that final holiday.

Ruby had gone downstairs for meals and tried not to cry when she saw the creamy butter set out in white bowls on the tables. She couldn't eat it any more and, in fact, didn't have much of an appetite for anything. Two days after Cain's proposal, she'd written to Edwin, telling him the news: that she had decided to say yes. He'd written back immediately—that same day judging by the date on the letter—setting out in sensible terms how happy he was to hear it. She had explained that she thought they should be married as soon as possible. She couldn't tell Edwin the reason why: that it was unthinkable for her to stay in her family's home after what her parents had decided for Clara. Her rage hadn't subsided since she'd waved Clara off on the train. It had merely calcified, stuck in her throat like a fish bone. She knew she could bring no more shame to her family, but she could no longer look her parents in the eye and see a real family. Their actions had struck at the very heart of love, of compassion, of any sense of security Ruby had ever had. The only way out, the only way to escape them, was to become someone's wife. With the heaviest of hearts and a dulled sense of her own future, she had agreed to go forward into a future she knew would be empty and loveless.

Ruby was acutely aware that she would be leaving every feeling of happiness and joyousness and love right here in Remarkable Bay, amongst the grains of sand and the sizzling rays of the sun; in the cooling night breezes and the blasting northerly winds; out in the ocean's depths and in the cries of the gulls.

'Is that everything?' Mrs Allen looked over the bags. 'There seemed to be more cases when we arrived. Oh—'

She glanced at her husband, who cleared his throat and looked away. Mrs Allen opened her purse for a handkerchief and turned away too, trying not to let her daughters see she was dabbing at her eyes.

'Well, come on then, girls,' their father instructed. 'Into the taxi.'

The driver opened the front passenger door with a flourish and a bow. Before they all got in, each member of the Allen family looked back to Mrs Nightingale. She stood at the front gate, looking slightly forlorn. As their parents said their restrained goodbyes to her, Adeline slipped an arm through Ruby's and tugged her down the street a little so their conversation wouldn't be overheard.

'This is it, Ruby,' she said. 'It's the end.' There was a hint of emotion in her voice, but it was well-concealed.

'Yes,' Ruby said, squeezing her sister's hand. 'Our holiday is really over.'

Uncharacteristically, Adeline dropped her head on Ruby's shoulder, and Ruby stiffened. She wasn't used to such displays of emotion from Adeline being directed towards her.

'No. What I mean is … this is the last time we'll be here like this. As sisters. You and me. And Clara, but she's gone already … oh, you know what I mean about Clara. She won't miss me. She's always thought I was silly and inconsequential.'

'That's not true,' Ruby started. But she knew it was true. Perhaps Adeline had more insight than anyone had ever given her credit for.

'Do you think she'll ever want to come back here for a holiday once she's experienced all that Melbourne has to offer?'

'I don't know, Adeline. All I know is that she loved it here, more than almost anywhere.'

'I've been wondering if her studies will be finished in time for her to come back for the wedding. It's only three months away and it's really not that far on the train. Do you think Clara will come home for the wedding?' Adeline looked truly perplexed, as if Clara's absence was constructed to hurt her somehow. In that moment, Ruby felt sadder than she had felt any day since Clara had been sent away. Not only had her parents ripped Clara from her family, they'd torn three sisters apart. Ruby wasn't sure they would ever recover from the schism. Clara's secrets must always remain hidden from Adeline. Ruby would forever feel torn between the two of them. How was that situation ever to end well?

'I'm not sure if she'll be able to get away, Adeline. We'll see.'

'Do you think she hates me that much that she would stay away on purpose?'

'She doesn't hate you, Adeline. You know that's not true. You bait each other, that's all.'

'I would like to have her in the wedding party. I want the three Allen sisters to be together one last time,' Adeline said excitedly. 'Have you thought that this time next year, you and I will both be married?'

Ruby hoped Adeline didn't feel her shudder. The two sisters looked down to the end of Ocean Street, where the road seemed to disappear into the sea, and breathed their last of the sea air for the summer. Ruby's premonition about the summer had been right, after all. This would be the final time she would holiday with her sisters or her parents ever again. And Ruby knew, in her heart, that she could never, ever return to this place.

'Girls!' Their mother called impatiently.

Adeline leant in and whispered in Ruby's ear. 'Shall we continue this tradition in years to come? Holidays at Remarkable Bay, I mean? With our own husbands and children? I'm sure the boys would think it was a wonderful idea. Won't it be lovely to be together again down here?'

'Yes.' Ruby patted Adeline's hand, reassuring her but sure in the knowledge that secrets would pull them from each other eventually. 'That would be lovely.'

The two Miss Allens said fond farewells to Mrs Nightingale, and stepped up into the taxi for the journey to Victor Harbor to meet the train.

As the car pulled away from the street, chug-chugging until it reached a travelling speed, Ruby took one last glimpse out the window to the croquet lawn and the sign marking the Harbour Master's Walk. Where Cain William Stapleton had proposed to her. Where she'd said no and her heart had broken. It was the spot where her true happiness lay, crushed in the sand like sea shells on the ocean floor.

She focussed on a figure and then gasped, smothering it with a hand so her sister and her parents wouldn't hear or turn to look. Cain was there, at the Walk, in his tweed suit, clutching a bunch of white carnations in his hand, his arm limp by his side. He was still golden, still lovely, but not smiling now for this final goodbye. His blond-brown hair caught the sun and gleamed in the light and his aqua-blue eyes tore into her.

She pressed her fingers to the glass. Cain lifted a hand to wave back, and then he was gone.

CHAPTER
28

2016

Roma had been too distracted to think about her for a while, too upset about her fight with Addy and too distracted by getting to know Connor.

But now the mysterious Miss Clara Allen was at the front of her mind once again, niggling at her, her name and her mystery part of a gnawing curiosity that wouldn't rest.

It was the day after she'd asked Addy to leave—although Addy had got in first and acted as if it was her idea—and the rain fell steadily throughout that grim Saturday. Roma had planned to make a start on the front garden, to pull out the half-dead and misshapen shrubs and reveal the original front garden layout amongst the cement pathways, but the rain hadn't let up. The sky was thick and grey and the streets were empty, and Roma's mood was as grim as the bay. She'd had some lunch, although she wasn't really hungry, and tried not to hear the sounds from upstairs of Addy packing. She'd made one trip downstairs to the laundry to shove some wet clothes into a plastic bag, and detoured to the kitchen for an apple without saying a word.

Roma needed the distraction of the past. Since her present was unsettling, she decided to spend some time investigating online, so she set herself up on the kitchen table and flipped open her laptop, her fingers clicking on the keyboard as she opened a search engine. She tried the simplest approach and typed in the words 'Clara Allen'. In a half a second, she discovered a sports reporter in Texas who was tweeting about a college football game. Then there was a cross fit instructor in Liverpool who was touting for clients with suggestive pictures of herself in poses which didn't seem entirely about exercise. Roma scrolled through pages and pages of search results with no luck returning anything that was meaningful or Australian.

There were bouncing footsteps in the hallway, then, 'Hey.'

Keira appeared, looking like a triathlete in her clinging fitness gear. She was incongruously carrying a plastic bag from the bakery on Ocean Street. 'The door was unlocked,' she announced and then hesitated. 'You don't mind me dropping by, do you?'

'Of course not. Come in.' Roma waved her over to the table. It would be nice to have a distraction from the negative energy flowing down the stairs.

'I've been waiting for the weather to break so I could go for a run, but it looks like it's settled in. And then I got bored so I thought I'd bribe you with cakes so I could hang out with you.' She put the bag on the table and Roma peered inside.

'You don't need to bribe me with cakes, but good call.'

'Where would I find some plates?'

'The cupboard on the far right. Up top.'

While Keira searched, Roma went to the coffee machine. She checked it was filled with water before slipping an aluminium pod into the slot on the top and pressing the brew button.

'No classes today?' Roma set two cups on the benchtop.

'I had two earlier this morning. Four people turned up for my ten o'clock class. Can you believe that? Four whole people! And they were all smiling when they left!'

Roma chuckled at the look of genuine amusement on Keira's face. 'How many turned up last week?'

'Only three. Four is so much better than three.'

'That's really great, Keira.'

As Roma fussed over the coffees, Keira continued. 'I knew it would take time. And I have nothing but time at the moment. But my new clients keep coming back and that's a vote of confidence in what I'm doing, don't you reckon? I've been thinking of doing some classes down on the beach when it's warmer, maybe in January when the holiday-makers arrive in all those other towns up and down the coast. I could put an ad in the local paper, spread the word online as well. It could be really great to get people to come down to the Bay with a towel and have them staring out to sea while they're exercising. Blue sky above. Warm sand underneath. What do you think?'

Roma brought the coffees and the plates to the table.

Keira put an iced finger bun on each one.

'You're evil.' Roma smiled.

'I know.' Keira laughed in response. 'So what do you think? Pilates on the Bay? That's it! I can't believe I came up with that name just like that. *Pilates On The Bay*. It's good.' She lifted her bun and stuffed it in her mouth for a huge bite. 'Oh, so is this.'

Roma picked at the coconut sprinkles stuck to the strip of white icing along the length of the bun. 'That's a great idea. Pilates on the Bay. I like it. I'd even come and you know I only do your classes twice a week so we can have wine afterwards at the pub.'

'I take that as a compliment, considering how terrible the wine is. Honestly, between you, me and Addy, surely we can convince them to stock some decent labels. McLaren Vale is only half an hour from here, for god's sake. It can't be that hard.'

Roma cheered inside. If Keira was talking about the wine at the pub, perhaps she was thinking about staying. 'That may involve many hours of research at a number of local wineries.'

Keira smiled widely. 'I see where you're going with this and I like it. So, have I interrupted you? Are you doing some online shopping or something?'

Roma pressed the space bar on the keyboard of her laptop to wake up her screen. 'I'm doing some research on this house and the people who stayed here. Wait a minute. I'll get the guest book I told you about and show you.'

Roma retrieved the volume from a shelf in the living room bookcase and returned to the kitchen, laying it out on the table next to her laptop. She opened it carefully to show Keira the first page and the handwriting.

'This is so old,' Keira said in amazement. 'And the handwriting is so beautiful. I wish I could write like that. You should see mine. I spent too many years taking notes in lectures. It looks like two pigeons landed on the page and did some breakdancing.'

Roma tapped the page with her forefinger. 'These are the names from December 1934.' The two women leaned in and studied the book. 'There she is. Ruby Allen, my great-grandmother,'

'And this Adeline. That's Addy's great-grandmother, right?' Keira asked.

Roma nodded. 'They were young women on holidays with their family during that summer. I do know that both went back to Adelaide and got married in 1935. Not long after they were here. I had no clue they stayed here at Bayview. It's strange isn't it, to think that they walked these halls. Sat in the big room overlooking the street to eat their breakfast.'

Keira looked at Roma, her eyes thoughtful and questioning

Roma continued. 'What we can't figure out is who this is?' They both peered down at the place where Clara's name had been scratched into the page.

'Clara. That's a lovely name, too.' Keira's fingers lingered there. She traced the script with an index finger. 'So no one in your family has ever heard of her?'

Roma shook her head. 'No. It's like she was here in 1934 and then disappeared.'

Keira rubbed at her arms. 'Ooh, I just got the shivers. It must be all this talk about disappearing. Being here in this old house. You'll be pulling out the ouija board next.' Keira glanced around cautiously. 'Do you think Bayview has ghosts?'

Roma scoffed. 'Ghosts?'

'Yeah, you know. Have you ever heard any strange noises? Any unexplained things that go bump in the night?'

'The only thing in this house that goes bump in the night is me when I get up to go to the loo. I don't believe in ghosts and I can't believe that you, as a scientist, can even mention them with a straight face.'

No, Roma didn't believe in ghosts, at least not the kind that appeared in the schlocky horror movies Addy worked on. She believed in ghosts of other kinds, of emotions that congeal inside of you, of secrets that sit in your gut and eat away at you, of memories that haunt you at night. Those ghosts were very real, still.

'It's all a bit of fun, Roma. Don't you love a good horror movie? Don't you love sitting down with some hot popcorn and scaring yourself shitless in the dark?'

Roma shivered. 'Not in the slightest. I can't believe you like them. Clearly, we can never be friends if that's your taste in movies.'

They laughed together and turned their eyes back to the guest book.

'Did she die soon after this, maybe?' Keira pondered. 'People died of things back then that we can't imagine now. Diphtheria. Appendicitis. Sepsis. Have you searched for a death record? I know that sounds morbid, but there should be one.'

Roma shrugged. 'I haven't yet. If Clara married and changed her name it might be even more impossible to find her.'

'What about your family? Don't they know anything about her?'

'I can't ask my parents any more. Addy was planning to ask her mother if she knew anything, but she hasn't mentioned anything to me yet.' Roma wondered if they would ever talk about Clara—or anything else—ever again. 'We weren't particularly close to all those other parts of our extended family. After the second world war, everyone drifted apart, according to my mother. My great-great grandparents lost all their money in a cattle investment up in the far north of the State, apparently, and things were never the same between all the branches of the family tree. You see, we used to be

quite well-to-do once. But it all blew up over money and one side
of the family didn't talk to the other side and then as the generations
went on, there were more sides than a … one of those mathematical
shapes with all the sides.'

Keira laughed. 'You mean like an octagon?'

'Exactly.' Roma thought about that history as she drank her coffee. 'There were as many stories about what really happened as there
were people. The real story got lost in a game of Chinese whispers
and my parents didn't really connect all the pieces until I started
school and met Addy. When her mother and mine met at the school
gate, they figured out they'd seen each other before, at a family
funeral I think, and they worked out they were distant relations.'

'That's so nice. Maybe you secretly knew you were related,' Keira
suggested.

'If we did, it wasn't obvious at first. We sat next to each other and
I didn't like her because she stole my first best friend. And then I
broke her favourite pencil. It wasn't until years later, when we were
teenagers and Addy's parents had just broken up, that my mum and
dad decided she could do with some time out from her horrible situation and she came down here to spend summer with us as well.'

'And then you became best friends again?'

'Something like that.' Roma turned her attention back to the
book. She was glad of this new and undemanding friendship she'd
managed to cultivate with Keira. It was so much easier than navigating the jealousies and rivalries of her relationship with Addy.
Maybe it was because she was a scientist, not a drama queen.

'Don't you have old family papers? That kind of thing?' Keira
furrowed her brow in concentration.

'Whatever we had from that side of the family was lost in a
bushfire.'

Keira's attention snapped back to Roma. 'How awful.'

'My grandparents survived, which was the important thing.'

'Of course. When was that?'

'In 1983, during the Ash Wednesday bushfires that terrible February. They lived in the Adelaide Hills near Norton Summit. We

were living down near the beach so we were okay. I wasn't even two years old, so I don't remember it.'

'So,' Keira said, reaching for the laptop. 'You said you were googling her name? This Clara Allen?'

'Yep.'

'You don't have a middle name?'

Roma shook her head. 'I didn't find anything.'

'Let me try something.'

Roma swivelled her laptop around. Keira did some quick typing and then stared at the screen, waiting for a page to load. 'It might be worth searching Births, Deaths and Marriages. I have to admit, I'm more used to researching birds, migratory patterns and aquatic environments but this might be worth a shot.' She waited while a page loaded. 'No, I don't want to register a birth.' Keira huffed and typed some more.

A birth. The words stung and Roma fought the tears. Out of nowhere the memories came flooding back. She'd spent so many long, fruitless years wishing and hoping Tom would change his mind and agree to have a baby. He had never understood her desperation and she couldn't seem to explain it in a way that made any sense to him. It was primal and hormonal, not logical. It wasn't rational, she knew, the way she had had everything mapped out in her head. What it would feel like to have a swelling tummy. The thrill of the first ultrasound. The thumping sound of the first audible heartbeat. The shopping for all those tiny jumpsuits that babies seemed to need by the dozen. All that desperate longing had come to nothing. They'd never agreed. The dream had consumed her almost every waking moment for years, had been the weapon she and Tom had used against each other, and suddenly, on the day of his death, she'd had to come to terms with the fact that her dreams of a child had died as well. She couldn't see into the future to imagine meeting someone else, to going through all that pain and heartache all over again, so she slowly had become resolved to the idea that she would never be a mother. Eighty years after Gertrude and Wilhelmina Smythe had signed Bayview's guest book,

she would be as much a childless widow as she assumed they had
been.

Keira sat up. 'Hang on, this looks promising. Oh, right. They
want me to pay.' She glanced at Roma. 'Do you want to pay?'

Roma frowned, her enthusiasm for searching for Clara dulled
by her memories of Tom, of children. Of how things had soured
with Addy. She suddenly wasn't in the mood for history, for looking
backwards at her mistakes. 'Not really.'

Keira turned the laptop back to Roma. 'There must be archives
somewhere up in Adelaide that would hold that kind of information. You could find a birth certificate for this Clara Allen, maybe.
It's what? Eighty-something years ago? It can't be too hard. They
must have digitised the records by now.'

Sadness swamped Roma like a wave and the laptop clicked as she
closed it. 'Maybe she's not related at all. Maybe she was an older
woman, a friend of Wilhelmina and Gertrude's.' Roma pointed to
their elegant signatures. 'Maybe they all came down here to find
husbands and found love with each other instead.'

Keira chuckled. 'It's hard enough being different in 2016. Imagine back then, in 1934? Imagine if you were gay or a lesbian or
anything else not considered *normal*?' Keira held her fingers up,
miming quote marks. 'So many people must have kept so many
secrets. What if Wilhelmina and Gertrude did love each other?
How could they ever be honest about who they were?'

'Not in their lifetimes I'm sure. And forget about being a gay
man. It was a crime to commit homosexual acts in South Australia
until 1975, later in the other states.'

'And it wasn't a crime to be a lesbian?'

Roma raised an eyebrow. 'The men who made the laws didn't
believe that women could have sex without a man.'

'That's the only kind I'm getting,' Keira scoffed. 'How do you
know all this stuff?'

'My brother Leo's gay. When he came out, my parents gave us
social history lessons over dinner.'

Keira dropped her chin into her hand. 'Damn.'

'Damn what?'

'I thought I might put the hard word on him at Christmas.'

Roma chuckled. 'Sorry. You're not his type. Although he might want some personal training while he's here.'

'I'll take any business I can get.' Keira sipped her coffee. 'You know what's interesting? This has made me realise that I don't know much at all about my family's history. My grandfather came to Australia from Europe after the war, all on his own. I've never met any of that side of the family, and my grandmother was adopted in Sydney. So our family tree is more like a shrub.'

'Do you have any brothers or sisters?'

'I've got a younger half-brother. My dad ran off with one of the other maths teachers at his school when I was twenty. They've got a son, Nate, who's five. And mum has step-children from her second marriage, but they're all older than me.'

'Sounds like that shrub is getting bigger all the time,' Roma laughed.

There was a jangle of bracelets in the hallway. Roma and Keira looked up.

Addy was at the doorway, glancing from one to the other. 'Hello,' she said, her voice cool and her face blank.

'Hey, Addy,' Keira said happily. When neither of the other two women said a word to each other, Keira looked at Roma, puzzled.

Addy crossed her arms. 'I'm all packed.'

Roma nodded and stared at her empty coffee cup.

'Where are you going?' Keira asked, turning in her chair to the door, where Addy seemed stuck.

'I'm leaving. I have a production job back in Adelaide. It's an ad. It's only a couple of weeks' work but beggars can't be choosers.'

Keira bounced to her feet and went to Addy, throwing her arms around her for a hug. 'That's great news about the job. What's it for?'

'A new IVF clinic. I'm going to be spending the next two weeks organising and wrangling screaming, shitting babies and their angelic parents. I can't think of anything worse. But a gal's gotta do what a gal's gotta do.'

Roma couldn't look up from her twisted fingers. She wanted to pick up her laptop and toss it across the room. 'Safe travels, Addy.'

'See you, then,' Addy replied. She turned and left. A moment later, Roma and Keira heard the front door slam.

Roma took a deep breath. There was no mention of coming back. Not a word of thanks. Maybe they'd been flogging a dead horse. Perhaps there was no friendship left with Addy. Roma had said goodbye to people before, loads of them. Addy, a million times. University friends who'd left Adelaide and never returned. Her grandparents. Her parents. Acquaintances who'd drifted away. Leo, when he'd moved to Sydney. Old, old friends when Tom had died. Roma was good at losing people. This wouldn't hurt one bit.

There was a hand covering hers. It was Keira's. 'Are you all right, Roma?'

She looked into Keira's eyes. There was something in the soft brown, the kindness, that undid her.

Keira sat silently with her as Roma dropped her head into her crossed arms and sobbed.

Addy drove down Ocean Street to Blake's shop and pulled up out the front. It was five minutes to five and still raining. She knew he closed the place at five so she waited in her car. She needed Blake this one last time. She needed somewhere she didn't have to think and that was his bed. Or his kitchen table. Or the sofa, or outside on a blanket on the back lawn. Once, it had been his car. In three nights, they'd fucked everywhere and often. Every night since the first time, fast slow, every which way. It was so much easier than talking. She didn't want to talk much and he hadn't pushed, which she couldn't figure out because lawyers were normally full of smart talk and words, but she liked it. He was still. Yes, that was a word for him. He used his body to speak to her and that said all she needed to know.

And he'd taken her straight to his bed, exactly as she'd wanted him to.

Now, after, they were lying together in the peaceful quiet of the twilight. The rain had stopped hammering on the tin roof and there was a beautiful and tranquil red sunset over Remarkable Bay. Outside, through Blake's bedroom window, she could see the first stars shining above. Addy tried to focus on just one. *When you wish upon a star.* She blinked. Another lie from another movie. Her dreams had never come true. Not once, no matter how hard she had wished them to.

Blake moved next to her. She hadn't told him she was going. She was going to. Right now.

'Blake?' He draped an arm over her body, pulling her close. They were both tired, having worn each other out one more time.

No words, just fucking. Keep moving. Be a fast-moving target. Don't let anyone in.

'What?' His voice was deep and sleepy and it sounded so good. He softly kissed her shoulder.

She tried to focus on what she had to say instead of the warm press of his lips.

'I'm leaving. Remarkable Bay, I mean. I'm going back to Adelaide.'

She could have sworn he stilled, tensed, his body all around her stiffened. 'When?'

'Now. My car's packed.'

She tried to kiss him but he turned his head to the side. 'Were you going to tell me?'

'I'm telling you now.' She laid her cheek against his chest, listened to his heartbeat. 'I got a job. The person who was supposed to be doing it is stuck in Bali. The planes aren't flying because of the volcanic ash cloud. I start tomorrow.'

'Well,' he said slowly.

'Yeah,' she replied, gliding a hand down his chest and stomach and hips to his cock, needing him to know that she wanted him again, needing to distract herself from the wave of something rising, a torrent of confounding emotions she didn't want to feel.

He let go of her. Got out of bed.

'Blake,' she implored. 'Come back to bed. One last time.'

He looked over his shoulder as he slipped on the jeans and T-shirt that she'd tossed across the room a couple of hours ago. 'You've got to go, remember? I'll see you to your car.'

Addy sat up slowly, pulled the blankets to her breasts. 'Blake ...'

'I've got some leftovers. I'll pack them up for you to take home. Make sure you eat.'

Addy drove away from Blake's with leftover curry and pappadums. The taste of Blake on her lips. And regret about Roma pounding in her head like a migraine.

CHAPTER
29

'I'm sure he doesn't like me. He barely said two words the whole time.' Roma carried a stack of dirty plates to the dishwasher, which Connor was loading.

He threw her a warm smile. 'You expect conversation from a fifteen-year-old boy? You have a lot to learn. If I get a grunt or two I'm delirious.'

She did have a lot to learn about Connor and about Angas, about the way they talked to each other, a shooting-the-shit style that revolved around Connor ragging on Angas for being a stinky slob and Angas returning fire with barbs about his father being old and past it. They'd been putting on a show for her, she knew that, and it filled her heart with joy to see how much they loved each other. Her eyes had pricked with tears more than once.

It had been Connor's idea to ask her over for dinner with Angas. He didn't say it, but she knew this was his idea of taking it slow, waiting for her. He'd made it clear what he'd meant when he'd told her he would wait: that when she was ready for another man in her life, he wanted it to be him.

And in the meantime, dinner with Connor and Angas was just another Saturday night. Nothing big or overblown or symbolic. It was just fish tacos and a colourful salad, with lemon slice for dessert, of course, which was all delicious. Despite Connor's reassurances that this was just a meal and it was just Saturday night, the evening had felt like some kind of audition for them all. Connor was trying her out on Angas. And Connor was trying her out for himself. She understood it was an important step for Connor to invite a woman to his home. She remembered what he'd said about the two women who'd been in his life since his divorce, that one couldn't stand Angas and the other one had tried too hard and Angas ended up hating her.

Roma tried to remember being fifteen. It was the summer of the end of things with Addy. Roma had been studious and cautious, while Addy had been wild and self-obsessed. Angas didn't seem to be either of those things. He was a boy, or rather, that combination of boy and young man that fifteen year olds are.

'What's the matter?' Connor closed the dishwasher and reached for her arm. 'You're frowning.'

'I'm not frowning.' Roma created an exaggerated smile instead.

'You are so frowning. You get those two crooked little wrinkles between your eyebrows.'

Her fingers flew to the spot. 'Now you're saying I've got wrinkles?'

'It's only fair,' Connor replied, poking her arm playfully. 'You've pointed out my grey hair on more than one occasion.'

Her gaze lifted to his jaw, where there were streaks of grey in his dark stubble.

'See? You're doing it again!'

She laughed and he did too, and they stood on either side of the open door of the dishwasher, looking at each other. His sparkling eyes and his warm smile said so much more than words could and Roma felt a flush of awareness heat her face. She knew how important this was. She'd been invited to dinner with his son. This meant something to Connor. It meant something to her, too.

He had laid his cards on the table. The next move was up to her.

Angas pushed his chair back from the table and stood. 'Dad, I'm going back to my room, all right?'

'Sure.'

Angas was at the doorway when Connor called after him. 'Hey. You going to thank Roma for the slice?'

'Thanks, Roma,' he said without looking back and then Angas disappeared into his room.

Roma leaned down and closed the dishwasher door. 'I don't know much about kids. Teenagers. Boys. Whatever you call a fifteen year old.'

'Join the club. But you did bring lemon slice for dessert. And I don't know about Angas, but it definitely has some magical powers over me.'

Roma looked up into his aqua-blue eyes. Such a happy face. Such a happy smile, all for her.

If she wanted it.

And she still wasn't sure.

'Thanks for dinner. It was really great.'

'You're going?'

'Yeah, I think I should.'

Connor was disappointed, she could see it on his face. 'I can't tempt you with another glass of wine?'

Roma shook her head nervously. She wanted to stay. She really wanted to stay. 'No, thank you.'

She crossed the room and picked up her mobile, tucked it into the pocket of her jeans. Connor followed her down the hallway, past Angas's loud music and then to the front door. Outside, under the stars, they stopped and looked upwards. Bright and constant for a billion years, they flickered and watched over Remarkable Bay.

'I never get tired of this,' Connor murmured, craning his neck back to take it all in.

'Me, neither,' Roma whispered. Perhaps this moment was the reason she had come to Remarkable Bay. With her heart beating fast and her imagining a future for herself she had never thought possible, she felt on the precipice of her new life. If she had the courage to reach out for it.

She turned to Connor, smoothed her hands over his chest. She felt his lungs expand and then still. He was holding his breath, as was she. She took a step closer and their bodies were touching. When she pulled the fabric of his T-shirt into her hands and tugged him closer, his hands found her hips.

And then cautious, scared, by-the-book Roma Harris took the biggest leap of her life and kissed Connor Stapleton.

The next day, Roma really threw her rulebook out the window and asked Keira if she wanted to move into Bayview. She couldn't explain why it seemed like a good idea, but it felt somehow right. Keira was easygoing, fun to be around and undemanding in her friendship and since Addy had gone back to Adelaide Roma had missed having another person in the house. Perhaps that was the biggest surprise for her—the fact that she liked company. And now perhaps she was ready to change gears, to create the next part of her life with new people in it. Keira and Connor could be those new people and she could be renewed around them. It was a relief to be with someone who didn't look at her like the lonely widow she was. It was also a relief not to feel like the lonely widow.

Kissing Connor had definitely had something to do with that. When he'd held her cheeks in his hands and she'd slipped her arms around him, something fell into place. Something that felt ancient and new all at the same time.

As Roma walked down Ocean Street at five minutes to nine, with a spring in her step that had been missing for so many years, she was hoping to catch Keira at the end of her morning Strength for Seniors class. The oldies liked to be up early, Keira had explained, and it was becoming one of her more popular sessions. Roma figured one of the joys of being retired might be that you didn't have to get out of bed early if you didn't want to. Staying in bed until ten with a good book was high on her bucket list for her senior years.

Some might see what she'd done, the move to Remarkable Bay with no job and no plan, as retirement, but it was nothing of the sort. It was a hiatus, she'd wanted to explain to everyone. It was a break from the real world and all its burdens and memories and regrets, one she so desperately needed until she could sort out in her head and her heart what she wanted to do in the next stage of her life.

Roma knew she would have to make a decision about work soon. She had money behind her, but it wasn't as if she'd won the lotto and she'd spent a few thousand of it already on the house and living expenses during the past three months. She would have to go back to work soon but she could survive into next year and would think about it then. Perhaps it could be the focus of her New Year's resolution. But she could see a future for herself finally. The feeling was akin to lifting one's legs out of quicksand: what had slowly been dragging you under was no longer a weight.

It was freeing, this feeling she'd woken up with on a sunny Friday morning. And whether it was Addy being gone and taking all that emotional drama with her, kissing Connor or deciding to invite Keira to move in, Roma felt better than she had in a long time.

When she reached Keira's studio, people were just leaving. Roma lost count of the cheerful smiles, some of which were returned to her as she waited by the door.

'Hey,' she called out.

'Hey, yourself.' Keira switched off the music and leant over to pick a mat off the floor. As she rolled it up, she looked at Roma, her face bright and her eyes smiling. There was a new understanding in her look. Keira had comforted her when she'd burst into tears after Addy had left. They'd taken a step forward in their friendship and had crossed the line from acquaintances to friends, and Roma couldn't have been happier about it.

'How were the oldies this morning?'

'Be careful. Some of them are more flexible than you.'

Roma scoffed. 'That can't be true. I'm at least thirty years younger than most of them.'

Keira shrugged. 'Sorry to say, but it is. Even with all the reno work, you've spent too many years sitting behind a desk. You need to loosen up, girl.'

If only Keira knew how true that was. 'I'm trying. I really am.'

'Good.'

'I'm actually here to ask you about something.'

Keira played with her ponytail. 'What's that?'

'I'm wondering if you want to come live at Bayview.'

Keira took a step back in surprise. 'What?'

'I know this might be totally out of the blue but Addy's gone and you're living in a daggy shack and I have all those rooms.' Roma felt suddenly nervous. She waited, knitting her fingers together behind her back.

'Wow. Really?'

'Yes. Really. It's not often in your life you meet someone and you just know you're going to be really great friends. I think we're going to be really great friends, Keira.'

Keira came to Roma and threw her arms around her. 'I'd love to.' She released her grip and laughed. 'It's so close to the studio and the beach. I love your house, you know that, right?'

'I love it too.'

Bayview was working some kind of magic that Roma couldn't see, but it was exactly the magic she had longed for it to cast on her. A new life, a hope for a new future, the next stage of her life. It all felt so close now she could reach for it and it wouldn't slip away.

Keira looked to the ceiling, bit her lip. 'I'm on a month by month lease so ... I could move in four weeks? That should be enough notice. I don't have much stuff. My place was furnished when I rented it and I'd sold off a whole lot of stuff before I left Canberra anyway.'

Roma thought of the bed Addy had bought for the room she wanted to use as her permanent summer bolthole.

'I might have a spare bed.'

'Well, we have a deal then. Except for how much rent I'll be paying.'

'Mates' rates,' Roma answered. 'We can sort that out when you move in. Let's just say I'm happy to subsidise the activities of the only Pilates instructor in town, given that I need to loosen up a bit.'

Keira laughed. 'I think you're getting there.'

Roma sighed. 'Me too.'

Addy had been at work for one day on the television commercial for the city's latest IVF clinic when things started arriving for her in the production office. On that first day, Tuesday, it was flowers. No card. She'd assumed the card had got lost and when she went in to the producer Sally's office to check if they were a gift from her for coming back to work so quickly, Sally had looked at her blankly.

'They're not from me, doll. But they're beautiful.' They really were. They were a bunch of red, yellow and orange gerberas surrounded by strappy leaves and tied with a piece of brown string. Addy guessed they were from that arsehole Jack Andersson. It would be just like him to send flowers without a card. Who else would be sending her flowers? In her furious anger, she handed the bunch to a passing production assistant.

'Happy birthday,' she said to the young woman with skin-tight jeans, Converse sneakers and a singlet top, which revealed her full sleeve tattoo. She took them but looked around as if she had just been punked.

'It's not my birthday,' she said.

'No? It will be one day. Take 'em.'

On Wednesday, a dozen bottles of wine arrived, a selection of premium whites from the Adelaide Hills. Again, there was no note. She was way too mercenary to give those away, so she took them home and drank a bottle that night all by herself. A half-drunk text to Roma and Leo later that night revealed it wasn't either of them.

On Thursday, it was chocolates. Specifically, a box of hand-rolled truffles. And damn, they were her favourite. Again, no note. She suspected now that the gifts weren't from Jack. He wasn't the kind of man to send a special gift and not expect the credit. It would have burned him up not to have had a phone call to thank him, so Addy knew it hadn't been him. Which meant there was only one other person who would be sending her flowers, wine and chocolates. And that was Blake Stapleton from the Remarkable Bay Surf Shop.

Addy had thrown herself into production on the television commercial with the gusto she was known for. She revelled in the long hours and the organised chaos of organising crews and locations and families to film. If she was thinking about booking editing time and dollies, she wasn't thinking about all that she'd left behind in Remarkable Bay.

She couldn't even say it out loud to herself, but she missed Roma. She was angry at her, sure, for what she'd said during the argument, but couldn't blame her. Roma was still grieving for her dead husband. Of course she would be. How could she get over a love like the one she shared with Tom? Addy remembered their wedding, at a beautiful winery in McLaren Vale, and had watched with envy at the way they'd looked at each other during the ceremony. Still so young, they seemed perfect together. How do you get over losing a love like that? Addy asked herself. She didn't know. And she had a feeling she might never know. She wasn't built for long-term relationships. Maybe that was it. Her attention span was too short so she kept moving.

She'd kept moving and come back to Adelaide, thrown herself into her work, but she couldn't forget Blake Stapleton. Her body literally ached for him. She'd never experienced yearning before, but now knew what that felt like. It was a craving worse than when she'd given up smoking; a desperate need for him. And not just his body, but his calm stillness. And then she remembered what she'd said, about not needing him to cook her dinner or buy her wine or chocolates or flowers, that she was a sure bet.

Flowers. Wine. Chocolates.

When she got home late that night, her back aching and her eyes stinging from tiredness, Addy ate a few of the chocolates. Well, maybe twelve of them as she sat on her sofa and caught something mindless on TV to relax before crashing into bed for the six hours sleep she would squeeze in before having to be up at the crack of dawn to be back in the production office. Such a glamorous life. She had so much work to do the next day. They were still having trouble finding couples who'd successfully gone through IVF and who were willing to share their difficulties and successes on camera. People wanted to keep their secrets. Addy understood that better than anyone.

On Friday morning, she pulled up in the production offices' parking lot at seven, juggling her handbag stuffed with papers and her devices, and a takeaway coffee. Her head was full of the things she had to do that day. So she hadn't been expecting the surprise that was waiting for her.

It was Jack Andersson.

CHAPTER
30

Addy gripped her car keys in her hand.

Jack.

The hairs on the back of her neck prickled and her heart picked up, pounding hard and fast. It made her sweat and tightened the breath in her lungs. What was he doing here? He was supposed to be in Melbourne, not here. It was the only way she could come back to Adelaide, knowing that he was eight hundred kilometres away from her. How the hell did he know she was working here?

Jack stood by the back door to the large old warehouse, surveying the empty parking lot. He knew Addy was always the first to arrive at work, that she liked the extra time it gave her to look at last night's emails, check for messages and plan the day ahead. Her car was lonely in the corner and Addy knew that they were the only ones there.

He waved. He was dressed head to toe in black, so Melbourne already, and had a leather satchel slung over his shoulder. Addy recognised his favourite battered leather jacket. He wore it because he believed it made him look like a real director. She ground her teeth together. Pity there wasn't a real man underneath it.

He was in the way. He'd obviously planned it that way. She would have to get past him to go into work. She stayed where she was.

'Addy.' He called out her name, as friendly as if he'd just seen her yesterday.

She needed to remain calm, to keep her head. She slipped a hand into her bag, not letting go of her keys, needing to reassure herself that her mobile phone was right there if she needed it. The cool metal casing under her index finger was reassuring.

She took a deep breath, trying to find strength. 'What do you want, Jack?' Her words hung in the air and echoed in the empty parking lot.

He took her in, his eyes grazing from her head to toe as if he owned her, as if it was his right to look at her that way. She stayed where she was, trying to keep a safe distance between them although, in her experience, there was no safe distance with Jack.

'You look good, Addy.' He always did it this way. He started with the charm.

'What are you doing here?'

'Aren't you happy to see me?' He came closer. Addy stepped back.

'You need to go. You need to leave me alone. If you'll get out of the way, I have to get to my desk. I've got work to do.'

'Oh, c'mon, Addy. It's been too long. Aren't you going to say hello? What's got into you?'

'Just leave, Jack. Go back to Melbourne. Get out of my way.' She positioned one of her car keys between her curled fingers, held on tight to it.

'I'm just here to talk.' And then she could see the change: the narrowed eyes, the edge in his voice. He pulled his shoulders back, and the shape of his lips transformed from a smirk to a snarl. His eyes narrowed, not in curiosity but in rage. 'I've come all this way from Melbourne. I've been driving all fucking night and I haven't had any sleep and I've drunk way too much shitty coffee. All to see you.'

'You have to leave,' she replied.

Jack laughed bitterly. 'You're working on some piece of shit TVC when you could have been working for me on my series in

Melbourne? What the fuck, Addy? I needed you on that show. You turned your back on me, you know that?'

She could hear the tension crackle in his voice. Her fingers gripped the keys. Her heart pounded in her ears. 'I was busy, Jack.'

He walked towards her, slow steps, menacing steps. 'Don't you know who I am, Addy? I am Jack Andersson.' He slammed his palm against his chest. 'I'm on my way. I've got an agent in LA. Did you know that? Huh?'

He was in her face now, snarling, angry. She swallowed, tried to breathe.

He reached for her, grabbed her upper arm, his big fingers digging into her, through her denim jacket, right into her skin. He was holding her so tight he was almost lifting her off the ground. Addy could already feel the bruises coming up, and the pain throbbing in the sensitive skin.

'You haven't returned my fucking phone calls. You wouldn't come to Melbourne. What the fuck is wrong with you?'

'Let go,' she said quietly, forcefully. 'You're hurting me.'

Don't make him angry. Don't make him worse. You know what will come next.

'I'm hurting *you*? What the fuck, Addy? How do you think I felt when you walked out on me, huh? It. Was. Fucking. Agony.' Each word was spat in her face. Each word saw a tightening and twisting of his grip on her arm. 'How the fuck could you?'

Addy breathed hard, glanced around. Please someone, she begged silently. Please come. But it was too early. She knew no one else would arrive for at least half an hour.

'Who is he? Huh?'

'What are you talking about?'

'His name. What's his name, Addy? He's the reason you didn't come to Melbourne, isn't it? Because you're *fucking* someone else. I chase a job and you're chasing some other guy's dick.'

Addy was turning in on herself to try to ease the pain, pain which was now stinging her eyes, thickening her tongue, tightening her throat.

And it rose up in her like a roar. Don't let him do this to you. Not again. Not ever again.

'Get your fucking hands off me,' she snarled as she jabbed at him

His fingers slackened and he splayed two hands on his stomach and yelped. 'What the fuck have you done?' He gasped, breathing fast, bending in the middle. She saw a weakness exposed and she turned slightly, taking her weight on her back leg and kicked him. She didn't have a word for the satisfaction she felt kicking him in the shin with a heavy boot.

'What the heck is going on?'

Sally. Her dear friend Sally. Her voice was in Addy's ear and she saw a flash of bright purple and then Sally was between them. The producer shoved her phone at Jack.

'I'm on the phone with the cops, Jack.'

Sally looked over her shoulder at Addy. 'They're on their way. You all right?'

Addy couldn't seem to move. The throbbing in her head was loud, like headphones full of rock music pounding in her ears, and she was shaking so much her keys were jangling in her hand.

'Addy?' Sally's voice was filled with caution and concern.

Addy's tongue was thick. She felt the throb of pain in her arm now and tried to shake it out but that only made it worse.

'The cops?' Jack moaned. 'Good. They can charge Addy. You mad bitch,' he shouted. 'Look what you've done to me.' He turned to Sally, jabbed the air. 'That fucking bitch stabbed me.'

Addy glanced at the big brave Jack Andersson now, as he doubled over, wincing and clutching his stomach. It took her a minute to remember. She looked down at her car key, still gripped between her fingers, sticking out like one of Wolverine's metallic claws. There was blood on it, bright red, at the tip.

The blood.

She felt woozy, closed her eyes, saw her reflection in the mirror. She was back at her house. It was the night she'd broken up with Jack. She'd run to the bathroom, terrified, and locked the door behind her, fumbling with the lock, standing there in her bare feet, shaking and frightened. Was that her in the mirror? Her auburn hair was tugged into knotty clumps. Around her neck, a rough, reddish ring from where his hands had gripped her, shoved her, tightened around her. She was cataloguing the damage, running through it like a production schedule. Under her chin, a scrape and a sting and blood. On a cheekbone, a slash, where his ring had crunched against bone when he'd backhanded her. And her eyes. Hollow. Lifeless. Where had she gone? Who was this person staring back at her, this ghost?

There had been no sign of Addy McNamara in those hollow eyes.

She had tasted blood and looked down. On the gleaming white of the bathroom sink drops of blood smoothed into watercolour smudges and streaked like rain on a window. Except the rain was blood red. The memories ripped at her.

Sally spat the words out. 'You are such an arsehole, Jack.'

And then the police car arrived with a squeal of brakes and a light that flashed red and blue and reflected in the windows of Addy's and Sally's cars. There was the sound of slamming doors and heavy footsteps on the asphalt and an unfamiliar male voice speaking into a two-way radio. One officer went to Jack. One came to her.

'Are you all right?'

Addy glanced from the officer to Sally. Her mouth opened but she didn't hear any words come out. There was a ringing in her ears.

'I'm the one who called,' Sally said, then she leaned over and looked directly into her friend's eyes. 'I saw it all, Addy. I waited in my car and called them.' Her voice dropped. 'This is your chance to tell them *everything*.'

Tell them everything. Sally knew. Oh god, she knew. Addy felt her insides shrinking, hollowing out and filling up with shame. Heavy as concrete.

Sally reached for her hand. 'I mean it, Addy. Please. For the love of god, before he does this to you again or does it to someone else. Tell them everything.'

The police officer nodded at Sally. 'I'll have to ask you some questions, too.' Then she turned to Addy. 'What's your name?'

Addy's eyes swam with tears. Now the police were involved. There would be interviews, questions, reports and maybe charges. God. She'd stabbed Jack. She was going to be arrested.

'Addy McNamara. Adelaide McNamara.'

'Do you know that man talking to the officer over there?'

Addy nodded. 'We used to be in a relationship.'

'Has he hurt you before?' The officer's voice was quiet and undemanding, and Addy knew all the questions had to be asked, but they still felt like an intrusion.

When Addy hesitated, Sally squeezed her hand. 'This is your chance, Addy. Please tell them.'

'Yes. He's hurt me before. He's hit me before.'

'You'll need to be medically assessed,' the officer said quietly.

'I can take her to hospital, get her checked over,' Sally said quickly, fiercely.

The officer looked at Addy knowingly. 'We'll want the evidence documented so we can take this further.'

Addy nodded, feeling at once half asleep, and half as if she would never sleep again in her life.

Her mask had cracked and shattered. She couldn't hide behind it any more.

She looked past the officer and Sally. Jack was being pushed into the back seat of the police car. The lights on top of it were still flashing but there was no noise from the sirens. Everything was silent except for the beating of her heart in her ears, the pressure of it in her chest so big it felt like her ribs were cracking. The stinging, swelling and bruising in her arm had begun to throb now in time with her heartbeat. After so long, she was now feeling everything. Every blow. Every hurled insult. Every taunt. Waves of hate and rage began to crash all around her and she felt as if she were drowning in it all.

It was all over.

The glittering and glamorous life of Addy McNamara had been a joke and a lie and now everyone would know it.

* * *

Addy went back to work the next day and the days after that until the commercial was done. The completed product was a soft-focus piece of propaganda about the success rates of in-vitro fertilisation and the joy having children would bring to a sad couple with empty arms and big wallets. She'd found the perfect, photogenic happy couples and their perfect, photogenic children and the director had done a brilliant job of capturing every smile, every look of love and every hug in a style that would out-schmaltz Hollywood.

Going back to work had helped. There was only one thing Addy prized about her fucked-up life and that was her professional reputation. She had to keep going. She had only ever had herself to rely on and she needed to work. She couldn't walk out in the middle of a job just because the rest of her life was a mess.

Sally—her rock—hadn't breathed a word about what had happened and fortunately it had been too early in the morning for any of their colleagues to see the events in the car park. After the police had completed the interview she'd gone to hospital, as the police requested, and Sally had waited while Addy was examined, interviewed, photographed. She'd agreed with the police that she should ask for a restraining order and one was granted.

But that piece of paper, that threat that if Jack came close to her again he would face the consequences, didn't make her feel any safer. He'd assaulted her in her own home before. And he'd tracked her down at work. Now nowhere felt safe.

On the final day of post-production, once she'd closed her files, tidied up the budget and organised the final payments to cast and crew, Addy went home and called Leo. Maybe she would go to Sydney for a while, so she could get away from everything that had happened in Adelaide. There weren't many other options available to her. She didn't feel that she could return to Remarkable Bay, not with the way she'd left things. That gnawed at her too, the schism with Roma.

Sydney looked like the only option. And she could do that: she could go to Sydney and be the old Addy again.

Leo picked up her call after three rings. 'Hey, Addy.'

She took a deep breath. 'Hi, Leo.' She tried to sound breezy and vivacious, the old Addy, but when her bottom lip quivered, all her pretend confidence drained away. She was so tired. She couldn't do this anymore. She couldn't hide. How to find the words to tell him the humiliating truth?

'You all right?'

The truth, Addy. Finally, the truth. 'No, not okay.' And when the tears welled she let them fall, hot on her cheeks, drizzling down on to her chest, dampening her T-shirt.

'Are you crying, Addy? What's happened?'

'I was assaulted.'

'What the hell? Have you called the police? Are you okay?'

She sighed, deep and long. 'It was Jack.'

'Jack?' Leo's voice hardened. 'The director Jack?'

'Yes. He came to my work and threatened me, hurt me.' And then the words and the story tumbled out of her. About how he'd hurt her before. About the police charges against Jack. The restraining order. Leo listened with a silent fury she could feel all the way from Adelaide.

'Where are you, Addy?'

'I'm at home.' She glanced around her living room. It didn't feel like home any more. It had been poisoned, invaded, its walls breached and her safety compromised. She knew she would never sleep well in this house ever again. The memories sat heavy like wet fog in every room.

'Is there anything you need me to do?'

'No. I don't think so. Except …' She swallowed a sob. 'Don't tell Roma, okay?'

Half an hour later, Roma was on the phone to Connor. She knew he would be at work. She wasn't sure if she needed him as a lawyer or a friend, but she needed him.

He picked up quickly.

'Excuse me,' his words were muffled, then clearer. 'I'm sorry. I'm in the middle of something.' She knew his words were code for, *I'm with a client.*

'I'm so sorry. I know you are. Call me when you can.' Roma hung up and paced the kitchen, not knowing if she needed a coffee or not. She decided she would make one anyway and busied herself loading the coffee pod and waiting for her cup to fill. Since Leo's call, Roma had worried herself into a splitting headache. He'd called her the minute he'd hung up from Addy and proceeded to tell her everything. Roma's head swam with all he'd said: assault, police, history of domestic violence, hospital.

'Oh, Addy,' she whispered to herself. Addy had kept her secrets so well. Roma would never have guessed that her strong, courageous, take-no-prisoners, no-bullshit cousin Addy could have suffered in so much silence. Why had she not told anybody? Why had she not told Roma?

And then Roma realised what a hypocrite she was. She had her secrets too, secrets so painful that she'd told no one. There were words she'd never said out loud, things she'd kept from Addy, from Leo, from Tom's family, from everyone. It had been easier to grow scar tissue over her own pain and hurt than it had been to tell any other living soul.

As she sat at the kitchen table holding the warm coffee cup between her hands, she realised how awful she'd been to Addy. The horrible guilt of what she'd done was like lead in her stomach. Why did women do that to each other, she wondered. Why did women judge each other, pick each other apart at the seams, tear each other to shreds?

The front door slammed. There were heavy, striding footsteps in the hallway and then Connor was next to her.

'What's happened? Are you all right?' He kneeled down on his haunches to look her directly in the eye. Already so familiar to her, she studied his face. His hooded eyes dark with concern. His mouth tense and worried. His steadying hand firm on her shoulder.

'You left the office?'

'Of course I did. I could hear it in in your voice. Something's wrong. What is it, Roma?'

She wiped the sudden tears. 'It's Addy. I think she might need a lawyer.'

He stood, held out a hand to Roma. 'Let's go.'

CHAPTER
31

It took Roma and Connor an hour and a half to reach Addy's house, a small, one-bedroom cottage on the eastern fringe of Adelaide. They fought the afternoon traffic the whole way, with Connor patiently waiting at lights and negotiating traffic jams.

He was similarly patient with Roma. Before they'd got in the car, she'd told him what she knew, and his grim-faced response told her more than words ever could. She hadn't felt like talking much on the trip, and he hadn't pushed it or asked any more questions. She'd sat in the passenger seat and stared out at the passing views, trying to distract herself with the tall trees around Mount Compass, the steep road down the Willunga Hill and past the rows of grapevines in full leaf through McLaren Vale. Using his bluetooth, Connor had called Angas and told him he should defrost something from the freezer for dinner, and that he wasn't sure when he would be home but to call if he needed anything. He'd then phoned an old contact in a domestic violence service, asking questions about what kind of support would be available, what they would suggest Addy's next steps should be.

Roma took some of it in, but not all. She was trying to gather all her courage to be strong for Addy and still wasn't confident she had enough of it to break through Addy's defences. Addy could duck and weave like an Olympic boxer. She obfuscated, distracted herself and others with her personality and her wit. She was a skilled actress, Roma realised, worthy of an Academy Award. She'd been playing a character for so long, Roma wondered if Addy knew who she really was.

Connor's hand was on hers. They were almost there. 'You okay?'

Roma sighed, her shoulders shook. 'I think so. I'm not sure if I know what to say to her.'

Connor's mouth dipped at one corner. Up until then, she had thought he might be physically incapable of frowning. 'How about something like, "Jack is a fucking arsehole and he should be in jail."' He checked the rear-view mirror before turning left into Addy's street.

Roma smiled, squeezed his hand. 'Works for me.'

When Addy opened the front door, Roma blurted out, her voice quivering with nerves, 'Jack is a fucking arsehole and he should be in jail.'

Addy looked wide-eyed at Roma, registered that Connor was by her side, and then burst into tears.

They took her inside and settled her on the sofa in her tiny front room. There were large framed movie posters on the walls from films Addy had worked on, and quirky objects on the mantelpiece, including a film can with black signatures scrawled on the metal. There were framed photos, including one of Addy wearing an Akubra with red dirt behind all the way to the horizon. Roma hadn't been in Addy's house before and as she took in all the markers of the glamorous life Addy lived, she realised how different it was from her own. Addy was successful, she could see it in all the paraphernalia: her name in the small print on the movie poster; the photo with a famous actor on a side table. It was a big life Addy lived. Maybe that's why the fall seemed so much harder.

Connor had discreetly offered to make coffee, leaving Roma and Addy alone to talk. When Roma went to find a box of tissues, she found Connor sitting at the kitchen table, talking on his phone.

'I'll call you back.' He hung up on the call and looked up to Roma with a million questions in his eyes.

'I'm looking for tissues,' she said quietly. 'I think we're going to need them.'

He reached for her hand. She put hers in the strong warmth of his. 'I'll wait here until you need legal advice. But judging by the state of her, I think there are a few other things you need to talk over first.'

Roma leaned down and kissed his cheek. She let herself linger, hoping the kiss would show him how she felt.

He smiled up at her, this lovely man.

'I can't thank you enough.'

'Take as long as you need with her.'

The tissues were in the bathroom on the pristine white vanity and Roma returned to Addy and handed over the box before sitting next to her on the overstuffed sofa.

Addy stared ahead, not meeting Roma's eye. Her voice was brittle. 'I'm assuming Leo called you.'

'I thought you might need someone to talk to, that you might need some help. I can't believe what's been happening to you, Addy. Hell. There are no words, really.'

Addy reached for a tissue and blew her nose. She leaned back into the sofa and pulled her thin legs up to her chest, hugging herself. 'You know, Romes, I feel like I've been living in a biopic about someone else's life. Someone who's a total idiot. I don't know how this happened to me, Roma, how I got into this situation. I really don't.'

Roma hesitated. 'Connor said something to me before we left Remarkable Bay.'

Addy listened, dabbing her balled tissue under her eyes to blot the tears.

'"It's always the charmers," he said. 'He told me he's seen it a hundred times in his practice in DV cases. These guys, guys like

Jack, are smart and loving at first, and they're so convincing that women get drawn in and no one on the outside would ever believe they were capable of this. They manipulate and they lie, Addy. And when they don't get what they want? They hurt and destroy.'

Addy sniffed, her throat sounding clogging with tears. 'I thought I was smart too, that something like this would never happen to me. But it was so slow, like a drip feed, you know? I didn't put all the pieces together until after, when I was being interviewed by the police and they began asking me all these questions. Had he ever stopped me seeing my friends? Tick. Yeah, he had. He wanted it to be just the two of us and I thought that sounded romantic, right? And then they asked me if he'd ever threatened to hurt himself if I left? Tick. Had he ever said he would kill me if I left?'

Roma stilled, trying to take all the revelations in. Her head was spinning at the idea that people could do this to each other, that a man could do this to a woman he professed to love.

Addy's voice trembled, her small frame shivering. 'He almost did kill me.'

'Oh god, Addy …' Roma said, her own tears clouding her vision. Addy's face was blurred, like she was an apparition.

'I found out he'd been fucking someone else. I saw him. And … and I told him it was over, that I was leaving. He mysteriously couldn't see why his screwing around was any of my business.' Addy's expression was distracted and faraway, her voice small. 'I kind of suspected it, but I was trying to be all too-cool-for-school about it. We creative types aren't like other people, right? We're *different. Artistic. Dramatic.* Well, that's a crock of shit. Turns out we're just like everybody else, but other people don't get to shroud their bad behaviour in glamour and celluloid.'

Roma scrambled for questions. 'Did you love him?'

Addy took a deep breath. 'I thought I did, but love shouldn't involve standing over your bathroom sink watching blood drip down the drain, should it? Or feeling someone's hands around your neck so tight you almost black out?'

Roma gripped Addy's hand.

'I don't know what love is anymore, do you? I've never had trouble finding someone to fuck. But Jack? I thought he was different. He wanted to stay after the sex. He wanted to talk, god could he talk, and that was different for me. I hadn't ever had that before. But when it all crumbled to pieces, I eventually realised the thing he wanted to talk about most was himself and when I got bored and impatient with that, he found someone even younger to be the president of his fan club.

'So, after … I went back to work, trying to pretend nothing had happened. It's amazing the lack of curiosity people have about a woman with a black eye. I lied and told everyone I'd tripped on my high heels and fallen down the front step on to the veranda and everyone laughed and believed me. They laughed and believed me.' Addy looked into Roma's eyes, searching for an explanation for how people can be so blind. 'On the day the finance on the film was pulled, Leo called me and told me that you'd bought Bayview. He thought you'd gone mad and sent me down to Remarkable Bay to keep an eye on you.'

Roma smiled a half-smile. 'I think Leo was right.'

Addy wiped her eyes. 'The truth is, you were a convenient excuse to get away from all the bullshit up here in Adelaide. I thought if I could just stop for a little while, breathe, you know? I might find myself again. Put everything behind me and find the strength to face it all. But it turns out I'm not very good at stopping. I started something with Blake that I shouldn't have and you and I were fighting … and I've made a mess of everything, Roma.'

'I wish you'd told me.'

'How could I? I was humiliated. And you? You've lost a husband. How can what I've been through compare with that?'

'God, it's not a contest, Addy. It's all grief with different shades.'

'And when we fought and you accused me of being perfect, of having the perfect life … I kind of lost it. I went straight back to my default position and that was to run.'

Guilt stabbed at Roma. 'I was judgemental and jealous and hurt. I'm sorry.' She held Addy's hand and Addy squeezed it back.

'Why were you jealous of me?'

'I've always been jealous of you. Didn't you know that?'

'No, never. I thought you looked down your nose at me because you're so much smarter than I am.'

The two women stared at each other for a long moment.

'I've never thought that, Addy. Not once.'

'Why have we done this to each other?'

Roma thought on it. 'I don't know. But I want it to stop.'

'So do I,' Addy replied.

They heard footsteps and Connor brought them their coffees, two mugs on a tray alongside a bowl filled with chocolate biscuits. He glanced at Roma before leaving them alone again.

Addy watched him leave. She slowly closed her eyes and shuddered. 'Did you tell him absolutely everything?'

Roma knew this was no time for fudging the truth. 'Yes. It's lawyer-client privilege, Addy. He's a safe pair of hands.' When Addy's bottom lip quivered, Roma added, 'I thought you might need some legal advice and, frankly, I wasn't in the right frame of mind to drive up to Adelaide by myself. Do you think you're going to be charged for stabbing Jack?'

'The police said they understand I was acting in self-defence. This kind of clinched the deal.' Addy gingerly pulled up the sleeve of her long-sleeved T-shirt to reveal the bruises on her upper arms. On the underside, there was a huge circular black-and-blue mark, the size of a man's thumb. On the other side of her arm, where her pale skin was dotted with freckles, four fingers had obviously dug in hard, creating deep black bruises. Addy winced. It clearly hurt to move and the sight of the injuries shook Roma to fresh tears.

Addy stared at her feet for a while, and Roma waited.

'What are you going to do now?'

'I don't know.'

Roma saw the honesty in Addy's eyes and realised it was time for some of her own. Hadn't secrets done enough damage? She vowed: no more. She needed to lift this weight from her life if she was to bring Addy back into hers, if she wanted to make room for Connor, and for Angas, and for Keira. For people she loved and who loved her. For people she was growing to like very much.

'I need to tell you something.'

Addy turned to her, puzzled. 'Is it about you and Connor?'

'No. It's about Tom.'

'Okay.'

Roma took a deep breath in. 'I have this dreadful guilty secret about what happened to him.'

Addy's eyes widened. 'Are you sure you're not the one who needs the lawyer?'

'No, it's not that.'

Roma reached for the bowl of chocolate biscuits and rested it on the sofa between them. She took one, bit into it.

'I haven't told anyone the real truth about Tom and me. About where we were, what was happening with us when he was killed.'

Addy didn't say a word, just stared earnestly into Roma's eyes.

Roma steadied herself. 'The truth is … we were about to separate when he died. Things had been terrible between us for a couple of years. Looking back now, I thought that the worst thing that could ever happen to me would be the breakdown of my marriage. It felt like we were fighting in quicksand. The more we argued, the more we sank into this horrible, hurtful pit until we couldn't even be bothered to fight any more. We didn't talk. We didn't make love. We didn't do anything together. We couldn't even agree on a TV show to watch that we both liked. Finally, I couldn't stand it anymore. The loneliness was overwhelming and I decided I had to make a new life for myself without him. The night he died, I'd told him I wanted to separate. We had an awful fight. I said things … I said such horrible things that I can never take back and he grabbed his car keys and slammed the front door and drove off.'

'Oh, Romes,' Addy reached for her hand.

'And he died with all those horrible things in his head. Words that I'd put there. And I still feel the whole thing is my fault. Maybe some dark, evil part of me willed it to happen because I wasn't happy.'

'That makes no sense. You must know that.'

'The only reason I could afford to buy Bayview and run away was because Tom died. I sold our house in Adelaide and we only owned that outright because he'd inherited the money from an aunt who didn't have children of her own to leave anything to. And with his life insurance and some superannuation, I had enough money.' Roma felt the sobs rising in her chest and swallowed them away. 'I didn't want to be married to him any more and I ended up with everything. How do you think that makes me feel?'

'Roma, you didn't kill him. That drunk driver did. He went to jail for it, remember?'

'He wouldn't have been in the car if I hadn't told him. If we hadn't argued.'

'You think you should feel guilty about that?'

'Of course I should.'

'Listen to me. How many years were you together?'

Roma thought on it. It was eighteen years since they'd met and they were married three years after that, right out of university. 'We were married for fifteen years.'

'That's five times longer than your average Hollywood marriage. Relationships end,' Addy said, her voice full of a simple sympathy that Roma had never heard in it before. 'Even good ones. Wasn't it good in the beginning?'

'It's hard to remember if it was ever good.'

'You married him. It must have been good or you never would have accepted his proposal, right? I was at your wedding, remember? It looked like the real thing to me. You loved each other. Everyone could see it. I was so jealous of you I snuck off to the loos and cried.'

'You did?' Roma whispered.

'I've never had the real thing, Roma. Men have always wanted to fuck me but they never want to stay. And judging by Jack, I'm a terrible judge of character, anyway. You have that thing. You always have. People love you.'

Roma thought back to her wedding day. She had loved Tom. She knew it was the truth that there had been good times, but she'd lost sight of them in the mire of the bad ones. She had forgotten how to trust those memories. 'I'd forgotten that we were happy, for a long time.'

'So what happened?'

'Everything and nothing. He didn't want kids. I do. Did. And it became this tool we used against each other. I'd just turned thirty and I really wanted a baby. I couldn't turn it off, that heartsickness about being childless. He wanted to travel more and he knew we couldn't do that with a baby.'

'Do you still want to have a baby?'

Roma blew out a breath. 'That dream died when Tom did.'

'What about the lawyer in the kitchen?'

'I thought he might want to run a million miles from the widow with dead husband issues, but no.'

'He likes you.'

'You know I've only ever slept with one man? And now I'm thirty-five and I don't know what to do. I'll probably be bad at it. Maybe that's what the problem was with Tom and me. Maybe it's me.'

Addy threw an arm around Roma and held on. 'You can do whatever you want. The only one judging you is *you*. Tom died in an *accident*, Roma. You didn't want him to die. You didn't cause it. It happened because it happened, not because you were unhappy. And now, it's been three years. You can reach for happiness, you know, if it's there, dangling in front of you. It's a shot at the new life you're after. Take the chance.'

Roma smiled and breathed deep, years of secrets flowing out of her. 'Please come back down to Remarkable Bay. It's almost Christmas. Leo's coming home. It's summer. And we can keep you safe.'

Addy's bottom lip trembled. 'I'd love to.'

CHAPTER
32

1935

Stuart—Allen On the 26th of June, 1935, at St Bartholomew's Church, the marriage was celebrated of Ruby, eldest daughter of Mr C. and Mrs H. Allen of North Adelaide, to Edwin, younger son of Mr X. and Mrs M. Stuart of Walkerville.

The notice in *The Advertiser* cost two shillings and sixpence and Ruby's parents were more than delighted to spend such a small amount of money to announce her nuptials so soon after the marriage of their middle daughter, Adeline. Publicly, at least, it was a very happy year for the Allens. By the time of Ruby's wedding to Edwin, Adeline had been Mrs James Stuart for two months. She lived across the city from her parents in an elegant sandstone villa with four bedrooms and separate rooms for the servants, a cast iron fountain bubbling happily in the neatly tended front yard, in a leafy street just on the edge of the parklands which ringed the city's square mile like a gum tree-filled moat.

Already an experienced wife of a mere eight weeks, Adeline had been full of advice for her sister's wedding. As the sisters walked the busy autumn streets of Adelaide, red and gold leaves swirling at their feet, they shopped and planned. Ruby had held her tongue when it all began to sound like more of a gloat than anything else, but she grew to enjoy spending time with Adeline, listening to her chatter about how wonderful married life was, how mature and worldly it felt to be running her own household and how, even if James did work very long hours, it was all for her, for their future children, for their family. Ruby didn't comment about the fact that James was away from home so much. According to Adeline, days were spent in the office, of course; three or four evenings a week he was at the club or at meetings; and on weekends he played golf on Saturday afternoons and often stayed for dinner at the clubhouse afterwards. Ruby had said nothing, other than to offer a sympathetic click of her tongue, agreeing with Adeline that it must be lonely, that she must miss James terribly. Ruby had no idea whether or not her own married life was to be the same and supressed the feeling that she might not mind Edwin's absences at all.

Ruby had simply half-listened while Adeline talked and fussed. It was comforting, this sister time. She let herself enjoy something happy after so many months of despair about Clara.

'You'll want Japanese lilies for the bouquet, Ruby, and lots of them. Pink roses are too old-fashioned.' There had also been advice on the wedding dress (white not ivory), the decision to wear a headdress (again, so 1920s) and the particulars of the food at the reception and the decorations atop the wedding cake. Ruby had ignored most of it. Unlike her sister, Ruby hadn't invested all her hopes and desires in this one day.

Once they'd returned from Remarkable Bay to a sizzling Adelaide, life had changed irrevocably for Ruby. Clara wasn't mentioned, as if the mere utterance of her name would bring further bad luck on the family. It felt to Ruby that her sister had disappeared off the face of the earth. She wrote to her twice a week but nothing came back. Letters filled with pleas to Aunt Jane were answered with explanations that Clara had her own mind, that she was faring well and would write when she chose to. There was not even a hint in her letters about the true situation. Perhaps she was afraid the servants might open them and Clara's shocking true secret would be revealed, that their cover would be blown with the slice of a sterling silver letter opener and a loose tongue in the kitchen. With Clara gone, the house was far quieter than it had ever been, filled with a sombre seriousness that weighed down on them all like a black cloak. Adeline had been far too busy with her own wedding plans to really notice that Clara wasn't there to scoff at her frivolousness. Their parents had formed a united front, quiet in their grief, if they felt any at all. Ruby had become increasingly convinced that they didn't. They had closed in on themselves; they were both more reserved in their behaviour, far stricter than they had ever been in controlling when their remaining daughters were out, who they were seeing and what they were up to.

Once Adeline was married and gone, Ruby had hated her loneliness in her parents' house. There were reminders of Clara in every corner. The mystery of the baby still haunted Ruby. When she sat in her room reading, when she walked through the parklands, when she sat with Edwin talking over their future, it was all she could think about. How had her sister become pregnant? Was it going to be a boy or a girl? Would it be given to a loving family?

If her parents had answers, they had never shared them with Ruby and, as Clara's absence stretched into months, her parents' callous and indifferent treatment of their youngest daughter ate at her. The cool stone walls of the family home seemed to be closing in on her, the birdsong from the tree in the front yard was cruelly taunting now she didn't have Clara to identify its composer.

Ruby found herself longing for her own escape. She'd known all along that her wedding was a practical choice, not a dream come true. There was a part of herself she'd had to shut away once she'd agreed to become Edwin's wife, the part in which she had hoped happiness would flourish and love would grow.

Ruby Allen and Edwin Stuart's ceremony was conducted on a cool June Saturday afternoon and the church was decorated in sprays of autumn flowers, which cheered her. The only instruction she'd given her mother was no carnations, especially not white ones. Her gown was lovely, made from ivory velvet to suit the cool temperatures, in a princess cut that swept into a long train, with sleeves that ended in points over her hands. The bodice featured a modest peter-pan collar, and it draped becomingly over Ruby's slim figure. She carried a bouquet of twenty-five Japanese lilies tied with an ivory ribbon. Adeline's choice suited her. She had stood by Ruby's side at the church wearing a delphinium-blue chiffon velvet frock, tight fitting and elegant. James was Edwin's best man, looking gallant as always in a black suit, and that was the little party. There was no flower girl or a ring bearer. Adelaide still hadn't shaken off the austerity of the depression, so things remained simple, even for the grandest families. Ruby and Adeline's parents had sat quietly in the front row, looking half-heartedly happy; their mother in her best fox fur, their father in his darkest suit. The only hint of any emotion from her father had been the quietest little sniff as he walked her down the aisle.

Ruby didn't think of Cain Stapleton during the morning of her wedding; nor when her mother helped her dress; or sat with her and her father in the car to the church. She didn't think of him when she walked down the aisle, her arm in her father's, nor when she was exchanging vows with Edwin. She didn't think of him when Edwin sniffed and shed tears during the ceremony, during which they offered to love, obey and honour each other until death do they part. He didn't cross her mind on her wedding night, even as Edwin kissed her and they lay together for the first time.

But she thought of him every day after that and every week and every month. When she and Edwin moved into the house his parents had bought for them in Norwood, just to the east of the city, she looked at the bluestone home and thought of a dairy farm, rich green grass and black-and-white cows. When Edwin dutifully carried her across the threshold, his cheeks blazing red, she had closed her eyes and wished they were Cain's arms around her instead.

She tried hard. She had taken notes from Adeline about what a modern wife should do. She studied the new recipes for casseroles in the *Women's Weekly* and Edwin had seemed to like them. She read and involved herself more heavily in her mother's charities. But it was not enough. She found herself floundering, aimless.

Nothing could replace the loss of a sister and nothing could fill the place in her heart in which she was sure Cain Stapleton still belonged. Ruby felt she would always have a piece missing from her young life. The events of the summer had stripped her of her youthful innocence about the world and her place in it.

In July, one month after her own wedding, her parents received a phone call to inform them that Clara had had the baby. It was a girl but she was given no name. All they had said, when Ruby had begged for more details, was that Clara was well. The baby was born healthy and had already been delivered to a real family. That night, Ruby sobbed herself to sleep, wishing with all her heart that she could be with Clara to comfort her, to ease the pain she must be feeling at having to give away her child.

When Ruby asked her mother when Clara was coming home, there was no definitive answer.

'Soon,' she'd been told.

'When is soon?' Ruby had asked impatiently, sensing the obfuscation in her mother's tone.

'When she is ready, Ruby, and not a day before.' Ruby knew what that really meant: when all signs of the baby were erased.

August was wet and cold and Ruby stayed in. She wasn't in a mind to do any visiting and filled in her time with books and the latest recipes. A month later, another letter from Aunt Jane arrived and when she was summoned to her mother, she was apprised of the news that Clara wasn't coming home to Adelaide. Aunt Jane had written explaining that she'd been out at a luncheon in Double Bay and had returned home late in the afternoon to find that Clara had packed her bags and left. She'd placed a note on Aunt Jane's elegant French-polished dining table, which explained that she was going to London to start afresh.

The words swam in Ruby's ears.

To start afresh. Clara was never coming home.

Her parents explained Clara's continued absence to Adeline by saying that Clara's studies had led to an offer at a university overseas. Adeline had shrugged her shoulders and displayed no further curiosity about her sister.

Secretly, Ruby wrote to Aunt Jane, begging for an address for Clara or for some more information.

I miss her dreadfully, Aunt Jane. I need to know she is well, that she is happy in her new life.

Aunt Jane could offer no more information, only to say that she missed her niece as much as Ruby did and had been hoping for letters herself, but nothing had come.

On the day that would have been Clara's nineteenth birthday, Ruby travelled across the city to see Adeline. Her visit was unannounced, but today of all days, Ruby needed her sister. She needed to say Clara's name to someone, to reminisce about her with someone who remembered her. She hadn't seen much of Adeline since Ruby herself had been married. It was sometimes weeks between visits from Adeline. Even after they were married, in their own homes, not more than a tram ride away from each other, Adeline rarely came. At first, Ruby was hurt. She'd lost one sister to the saddest of circumstances. But to drift apart from her only other sister when they lived so close? There had never been cross words, nor an argument, but even the brothers seemed to lose touch with each other. Ruby had always known that charming and witty James was very different to the reserved and circumspect Edwin, but those differences were emphasised once they became husbands.

The silver birches in Adeline's front garden were coming into leaf and they rustled in the spring breeze. The first roses were blooming and the rosemary hedge around the ornate fountain scented the air.

A girl answered the door, a young thing with wide and scared eyes. She couldn't have been more than fifteen years old.

'Hello, Mrs Stuart.'

'Hello, Patsy.'

Ruby waited to be invited in but Patsy gripped the doorknob and hid behind the half-opened door.

'Whatever is the matter?'

'Nothing, Ma'am.'

'I'm here to see my sister,' Ruby said.

'I'm afraid that Mrs Stuart is resting,' the girl answered nervously. 'She asked me to send away anyone who calls.'

'But I'm not anyone.'

Later, Ruby couldn't remember why she'd been so insistent, barging past the girl and scurrying down the hallway to Adeline's bedroom, but she'd had a sense. The door was closed but Ruby went in without being announced. The curtains were drawn and Ruby could just make out Adeline lying in her bed. Her auburn hair was a spray on the crisp white of the pillows under her head. She appeared to be still in her silk nightgown, her thin frame covered with a thick blanket. Ruby rushed to her side.

'Adeline,' she gasped. 'What's wrong?'

Her sister had a purple, swelling mark on one cheek and a blossoming, purple-and-yellow bruise under her puffed-up right eye.

'It's nothing,' she said, reaching a hand out to her sister. Ruby felt the hard grip of her fingers. 'I fell in the bedroom. I wasn't watching where I was going and I tripped over one of James's shoes. He has such big feet, Ruby. His shoes are enormous.'

Ruby stammered. 'Have … have you called the doctor?'

'Yes, James did. He came here to see me yesterday. Lots of rest and a cold poultice and I'll be fine.'

'Surely you should be in hospital, Adeline. Look at the state of you. What did mother say?'

'No!' Adeline gasped. 'Don't tell her. Not yet.' Her frown became a knowing smile. 'You see Ruby, It's just that I'm a little clumsy at the moment. I'm … I'm having a baby.'

Ruby's heart swelled. 'You are?'

'Yes. A few more weeks and I can tell mother and father. And James's family, of course. You're going to be an aunt, Ruby.'

Ruby wanted to be happy for her sister. She really was happy for her. This was everything Adeline had always wanted: to be married, to have a husband, to live in a nice home with all of life's luxuries and enough babies to fill every room. But the words she couldn't say sat on her tongue, heavy. *I am already an aunt.*

'You must be tremendously excited, Adeline. And James, too.' Roma reached for her sister's hand, gently held it. 'A baby. Well.'

Eight months later, Adeline delivered a baby girl. Six pounds four ounces. Her name was Mary.

In June 1936, one year after her wedding, Ruby became a mother. She too had a daughter and named her Eleanor Elizabeth. Edwin was a proud father and his own parents showered gifts on their second grandchild, who they hoped to see more often than their first. Little Eleanor, born out of a marriage her mother had settled for, conceived in respect rather than passion, was loved by everyone and by no one more than her mother.

Eleanor was a placid baby. She smiled and cooed and took to the breast without fussing. Ruby could never remember her crying for more than a few minutes at a time, and only with good reason.

It was only in the quietest times they shared, when Ruby nursed her tiny baby, stroked her head, rocked her as she sat in the old wooden chair in the nursery, that she shed tears and wished someone else was her father.

CHAPTER
33

2016

In the second week of December, Addy returned to Remarkable Bay. As she pulled up outside Bayview, or Roma's folly as she'd fondly grown to think of it, she sighed and smiled to herself.

It strangely felt like coming home.

She peered through the windscreen and up at the big house. In the early evening light, it didn't look glamorous. It still needed a paint. The front garden was kind of unruly, and she wondered if Roma had got around to cleaning all the cobwebs from under the front veranda. First impressions were important, she knew that. And she'd become a master of first impressions over the years. Maybe that could be her gift to Roma, her way of saying thanks for everything.

Who would have thought that Remarkable Bay—the pimple on the backside of a town in the middle of nowhere—would be the place she could go to seek solace and protection? There was no night life to speak of and there was nothing for miles around which even in the slightest resembled a day spa. The pub still served up cask wine and she wasn't even sure where the nearest boutique was. Despite all that, it was the only place she'd thought to come when it was clear she had to get out of Adelaide for a while. It felt safe and, mysteriously, like the home she'd been missing for twenty years.

Maybe she had changed after all.

Addy looked up. Roma and Keira were coming out of the front door, laughing with each other, and she was struck by how similar they looked. Roma's black hair was collar length and wavy. She was tall, curvier now than she used to be, and broad-shouldered. Keira was the same height but athletic and slender, her mid-brown hair pulled up in a high ponytail. They shared the same pale skin and heart-shaped face. Maybe that was it. But it was the eyes, too. The knowing eyes that Addy had always turned away from, as if Roma had always been able to peer right inside her and see her secrets.

'Hey!' Roma called as she walked through the front gate.

Addy shook her thoughts away. She was here. With Roma and Keira. Bayview seemed to be calling her home. She wasn't going to resist its siren song this time.

She opened the car door and skipped around to her two friends. 'I'm back.'

And then there were arms around her, Roma's voice in her ear saying, 'Welcome home, Addy,' and Keira was behind her and Addy felt her strong hands on her shoulders, pressing firmly into the knots that had stiffened her spine for such a long time.

'Let's get your things inside,' Keira said.

'And once you've unpacked, we've got a surprise for you.' Roma grinned and Addy didn't think she'd seen Roma so happy in a long, long time.

'It had better involve wine.' Addy rounded the car and opened the boot. 'Or I'm going back to Adelaide.'

They led Addy upstairs to one of the bedrooms that had been a junk room when Addy had left to go back to Adelaide. The last time she'd seen it, it had been filled with rolled-up carpets, ladders and unpacked boxes, and there had been a terribly ill-advised pair of geometrically patterned curtains hanging over the window.

She staggered through the doorway and stopped. Her bags hit the floor with an echoing thud.

'Oh my god,' she said in a whisper. 'I feel like I'm in the Hamptons.'

The room exuded cool and calm and Addy's eye followed the golden, honey-coloured floorboards to the large and inviting queen-sized bed on the right. The crisp white sheets and quilt cover were so smooth she thought a coin might bounce off it if she tossed one. Three patterned cushions, in china blue, sat in a row near the bedhead and a blue striped throw rug covered the end of the bed. A wooden table on one side held a stylish white lamp and a blue vase. The soft white of the walls blended into the painted pressed metal ceiling and sheer curtains hanging in front of the window fluttered in the sea breeze from the Bay. Behind the door was a white wardrobe, and a matching dresser with four deep drawers was decorated with an enormous bunch of flowers in a cut-glass vase. They reflected in the mirror hanging there and the blooms looked twice as big. Next to them, a white candle was softly flickering, exuding the scent of jasmine.

This was an oasis. She turned to Roma and Keira and didn't care one bit about hiding the tears streaming down her face.

Roma jabbed Keira in the ribs. 'I think she likes it.'

'Like it? I absolutely love it.' Addy searched Roma's face. 'When did you do all this?'

'In the week since I saw you up in Adelaide.'

'You did all this in a week?' Addy felt like extending her arms out and spinning around like Maria von Trapp on the top of a mountain. Or at least leaping face first onto the bed like Kate Winslet in Los Angeles.

'*We* did this in a week,' Roma explained. 'Me, Keira, Connor and Blake.'

'Blake helped you?'

Oh god. Blake. Then she remembered. All the gifts that had arrived at the production office when she'd begun work on the TV commercial. The chocolates, the flowers, the wine. She hadn't said a word of thanks to him. She would have to make that right, she knew.

'Yes. And those flowers are from him.'

Addy stilled. 'Blake sent those?'

'Yes. Aren't they gorgeous?' A cheeky grin lit up Keira's face. Addy blinked. That was it. It was the smile. She and Roma shared the same smile.

Addy steeled herself to ask the question. 'Does he know, Roma? Did Connor tell him?'

Roma reached for Addy's arm, laid a gentle hand there. 'No, he didn't, so don't you be thinking they're pity flowers or anything. All we said was that you were returning for the summer and he was happy to know you were coming back, that's all.'

Addy walked over to the dresser. The flowers were all white, as if he'd chosen them to match the room. Roses, carnations, lilies. The scent invaded her senses. 'They're beautiful.'

'There's a card,' Roma said quietly. Addy could see it was standing on the dresser, next to the vase. She lifted it and looked inside.

Welcome back.

Tears spilled down her cheeks. 'Whoa.' She turned back to Roma and Keira. 'This may spoil me so much I'll never want to leave.'

Roma and Keira exchanged glances. Addy tried not to read what was in them.

'Why don't you unpack and come downstairs when you're ready?' Roma rolled one of Addy's bigger suitcases into the room and positioned it at the end of the bed. 'We've got a surprise down there for you, too.'

'Give me half an hour to unpack.'

They left Addy alone. She gazed around the room, so peaceful, so quiet. Every single thing in it was beautiful and felt as if it had been chosen just for her. They'd been busy during the past week. She'd been so grateful to see Roma and Connor on her doorstep the day they'd driven up to Adelaide. Connor had given her really smart legal advice, in a matter-of-fact yet sympathetic way. He'd talked to the police, connected her with some support services if she wanted to seek counselling about what had happened to her and then laid out for her in clear detail what her next moves might be if Jack Andersson ever showed up again. She liked Connor a lot.

And Roma. She was so thankful to have cleared the air with her. Her wonderful, constant friend. She was so grateful that Roma was letting her in to the new life she was making for herself at Remarkable Bay. Her first instinct had always been to run, to obfuscate, to distract with shiny objects. But there was nothing shiny about her life any more.

Grief acted like a sieve. She wondered which of her friends would be left if they knew about Jack, about the violence, about her secret. Which of them would survive the sifting, the truth, and make it out the other end to stick with her? She knew she hadn't measured up in the past. She hadn't been by Roma's side when she'd lost Tom, that was for sure. She hadn't been able to deal with the depth of that sadness, the awful reality of what Roma was going through, so she'd done what she had always done. She'd run. And for that, she was determined to make amends.

Addy lowered herself on the bed, smoothing her hands over the crisp cotton, cool and clean under her fingers. How had Roma known that Bayview was what she needed? How was it that Roma understood her need for a safe haven? She let out a deep sigh. Of course Roma knew: she'd created Bayview as one for herself.

Addy had thought Roma was running from something when she'd moved to Remarkable Bay, that she'd been hiding from the world. But maybe this wasn't hiding. Maybe this was living. And it wasn't just getting out of bed and putting one foot in front of the other, going through the motions. She wasn't just opening her home to Addy, she was opening her heart, too.

Addy flopped back on the bed and stared up at the pressed metal ceiling. This really was a million miles from the rest of her life. This room felt safe. There were no memories here that could reach out in the dark and hurt her. Bayview felt safe too, off the beaten track and out of harm's way, a house full of love and affection and two women who would wrap their arms around her and protect her if she felt fragile or skittish. She hadn't felt that safety, that security, for a very long time.

Half an hour later, as the sun was setting over the bay and the breezes had settled for the evening, Addy went downstairs to find Roma and Keira in the living room. They jumped up from the couch and watched her reaction.

'What is all this?' she exclaimed.

A quick glance revealed they'd set up a welcoming party for her. On the coffee table there was a bottle of wine and a platter with olives, different cheeses, crackers and dried fruit. Next to the food was a stack of DVDs, ranging from black-and-white classics to the best of the recent English rom-coms. The soft lamplight cast a fuzzy glow in the room and the sofa, which she'd slept on when she'd come down to Remarkable Bay the first time, was covered in soft, decorative pillows.

Roma came forward and took Addy's arm, guiding her to the sofa.

'I'm not good at sitting around, I'm warning you,' she said.

'Get used to it, Addy,' Roma announced. 'Not that it's my job to boss you around but I'm going to boss you around. We—Keira and I—are officially looking after you.'

She fought the urge to resist but said, humbly, 'Thank you.' Addy hoped it would come naturally. She was sick of running. It was one of the things she knew she would have to change: she had to learn to confront her problems head on instead of avoiding them. The funny thing was, she was already doing it. Returning to Remarkable Bay didn't feel one bit as if she was running from them. It felt for all the world as if she was walking forward into a happier place, a kinder place, one in which people she loved cared about her and loved her right back, in spite of all her faults and her mistakes.

Addy sat and let herself sink into the soft cushions, and there was a long, deep sigh and she realised it was her. She let her head fall back on the headrest and closed her eyes. Keira sat herself down on one side of her, and Roma on the other. Addy laid her hands on her knees, palms up, and her hands were filled in an instant, with comfort, with protection, with perhaps the kind of love she'd been looking for all along. Being here in Bayview, with Roma and Keira, was beginning to feel like the perfect remedy for what ailed her.

'So, we've got all these movies.'

'You should have seen the look on the guy's face when we rented all these. I don't think he's had this much business in years!' Keira laughed. 'Which one should we watch first?'

Roma leaned forward and shuffled through the pile of DVDs.

'Roma wouldn't let me get any horror movies,' Keira said. 'She's a total killjoy.'

'Good,' Addy said. 'I hate them.'

Keira gasped. 'Aren't they your bread and butter? How can you hate them?'

'I've decided that there are too many women as victims in those kind of films, that's why.'

Keira frowned. 'Oops. Didn't think of that. About … sorry.'

Roma pulled out *Love, Actually*. 'What about this? It's coming into Christmas and this is all Christmassy.'

Addy shook her head. 'I don't believe in love. Next.'

Roma held up another cover. 'What about *Thor*? Mindless violence and Chris Hemsworth.'

Addy looked at her friends and laughed. 'Perfect.'

The next day, Roma woke early. She lay in bed for a while, half-heartedly reading a novel she'd left by her bedside table the week before, but slipped the bookmark back in after only a few pages. She tossed back the covers, slipped on a blue summer dress and her thongs and went downstairs.

She guessed Addy was still sleeping, cocooned in her bed. Roma had loved Addy's reaction to the makeover they'd completed for her. When she'd suggested the plan to Connor on the drive back down to Remarkable Bay the day they'd seen Addy, he'd roped in Blake before they'd even hit McLaren Vale.

She was unsure at first, not knowing how Addy had left things with Blake, but Connor had insisted.

'He wants to help,' he'd told her.

'Are you really sure?'

Connor had looked at her with a mysterious gleam in his eyes. 'Oh yeah. I'm sure.'

So they'd scrubbed and painted and sanded back the old dresser and the wardrobe and painted that, too. Keira had sewn new curtains—the ceilings were so tall and the windows so long that store-bought curtains weren't big enough. She'd also found the fabric for the pillows and sewn them too. When it was all finished, all four of them had gone to the pub for a meal and toasted their efforts. Angas had been working that night and delivered their meals with a smile.

All their hard work had been worth it, as Addy seemed to love her room. Roma walked across the kitchen to the coffee machine and flicked it on, slipping in a pod and watching it brew. Keira had already left for her Saturday morning Pilates class—Roma had heard her footsteps on the stairs—so she was alone.

Alone, but not lonely. And that was a good feeling, she decided.

After breakfast, Roma went next door.

Angas answered the door in a wetsuit. 'Hey, Roma.'

She didn't want to read anything into the fact that he'd used her name for the first time ever and, if she wasn't mistaken, he seemed to be smiling. Miracles never cease. 'Hey, Angas. You heading down for a surf?'

He flicked his eyes to his skin-tight neoprene and then back at Roma, a quirky smile on his face. She realised then, for the first time, that he had Connor's eyes. They shared the same aqua-blue gaze.

'Sorry,' she chuckled. 'Wasn't that a stupid question.'

'Yeah. Kind of. You looking for Dad?'

Roma nodded and felt her cheeks flush. 'Yeah. Is he home?'

Angas stepped back and made room for Roma to walk past him. 'He's in the kitchen.' Connor was sitting at the table with the

Saturday paper spread out before him, He was hunched over it, his elbows on the table, his glasses low on his nose. He looked up, saw it was her and smiled.

It hit her right where it was meant to.

'Hi,' he said softly and leaned back in his chair.

She went to him, stood close. He slipped an arm around her legs and she leaned down to kiss him on the lips. They kept it simple, knowing Angas was lurking and might make an appearance any minute. Connor pulled out the chair next to him and Roma sat down, her mouth tingling. She liked kissing him when they saw each other. It had begun during the work on Addy's room and she craved it now, his lips on hers, his arms around her.

'What's happening in the world?' She nodded to the paper.

'Same old, same old. How's Addy settling in? What did she think of her room?' Connor wore a look of pride on his face and Roma understood it. They'd created something beautiful together.

'She absolutely loved it. She cried, as Keira predicted she would. She liked Blake's flowers.'

Connor smiled knowingly. 'I think that was his plan. Did she crash last night?'

'We didn't let her wallow in her room for long. We had a little welcoming party, complete with movies and popcorn and there may have been a few bottles of wine consumed, which explains why she's still in bed.'

Connor reached for Roma's hair, smoothed it away from her forehead, his fingertips drawing intimate lines on her skin. The gentleness of the gesture made her heart beat faster.

'What about you? Are you suffering today, too?'

'Only a little. But seeing you makes me feel a whole lot better.'

Connor leaned in and kissed her and it was longer this time, deeper, closer. She liked it very much. When he finally pulled back, he rested his forehead on hers and met her gaze. Connor didn't have to say or do much to make her feel happy.

'Do you want some coffee? It might help with your head.'

'No, thanks. I've had one already.'

'Can I tempt you with breakfast then? How about bacon and eggs?'

He sure did know how to win a woman over. Ten minutes later, they were both tucking into the yellowest eggs and the crispiest bacon Roma believed she had ever had. Connor had toasted sourdough bread and there was a side of mushrooms that were equally as delicious.

'I could get used to this.' Roma took a last mouthful and placed her cutlery across her plate. There was nothing left but a smear of egg yolk on the white china.

Connor regarded her. 'And I could get used to having you at my table at breakfast time.'

She chuckled. 'Cook me brekkie like that again and you've got a deal.'

Connor looked down at his empty plate before reaching across the table for her hand. 'I'm serious, Roma.'

There was such steady strength in his fingers and in his voice. 'I know,' she replied. 'And I wouldn't be here if I didn't think the same.'

Connor lifted her hand and kissed the back of it.

'I want to thank you again for everything you've done. For Addy. With the police and her room. It's been incredible and way above and beyond.'

'It was nothing, really.' He was being modest, she knew that for sure.

'Oh, right. It was nothing,' Roma rolled her eyes and sipped her orange juice.

'Seriously,' Connor said with a furrowed brow. 'Addy did the hard work. She found the courage to tell the truth, despite knowing that it could still get ugly. Guys like Jack Andersson … let's just say they are control freaks to start with and sometimes getting the police involved makes things worse, not better. That doesn't make it right, and it doesn't mean she shouldn't have gone to the cops, but the reality is she'll have to be careful for a long time.'

Roma leaned an elbow on the table and cupped her chin in it. 'It's that serious?' Roma hadn't realised it but she could see it made sense, that men like Jack who manipulate and violate wouldn't suffer a blow to their egos without getting nasty again. The thought send a cold shiver through her and made her even more determined to protect Addy.

She stiffened her spine. 'Then there's no other choice, is there? She should move down here for good.'

Connor looked surprised. 'Hey, you won't hear me saying a bad word about Remarkable Bay, but the last time I looked it didn't have a thriving film industry. What about her job?'

Roma frowned. 'Good point. But I can't help but think this is the best option, don't you? All Jack has to know is that Addy's moved away. He won't know this address and if she keeps a low profile for a while, we might be able to protect her here. And there is the restraining order, right?'

'Which arseholes like Jack Andersson break all the time. It's catching them that's the problem. I've represented women who've had security cameras installed on their homes to catch their ex-partners on their property.'

Roma's mouth dropped open in shock. 'You are kidding me.'

'Not kidding. These guys just don't get it, Roma.'

She stared into her juice and pondered.

'Have you mentioned this to Addy?' Connor asked. 'Your plan for her to move down here, I mean. What did she say?'

Roma shook her head. 'No, I haven't. She's here to recuperate and rest. She'll be here for Christmas and we've vaguely talked about staying through January, but nothing's fixed. It's a bit of a one-week-at-a-time proposition.'

Connor gave her a look that made her want to kiss him hard. It was something like pride and lust mixed together and it softened his eyes and made one corner of his mouth lift in a half-smile.

'She's lucky to have you for a cousin eight times removed.'

'I'm lucky to have her.' And in that moment, Roma was grateful for all the people in her life. 'And Keira. And wait until you meet Leo. He's fierce.'

'He's your brother, right?'

'Yeah.'

'Should I be scared? Will he take one look at this small-town lawyer and single father and decide I'm not good enough for his sister?'

She scoffed. 'I decide who's good enough for me.'

'Glad to hear it.'

'He's coming home for Christmas. Are you and Angas doing anything special?'

'On Christmas Day we're having lunch with my folks in Victor Harbor and then he's flying out later that day to Sydney to spend a week with his mother.'

Roma gnawed her lip. She didn't have to second-guess what she was feeling. This was right. 'Would you both like to have Christmas Eve dinner with us at Bayview? We're celebrating the night before because Keira's going to Sydney to see her parents too.'

'Really?'

'You'd both be very welcome.'

'That would be great. And I'm calling it now: Angas doesn't get a say. He's either coming or he eats two-minute noodles for dinner.'

'You think he won't want to come?'

'He'll come. He likes you.'

'He does?' Roma felt ridiculously excited about the idea. If Angas liked her, she was definitely in with a shot with his father.

'He's not so sure about that lemon-stealing cousin of yours.'

They laughed at the memory.

'And ask Blake, would you?'

'Sure.'

'Good,' Roma said with a smile.

'Good,' Connor echoed.

Roma took in every part of his lovely face. His full lips, so sweet and warm, and his jaw, a shave away from being smooth. But it was his eyes, shining, aqua, mesmerising, that had entranced her from the first time they'd met.

'Did you get your eyes from your mother or your father?' she asked quietly, moving closer to him to stare into them.

'It's a Stapleton thing. I got them from my father and he got them from his and so it goes. We all have these weird-coloured blue eyes.'

'Weird?'

'Kids in primary school used to call me the Blue-Eyed Trevalla.' Roma guffawed.

'It's a fish with—'

'Big blue eyes?' she offered.

They laughed and the warm and homely sound of it echoed all around the room and reached into Roma's chest and settled there. The sound of laughter like that, the feeling of love it generated inside her, all said home.

'They're not weird eyes, Connor. They're anything but weird. They're kind of beautiful, actually. Hypnotising. I can't look away.'

'Why would I want you to?' He reached for her hand.

This all felt so new but it was so easy, somehow, and right. Maybe because she was ready for it now, open to letting someone into her life.

'So we've got Christmas sorted out then. What are you doing today?' Connor asked.

'I have a Pilates class later. Then I might see what Addy feels like doing. Maybe I'll take her for a long walk on the beach and a swim.'

'What about tonight, after dinner?' Connor held her hand.

Roma tipped her head to the side. 'Are you asking me on a date, Connor Stapleton?'

He grinned. 'I think it's about bloody time, don't you?'

'Yes,' Roma said, feeling an anticipation, a spark, a delicious rumble in her stomach. 'It's about time.'

CHAPTER
34

Addy slipped her hands through the plastic strips hanging over the door of the Remarkable Bay Surf Shop and stepped into a shop full of customers. She hadn't seen quite so many people in there before, but given it was a week until Christmas, she shouldn't have been surprised that business was brisk. She'd already noticed the change in Remarkable Bay since she'd returned. There were more people in the queue at the bakery and the supermarket was busy. There was more traffic on Ocean Street and, by early afternoon, there were sun shades dotted all over the sweep of the bay and people were enjoying the sun and the sand.

She'd been back a week and hadn't come to see Blake yet. She hadn't done much of anything. Roma and Keira had been pampering her with delicious home-cooked meals and easy conversations over movies and box sets of TV series that she'd missed the past few years. They'd made everything easy for her, and she wasn't sure how she would ever be able to thank them for the comfort they'd provided. She still needed time to work through what had happened to her, to figure out how she could avoid making the same mistakes again. And she still had to summon up the strength to tell her mother what had been going on. She wasn't strong enough for that yet, to cope with the judgement and the condemnation.

But she felt it was the right time to talk to Blake. When Addy saw him across the shop, she tried to ignore the shimmer in her chest and the memory of the taste of him on her lips. He was wearing his Remarkable Bay Surf Shop T-shirt over faded jeans and was busy serving a stream of people. She hung back and watched. He tucked bikinis and T-shirts into bags, measured bodyboards to be sure they were the right height for their buyers and gave advice to a middle-aged man hovering with great uncertainty near the surfboard racks. She waited and watched, lurked in the women's clothes section and enjoyed this glimpse of the Blake she barely knew.

She didn't really know him at all, this man she'd slept with after little more than a moment's thought. They'd barely had a conversation because he'd seemed so quiet and really, for what they were both after, words hadn't been necessary.

'Hey, how are you doing today?' Blake's booming voice echoed and she looked up, a wave of happiness rushing through her at the thought that he was addressing the greeting to her. But he'd rounded the counter and was shaking hands with a customer, a youngish dad holding a small girl in his arms.

'And how's this little one?' Blake asked happily. 'Haven't you got big? Mate, we've got to get her surfing sometime soon and I reckon I have the perfect board for this little grommet.' She looked on as Blake held out his arms and the child went to him happily, snuggling into his chest. As the two men talked, Blake gently rocked from side to side to comfort the little girl, who was clutching a stuffed brown kangaroo, and she sat comfortably in his arms.

So this is how you survive in retail in a small town, Addy thought. He listened, he helped, he was friendly and, most importantly of all, he was Blake with the smile and the laughing eyes. She hadn't noticed those things in him before she'd left Remarkable Bay. Or maybe they'd been there all along and she hadn't wanted to see it.

He was so much more than a quick fuck ... sex ... a diversion.

The trouble was, Addy wasn't sure if she had any more to give than that. She still felt broken, ruined by what had happened to her, unsure of her judgement and about whether it was at all wise to leap into something else right away with another man. Crack the surface of Addy McNamara and she wasn't sure what was left inside.

And then, as if he'd known she was thinking about him, Blake looked across his shop and saw her. He lifted his chin in a silent greeting and handed the little girl he'd been holding back to her father, with a few quick words and a goodbye wave to the toddler. Addy tried to look busy. She picked out a shirt from the rack and she was holding the hanger in her hand as he approached. When she tried to hang it back up, it tangled with the other hangers in a metallic dance. She wasn't nervous, no, not at all.

'Addy,' he said. His voice melted her nerves away. He was just a man she'd had sex with a few times. He'd done nothing other than be kind to her, feed her, make love to her and listen to her. She'd never felt frightened with Blake.

'Hi, Blake.'

He searched her face, perhaps waiting for her to say more, but she couldn't say a word. There was too much to say, too much to explain. Maybe one day she'd tell him everything. Or not.

He glanced away and then his gaze returned to her. 'I was hoping you might come by. Buy a bikini, maybe.' He grinned and she let herself smile, feeling lighter as some of the tension that had tightened her shoulders flowed out with a breath.

'You're really busy today. It's great.'

He looked around. 'Summers in Remarkable Bay. God love 'em.'

Addy realised that she might just be starting to love Remarkable Bay too. She looked past him as another couple of customers entered the shop. 'I'm sorry. I can see you're really busy.'

'They can wait,' he replied adamantly, watching her intently.

She looked up into his eyes. Such an unusual blue. Like the ocean on a bright summer's day and quite hypnotising. Why had it felt as if she'd never noticed them before?

Because she'd been too busy looking away, that's why.

'I came by to say thank you for the flowers. It was very thought-ful of you.'

'Glad you liked them.'

'And my room. It's beautiful, too.'

He grinned at her and those mesmerising eyes sparkled.

'I was happy to help with that.'

'I love it.'

'I had an ulterior motive, of course.'

'What's that?'

Another group of chattering customers, a giggle of teenage girls in very short shorts and long straight hair, entered the shop and when Addy glanced over to the counter, she could see the queue was already four people deep. 'You've got customers. We can do this another time.'

He reached for her shoulder, gently laid his hand there. 'Can I see you tonight?'

Yes. 'Yes.'

Something like a smile shone in his eyes. 'Why don't you meet me on the beach? At seven o'clock.'

When Addy spotted Blake later that day, he was coming down the steps to the beach at Remarkable Bay, carrying a bodyboard under his arm. It was bright orange.

Addy lifted a hand to shield her eyes from the still bright early evening sun to watch him. She'd brought a towel and a couple of cold beers with her. As she was waiting all afternoon, figuring out what to say to him, her first thought went to champagne. But she figured it might be nice to mix things up for a change. She could do a cold beer at the beach with Blake Stapleton on a warm December night. Yes, as a matter of fact, she could. This wasn't a wine bar or a nightclub and there were no film people within a million miles of this little piece of heaven on the beach, dissecting the latest film from the latest hot director or the latest grosses out of Hollywood.

There could be far worse ways to kick-start her new life.

When he reached her, he stopped and lifted his chin, smiled broadly. His teeth gleamed in the sun. 'Is one of those for me?'

She lifted a bottle towards him. 'You look like you had a hard day at the office. I thought you might need something long and cool.'

'Perfect.' Blake took the beer from Addy, twisted off the top and took a long swig. Looking up at him, she would never have guessed he was a lawyer once. He looked too tanned for the kind of work that required files and a desk. She couldn't imagine him being constrained in a suit and tie all day, or obeying the rules of a courtroom.

He sat down next to her on the sand and they stared out at the waves.

Addy sipped her beer and slowed down enough—because she was learning that now—to take this all in. The wispy streaks of cloud spun like fairy floss in the distant fading sky. The smell of the ocean and the squawk of the seagulls flying overhead, waiting, hovering, for a scrap of food. The wind in her hair tickling her ears whispered to her. And Blake was next to her, his legs kicked out in front of him, his bare feet covered with glistening grains of sand. The wind played with his hair, too, and the sun added another layer of tan to his brown skin.

Finally, she asked him, 'What's with the bodyboard. You going for a swim?'

He turned slowly to her. 'It's a present. For you. The colour matches your hair.'

Addy scoffed. 'You might have me mixed up with someone else. I don't know how to use one of those things.'

'It's good fun. Getting out in the water, skimming a wave, it gets you out of your head for a while. I figured you could use some of that.'

Okay. The elephant in the room was stomping on the sand in between them.

Her pulse thudded suddenly and she waited for it to be steady, feeling lightheaded and jittery. Like half a panic attack.

She steadied her breathing. 'Listen, Blake. The reason I wanted to talk to you was to say … we started something before I left. But we shouldn't have.'

He sat silently on the sand next to her, his gaze on the distant waves.

She waited for him to respond to what she'd said. He didn't.

She continued. 'I've been through something really horrible and I thought fucking my way out of it was the answer. Turns out, that wasn't such a great idea. When things have got tough in my life, I've always run. I've done it my whole life and I'm tired. I need to stop for a while.'

Blake crossed his long legs at the ankles, propped his hands behind him in the sand and looked up to the sky.

The half-panic attack became stronger. Addy fought off the pinpricks of terror that rose up her spine, thickened her tongue and prickled each hair follicle. Her heart thumped against her ribs and she tried to slow her breathing so she wouldn't hyperventilate. She knew why she was feeling this panic: the last time she given a man the kiss off, he'd tried to kill her.

'Remarkable Bay isn't a bad place to stop for a while,' he said quietly.

She exhaled. 'I think so, too.'

'If you want to stop. Get off the beaten track.'

'That's exactly what I want.'

'How long do you reckon you'll stay?' Blake looked at her. His eyes were serious, narrowed in a question.

'Roma says I can stay as long as I want. And how long is that?' She tried to laugh to lighten the mood. 'I don't know. How long is a piece of string? I don't have any work lined up for a while and, to tell the truth, the idea of working fourteen-hour days isn't so appealing any more. I needed to get out of Adelaide. I figure I'm just going to hang down here for a while and see what happens. I'm tired. So tired.'

She could see the concern in his serious eyes, in the flat line of his mouth. 'That sounds like a plan,' he managed.

'Blake … I came to the shop today because there are some things I need to say. For one, I never thanked you for the flowers and the chocolates and the wine you sent me.'

'I was wondering if you ever got them.'

'I did. But since you didn't send a card with them I thought at first they were from someone else. Someone else I have been trying to run a million miles from. And then ... and then everything imploded and I forgot. So, thank you. And I wanted to also say thank you for the work you did helping Roma and Keira and Connor with my room. It's really beautiful. You've been nothing but kind and lovely to me since we met.'

And I'm not used to that, she thought. How could she explain to him that she still harboured suspicions about a man who treated her that way? About any man who wanted her?

'It's easy with you and I won't lie about why I helped out with your room. Why I sent you the flowers and the chocolate and the wine.'

Addy couldn't comprehend what he was saying.

He continued. 'I would have done anything to get you to stay for a little while.' His words were so quiet they were almost lost on the sea breeze. 'Or maybe a long while.'

If her life was normal, this would be perfect. But it wasn't.

'You're a great guy. You're more than that, actually. But I can't get into anything with you or anyone right now. One day, I might be able to explain but for now ... I just need to be alone for a while.'

'That's a pity,' he said quietly.

'It's the way it has to be for my own sanity.'

'To be clear. You weren't just a fuck for me, Addy.'

'Which makes me feel even worse for dragging you into my mess.'

Blake took a deep breath and turned to her. His voice was serious and deep, rough around the edges, as if there might be more he wanted to say but was holding himself back. 'Jesus, Addy. You didn't drag me. I went willingly. Very willingly.'

'I can't be with anyone right now. Not until I get my head sorted. And when I'm ready, you'll be my first choice, believe me. But in the meantime, I could really use a friend.'

There was a smile in Blake's eyes. She'd said no, but only no for now. She liked his reaction to it.

'What about a boss?'

Addy stared blankly at Blake. He continued. 'You saw for yourself how busy the shop is at this time of year. Feel like working a few shifts and helping me out?'

What the hell was happening? She'd said no to more sex and wound up with a job offer instead.

'You're offering me a job?'

'Yep.'

'In the Remarkable Bay Surf Shop?'

'Yep.'

Addy pondered his offer. She sure could use the money. She'd worked retail before, in a cafe during high school. It wasn't such a bad idea. It would distract her, help her connect with the real world again. She could give some money to Roma for rent. And she'd be working with Blake Stapleton, the man-of-few-words shopkeeper turned white knight. The idea made her smile.

'On one condition,' she said.

He grinned. 'If you have wage demands, I'll have to speak to my lawyer. Which is me.'

'If you want me to come and work for you, I have to redesign the shop.'

He was silent. She tried to read his expression. Was it shock?

'C'mon Blake, it's kind of a mess. You've got too many racks in there with too much old stock. It's cramped and hard to move around and actually see what you're stocking. Some of those posters on the walls are older than me and the surf DVDs you're playing on the TV behind the counter? I didn't see one woman out there on the waves. You need to do a stocktake, put some of that old stuff on sale and retail the hell out of that space.'

Before she'd finished her lecture, Blake was holding out a hand. 'Deal.'

Addy swallowed. 'You're not scared off by all my bossiness?'

'No.'

'Oh. It's just that I'm used to organising people. It's kind of my thing.'

'And it's just what I need.'

'When can I start?'

'How about tomorrow?'

'Okay.' She smiled. 'Tomorrow.'

CHAPTER
35

1946

Mrs Ruby Stuart was coming out of the greengrocers on a lively shopping strip in the Adelaide suburb of Norwood when she saw Cain Stapleton for the first time in eleven years.

It was a busy Saturday morning, and she'd had to wait in line at the grocer's while Mrs Buttrose, who lived three doors down from her, had painstakingly gone through her list with the greengrocer. Six potatoes. Ten carrots. A pound of peas. Finally, Ruby was served and nestled her purchases at the end of the pram, careful not to squash her daughter's toes. She said her farewells, manoeuvred the carriage down the front step, jiggling Edwina, who giggled as she bounced.

Ruby turned right and said polite hellos to her neighbours as they passed. She walked slowly past the pharmacy and a dress shop on the corner that Ruby had favoured until things such as new frocks and hats had become frivolous and unnecessary. Her feet ached. She'd been up since five in the morning with Edwina, who had fussed over breakfast while her other children had fought.

To break up the battle, she'd dragged Arthur along with her on their outing too. He had a banana in one hand and the other was holding on to the side of the pusher. As they walked, Edwina's eyes fluttered shut and she fell asleep, and Ruby breathed a sigh of relief.

She'd left her older two, Eleanor and Dudley, at home. Eleanor was ten years old now, and she'd faithfully promised to quietly play dominoes on the living room floor with her brother until their mother returned. Ruby hadn't hesitated to believe them. Since the day she was born, there was a wisdom about Eleanor that had perplexed Ruby. It made her ache to see it, but her daughter was so much like her sister Clara that it seemed sometimes she might have been her daughter instead of Ruby's.

There was only twelve months separating her first two children and in so many ways they were like twins, with a secret way of speaking to each other that Ruby couldn't penetrate. Four-year-old Arthur was rambunctious and liked to get in between his older brother and sister, taunting and teasing, proud to be the instigator of fights which inevitably resulted in someone shedding tears. It was all a lot to manage. Edwina had been a terrible sleeper since the day she was born and in those long cold nights of pacing the floor, trying to get her daughter to sleep, Ruby blamed herself. Edwina had been conceived in a rush and born in a haze of shock and grief.

For Ruby had been eight months pregnant when the uniforms had knocked at her door.

Edwin was dead. He'd died in Sandakan.

She'd gone into labour right there on the doorstep, a moment after the two soldiers had asked her if she was Mrs Stuart, a moment after they had handed her a letter.

It had fluttered to the floor.

Arthur had been behind her, holding on to her leg, gripping it tight, and she remembered his fearful cries as she'd doubled over and moaned. Her mother was behind her a moment later and Jane, the housekeeper, had whisked Arthur away with a sweep of her arm.

Ruby didn't remember Edwina's birth, other than her doctor telling her afterwards that it had been quick, that it was a pity she wouldn't be having any more children because she was a good breeder with hips like that, quick labours and healthy babies.

And she'd stared up at him, gripping the crisp and thick white sheets to her neck, staring at his slicked-down hair, like brushstrokes of ink on his pate, his pince-nez on the bridge of his nose, the smell of antiseptic in her nostrils, and the flow of blood warm and thick between her legs, and there were no words.

My husband is dead.

My daughter, my tiny precious bundle, will never know her father.

The doctor had swept out of the room and on to another patient. Ruby had lain there in the dim light, the cool quiet, glad Edwina was in the nursery, and felt the tears streak her cheeks.

She'd gone back to her mother and father's house after that, for a month or two after Edwin's death and Edwina's arrival, but she couldn't stay. Her mother had clung to her grandchildren too tight, each of them filling the hole in her heart where Clara's baby should have been.

Ruby had worked had to create her own family so she could escape the one she'd been born into. Staying there would mean the previous generation would slip their arms around her neck once more.

She was now a widow with four children and sadly she wasn't the only woman in Australia to have borne a loss. But they were expected to get over it. The war was over and there was so much of the stiff upper lip in her circles. When she'd finally moved back to her home, her mother had helpfully gone through and tidied up the house, readying it for Ruby's return. Her way of cleaning up was to destroy all of Edwin's letters, telegrams and photographs. Any reminder of him was gone. Ruby didn't even have a wedding photo left. Her mother had done the same thing when Clara had gone to London and never returned: her clothes were given away, her precious books, including her volume of Gould's *The Birds of Australia*, was donated, and photographs and school reports and letters were thrown in the fireplace and burnt to ashes.

It had broken Ruby's heart but she couldn't find the anger to blame her mother, who had been getting progressively more forgetful and disoriented towards the end of the war, her behaviour increasingly strange.

If her mother thought that destroying all traces of Edwin would mean she would miss him less, she was mistaken. She had four children who were constant reminders of the life she and Edwin had made together. She had settled for Edwin. By the time he went off to fight, they'd created a partnership that was as good as any other marriage, Ruby had supposed. Edwin had been a kind husband and a loving father. They grew to respect and care for each other, and Ruby accepted all the responsibilities that went with being his wife.

When Edwin was gone, first to Townsville and then to Malaysia, she'd raised her children and soldiered on. Ruby started a group which would meet in her living room and they knitted pullovers and caps and waistcoats with buttons and V-necks. Scarves and muffs, balaclava helmets and sleeping socks; gloves, with or without fingers.

It had helped sometimes, knowing that she and her new friends were doing what they could to support the war effort and the troops. She was able to smile and laugh, imagining the boys in Europe opening the packages from home, and then pulling out one of her jumpers. Would he notice the dropped stitches on the left arm? Would he read her note, always anonymous, and smile?

With warmest wishes to you from Adelaide.

Ruby couldn't bear to think of the items she and her friends had knitted stained with blood or brains. She couldn't bear to think of them on the bodies of corpses, in ditches, blown to bits, buried in graves so far from home.

Edwin wouldn't have needed such things. He had been a prisoner of war for two years in the stinking jungles of Sandakan. No, Edwin wouldn't need a jumper or mitts or gloves with or without fingers.

But someone else's husband or sweetheart or son or father might, and that's what kept them all going. Ruby felt a long way from the young girl she was in that December of 1934 when she'd spent her last summer at the Bayview Guest House at Remarkable Bay. She thought of Clara often. Ruby did the sums in her head and realised Clara would be thirty years old now. She'd moved to London back in 1935 and they'd never heard a word from her since. In eleven years there hadn't been a letter or a telegram or a Christmas card. Memories were all she had left of Clara Allen. Ruby wondered whether she'd ever married and if she had other children. The little girl born in 1935 would be ten years old now. She had hoped that her sisters' children would one day be terrific friends of her own children, but that was not meant to be. She didn't know Clara's daughter and wouldn't know Adeline's children, Mary and Frances, if she passed them on the street.

The three Miss Allens had become strangers to each other. Since that day Ruby had gone to Adeline's house and found her face black and blue, there had been a great estrangement between them. She believed she knew why. When she'd left, Ruby had gone directly to her mother and father's house and told them what she'd seen. Adeline had then accused her of making up malicious stories and peddling gossip and had never spoken to her again. Ruby thought she might settle once she'd had her baby, but there had never been any rapprochement.

Ruby often thought back to their last day at Remarkable Bay that summer. Adeline had said, 'It's the end. This is the last time we'll be here like this. As sisters. You and me and Clara.'

How had she been so prescient? Adeline hadn't known then about Clara, about the secret the rest of the family was burdened with, and had never been let in on it. As far as Adeline knew, Clara had abandoned her family for the glittering lights of London and had selfishly never returned.

Their parents and Ruby let her continue to believe it and Ruby had never shared her secret fear of what Clara might have faced in wartime London. More than twenty thousand people had died in the Blitz. What if Clara had been one of them? Ruby had seen the images in the newsreels that screened at the cinema before the main feature. The devastation had been random and complete; the bombs shredding homes and buildings and debris and bodies, all scooped together into towering piles of bricks and death.

What if Clara had been one of the casualties? Would Ruby have felt it? Would she somehow know that her younger sister was dead?

Ruby had lost Clara and then Adeline and now Edwin. She was becoming stoic to the losses; her guarded heart had never been as open as it had been back in 1934 when she'd met Cain Stapleton at Remarkable Bay. All those girlish hopes for love and life had become fairy tales as unrealistic as Cinderella or Sleeping Beauty.

That summer of 1934 and 1935 seemed like eleven lifetimes away instead of eleven years.

And now, standing outside the greengrocer's, everything about it had come back to her in an instant.

Cain Stapleton was staring at her open-mouthed, just ten feet ahead of her on the footpath. His aqua-blue eyes were as mesmerising now as they'd been the first time they'd shone down at her at Bayview, when he'd been delivering Mrs Nightingale's milk and butter from his parents' dairy farm. She could still taste it, that butter. Cool and thick on her tongue.

Cain stopped, lifted a hand, touched the brim of his hat, and nodded. His eyes flickered and fixed on her, recognition curved his lips and then there was the warm smile she remembered.

Roma reached for Arthur, ruffled his hair, satisfying herself that he was still next to her. She needed to reassure him. He'd become scared of strangers, especially tall men, and she didn't want him to make a scene in the street.

'Why, hello Ruby.' Cain stepped forward.

'Hello, Cain.'

How was it that she hadn't seen him in all these years? He looked much older than she supposed he might, having seemingly aged so much more than the eleven or so years since she'd last seen him. She knew that the war had wearied so many people. There was grey at his temples and lines around his eyes. He wore a moustache and there was a scar on his left cheek that he hadn't had when she'd known him. She'd dreamt of him so many times, staring back at her in the cool water of Remarkable Bay, especially when Edwin was away, when she was alone, after all the children were finally asleep and there was nothing but peaceful quiet in her bedroom and streets dark and ominous from the blackouts.

She'd made a good life with Edwin. But it had never been the life she'd wanted.

This man standing on the footpath in a three-piece suit was the man she'd always wanted.

'Who's this, then?' Cain glanced down at her son.

'This is Arthur,' she said, her voice shaky. 'And here in the pram is Edwina.'

She saw the memory flash in his eyes. 'Two children,' he mused with a sad smile.

'Four, actually. The older two are at home.'

'You have four children?'

And she knew what he was thinking. That four children meant a long and happy marriage and love and all that went with that.

'Yes.'

'I'm very happy for you, Ruby,' he said, his voice serious and quiet.

'And what about you, Cain? Do you have a family?'

'Yes,' he said. 'Two boys. The Stapletons are cursed with boys, it seems.'

Not a curse, never a curse, when one of them is you.

Edwina stirred and Cain peered at her wriggling form, which made her cry again.

Ruby lifted her daughter out of the blankets and held her tight to her chest, rocking from side to side to comfort her.

Cain's blue eyes widened. 'She looks just like you, Ruby.'

'Do you think?' Ruby peered down into her daughter's teary face. 'I can't see it. Everyone says she looks like her father.'

'No, she looks exactly like you. She's a most beautiful girl.'

And they shared a moment which, when Ruby looked back on it, felt like an hour but wasn't more than half a minute.

A mere moment together, after eleven years of dreams, and this was all it was to be.

'Do you live locally? I don't know if I've ever seen you here on the Parade.'

'No. My wife Edith and I live on the farm, down at Remarkable Bay.'

Edith. She knew the name. 'Edith? Didn't Mrs Nightingale have a niece by that name?'

'Yes. Edith Robinson. We were married in 1937 after I finished university.'

If Ruby was looking for regret or revenge in his tone or his face, she didn't see it. Her heart swelled and tore at the same time. She was so happy that he was married, had a family and everything that went along with that. But it burned to know that it wasn't with her. It still burned. How dare she feel heartbroken at the news? She had no place, after what she'd done to Cain, to wish that he hadn't found happiness.

'Congratulations Cain. That's wonderful. And you and Edith are on the farm?'

'Yes. We did live up here in town during the war, when I worked at the Council for Scientific and Industrial Research looking into animal diseases. But we moved back a few months ago. Edith's a local girl and she wanted to go home. I'm here to see to my uncle's house. He died four weeks ago. His own son died in Africa during the war, so the house was left to my brother and me.'

'I'm so sorry to hear that.'

'Thank you.'

'And your parents?' Ruby asked. 'Are they still on the farm?'

Cain chuckled. 'Try keeping my father away from his precious cows.'

Arthur started to get restless, and he tugged on Ruby's hand. She looked down and scolded him. 'In a minute, Arthur.'

Cain held out a hand. 'Please, don't let me delay you. I know how young boys can be. Mine like nothing better than playing cricket for burning off all that energy. Little Christopher slogs the ball all around the property. He imagines himself to be a young Ray Lindwall, I think.'

'He sounds like a delightful young boy with lots of energy. I have one of those myself,' Ruby cocked her head towards Arthur, 'So I understand completely.'

Cain took a step closer. Ruby held her breath. She could smell the sea and taste the salt in her mouth.

'Ruby ...' he said quietly, deeply, and then paused. She didn't need to hear the words. She could see by the forlorn, longing look on his face what he meant. It mirrored her own feelings exactly.

'I know,' she whispered.

'I've never forgotten you.'

'And I'll always remember that summer,' she said, fighting the tears.

When he reached for her hand, she slipped her fingers in his. She remembered his warm strength. He glanced down and then looked back up quickly. She knew what he'd seen: that she wasn't wearing a wedding ring. She'd had to take it off when she was pregnant with Edwina because her fingers had swollen so much it would have to be cut off if she hadn't lathered it with castor oil and finally coaxed it off. She hadn't put it back on. There was no point. Everyone knew Edwin was dead. Everyone knew she was a widow.

And now Cain did too.

'Goodbye, Cain.'

He waited, as if he was struggling to say the words. 'Goodbye, Ruby.'

Ruby's heart shuddered as she walked away from the man she would love with all her heart until the day she died, 2 July 1981. She lay in a bed at the Royal Adelaide Hospital, surrounded by her four children and her grandchildren, with too many different names to remember, names that had sounded strange and modern when she'd heard them for the first time: Kylie and Belinda and Melissa and Natasha.

The youngest of all her granddaughters, Michelle, went into labour on the day Ruby Allen died and delivered a healthy baby girl just before midnight.

Her name was Roma Elizabeth Harris.

CHAPTER
36

2016

The French doors to the balcony off Roma's bedroom were wide open and the sheer white curtains were billowing in great puffs, like clouds. Outside, stars were bright in the night sky. Inside, Roma and Connor lay side by side. She was nestled in the crook of his arm and he was playing with her hair, winding the strands of it around a finger.

Roma had wondered for a while about what this would feel like, about being in her bed with Connor, about how it would feel after they'd made love for the first time. There were a few words floating around in her head, finding their way into her heart and lodging there like a feeling she never wanted to go away. Right. Easy. Wonderful. This man was wonderful. And that's how she felt now.

'Your hair's getting long.' She moved next to Connor, easing a leg over his, teasing her fingers through his ruffled hair. He held her tighter.

He stroked a finger up her arm. 'It's my way of sticking it to the man. I always get a kick out of the way visiting magistrates stare down at me from the bench. I consider it my minor act of rebellion. I know it's not much but it's all I've got.'

'Don't all the best revolutions start with hair?'

They laughed.

'You know,' Roma said, 'When I met you, I thought you were a real estate agent. I mean, who else wears a suit in Remarkable Bay?'

He chuckled. 'Ouch.'

They lay silent in the quiet. Connor kissed the top of her head and she felt his warm sigh against her hair.

'Can I tell you something?' he asked softly.

'Sure.'

'I've wanted you since the first day we met back in August, on that cold day at the bakery. When you apparently thought I was a real estate agent. No wonder you looked at me the way you did. With disdain.'

'I did not!'

'You did, too. And I don't know why but when I saw you, I had to say hello, and then I ran off at the mouth and no doubt looked like a total fuckwit. Thanks for not mentioning that, by the way.'

She pressed her lips to his chest, smiled against his warm skin. He was always doing that, lightening the serious with a joke, putting an exclamation mark on the things he said.

'You had food in a bag for Angas.'

'So you do remember.'

'Of course I do. After the woman at the bakery, you were the second person I spoke to in Remarkable Bay. '

'I don't know if this makes any sense, but I saw something in your eyes that day.'

What had he seen? Was it her pain? Her guilt? She breathed deep. Did she really want to know the answer? Hearing what other people thought of you wasn't like looking into a mirror and seeing your reflection. It was what people saw in you when you weren't aware you were being observed. The real you. The raw you.

'What was that?' she finally asked.

Connor turned so he was face-to-face with her. She didn't need any light to know what was in his eyes because she could feel it in his touch, in each caress, in each kiss.

'Your eyes were full of secrets. And sadness.' He stroked her cheek gently. 'And I don't know why, but I had to find out why you were so sad. I had to go and talk to you. This sounds ridiculous and like the biggest line you can think of, but I was drawn to you. It's so weird.'

Roma scoffed good-humouredly. 'You're not telling me you believe in fate or something?'

'Don't you?'

'No.' She hesitated. 'Well, I never used to. But I can't fight the feeling that Remarkable Bay somehow chose me. This rundown, weird-smelling house that I just had to buy. It brought me here and brought all these people into my life.'

Connor pulled her closer and she pressed herself against his warm and naked body.

'Ever since you told me that you used to come down here when you were a kid, I've been wondering how it is that we never met? All those summers you were here with your family and Addy and I must have been everywhere you were. I've been wracking my brain, trying to recreate every memory to see if you were there somewhere. On the beach. At the deli. In the surf shop.'

'Anything?' she asked with a smile.

'No, nothing. Maybe we weren't meant to have met then. I mean, if I had, I would have fallen madly in love with you right there and then and obviously would never have married Angas's mother or had Angas.'

'I know what would have happened if we had met. You would have fallen in love with Addy. Everyone always did.'

Connor held her tighter. 'I think this happened at just the right time, don't you?'

'Yes,' Roma said, thinking that perhaps there was a mystery about Bayview after all.

CHAPTER
37

1934

'Miss Clara?'

There was a knock on the door of her parents' front parlour and Clara Allen looked up from her chair. She'd settled in for the afternoon, glad of the peace with everyone else in the family out and didn't appreciate the interruption. Her mother and her sisters were out at John Martin in Rundle Street, shopping for new outfits for their holiday that summer at Remarkable Bay. It had been all Adeline had talked about since she'd seen the fashion parades at the Town Hall last month. That and her wedding next April.

Clara couldn't have cared less about the newest fashions from Sydney or London or Paris. She wasn't interested in rouging her cheeks or the latest lipsticks or whether or not Ruby should have her hair cut into the latest style, a bob, which sat bluntly in a straight line at the nape of her neck. Clara was far more utilitarian. She had only just turned eighteen, after all, and was more interested in a pair of sensible shoes she could wear when she was bird watching in the Botanic Gardens set amongst the parklands which ringed the city. Instead of a new lipstick, she would have much preferred a new pair of binoculars.

And now, her solace had been interrupted.

'Yes, Mrs Battersby?'

'It's Mr James Stuart.'

Clara pinched her lips together. Why was it her job to entertain the man who was to be her brother-in-law next April? She checked her watch. Where was Adeline?

'Come in,' she called hesitantly.

James Stuart entered the room slowly, wearing his familiar smile. He glanced around the room as if he hadn't seen it a hundred times before. The glass cabinets lined with ornaments. The tapestry-upholstered furniture. The ornate grandfather clock in its polished mahogany case which Clara's father had shipped from England two years before.

'Hello, James,' Clara said politely. 'Adeline isn't here.'

'Isn't she? That's a bother when I've come all this way.'

James had closed the door behind him and was taking slow steps across the room to her. He looked neat and polished as he always did, with his dark hair slicked back with whatever it was that young men greased their hair up with these days. His tweed suit was neatly pressed and his white collar gleamed. When Clara looked at his shoes, she could almost see her reflection in the leather.

Clara put her book down on the mahogany table next to the upholstered sofa and stood, to emphasise the point that she was not in the mood for conversation. 'I don't know when she'll be back.'

James adjusted his tie and smoothed down the flaps on his pockets. 'Mrs Battersby's just told me. I must have the time mixed up. I definitely thought I was to meet her here at two.'

The grandfather clock standing tall on the wall opposite the marble fireplace revealed he was ten minutes late as it was. Its shining silver pendulum swung, and Clara watched it, hoping James would get the hint that her time was precious, and leave.

Clara straightened her shoulders. 'She's caught the tram into town with mother and Ruby. They're shopping for outfits to take down to Remarkable Bay. Although I don't know why one would bother three months out, but still, I suppose I don't like shopping as much as they do.'

James was by her side. 'What are you reading, little Clara?'

'*The Birds of Australia* by John Gould. This is Volume One.' She sat down. There was no possible way James was interested in birds or nature but he turned the book towards him and casually flipped through the pages. When he closed the hard cover on the volume, he settled on the sofa next to Clara.

'Birds of Australia,' he said. 'Which one is your favourite?'

He lifted the book and passed it to her, moved closer so he could more easily see the illustrations. Clara opened the book to a well-worn page. 'This one. *Platycercus elegans*. The crimson rosella. Sometimes it's called the Adelaide rosella. They fly in to our front yard sometimes.'

'Pretty little things, aren't they?' James's voice seemed to be rather close to her ear. 'All those wonderful colours.' When his fingers traced through her hair, loose and curly on her shoulders, Clara squeezed herself against the arm of the sofa, away from him. She pushed her feet into the Persian rug and tried to stand up but he'd pressed his thigh against hers and trapped her.

'James, please. You're squashing me. Would you move over please? Shall I ask Mrs Battersby for some tea?'

After that, it all happened so quickly. He was so practised, as if he'd done it a hundred times before, that Clara had trouble later remembering in which order James had attacked her. Did he grab her throat first or press his mouth to hers? Were his probing hands scratching up her thigh and inside her petticoat before or after he'd groped her small breast? And when had he managed to free himself from his trousers? Before or after he'd ripped her underwear and exposed her to his fingers and his violence?

There were some things Clara wasn't confused about, so clear were they in her memory. He'd slammed her head back against the wooden end of the upholstered sofa so forcefully that she'd had an egg-shaped lump there for a week afterwards. She would never forget his ugly, threatening words, that she should tell no one or he would reveal her immorality to the whole of Adelaide and she would ruin both her sisters' happiness. And, as he moved on top of her, she dared not make a noise, dared not scream in case Mrs Battersby walked in and saw them, and then he whispered crude things in her ear as he slid a hand between her legs. She stiffened, every muscle rigid with shock about what was happening to her, and the scream that she felt rising up from her lungs was silent, and he was on top of her and pushing between her legs, forcing himself inside her, and there was pain and he groaned and then she remembered him exhaling into her ear and he smelt of tobacco and she choked on the smell.

When James got off her, pushing down angrily as he levered himself up, he tidied his clothes and harshly suggested she do the same.

'Tell your sister I stopped by and that I was so sorry she wasn't here.' He leaned down towards her, placing a hand either side of her head, pulling her hair tight, and she gasped. 'And this is our little secret, Clara. Remember that.'

The man smiled at her and she felt nothing. When his jacket was buttoned and his tie straightened, he turned to leave but tripped and stumbled on Gould's *The Birds of Australia*, which had fallen to the floor, spread open to Clara's favourite page. He kicked it across the room before looking back over his shoulder and sneering.

'Lovely seeing you this afternoon, Clara. Tell Adeline I couldn't wait.'

James Stuart closed the door quietly as he left and she heard him call a traitorously cheerful goodbye to Mrs Battersby down the long hallway as he departed. Clara waited, unable to breathe, her heart pounding behind her eyes, a strange and guilty dampness between her legs. It was only when she heard the wrought-iron gate latch close behind him, and long footsteps past the parlour window, did Clara begin to shake and cry.

CHAPTER
38

Rain lashed Sydney on 22 September 1935, the day Clara Allen leapt over The Gap and into the pounding Sydney winter sea two hundred and eighty feet below.

She was a smart girl. She'd planned everything meticulously so there would be no suspicion about what she'd done. After what had happened, she did not want to be the cause of further shame or embarrassment to her family. She'd waited until her Aunt Jane was out shopping and had then written a letter, within its pages details of her plans for a new life in London; that she had booked passage on a P&O liner and was setting sail that day. She'd implored her aunt to understand that she hadn't wanted another farewell, after all that had happened, and promised to write once she reached England. She'd packed all her belongings in her single suitcase and left it in the foyer of a hotel in Kings Cross. There would be no remaining trace of her left. Just as there was no remaining trace of her child.

The child who must never know her history.

Two aunts who must never, ever know who her father really was.

Clara had never held her baby, had never seen her face or touched her soft little body. The infant had been whisked away from her mother as soon as the umbilical cord was cut and she had disappeared, had been wrenched from her, as if Clara might stain the baby if the little one were to cast her eyes on her shameful mother. As if her shame might also shame her baby.

Clara had said goodbye to her family nine months before. She'd said goodbye to her Aunt Jane that morning with a kiss on the cheek and a wave at the front door. And she'd said goodbye to her baby with wet tears and a broken heart.

She was inured to goodbyes now.

All Aunt Jane would know was that Clara had departed for London for a grand adventure. It was best this way. Clara had felt so alone. Without her family, without her baby, she was hollow. There was to be no more joy in her life. There was nothing but fear of being found out and misery and shame and guilt about what had happened to her drowning her.

Clara looked up into the rain. A seagull fluttered overhead, stalling, waiting, and she remembered all those summers at Remarkable Bay.

She smiled at the bird in the moment before she leapt.

The next day, the papers reported that a well-dressed middle-aged man had been walking his dog when he'd seen a woman in a billowing navy skirt standing on the eastern Sydney cliff top at Watson's Bay. He'd been disbelieving and distraught when she'd stepped over the edge and disappeared into the churning water below, her skirt flaring out like a parachute as she leapt.

It hadn't saved her.

The police were alerted with great haste and had set out in a steamer for a rescue. When her body was dragged aboard the boat, there were no papers or no identifying jewellery.

She couldn't have been more than eighteen years old, perhaps twenty, it was reported later. She was never identified and there was speculation for a week about who the mysterious flying young woman in the navy dress had been, until another scandal gripped Sydney.

No one came forward to claim the mysterious young woman and she was later laid to rest in a pauper's grave, with no burial marker, no name, no identity, no history.

It was as if Clara Allen had never existed.

CHAPTER
39

2016

When Roma woke on Christmas Eve, stretched and yawned, blinked herself awake, she could hear Christmas carols.

The sound of cheesy Christmas songs was drifting up the staircase, along the upstairs hallway and into her bedroom.

She stilled and listened. It was Michael Bublé, she was sure of it, crooning about Christmas and sleigh bells and reindeer. Not entirely appropriate for a thirty-five degree day in her little beachside town on the south coast of Australia, but comforting none the less.

There were sleepy footsteps in the hallway and then a knock on her door.

'Come in,' she called.

Keira was in her workout gear already.

'You going for a run?' Roma yawned.

Keira snorted. 'I've *been* for a run.' She cocked her head at the door. 'You hear that?'

'I'm pretty sure it's Michael Bublé,' Roma said, slowly sitting up, pushing her hair from her face.

Keira sat on the end of her bed. 'And he's singing Christmas carols.'

'Well, it is almost Christmas, you know.' She'd been thinking about the holiday a lot in the weeks leading up to it, since Addy's return, since her invitation to Connor and Angas. It was getting easier. This would be her fourth Christmas without Tom and the sixth for her and Leo since their parents had died within months of each other. And while she would never forget them, and they would always be missing at this time of year, she found some joy in the fact that she'd found a new family to share this special time with. This year would be her first Christmas with Addy in about twenty years. Keira wasn't just a housemate anymore: she already seemed like part of her family. And then there was Connor. And Angas. And Blake. They'd all really got to know each other while they were doing up Addy's room and she had loved watching the Stapleton men banter with each other, tease and joke, and it had been fun to see Angas increasingly able to turn the tide on his father and his uncle with barbs of his own.

This was a new beginning in a place in which she'd never expected to do anything but hide. She had left her world but a new one had come to her, in all its messy glory, with its baggage and memories and complications and history. Bayview had worked some kind of magic on them all, she realised.

The music downstairs seemed to get louder and Roma and Keira chuckled.

'You think she's trying to tell us something?' Roma said. 'Like, get out of bed?'

Keira's expression became serious and she started to speak but stopped. She dropped her eyes to her hands.

'I've been meaning to say, Roma.' When she looked up, her eyes were wet with tears. 'I wanted to say thanks for changing all your plans and moving the big dinner to Christmas Eve just for me. You should have heard Mum when I called and told her I'd be coming to Coffs Harbour on Christmas Day in time for dinner.'

'They were excited, huh?'

Keira rolled her eyes. 'I thought my mother was going to have a heart attack. She loves Christmas so much and I've missed a few over the years. This year ... I don't know, I feel like going home. Everything that has annoyed the crap out of me about her seems like nothing when you realise what other people have gone through.' Keira sniffed. 'You with Tom, and you and Leo losing your parents. Addy with all that horrible bullshit she's been going through. Whatever gripes I have with my bizarre, dysfunctional family seem like first world problems right about now. I figured out something. No matter how crazy my parents are, I should hang on to them while I've still got them, right?'

Roma reached for Keira's hand. 'Absolutely. And you can always come back here to a whole new group of people who love you.'

'Oh, I'm coming back. A week with my mother will be more than enough.'

'You know what I like about living now, in this time in history, in this country?' Roma looked up to the ceiling as she thought. 'We're not bound by the old rules about what was acceptable or not. We don't all have to do the washing on a Monday like our grandmothers did or risk the vengeance of neighbourhood gossip. All those terrible things that families kept secret are now things we celebrate. Nowadays, we get to choose who we love, although some still can't *marry* the person they love, unfortunately. And if we want to, we can sell up everything in the city without a man's permission and move to Remarkable Bay. And the only thing people are gossiping about is how much I spent on this place.'

Keira looked around the room. 'I love this house, you know.'

'Me too. I don't think I ever want to leave.'

'Why would you?'

'I'll run out of money one day. Maybe sooner than that.' She laughed. 'So I'm going to have to come up with something.'

Keira got up from the bed and walked to the French doors, slipped through them and went out to the balcony.

Roma got out of bed and followed Keira outside. The sky was already the brightest of blues and the north wind was crisping everything it touched. Past the reserve across Ocean Street, they could see people already on the beach, and the white caps of three-foot waves were already moving in rhythm on to the sand.

'I've got an idea,' Keira said. 'What if—'

'Where are you two?' She was interrupted by Addy, who had poked her head through the curtains and was staring at both women indignantly.

'We're enjoying the view,' Roma called.

'Haven't you heard the music?' Addy all but stomped her feet.

'How could we *not* hear the music?' Keira said.

'I've got a surprise downstairs. I've been waiting ages.'

Roma and Keira exchanged glances. 'We're coming.'

Addy had transformed Bayview's kitchen and dining room into a movie set for a movie about Christmas. A real fir tree stood in one corner, stylishly decorated with nothing but gold baubles, all of the same size. Tiny fairy lights had been strung from each corner of the room, criss-crossing each other, which made the ceiling look like the night sky. The dining table was covered in sparkling swirls of tinsel, and multi-coloured crackers lay diagonally across each plate. Right down the centre was a row of mismatched white candles of different heights and shapes, and tall glasses stood sparkling at the top of each setting. Gold angels hung in each window and a poinsettia sat bright red on the kitchen counter.

Addy turned down Michael Bublé and turned to see their reactions. 'Well?'

Roma was still trying to take it all in. 'Were you up at the crack of dawn or something?'

Addy sighed happily. 'I stayed up last night after you two crashed. I wanted to give you both a surprise for Christmas Eve.'

'Mission accomplished, sister,' Roma said with a smile.

'Best Christmas present ever,' said Keira.

'Think of it as my way of thanking you both. I haven't had a Christmas with family in so many years I can't remember. This year, finally, it feels like something I want to celebrate. I'm down here. I have a job and I get to hang out with the both of you.' Addy gave Roma a meaningful glance.

'It's beautiful, Addy, it really is.' Roma teared up. She felt exactly the same. This year, there was something to be thankful for. There were two people right here to be thankful for: her oldest friend and her newest friend. Her housemates. Her family.

'To be honest, I've never liked Christmas much,' Addy said, staring at the twinkling lights on the tree. 'Not since I was about fifteen, anyway. My parents inevitably argued about who would get me and then whoever won seemed as if they didn't really want me there in the first place. I always felt like the mysterious Christmas gift that no one wanted once they'd unwrapped the pretty paper and found out what was inside. And in the past few years … well, in the past few years I've been a bit of a Grinch as well.'

Roma felt Addy's shoulders rise and fall. She hadn't felt much like celebrating either since Tom had died. Leo had encouraged her to come to Sydney—insisted, more like it—but she'd stayed home instead, telling him that she didn't want to leave her dog, Charlie. Tom's parents had of course asked her to their house for lunch, but after the first year turned into a grieving reflection on all they had lost, she couldn't go back there again.

This—this house, this room, these women—felt more like Christmas than anything she had felt in a very long time.

'It really feels like Christmas now, don't you think?' Addy looked around at her work.

Roma laid her head on Addy's shoulder. 'It really, really does.'

They moved to the counter and sat on the stools opposite each other. Roma still in her sleeping T-shirt, Keira in her workout gear and Addy in the black top and yoga pants that she wore to Pilates. A warm breeze played with the baubles on the tree, and they swayed back and forth. The lights over their heads tinkled against each other like distant Christmas bells.

'Coffee?' When both the other women nodded, Keira got to work behind the coffee machine.

'I can't believe it's Christmas,' Roma said. 'When I moved down here in August, I couldn't imagine the end of September, much less all this. A real tree, stylish decorations a la Addy McNamara, and two housemates.'

Addy propped an elbow on the bench and her chin in her hand. 'Has it helped, do you think, moving down here?'

Roma thought on it and nodded. 'So many good things have happened. If Leo hadn't thought I'd made some totally ridiculous real estate investment by buying Bayview in the first place, he wouldn't have asked you to come. And then we wouldn't have met Keira.'

'Because it's all about me, isn't it?' Keira laughed. 'Don't you see what Bayview has done for you two? Maybe this house has magical powers. Maybe it knows things we don't and is trying to make amends for something.'

Roma nodded to Addy. 'She's been watching too many horror movies. She'll be expecting green slime to come pouring out of the walls next.'

Addy shivered. 'Houses have history. Why wouldn't this one?'

Keira put three cups on the table and fetched the milk from the fridge. 'We never did figure out the mystery of Clara Allen.'

'No, we didn't.' Roma said as she sipped her coffee. She'd thought a lot about Clara, Ruby and Adeline since they'd found the guest book. Who were those women from so long ago? What had they wished for themselves in 1934? She didn't know about their loves, their passions, their secrets. All women had secrets, Roma knew too well, so what had they carried to their graves? If she'd had children herself, would she have ever told them the truth about her life, about Tom? No, she didn't think she would. We whitewash our histories. We rewrite them to suit. We edit out all the painful things and we pass down fairy tales. That's what parents do for their children and their children's children.

Roma knew better than anyone that everyone had secrets, and some she would carry with her to the grave. Perhaps Clara Allen was the same, whoever she was.

Roma did know that she wouldn't be sitting in Bayview right now if it wasn't for Ruby Allen and the choices she had made in her life. If Ruby hadn't married her husband Edwin, Roma's grandmother would never have been born and if she hadn't married Peter, her own mother wouldn't have been born and so on down the line it went. Whatever choices they'd made, Roma was grateful for them now. Everyone has secrets, and maybe Clara Allen was protecting her own. It wasn't inconceivable to think that Clara had moved away from Adelaide and had never returned. The family was well-to-do in those days: perhaps she had travelled the world and had adventures that Roma never would, although she had all the freedom and resources to do it if she wanted to.

'Maybe Clara was a nobody,' Addy said with a sigh and then clarified her words. 'Oh, you know what I mean. A simple girl. Perhaps she had a holiday one summer a very long time ago at Remarkable Bay and then went back to her life. Got married, changed her name, had a family, did all the normal things. What else was there to do in those days?'

'Maybe she did,' Roma said.

Keira glanced around the room. 'Maybe she wouldn't want us to know, whoever she really was. Maybe there are secrets we're never meant to find out.'

Addy smiled sadly. 'Sometimes people don't want to tell anyone the truth, for a whole range of reasons. I don't know, maybe it's best we never found out who she was. Sometimes there are skeletons in closets because people want them to stay there.'

'Oh,' Keira rubbed her arms. 'I just got the shivers.'

'You've been watching too many horror movies,' Roma joked.

'No, really,' Keira said, wide-eyed. 'You didn't feel that?'

Addy and Roma looked at each other. They shook their heads.

'So when did you say Leo was arriving?' Addy asked, turning her attention to Roma while she drank her coffee.

'His flight lands about midday, but he's hiring a car and doing some tasting in McLaren Vale on the way down. Which means that we'll have some lovely wine for our Christmas dinner.'

Addy clapped her hands together. 'We'd better get started on the food then.'

'Oh no you don't.' Roma took Addy by the shoulders and gently pushed her towards the kitchen door. 'Keira and I will get everything started. You've done enough already, so why don't you have the first shower? I'll pretend that I know how to stuff a turkey.'

Keira head snapped towards Roma. 'You've never cooked a turkey before?'

Roma bit her lip. 'No. Is that bad?'

Keira laughed. 'You might have mentioned it when we lugged home that five-kilo bird yesterday.'

'Well, I thought it seemed Christmassy. A turkey with all the trimmings. This is a special Christmas. It's my first in Bayview. Addy's here. You're here, Keira. Connor and Angas are coming.' Roma glanced at Addy with a grin. 'And Blake. And Leo's coming from Sydney. This year is special.'

Keira looped an arm around Roma's shoulders. 'Let's go consult Dr Google and get this figured out, shall we?'

CHAPTER
40

To the tune of a further selection of cheesy Christmas songs Roma had downloaded on to her iPod, they worked through the morning. They wrangled the turkey, argued good-naturedly about the cooking instructions, made stuffing (minus the chestnuts which Roma hadn't been able to find at the local supermarket), peeled potatoes and pumpkin, set jelly and made custard for the trifle, peeled prawns for the entree cocktails (because why have a seventies-inspired kitchen if you weren't going to go retro with at least some of the food), and sipped a champagne cocktail at midday to celebrate their progress.

They repeated the champagne cocktail at one, two and three o'clock as well to celebrate further progress and, when Leo arrived at four, they were sitting around the kitchen table, all the work finished, basking in the glow of what they'd achieved and revelling in the scent of the roasting turkey.

'Leo!' Roma jumped up from her chair and went to her brother, throwing her arms around him for a huge hug. It was so good to see him, and she hoped he could see how different she was now, how much happier.

'Have I interrupted something?' he choked out, barely able to breathe with the air being squeezed out of him.

'Leo the Lion,' Addy called out and she too went to Leo, hugging him.

'Something smells amazing,' he said when they finally let go. He looked around the room. 'Wow. This really is Christmas.'

Roma took his arm and dragged him forward. 'Leo, this is Keira. Keira, Leo. She's the one I told you about. The scientist-slash-sadist who has the Pilates studio.'

Keira stood and when Leo extended a hand she reached up and kissed his cheek instead. 'Put away that hand. I feel like I know you already.'

Leo looked a little surprised, taken aback by the noise and camaraderie of the three women. He propped his hands on his hips and smiled at them, noticing the half-empty bottle of champagne on the table. 'I see you started without me.'

There were footsteps in the hallway and a voice called out, 'Mate, where do you want the wine?'

'In here, Dylan. The end of the hallway.'

Keira looked at Roma, wide-eyed. She mouthed, *Dylan?*

A tall man, with short blond hair and a strong jaw, walked in to the kitchen carrying a box of wine in his arms. He glanced around and smiled at Roma, Addy and Keira.

'Over there, by the window,' Roma instructed. 'Thanks.'

They watched Dylan bend down and slowly position the box by the wall. As the women admired his arse, the bottles clinked together and Roma grinned at the blush in Keira's cheeks. He turned, slipped his hands into the front pockets of his jeans and smiled at everyone.

Leo clapped his hands together. 'For god's sake, stop staring at the man's arse.'

'We were not!' Roma insisted.

'We were so,' Addy snorted. 'And we're allowed to stare at your boyfriend's arse, especially when you bring him to Remarkable Bay for Christmas and when he's that hot.'

Dylan looked at his shoes, grinning.

'He's not my boyfriend,' Leo huffed and rolled his eyes.

'Aw,' Addy teased. 'Did he turn you down? Too old for him?'

Dylan laughed out loud. 'I'm straight.'

All three women laughed so hard the happy noise filled the kitchen.

Leo rolled his eyes. 'Dylan? That's my sister, Roma. Addy is our incorrigible kind-of-cousin. It's complicated and I'll explain later. And this is ...' Leo looked at Keira with a raised eyebrow. 'Kelly? I'm getting that wrong, aren't I?'

'Keira,' she said. She lifted a hand and waved to Dylan who smiled warmly back at her.

Leo walked over to the counter and slipped an arm around Roma's shoulder. She leaned into him, so happy to see him, so happy to have him at Bayview for Christmas. He looked down at her with what seemed to be relief in his eyes.

'Since this Christmas is all about widows and orphans,' he said, 'I thought you wouldn't mind if I brought this guy along. The poor bastard faced spending Christmas all alone in some terrible English-themed pub in Sydney crying into a beer and dreaming of snow, so I took pity on him.'

'It's true.' Dylan nodded, smiling. 'I just can't get used to these appalling Australian summers. All the sun. All the seafood.'

Everyone laughed and Dylan's tanned face split in a grin. 'Thanks for letting me barge in on your dinner, Roma.'

'You're very welcome. I'm glad you came.' They shook hands and then he did the same with Addy and Keira.

'Whereabouts in London are you from?' Keira asked.

'From Kent originally, but I lived in Wimbledon before I came out to Australia.'

'Wimbledon, huh? I love the tennis. What's it like going to see it in real life?'

'Living in Wimbledon doesn't mean you get tickets, unfortunately. I've never been.'

Keira looked down into her champagne glass and Roma saw the look. Dylan had held her gaze for just one extra moment and

Keira's blush coloured her cheeks. Roma looked at Leo. He'd seen it too. They shared a knowing smile. Leo had done it again. He'd sent Addy to Roma when she'd moved down to Bayview, lost and alone. He'd sent her to Addy when she'd been assaulted.

Roma turned her face towards him and whispered into his ear, 'I'm so glad you've come.'

He nudged her in the side. 'So how about a tour of Casa del Disaster?'

Ten minutes later, Roma and Leo were on the balcony, looking out over Remarkable Bay, the late-afternoon sun creating sparkling diamonds on the water. A mild sea breeze played with Roma's hair and Leo sucked the salty air into his lungs. He leaned his elbows on the railing and took in the view.

'I didn't get it when I looked at this place on the internet, but I damn well get it now.'

'Get what?' Roma asked.

'You. This house. I really did think your grief about Tom had driven you mad. I mean, who does this? Who buys a rundown guesthouse in a dying seaside town? And you?' He pointed at his sister with a grin. 'The most cautious person I know. You, who's never done anything spontaneous in your life without analysing it a hundred times.'

Leo was right. She had been that kind of person. But she'd been liberated from that, with all that had happened to her. Being cautious hadn't prevented her marriage from disintegrating, hadn't stopped the car that night that had hit Tom and killed him. It hadn't prevented her parents dying from cancer. It hadn't helped with her overwhelming grief in the years since.

He was serious now, his eyes narrowed, as if he finally understood his sister. 'I get it now, why you moved down here and bought Bayview. Look at all those people downstairs. You've brought everyone together. You've got me back from Sydney for Christmas for the first time in a long time.'

'I wanted it to feel like Christmas again,' she said simply.

'Hope you don't overcook the turkey.'

She smacked his arm good-naturedly. 'So tell me. What's Dylan's story?'

'He sits at the next desk to me. He's a really great bloke. You know, for a Pom.' Leo chuckled. 'He met an Australian woman in London last year, fell madly in love with her and did this really big atypical English thing and threw everything in over there to come to Sydney to surprise her. Poor bugger. Turns out she was engaged to someone else. But he already had his visa and decided to stay anyway. He absolutely loves it here. I reckon he'll be barracking for Australia in the cricket before too long.'

'I'm glad you brought him with you.'

Leo raised an eyebrow. 'I think he might be glad he's come, too.'

Roma smiled. 'You saw that, too?'

'I thought he might be good for Addy, but I don't think that's going to happen.'

'No. You're right there. There's someone here in the Bay who likes her a lot, but I think it'll take her some time to trust someone, to want a man in her life again, after what she's been through.'

'For a pretty damn good reason. What's he like?'

'He's solid. His name is Blake. He's Connor's cousin and he used to be a lawyer but he owns the surf shop now.'

'Connor. He's the guy next door, right?'

Roma felt the heat in her own cheeks, felt a flood of happiness well inside her.

'Judging by that look on your face, it's serious.'

Roma concentrated on the distant ocean, the white caps, the blue sky and the Norfolk Island pines swaying in the distance.

'It might be. He's got a fifteen-year-old son. Angas. I've got my baggage. We're taking it slow. We're being careful.'

'Is that because of his son or because of you?'

'Both. I really like him. He's a lawyer, too. He helped Addy with everything after she was assaulted. He's coming to dinner tonight. And so is Blake.'

'Did you at least organise me a blind date?'

Roma laughed. 'I thought you had a thing with your personal trainer?'

Leo sighed. 'I did. I'm back on the market. Hey, I've been meaning to ask. Did you ever do any more digging about that woman in the book? Clara?'

Roma shrugged. 'No, not really. I don't know what I was expecting to find, to be honest. After everything that's happened, I kind of need to put the past where it belongs. If I look back, I think of Tom, and then I think of Mum and Dad, and it makes me too sad. I need to keep shifting gears up, you know? This is a new life for me, a second chance. I need to keep looking out to the horizon instead of at my feet.'

Leo searched her face. 'Tell me something, Romes. After everything that happened to you up in Adelaide, why was it that when you decided to find that new life, you chose Remarkable Bay?'

'I've asked myself that a lot. But I don't believe in fate, if that's what you're implying. That would mean there was some pre-ordained plan to all life's tragedies. I think it's nothing but a coincidence.'

'What's a coincidence?' Addy appeared with a bottle of champagne and three glasses. Leo took the bottle from her and poured.

'Leo was asking me if I thought there was some grand plan behind me buying this place. Like it was in the stars or something.'

Addy looked at Leo quizzically. 'Since when did you become the romantic?'

He shrugged. 'I can see the difference in her, and in you too, Addy. Maybe there's something about this house, about Remarkable Bay.'

Roma and Addy shared a knowing look. In that moment, they knew there was something in what Leo was saying. They'd felt it. It had pulled them back together when they'd needed each other the most. It had reunited their family.

'I think the house is working its mysterious magic again, downstairs in the kitchen. You should hear Dylan and Keira. They're getting on like a house on fire. It turns out they used to drink at the same pub when Keira was backpacking and worked in London for a little while. She's telling him she'd love to go back and he's saying he can't imagine why and that's when I left them to it.'

'Well, well, well.' Roma nodded.

Leo laughed and raised his glass. 'Cheers.'

As they toasted, Blake walked through the front gate. 'Hey,' he called up to them

Addy peered over the railing. 'Hey, Blake. I'll come down.' She shot Roma and Leo a warning look.

'Don't,' she said with a smile and went back inside.

Roma and Leo clinked their glasses together in a toast, celebrating family and friendship and summers past and summers future. Roma had a feeling the summer of 2016 was going to be her best year yet.

CHAPTER

41

On Christmas Day, Roma woke in her new skin. Feeling like a snake that had shed its old one, she stretched, felt revived, still with the same wrinkles and freckles she'd gone to sleep with the night before, but taut, alive, bristling with an energy she hadn't felt perhaps her whole life.

This was changing gears. She could feel her life moving forward. Finally. She'd been stuck for so long, or adrift maybe, that feeling anchored was euphoric. Finally, she knew herself. She knew what she wanted for her life.

It had been so long in coming that she had lost hope that it ever would.

'Roma.' She blinked her eyes open against the morning light. It was Connor's voice drifting up to her room from the front gate. Naked, and feeling his touch all over her body still, she pulled a sheet around her, slipped through the open French doors and the softly billowing net curtains and stepped out on to the balcony.

She didn't care if there were people down on Ocean Street who might see, who might look up and wonder about the woman with the pink cheeks and the tousled hair and the beaming smile, look-ing for all the world like a middle-aged Juliet smiling down on her grey-at-the-temples Romeo.

'Good morning,' she smiled, and she felt alive from her toes to the roots of that tousled hair. Connor was grinning up at her, a bunch of roughly picked flowers in his hand. There were gazanias and little white seaside daisies and coprosma leaves. It was messy and spontaneous and she loved it.

'They for me?' She cocked her head at the flowers.

'Yeah. It's not much but I had to improvise. It's the thought that counts, right?'

His every thought did count, had from the first time they'd met when he'd welcomed her to Remarkable Bay. 'I suppose I'd better let you in then, huh?'

When she met him at the front door, he wrapped his arms around her and pressed his lips to hers, soft and fierce at the same time. She had made a good choice this time, she knew. She hugged him tight, slipping her arms around his waist, pressing her cheek to his chest, making a place for herself in his arms and in his life. She felt that flutter, the same one that appeared every time she saw him. It was a lightness that settled on her when he was near. And perhaps that's what love felt like. An exhale. A breath. A softening.

He held her at arm's length, studied her face. 'You good?'

'Why wouldn't I be?'

The flicker of doubt in his eyes told her he needed reassurance. 'Thought I'd better come and check you hadn't woken up with any regrets.'

'Not one.' She slipped a hand in his. 'Come back to the kitchen and I'll make you breakfast.'

Connor put the flowers in a tall glass and Roma took bacon and eggs from the fridge, a frypan from a cupboard, and began mak-ing breakfast for them. Connor slipped some sliced bread into the toaster and then nestled in behind her, resting his chin on her head, nuzzling her neck, kissing her ear and whispering, 'What if we eat breakfast after?'

She teased him. 'After what?'

'After I check you have the capacity this morning, after last night, to enter into a legally binding agreement?'

It wasn't quite the answer she was expecting. "Wow, lawyer talk. Very hot. Or maybe it's the bacon.'

'There's something I need to talk to you about, if you have the aforementioned capacity, that is.'

'Why wouldn't I have the aforementioned capacity?'

Connor nuzzled her cheek. 'Thought I might have fried your brain last night. You fried mine.'

There were light footsteps, then, 'Get a room you two.'

Addy pulled out a chair and sat at the table. Her silk kimono was hanging loose from her shoulder, revealing a white singlet top and her long, pale legs. Her curly hair was fuzzy and her face was bare of make-up.

Connor exhaled loudly in Roma's ear, his desire and frustration evident, and reluctantly let her go. 'Good morning.' She took four plates from the cupboard and set them on the counter.

'Morning,' Addy said sleepily.

Then the front door opened and closed and there were more footsteps, heavier, a longer stride.

'Morning,' Blake announced.

'You here for breakfast, too?' Connor said, puzzled.

'I can smell the bacon from my place. Make mine sunny side up.' Blake sat down next to Addy, dwarfing her at the table. He was in boardshorts and an old Remarkable Bay Surf Shop T-shirt. Roma saw the way he smiled at her and noticed Addy's flushed reaction.

'I'm going to be needing one of those T-shirts, you know, now that I'm on staff.'

Blake looked down at his. 'I'll see what I can do.'

Roma laughed from the stove. 'I can't believe you two.'

'See what happens when you try to run away from it all? You wind up with a job.'

Roma smiled at Addy and Connor nodded at Blake.

'Well, well, well,' Connor said.

Roma put some more bacon in the pan and watched it sizzle before looking over her shoulder. Addy. Connor. Blake. Something had happened to her in Remarkable Bay. Something, well, remarkable. When she bought this old house, the reasons were a mystery to her. She'd never been spontaneous in her whole life. It was still a puzzle to Roma why she'd done what she'd done, what twist of fate and circumstance had led her to this point in her life and why.

Perhaps there were secrets in these walls that spoke to her, without her knowing. Was that even possible? Was there love in every brick and every room here, which had just been waiting for the right people to bestow it on? Maybe it was the love that had seeped into the walls of the house over its one hundred years, and it had all been waiting to leech out, to absorb into someone whose heart was empty and broken, to entwine its tendrils around those in her life and pull them closer to her and to each other. To reinstate a family around her, a community of people she cared for and who cared for her.

Was it Bayview that had healed her? Was it Addy? Was it Leo and his caring concern from so far away? Was it Keira? The beach and the ocean and the clean winds? The fresh air?

Keira arrived in her running gear, barely having raised a sweat from her regular morning run, just as plates groaning with bacon, eggs, wilted spinach and juicy brown mushrooms were being served. Dylan was right behind her, still puffing.

Addy looked up. 'You two been for a run?'

'Yeah,' Keira said as she looked up at Dylan. 'I was showing him the sights.'

'Bloody hell, it's gorgeous here.' Dylan pushed a hand through his hair. 'Is there anything I can do to help?'

'No. Take a seat,' Roma said and Connor slipped a plate in front of him. He groaned. 'I'm starving and this looks amazing. Thanks, guys.' Soon, everyone was at the table and salt and pepper and tomato sauce were changing hands as they began to eat, in companionable silence, in each other's easy company, taking it easy on a Sunday morning, Christmas Day, in Remarkable Bay with no

deadlines, no early morning shop openings, no production meetings, nothing to drag them away from this.

Roma loved this, having everybody here.

Then Angas arrived, as if drawn by the aromas of breakfast 'Hey,'
he said.

Everyone at the table called in unison, as if rehearsed, 'Morning,
Angas.' He seemed stuck to the floor at the entrance to the kitchen.
Connor glanced over at him. 'You want some eggs? Juice?' Connor
looked over at Roma, a warm smile on his face. She returned it.

'They're really good eggs, Romes,' Keira added.

'You guys should cook breakfast for a living, you know that?'
Blake said, as he pushed his plate to the middle of the table.

Roma leaned back in her chair. 'Funny you should say that. I'm
going to.' She smiled at Keira. 'It was all her idea.'

'Who's had an idea?' Leo shuffled in, sleepy-eyed and hung-over.
He pulled up a chair next to Blake. Angas stole a crispy piece of
bacon from his father's plate and hovered near his chair.

'Keira and me. I'm going to apply for planning permission to
turn Bayview into a bed and breakfast. Just weekends for now.
We've got enough space, that's for sure. Keira and I are going to
run it.'

Connor looked at Roma with shock and surprise in his expression.

There was a clatter of cutlery. It was Addy. 'What about me?'

'What about you?' Roma asked.

'Are you kicking me out?'

'No.' Roma leaned her elbows on the table. She knew Addy
needed to find a home as much as she had. 'I was going to ask you
if you felt like giving up your glamorous movie life and would consider staying in Remarkable Bay and running it with us.'

Addy's blue eyes shone with tears.

'I don't know. I've got a career. A job I love.' Addy paused. 'Used
to love.'

Roma shrugged. 'Think about it. I reckon we could make this
place something amazing. We've got plans, you see.'

The room went silent.

'As well as being a cruel Pilates instructor, Keira is an environmental scientist.'

Keira picked up the thread. 'I thought we could do some local walking tours along the beach and through the dunes, to show people the bird life, the mangroves. I want people of all ages and interests to come to Bayview. From the honeymooners to the twitchers.'

'The what?' Angas asked.

'The bird watchers,' Connor explained. 'This area is rich with birdlife and they come down here a lot to take photos of birds. It's a thing.'

'I can fit all this around my classes at the Pilates studio. Things are starting to build up. A couple of the retirement homes in Victor Harbor have arranged weekly day trips to bring their residents here for fitness classes. That was a great idea of yours, Roma.'

'And Blake, what about you? Could you offer surf lessons?'

He looked at Addy, raised an eyebrow. 'Sure. Angas. You in?'

'Sure, Uncle Blake.'

'We can do this, all of us.' Roma looked around the room at everyone she loved. 'We can bring Remarkable Bay back to life. I don't want to go back to the city. I want to stay here and yes, I'm manipulating you all into staying too. Because I've found the place where I belong. And it's here with all of you.'

Roma felt her life changing up into another gear. The past was the past now, settled into its dust. She had made peace with her choices and her disappointments. She had made a future for herself here, with the people she loved the most. This family, her new family, was going to make her happy because she was ready to open her heart to the possibility that she deserved it.

Connor was behind Roma and he slipped his arms around her. He pressed his lips to the top of her head and she reached for his arms.

'I like this idea a lot,' Blake said. Then he turned to Addy. 'Have you decided?'

'I'm thinking,' she said, chewing on a nail.

Blake leaned in close. 'Stay.'

She fidgeted in her chair. 'This is my decision.'

'I know it is. I just want you to be clear on where I stand. On what I want.'

Addy looked to Roma. 'I'm thinking seriously about it.'

'I know you are,' Roma said.

Connor let Roma go and paced up and down across the room. He suddenly looked like a lawyer about to make a case. 'It looks like things have worked out for everybody. Roma and Keira have a new business. Blake and Angas get to give surf lessons. Addy is still deciding but it looks like you've got a life here if you want it, in more ways than one. Which leaves …' Connor looked around the room. 'Me.' He crossed his arms and looked at Roma.

'You're asking what's in this for you?'

'Well. Yes. I'm asking what's my part in all of this?'

Keira looked confused. 'Aren't you providing all the free legal advice?' Addy laughed. Blake chuckled.

Roma thought about it. 'You're my … boyfriend?' Then she scowled. 'That word is so wrong for us.'

Connor ran a hand through his hair. 'I came over here this morning to ask you something, before the rest of Remarkable Bay arrived to freeload for breakfast.'

Roma sipped her coffee. 'And what was that?'

Connor reached into the pocket of his shorts and pulled out a yellowed handkerchief. 'This was going to be so much more romantic. I had plans to drag you down to the beach and do this down there. But, no. Looks like this is going to happen here. In this Christmas wonderland.' Everyone looked up to the lights strung above them. Blake leaned across to the switch and flicked it on.

Addy gasped. Keira clutched her hand to her chest.

Roma couldn't breathe

Connor looked to his son. 'Will you give the old man permission, Angas?'

Angas shrugged. 'As if I could stop you.'

Then Connor got down on one knee. Chairs scraped on the floor as Addy, Keira, Blake and Dylan positioned themselves to get a better view.

'You're kidding,' Roma whispered.

He looked up at her, laughing. 'Not kidding.'

'Bloody hell.' Roma covered her face with her hands. When she found her breath and peeked through her fingers, Connor was unwrapping the yellowed handkerchief. He presented it to her like an open flower. Resting in the middle was a thin, dull gold band.

'I was wondering if you'd like a husband.'

'Connor …'

'Angas and I paid a visit to my parents yesterday. I told them all about you.'

'You did?'

'He was so embarrassing,' Angas added.

'I told them that I love you and I want to marry you. And then my mother goes to her china cabinet and pulls this out. Turns out it's my great-great-grandmother's wedding ring. She said I should give it to you. So I am.'

Roma picked it up and held it up to the light from the window. It wasn't fancy. It was worn and simple, as if it had been waiting a long, long time to be slipped back on to a woman's finger.

There wasn't a sound in the room but her heartbeat.

'C'mon, Roma,' Connor pleaded jokingly, 'You'd better make a decision. These knees have surfed too much to kneel like this any longer.'

Roma heard the word *yes* slip from her lips but it felt like the house had whispered it, not her.

'Yes, Connor Stapleton. I choose you. I choose this life with you. I will marry you.'

And then she heard nothing else but a happy roar and they were both engulfed by the people who loved them the most in the world. Angas, as tall as the adults, managed to get in between them, and Connor kissed him loudly on the forehead.

'You're stuck with him now,' Angas joked.

'And I'm stuck with you, too,' Roma replied, pulling him in for a hug.

'Bad luck,' he added with a smile.

And then Addy pushed into the middle of the huddle, cupped Roma's cheeks in her hands. 'I've decided. I'm staying, Roma. You and me and Keira here, in this house. Can you imagine what our great-grandmothers would think if they knew we were back here?'

And the house shifted and settled, creaked.

A family had found her.

ACKNOWLEDGEMENTS

One again, I would like to thank my family. To my mum, Emma Purman, who would hold the official title of President of my fan club, if I had one. At home, aka The Land of the Giants, I thank Stephen for support, love and wine. To Ethan, for being my assistant in the kitchen so I have more time to write. To Ned, for the jazz guitar background music while I type. To Clancy, the rock god, for the drum solos which keep me writing fast. And to Charlie, for staring at me adoringly while I write. (To clarify, sons don't stare adoringly at their mothers. Charlie's the dog.)

To my wonderful friends, Linda Brown, Amy Matthews, Trish Morey and Bronwyn Stuart: you ladies kick butt in a thousand different ways. To Kate, who generously let me ask her about grief. To Sally, who answered my questions about the world of film production.

Thanks to Sonya Feldhoff from ABC 891 Adelaide who ran a competition during Adelaide Writers' Week 2016 to give a listener the chance to name one of the characters in this book. Thank you, Amy Mann, who chose 'Edith Robinson'. The name Edith runs through four generations of Amy's family. I was so thrilled that the contest threw up something so absolutely fitting, not only to the 1930s when part of this book is set, but to the theme of great-grandmothers and great-granddaughters which is intrinsic to this book. You'll find Edith Robinson within the storyline set in 1934.

I would like to thank 891 listeners who were so generous when I appeared on Sonya's program asking for information about guest houses on South Australia's south coast, and memories of holidays there in days gone by. People sent me letters, source material and tips on where to find information. A big thank you to the staff of the Victor Harbor Library, who were so helpful when I was researching this book. The recordings from the Victor Harbor Oral History Project and 'Beside the Seaside' by Rob Linn were particularly helpful.

To the amazing team of women at Harlequin Australia: Michelle Laforest, Cristina Lee, Sue Brockhoff and Jo Mackay. I'm down on bended knee to Annabel Blay, my stupendous editor. You're stuck with me from now on, Ms Blay.

And finally, to my readers. Your messages, emails and reviews are such a reward. I'm so very grateful that I get to do what I do. When my ideas seem flat, when my blank screen stares back at me and when I think I'd rather go and eat chocolate instead of typing one more word, the idea that you are all waiting for my next book keeps me going.